IT'S COMPLICATED

KINDLE ALEXANDER

TRADEMARK ACKNOWLEDGEMENTS

The author acknowledges the trademarked status and trademark owners of the trademarks mentioned in this work of fiction.

NOTE FROM THE AUTHOR

It's Complicated has been fully edited by a team of trained editors but no manuscript is perfect. Please email me with any mistakes you find at kindle@kindlealexander.com.

This is not a military bible – please don't use it as such. Creative license was taken with this story. It is a work of fiction.

SPECIAL THANKS

Mari Carr

Thank you for letting us into your world. It's a dream come true to work with so much talent.

Let us know when you find Mari's characters in It's Complicated.

DEDICATION

Kindle, you are forever in our hearts.

Perry, you're missed every day.

CHAPTER 1

Julian Cullen stood behind the wall of one-way mirrors in his office at Reservations, the nightclub he managed. He assessed the new tables and barstools as he looked down over an almost empty main floor. The cleaning crew scuttled around, hard at work this morning, making the place as pristine and as close to perfect as possible.

Reservations had a standard of excellence to maintain, and Julian worked day and night to ensure each employee on his team understood their role in meeting those expectations. From the club's janitorial service to the attached restaurant's kitchen staff, Julian demanded they all measure up. If they didn't, then he cut them loose.

This club had reason and purpose. It saved lives. It had saved his.

"Did you walk away again?" The deep, husky voice drew Julian from his musings and back toward his desk, where the red light showed the speakerphone still active. *Shit.*

Now Julian had two options. One, stay quiet and let his boss, Thane Walker, owner and operator of Reservations, believe he had indeed walked away from their conversation like he had done many times before while being censured. Or two, confess he'd been lost in thought about the argument he'd had with the incompetent master chef a few minutes ago.

Of course, the disagreement hadn't gone well for the chef. Julian had fired the belligerent man on the spot. It didn't matter to Julian that he didn't have any jurisdiction over the restaurant side of Reservations.

Julian rolled his eyes, then let one of those intensive, counseling-learned sighs build in his chest. He inhaled a deep centering breath and held it, closing his eyes to let the calm descend over him like a comforting blanket. The exhale gave way to a slow release of the tension that had invaded every muscle in his body. Weird how something so simple had become his key method for getting through his day-to-day life.

He opened his eyes, a smirk tugging at his lips as he turned toward the office desk, talking as he went. "I may have tuned you out. Did you say my raise for the new position is going to be S-class money or Bugatti money?"

Thane's harsh laugh echoed from the speaker, the following harrumph let Julian know he'd played the moment properly. He'd distracted Thane. Julian was nothing if not capable of being a massive distraction.

"With as big of a pain in the ass as you are, you should pay me to work there. Why did I ever think it was a good idea to offer you a regional position? You used my good mood against me. I think you should lower your salary expectations to the range of a used Civic, maybe a late '90s model if you're lucky, and that's only if you quit pissing everyone off."

Julian's grin brightened as he realized Thane didn't know what had happened this morning with the so-called master chef.

Thane couldn't be any farther than about mid-flight on his way back to his corporate office in Ellicott City, Maryland. If Julian didn't mention the incident, he might get a couple hours of peace before his boss exploded on him.

Though, sparring with Thane was one of Julian's favorite pastimes. Especially now that Thane had finally eased off on treating Julian as if he would shatter at any given moment like a fragile piece of crystal teetering on the edge of a table. The kid-glove treatment had needed to end well before now. That was most likely the real reason he kept stepping outside his job description to make sure all the parts of Reservations worked cohesively with excellence as their goal. Julian wanted to prove to everyone around him that he wasn't the same shell of a man they had first met. Or perhaps Julian was just a first-rate asshole. He casually shrugged a shoulder, liking that last option the best as he walked across the office to the desk chair.

"Answer my question, Cullen. What do you really know about the Marlboro Man?" Was that what they'd been talking about?

At the reminder, a new annoyance built inside Julian. Why did Thane even care? The Marlboro Man had easily passed the rigorous background checks to become a member. Julian had danced with the cowboy last night. End of story. Nothing more mattered.

"Stop digging around in my love life…" The words were out of his mouth before he could stop them. Who was he kidding? He didn't have anything close to resembling a love life. Hell, he didn't even have a relationship with his own damn hand. How pathetic was that?

Thane meant well, but it wasn't enough to ease the sudden burst of frustration.

If Thane didn't like the way Julian stepped outside of his position… Well, Julian was damn well sick of Thane Walker's constant hovering.

"Unless you've changed your mind and we're back on. All you gotta do is ask and you will receive. You know how well I can suck a di—"

"Stop," Thane said, interrupting him. "I'm a married man."

Julian cocked a brow, staring at the phone. Married? *Pfft*. Thane wished he were married. Besides, there would be no Thane and Levi without Julian. He'd introduced the two. Thane needed to show a little more appreciation for what Julian had placed in his path.

"No, you're not married."

"Thanks for bringing up such a sore subject." Thane, the mover of mountains, caregiver to the world, had met his match in Levi Silva, one of Reservations waiters. Julian couldn't deny how much he had enjoyed watching his overly confident boss chase after the waiter day and night. Thane needed his arrogant ego knocked down a peg or two, no matter how good a guy he always tried to be.

"I have Beckett St. Clair's file in front of me. I don't see why everyone thinks he's so nice-looking. There's not a lot of information here, and he's come out of nowhere. What do you know about him?" Thane asked.

Julian kept his lips zipped about the ruggedly handsome beauty of Beckett. The waiters had almost immediately given Beckett the moniker of the Marlboro Man, and it fit. The guy towered at a soaring six-four of solid muscle, and he was masculine as hell. He pulled off elusive and mysterious better than anyone Julian had ever known. And, goddamn, the guy had swagger. Beckett's self-assured strut had the club patrons turning to watch that man leave at every opportunity.

Beckett was everyone's type, no matter what Thane insinuated.

Should he confess to Thane that he'd already been digging around in Beckett's background? The Marlboro Man had given Julian his undivided attention for months. Julian hadn't missed the way Beckett watched him. He loved the weight of the man's stare. Soft smiles and little pleasantries here and there always made Julian's night so much lighter. Julian found himself moving about the club, just to be noticed. Something he hadn't even contemplated since…before.

There would have been a time he would have been all over that hot cowboy, but not anymore. Men and dating were a hard pass. So off Julian's radar that he couldn't remember the last time he'd done either. A self-imposed exile from sex was a hard pill to swallow for someone who had previously lived to get off. Giving and receiving pleasure had been his only priorities in life.

In what strange twist of reality would anyone from his past believe that Julian Cullen had gone celibate?

This new, careful Julian needed the reassurance that the Marlboro Man was harmless. Trust came as a hard commodity these days. He had enlisted Tristan Wilder's help to dig deeper into the man's past. A secret he chose to keep from the well-intentioned Thane. If Thane had any inkling of Julian's uncertainties about Beckett, he'd have already kicked the guy out of the club and revoked his membership. They didn't need that kind of bad press right now.

Besides, none of it mattered. Julian tried for nonchalance as he spoke his truth to Thane. "St. Clair's been a member for months. I danced with him last night at a celebration that your man, Levi, invited him to participate in. He gave me a compliment. I liked it. That's all." He hoped his tone conveyed that Thane had overstepped his boundaries by letting his protective side get the best of him.

"Three times, Julian. You danced three long dances with him. I watched you. You were into it." Thane's exasperation rang clear in his words as if Julian were a petulant child. "Anyone you date needs to be thoroughly vetted; I won't have it any other way. They haven't caught the guy who hurt you. I refuse to take risks where you're concerned. Hell, we still don't know the motives behind your assault. The private investigators have nothing, which means it's most likely a serial predator. But what if it was personal, and he's waiting—" Thane abruptly stopped the commentary he'd given Julian at least twice a month since the assault.

Thane wore the protective daddy bear cloak with pride. Julian allowed it only because he silently agreed. But how long could he go on like this? Living without actually living, waiting for something that might not ever happen?

"I'm sorry to bring it all up again. What happened to you just gnaws at me. I can't let it go." Thane had been Julian's champion from the minute he'd missed their regularly scheduled "date" because his ass was lying unconscious in a hospital bed, fighting for his life. Thane had gone out of his way to find Julian when so many others would have never thought twice about his absence. Then Thane had taken over his care. He owed Thane everything. The expensive healthcare system wasn't there for people like Julian. It had taken everything Julian had plus a whole lot of Thane's aid and influence to get him back on his feet.

It never took long for all the guilt to come flooding back and begin crushing him from the inside out.

Fuck.

Julian had no idea how long he'd sat there quietly contemplating Thane's rehashing of the past before Thane spoke again.

"Julian, did you leave me this time? I probably deserve it if you did."

That brought a smile to Julian's lips, and he took the opportunity and promptly changed the subject. The path they were on would get them nowhere fast. "I'm not sure I want to move to Ellicott City. You guys keep having those once in a thousand year floods. How many thousands of years have you knocked out now? I feel like I'd need some swimming lessons or something."

Thane barked out a laugh. "I love this area, I swear I do, but that last flood may have done me in. I've got to stay local for Levi. Luke's registered to begin school here... I've liked being able to walk to work, but my staff can't continue to have their safety at risk. It's a hard decision."

Julian's grin grew as he listened to one of his naughtiest former clients talk about his newly domesticated life. He was happy for his boss. Thane had taken Luke's guardianship as seriously as he'd taken anything. Not that Luke, Levi's teenage brother, needed much looking after. The kid was rocket-scientist smart and as fundamentally good a person as anyone Julian had ever known.

"Let me dig deeper into this Beckett St. Clair. He's too interested in you. We need to get ahead of this," Thane said quietly. "I have a bad feeling about this one."

"Lord, Walker, no one needs this much negativity in their lives." Julian guessed it didn't really matter if Thane poked around in the cowboy's background. He'd learn what Julian already had learned. "Do whatever you've got to do."

"You gave in too easily," Thane countered, skepticism coloring his words.

Julian rolled his eyes, then brought his palms up, running them over his face. He didn't give in, and Thane doubted him. Then he gave in, and Thane doubted that.

Suddenly, firing the master chef seemed like a far easier conversation to have.

"Have you heard from Franklin?" Julian asked.

Silence held between them for maybe ten long seconds.

"What did you do, Julian?" Thane clipped out.

Thane knew him so well. Julian gave a small smile as he said, "We've lost our quality of food service. Plate presentation is down. I've heard gossip that some of our dishes are mediocre at best. As it turns out, that's all on Franklin. He's not maintaining the standard we expect. I did an impromptu quality check myself during prep this morning. I felt like the complaints were warranted and fired Franklin because he's seriously a gigantic jackass. I've already sent an email requesting Dishology's training department send someone over for tonight's meal service—"

"Goddamn it, Julian. You do not have the authority to fire anyone without the GM's involvement. You have absolutely no say in anything happening inside the restaurant. Why can't you get that through your thick head?"

"I can't help that *your* kitchen manager ran this place like a food truck." Julian warmed to the new topic, grinning broadly. Thane cut him right off again before he could get on a roll.

"No. Julian, listen to me. There are employment laws at play here. Dishology has policies that must be followed. You're pissing me off with this, and you won't fucking stop. It's never-ending."

Julian pushed to his feet, done with this conversation. He didn't care in the least about Thane's ire. He saw himself as Thane's eyes and ears at Reservations. He took the role seriously.

He left the office, letting the door swing shut behind him. He made it as far as the bottom step before his cell phone vibrated in his pocket. Julian grabbed it, sending Thane's call to voice mail. He'd give Thane time to cool off and see that Julian had made the right decision. Protocols were all well and good, but Reservations had a reputation to protect.

Franklin was a douche who'd be better suited for meal prep at the local fast-food restaurant. Maybe. Nah, Franklin wasn't even Mickey D's material. Julian had always liked their french fries and would hate to see the quality compromised.

CHAPTER 2

Beckett St. Clair drove the last leg of his journey home, traversing the long gravel road to the main lodge of his survivalist camp, giving a jaw-cracking yawn as he went. His elbow hung out the window of his pickup truck and the fresh, cool morning air hit his face. He needed sleep, something that wouldn't happen for several more hours, until he'd tackled some of his responsibilities.

He was itchier and grittier than after a weeklong survival training course in the mountains. The dress clothes he now wore always made him feel that way. Pressed slacks, clinging dress shirts, and silk ties…ugh. Why would anyone willingly subject themselves to this wardrobe every single day?

Beckett shuddered, glancing down at his tight-fitting ensemble. The smart thing would have been to make a quick stop to change into the jeans and T-shirt he'd brought along yesterday when he'd decided on this last-minute run to the club in Coronado. But he'd rushed aboard his plane and taken off for his home in Northern California, intent on making it back early in the day.

The trip back and forth had become a habit. But admittedly he'd pushed his leaving time as far as he could last night, all so he could stay a little longer in the company of a set of piercing eyes that touched his very soul. He'd left his personal plane at the hanger of the family airstrip, a good mile and a half from the main lodge.

His grin spread. Thank goodness he hadn't talked himself out of going yesterday. He'd been teetering over the decision because it appeared the nightclub's manager just wasn't into him.

Beckett had held out hope—fed by his deep infatuation—that Julian only needed to look his way, just one time. That when he finally did, surely, Julian would see what he'd been missing and fall to Beckett's feet. That had him chuckling to himself. At least he could dream. His smarter and more logical side recognized that it had been three months with not one single sign of encouragement. If Julian was going to acknowledge him, it would have happened two months, three weeks, and two days ago.

Hell, Julian paid less attention to Beckett than he did anyone else inside that bar.

Until last night when Beckett had the breakthrough he'd been waiting for. Out of nowhere, Julian's extraordinary gaze zeroed in on his and Beckett's world tilted on its axis.

Even now, remembering their moment had butterflies fluttering inside his belly, the muscles quivering and tightening in anticipation.

They'd shared three dances together, and their chemistry couldn't be denied. When had dancing with a man been such a binding, physical force?

Never. That was when.

Until last night.

Images of the most handsome man he had ever seen played in Technicolor inside his head as the truck hit a rut and bounced him around the seat.

Julian Cullen—a man almost too stunning for his own good.

That gaze, his pouty lips with that sharp-witted tongue, the slight indent in his chin…

Beckett had always liked his men on the big and beefy side. Julian had shown him exactly how wrong he'd been.

A single glance of Julian on his first visit to Reservations had triggered an all-consuming reaction. He'd heard about the club from one of his clients and casually started digging for more information. Beckett hadn't been out all that long. At thirty-three years old, it had taken him longer than most to make peace with his own being.

He had almost backed out of going to Reservations for a variety of reasons. One, he'd hidden for so long that it took some adjustment to be around so many openly gay men. The other bigger reason was their dress code. Beckett did *not* like to dress up.

He'd added his Stetson to his new high-dollar suit just to feel the slightest bit more like himself. If he hadn't taken the time to complete the long membership forms and spent the several thousand dollars on the entry fees and clothing required, he probably would have changed his mind as he'd stood staring at his reflection before heading out that first night. Thinking back over that initial visit, he could see what a mistake that would have been.

At the time, he had thought all the vetting Reservations did for its club members was overkill, but when he'd walked through the front doors of the club for the first time, he recognized what they were trying to accomplish. And it worked. It gave men like him, gay men, a place to safely meet. Not that he'd met too many available guys there, but Julian took that blame.

When he'd surveyed the elegant nightclub, taking in every bit of the opulence, his heart had almost leaped from his chest when his gaze landed on the gorgeous manager working at his perch at the end of the bar.

For those who didn't believe in love at first sight, they were flat ass wrong.

The object of his desire was his exact opposite. Julian leveled out on the high-end of being an extrovert. Full of life, and so very clearly the energy behind the club. Julian's mouth— Beckett shook his head just thinking about it. That damn sassy mouth had a comeback for everything.

Julian was also annoyingly elusive. Every night that Beckett spent in Coronado, whether there for work or an impromptu visit like last night, he'd sat inside the club, spending wads of cash and watching Julian flirt with every man in the place. Every man except for him.

Nothing in Beckett's life seemed to matter more than catching a glimpse of the blue-eyed manager. After last night, when they'd shared three dances together, that truth crystallized even more. Tingles radiated through his body and down to his fingertips where he clutched the steering wheel just thinking about Julian's beautiful face inches from his as they moved together on the crowded dance floor.

Fuck, Julian was sexy.

Their dances last night had to mean Julian had noticed him on more than a superficial level. He'd felt the moment Julian's body relaxed into his. Beckett had never been more alive than when he'd held Julian in his arms.

Much like he had done over and over on the trip home, he zoned out, reliving every second of the night. He'd shocked the shit out of himself when he'd followed through with his *Be Bold Initiative* by accepting the private table invitation to celebrate Levi's big night. He'd become fast friends with Levi after joining Reservations and his standing table wound up in Levi's section. Levi's boyfriend and owner of the club, Thane Walker, didn't seem too keen on Beckett being included in the party. That was putting it mildly, but he had ignored Thane and stepped outside his comfort zone in his effort to encourage Julian to notice him.

Beckett replayed the raspy lilt in Julian's alluring voice as he'd said, "You sure stare a lot. Is there a problem or something?" Those words— No, it was Julian's husky tone while calling him out that would be etched inside his heart forever.

"Surely, you have to be used to men starin'. You're gorgeous." Beckett had inwardly cringed at his choice of words. *Gorgeous?* Where had that even come from? He never used words like that. In the middle of his mental beratement, those soul-destroying eyes twinkled with mirth. He had only thought Julian had dumbfounded him before. He'd been so wrong, because in that moment, he'd lost all of himself to that beautiful man.

"Oh, direct and smart. I like that in a man."

Beckett grinned to himself, remembering the goose bumps when Julian's arm slid around his back, urging him out onto the crowded dance floor. He'd removed his suit coat, tossed it aside, and danced with Julian. Something he didn't often do, but boy, could Julian move. It didn't matter that Beckett might not know the right dance moves. For maybe twenty minutes, he and Julian had stayed glued together under the flashing club lights.

Julian danced against Beckett like he had every right to be there. He wasn't wrong. Julian could sidle up next to Beckett anytime he wanted to. But something about Julian changed in front of Beckett's eyes. Julian transformed from a hardworking, take no shit off anyone manager to a master seducer. Beckett had been caught in Julian's spell, turning to putty in his hands.

Any perspective Beckett had managed to use to tamp down his feelings about Julian slipped from his emotional grip as he'd wrapped his hands around Julian's surprisingly hard body. Beckett's dick had punched against his zipper, aching with the need Julian provoked in him.

Those might have been the best twenty minutes of his life.

Julian had ground those perfect hips against his groin then suddenly stopped moving as if he'd been unaware of his actions. For several seconds, Julian's entire body became rigid before a confused look crossed his face and he bolted. Julian had dashed away without so much as a goodbye.

He had no idea what caused Julian's panic. Had Julian felt how hard Beckett's cock had been? Beckett forced the memory to end right there as his insecurity rushed back in waves.

The van heading his way pulled his thoughts to the present. He hadn't expected to see his company's passenger van so early in the morning. He flipped through his mental calendar, not remembering any clients arriving on the schedule that morning.

Beckett pulled to the side of the single-lane road and lifted a hand in greeting as the driver—a guy who'd been employed by them for the last fifteen years—passed by. Then, surprising him further, their second van came around the corner a little faster. Beckett rolled slowly forward, letting that van pass him before continuing. As he took the curve leading to the main lodge, several small groups of people came into view. They had gathered, along with their gear, in the front yard of the lodge. He racked his brain, trying to remember what training he'd forgotten.

As he pulled his truck into the gravel parking lot of the main building, he saw his father and their lead instructor, Randy, moving from group to group, clipboards in hand. Beckett cut the engine and jumped out of the truck, sending the door flying shut without a backward glance. He hoped he hadn't left them shorthanded when he'd taken off yesterday afternoon.

He scanned the people, taken aback by what he saw. This didn't look like their normal client demographic.

"Don't you look fancy," his father called out when Beckett came within hearing range. His old man's gruff voice might sound angry to the others based on the deer in the headlights looks snapping his direction, but Beckett wasn't bothered by his father's teasing ways.

Years ago, he and his father had turned their hobby into a thriving survivalist training camp. A place where they trained real-time, real-life survival techniques. With long hours and loads of hard work, they had managed to build that small company into a leading survival training school. They worked with private security firms, law enforcement, and the military. The last one was the reason for Beckett's visit to Coronado in the first place.

He suddenly remembered his father's middle of the night, bright idea from not less than a week ago. Since his father's recent mild heart attack, things had changed. His father could no longer assist with the more rigorous training classes. That had been damn hard on the old man's psyche. So, his father decided to open their camp to individual, private pay clients.

Over the last couple of years, the number of everyday people wanting to learn basic survival skills had increased exponentially. All the survival shows on television and YouTube no doubt drove the wild phenomenon. They had been inundated with inquiries from people who wanted to learn to "live off the land." They hadn't considered taking on novice trainees at the time, something outside their current business model. But the idea that there were people out there that wanted lighter training had been the concept behind his father's idea. His father wanted to teach a basic, rudimentary beginner's course—a three day, learn to live off the land excursion.

Beckett hadn't realized that they had gone from the idea phase to implementing the training. Could his rough and tough father handle the basic needs of a newbie trainee? Beckett's brow furrowed as he thought of the hard time their seasoned instructors had had in keeping up with his father.

If Beckett didn't have his own training class starting tomorrow, he'd volunteer to take the group out himself.

"Who's helping you, Dad?"

"Paul and Walt."

Oh, not good. Both men were part of their lawn crew. Beckett looked around the yard, counting twenty-five people. They wore their brand-new walking shoes and backpacks with their cell phones stuck in their palms. None looked as if they knew what they were really getting themselves into.

Beckett slapped his father on the shoulder and gave a gentle squeeze in greeting. "Randy and I can head out with you today and stay overnight. We've got to be back in the morning to take my class out. Sound good?"

"Do I get a say?" Randy asked.

"Only if it's a yes," his father cackled while continuing to complete the legal liability forms each person needed to sign.

Beckett took one of the clipboards out of Randy's hands and a couple of ballpoint pens. Sleep just got a whole lot less likely.

CHAPTER 3

How could it already be time to wake up?

Exhaustion clung to Julian, muddling his mind as he tried to assess the time without opening his eyes. He'd closed Reservations and gotten home at a little past three in the morning. It had taken some time for him to unwind. Sleep was always a tricky game these days, but he'd finally made it into bed and had actually fallen asleep. Surely, it wasn't time to start his day again.

Julian swore he lived in the movie *Groundhog Day* where every single day was the same thing. At times, he felt like he'd never escape whatever had such a tight hold on him, and other days, he appreciated the monotony. Living the same day over and over again had kept him safe from—

Yeah, not traipsing down that rabbit hole of crazy thought again.

No matter what woke Julian, he planned to go back to sleep. He concentrated on wiping his mind, clearing it of anything other than sleep. He drew in a deep breath and relaxed his body on the exhale, letting the tension go, tucking his hands underneath the softest pillow he'd ever slept on—a pillow he'd swiped from Escape Coronado. The resort didn't skimp on anything.

He needed to find a way to get his hands on those penthouse-quality sheets. A small smile tugged at the corners of his lips as he wiggled into the cushioned pillow-top mattress.

Had he totaled the bar's sales receipts before leaving?

Julian's brow furrowed as he tried and failed to recall the sales numbers. Weird, he always remembered the revenue Reservations pulled in each night.

Stop.

Sleep.

What had he read about the breathing techniques for sleep? Deep inhale, through your nose, for a four count. Hold it while counting to seven, then release slowly for eight.

Again.

Julian inhaled, letting the cadence of his breath lull him back to the edges of sleep.

It worked the same way as the breathing techniques he used every day. How could something so simple, an involuntary part of his minute-by-minute existence, be such a healing tool when used with intention?

But did it really help heal, or was it merely a bandage designed to cover a big, festering wound?

Goddamn it.

Clear your mind, asshole.

His mattress shifted, and his neatly arranged blankets were tugged from his body. *Right.* Julian blew out a breath and turned from his side to flop to his back. He cocked a brow as Woofer came to stand over him, lowering his face to look Julian in the eyes. Hot breath fanned Julian's cheek as deep brown eyes pleaded for his attention.

"You're the worst emotional support animal on this planet."

Woofer's tongue flopped out in response to those words. Julian instantly woke, bolting away, rolling to the side of the bed, knowing a long, wet lick was on its way if he didn't take action. He drew the line at having wet dog mouth slobber all over his face.

Julian already had to deal with dog hair and destruction all over his small yet super-tidy apartment. Woofer had no boundaries at all. Which was Julian's own damn fault. He wasn't consistent with the dog as they had instructed him to be. Woofer was supposed to help ease Julian's anxiety, but sometimes he wondered if maybe they had exaggerated the extent of Woofer's obedience training. The damn dog thought he owned the entire place.

How Julian had ever been talked into getting a trained emotional support animal was beyond him. Unless emotional support meant anytime he sat down, the hundred-pound German shepherd sat on top of him, then they needed to redefine the term.

Julian slid his slippers on as he got to his feet, reaching for his robe at the end of the bed. With a glance at the time as he tied the belt in place, he finally acknowledged the dog.

"It's five thirty in the fucking morning. What the hell's wrong with you? Why do you always have to go outside before the sun even comes up?"

The dog completely misread Julian's tone. Woofer spun around excitedly in circles, pawing and crumpling the sheet and blankets under his enormous body before he leaped off the end of the mattress. His nails scrabbled on the tile floor as the dog darted for the back door. Julian ran his fingers through his hair as he padded along after him.

Woofer had been given to him on a one-month trial basis. That had been three months ago. Every time Julian decided he wasn't the right person to take care of another living being, especially an untrained, imbalanced oaf of an animal, Woofer gave him one of his special soul-warming, deep, brown-eyed stares that Julian couldn't say goodbye to.

Apparently, Julian had a thing for beautiful whiskey-brown eyes.

Don't think it.

Do not fucking think it.

"I'm serious. It ain't happening. Stop the bullshit," Julian scolded himself. Of course, it happened anyway. Dwelling on Beckett's deep brown gaze stole Julian's ability to think for one maybe two long seconds. The sexy cowboy filled his thoughts more than he'd ever willingly admit, especially to Thane.

Beckett smelled amazing. He could never quite place the exact scent of cologne the cowboy wore—

White-hot pain seared up Julian's foot and leg. *"Fuck!"*

He'd misjudged the ridiculously large ottoman and clipped his toes on the edge.

Julian doubled over, grabbing for his foot. *Hell, that hurt*! Julian's ass landed on the edge of the cushion that instantly wobbled then slid out from underneath him, dumping Julian on the floor.

He'd probably broken his toe on that stupid ottoman. His living room was just too small for his old, oversized, stupidly expensive furniture. His place in LA had been three times bigger than this one.

He sighed. He had never envisioned his life this way. As Julian's toes throbbed, he looked around. Maybe his beloved LA pad was actually four or five times bigger than this one and certainly more modernized. Nothing like this cheap-ass nineties remodel of the seventies original build.

How did working-class people make it through their lives under all this oppression?

It could be the reason his parents were so damn uptight all the time.

Oh God no. He refused to think about his awful biological

family right now.

Julian dropped his head back on the toe-assaulting ottoman as the dog's wet tongue swiped across his cheek. He let go of a sigh and tucked his chin to his chest, feeling defeated as Woofer's head dropped to his lap. The shepherd's big body followed, settling on the floor beside Julian as if he weren't the exact reason Julian had gotten out of bed in the first place.

He was helpless to do anything more than run his fingers through the thick fur and pet the dog who tried to comfort him.

"Come on." Julian pushed up, getting to his feet as he reached for the leash hanging over the outside patio doorknob. He locked the metal latch in place on Woofer's collar. The animal forcefully tugged Julian out the door.

A balmy breeze coated his skin as the sun's rays barely peeked through the overcast sky. Woofer took off, the leash's lead rope sent whizzing as the dog ran. Julian quickly clasped the small handle, holding on tight. He'd learned this lesson the hard way.

He was jerked forward several steps before he planted his feet on the ground, causing Woofer to only make it so far without Julian having to walk the rest of the way toward the patch of grass close to the curb.

"Make it fast."

Julian had no idea why he always averted his gaze to give Woofer privacy, but he did by turning his back away from the dog, looking down the street as a car's headlights came around the corner. He let his thoughts shift back to Beckett's mesmerizing eye color. They really did look like iced whiskey.

A smoke-colored Charger drove slowly by, flexing its muscle by giving a rev to the engine. The color caught his attention seconds before a sharp pain pierced his brain, sending an icy chill racing down his spine. Brief flashes of multicolored lights zipped and zinged through his mind while confusing images played like a slideshow behind Julian's eyelids. He was dancing and felt woozy. Loud thumping music and the stench of cigarettes and booze assailed him.

Something was very wrong.

The dance club's lights blur as dizziness overwhelms him.

Julian stumbled backward from the weight of the memory.

A barrage of images crashed over him like waves during a storm. As one ebbed another flowed forward with unrelenting impact.

A dimly lit dingy hallway.

Ugly wallpaper.

Men's voices—several of them.

Julian couldn't catch his breath.

The here and now slid back in place in slingshot fashion, sending Julian's balance reeling. Back in the early morning, standing outside his condo. His building was on one side of him, Woofer on the other. The paralyzing pain in his head left his vision blurry, while darkness danced around the edges, making him so unsteady.

Shit, he was about to pass out.

"Dude, are you okay?" The voice sounded a million miles away. Julian's knees gave out, and the world tilted as he swayed backward, helpless to stop his fall.

Julian jerked, startled awake by the motion. He struggled to lift his head, snapping his eyes open, disoriented as to why he was lying on the ground.

His neighbor, a guy he'd nodded at a couple of times, hovered over him, his cell phone at his ear. The guy looked worried as he pushed at Woofer with his free hand. Woofer didn't budge a single inch as he stood guard on Julian's other side, peering directly into his face.

The throb in his head had grown tenfold since opening his

eyes. Julian tried to push himself up off the hard concrete beneath him. He could only manage to turn to the side as his stomach roiled.

"Stay down," his neighbor instructed, concern lacing his words. "You took a hard fall. I called 911. They're on their way."

"What happened?" Julian asked, his voice weak and raw. He reached for the back of his head, a hard knot about the size of a golf ball protruding from his aching skull. "Am I bleeding?"

"No, I don't think so."

"What happened?" Julian asked again. Woofer crowded against Julian's body, whining beside him as he offered his own brand of support.

"I don't know. I just saw you teetering and down you went."

Yeah, Julian got that much. He fought the rising nausea and forced himself to a sitting position. Saliva flooded his mouth, and he prayed he wouldn't vomit on top of everything else. His head hurt so damn bad, though. The barrage of sirens barreling toward them didn't help the pulsing pain thumping through his head.

"Can you cancel the police?"

"They're bringing an ambulance. You hit your head pretty solidly on the concrete. You should be checked out." His neighbor reached for Woofer's leash. "Let me take him inside." He pulled, but Woofer stayed planted in his spot. The dog didn't budge one single inch as he hunkered down beside Julian. "Come on, big guy."

Julian reached for the German shepherd, petting his head. "Go inside for me."

Woofer knocked his nose into Julian's shoulder, urging him to follow. His neighbor tried again, giving another solid tug on the leash, but the dog fought to stay by Julian's side. It was endearing even though he didn't like the damn dog at all.

"Let him stay. He's a support animal. This is what he does. He won't leave willingly."

A police cruiser pulled to the curb, followed by an ambulance. This wasn't the first time he'd been intimately involved with either of those vehicles.

Julian lurched forward, throwing up in the dew-damp grass beside him. So much for avoiding that humiliation.

Luckily for Beckett, he and the group of newbie survivalists had only had to hike up the side of the mountain for about three miles before his father had stopped and made camp for his introductory survival training course. Surprisingly, his father had a solid read on his students and had preplanned the area for their arrival. He'd chosen the perfect distance for the beginner group: close enough to the main lodge for anyone who might need to be taken back but far enough away to discourage anyone in the class from leaving on their own.

What the survival 101 training hadn't done was provide Beckett with a good night's sleep. He hadn't gotten more than a couple hours of shuteye all night long. There had been a low-level buzz from the trainees. Excitement, fear, and nervousness fueled many students who stayed awake until the wee hours.

Beckett walked the trail back toward his home, lifting his face to the early morning sun, letting its soothing warmth coat his skin. He left his dad and their lawn crew behind to wrap up training, secure that the newbies were in good hands. His sure-footed steps guided him over the rugged terrain, a path he knew by heart with as many times as he'd hiked the trail over his lifetime. Nothing filled his soul with peace more than the majestic, almost untouched energy radiating from the mountains.

The crisp breeze slid over his skin heated by the excursion of climbing down the rocky slope. The cleanest air anyone could ever breathe added to the allure of the moment. Whenever possible, Beckett started his day outside, taking a hike, clearing both his head and his heart. He loved the dawning of a new day filled with hope and possibility.

Mother Nature didn't seem to care about the struggles of the world. She started fresh every day, so he aimed to do the same.

"You're being quieter than normal," Randy said. The crunch of dry leaves under their feet and the chill of the mountain air added to the soul-inspiring tranquility of the morning hike. Randy was Beckett's lifelong best friend. They'd joined the military together. Then later, Beckett had recruited Randy to work on their survivalist instructor team. It had been the best hire of his life. Randy had a way of getting results out of even the most difficult trainee.

Off-duty, though, Randy was a talker.

Beckett, not so much.

Their downtime had become a balancing of their strengths. Randy handled the heavy lifting of incessant chatter while Beckett gave a few grunts and groans here and there, not ever really paying much attention to what Randy said. It worked well for their friendship.

"Are you listening at all?"

Beckett tuned back in. He guessed he wasn't grunting enough to keep Randy talking. "Yeah."

"Your old man did a good job. You know he arranged all this by himself in less than a week. The tents were a good idea. I was shocked that most of the class didn't know the proper way to erect one."

Beckett didn't respond. He focused on keeping their steady pace, navigating the rocky terrain down to the base of the mountain.

"I liked that he wants to add a new intermediate class for those who graduate from this one. I was skeptical when I first heard his idea."

Beckett had to agree.

Years before Beckett was born, his father had made a career out of the military. He'd served in the United States Navy as part of the first SDV teams under Naval Special Warfare Command. He led reconnaissance missions, was beloved by many. Still, there wasn't anyone on the planet who idolized his father more than Beckett. Watching his father getting older, having serious health issues, and being restricted from what he loved to do came with its own set of fears.

"Your old man told me you've been distracted lately. He thinks it has something to do with all those fancy clothes you keep buying. I said you've finally decided to spend some of that money you've been sitting on, so you'll look good at his funeral."

Beckett stopped in his tracks, tilting his chin over his shoulder, and gave Randy a menacing glare. The thing about talking too much was that a person eventually said stupid shit. Randy did it all the time. Take this moment as a prime example.

"Sorry," Randy said, lifting his hands in surrender. "It was funnier when I said it to your dad. He got a real kick out of it."

Beckett pointed a finger in Randy's face, daring him to say another word. "Don't fucking talk about him dying. That shit's not funny."

Randy lifted both hands higher in the air. When Beckett didn't give in right away, Randy rolled his eyes then reached out to shove Beckett to get him moving. "So why have you been so distracted lately?"

"I don't want to talk about it," Beckett grumbled, bounding down the last few rocky steps. He only had about a quarter-mile walk to his cabin. Randy could hike the rest of the way to the main lodge by himself. Beckett needed time to recoup before heading out again this afternoon.

"You not wanting to talk about something? What a shocker. Did your old man tell you the pot farm paid in full?"

That had Beckett slowing his steps to let Randy catch up.

"No, I don't think so. When did they do that?"

"I guess it was unexpected. Those two guys that bought y'alls land drove out yesterday afternoon."

Beckett couldn't help but look in the direction of the pot farm in the distance. If he squinted his eyes and the sun was in the right position, he could maybe see the large greenhouses from where he stood.

What a trip. When his father had first talked about the possibility of splitting up the back part of the property that had been in their family for over a hundred and fifty years, Beckett was fully against the sale. A century and a half was a long time for something to be passed down from generation to generation only to be sold off for no valid reason.

Then Beckett heard about the pot farm intending to settle there. His father shocked him by even considering the idea. His old man had always been a firm believer that any kind of drug was a bad thing. But somehow, the buyers had talked his old man into selling, probably because they'd agreed to the enormous asking price.

Beckett hadn't told anyone at the time that he'd done a side hustle on the deal, becoming a silent investor in the pot farm's business, enabling the guys to buy large pockets of land all over the United States and Canada. That one hastily made investment had changed everything for Beckett. The investment had quickly become profitable. Beckett had made millions of dollars, and the income continued rolling in with no end in sight.

The closer they got to his cabin, the more Beckett relaxed, and Julian's blue-green gaze returned to the forefront of his thoughts. Julian's eyes were multidimensional with iridescent shards of crystal flakes inside their depths. Beckett bet Julian was a sight to behold when those unusual eyes heated with lust...

God, Beckett had it bad. Once he'd decided he no longer wanted to live a life without love, he'd gone in the complete opposite direction and set his sights on the most beautiful man he'd ever seen. Pretty lofty goals and desires.

A yawn tore free. Beckett glanced up at the position of the sun to judge the time, maybe not quite seven o'clock in the morning. He didn't need to be at the main lodge until noon. His latest round of clients didn't arrive until two. They were part of his newest contract with the military. Those elite soldiers coming to train were some of the most intense they had ever hosted. He'd only be gone for three days, but they would be a tough seventy-two hours.

Maybe Beckett could squeeze in a couple hours of sleep before the new class arrived. If those mesmerizing eyes would leave him alone long enough to doze off.

"I'm gonna grab some coffee before I take the jeep to the main lodge," Randy said, still right behind Beckett.

"I left my truck there yesterday. I need the jeep."

"I'll be back to get you at eleven thirty." Randy rounded past Beckett to climb the steps to his porch, pushing open the front door.

Beckett, with the help of Randy and his father, had built this log cabin about five years ago. Nestled in a thick grove of large trees with a million-dollar view of the mountains just past the folding glass panel doors covering the length of the back wall. Perfect for him.

"What the fuck, St. Clair?"

Randy stopped short in the doorway, blocking Beckett's entry. He had no idea what Randy saw and shoved him between the shoulder blades to get him through the door. Randy stumbled forward as Beckett looked inside. The clothes he'd ordered had arrived and been placed in the center of his living room.

"Stop making such a big deal about it," Beckett muttered, sending the door slamming shut behind him.

His buyer from J.Hilburn sent a rack with six new suits in various colors, several pairs of pants, dress shirts, casual wear, and eight shoeboxes if he counted correctly in the quick scan. Beckett bypassed the new clothes, even though he really wanted to take a closer look but refused to listen to Randy go on and on, wondering then guessing what Beckett was up to.

"These don't look like you," Randy said, doing a complete three-sixty around the rack. His dirty fingers scooted the hangers around to get a better look. "You had to have met someone to go to this much trouble. Does he know you're a jeans and T-shirt kind of guy?" From over the rack, Randy looked at Beckett, confused. "When do we get to meet him? It's a guy, right?"

Beckett decided against relaying the fact that his infatuation remained one-sided. All this trouble for the sole reason to get Julian to pay attention to him. It seemed pathetic and needy, so he kept his lips shut tight and thoughts to himself.

"I'm gonna catch some z's. Make yourself some coffee, but don't lose track of the time. Be back here in four hours. Don't be late. It's the new military contract. We've got to be ready for them. You know they'll test us." Beckett went for his bedroom, letting the door shut as he listened to more scraping of the hangers against the rod.

Clear plastic covered each suit, but he still worried about gunk and dirt getting on his new clothes. There was a small fortune in clothing sitting in his living room.

"Keep your grimy hands off the material," Beckett called out through the closed bedroom door then headed into his bathroom.

CHAPTER 4

Three days later

"Whenever you're ready, Julian."

Several days had passed since the "incident". A term Julian coined to describe whatever the hell had happened to him a few mornings ago, but the revealing pieces of the flashback still haunted him. He'd honestly rather forget about the "incident" than acknowledge the extreme panic and anxiety those little bombs of revelation had caused.

Julian stood at the window, staring out at the tranquil scene of a small flower garden right outside the office of his counselor, Sarah Campbell. He found it soothing to watch nature do its thing.

Most of his sessions were done just like this. It gave him a sense of calm. Something about the green grass and pretty blooms spoke to his heart. The birdbath, where actual birds frolicked, made him feel healthy and whole. A displaced memory from his youth tried to form, but it never fully materialized.

"You're pushing," Julian finally answered, crossing his arms over his chest as he turned to stare at the older woman sitting nearby. His shrink, who'd been working with him since the...

Why did he struggle to call his assault an abduction?

His ironclad internal protective barriers slammed down in place, not allowing Julian to dig any deeper as to why he struggled to verbalize the truth.

Sarah looked like she always did: a patient, kind, well put together person. He often wondered if that was a facade or whether she, in fact, led a basically normal life.

"We're thirty minutes into your session, and I've stared at your back the entire time."

Julian lifted his gaze to the clock on the shelf, surprised at the time. He hadn't spoken a single word since he'd entered her office. But he felt calmer than he had in days and didn't want to spoil the peace building inside his soul.

He lifted a hand to carefully touch the goose egg on the back of his head. It was smaller now, but more painful.

His gaze narrowed as his defenses zeroed in on Sarah, hoping to get a rise out of her rather than have her focus on him. "It's the ass, right? My bubble butt slays. Men and women alike pant after it."

Julian twisted his waist to let her see his ass from a side angle, his hand sweeping past to show it off while watching her closely. Her passive facade never cracked. Not ever. She lowered her head to write something on the pad of paper in her lap. She was real old school. She didn't believe in technology or electronics; she considered them a privacy issue and avoided them as best she could.

"If this is how you'd like to spend the last fifteen minutes of your time, that's your call, but I'd like to know more about your injury. What happened?" Her keen gaze lifted back to Julian.

He stayed rooted in his spot, crossing his arms over his chest again as he said, "The dog you insisted I get has bladder problems, or he's a new breed of nocturnal animal. Why does he always need to go outside in the early morning hours, right before dawn? Do all dogs do that?"

She nodded to the chair across from her, encouraging him over. "I've told you the service animal was only an experiment. They aren't for everyone. You don't have to keep him."

"I like to think of Woofer as a stray. You know, like I'm saving him from the streets. Makes me like him more," Julian replied, taking the few steps to the chair, landing his ass on the soft cushion. He crossed one leg over the other, mimicking her pose. "Honestly, I thought service animals were trained beasts, docile to their core. If that's the case, mine's defective. And costing me an arm and a leg. I work too much. I'm paying people to walk him every day. Woofer has play dates. He's popular. All these dogs and their owners want to play with him. His schedule's busier than mine. And he's eating me out of house and home…"

"You're making him into a pet, not a service animal. We've talked about all this. Tell me what's happened, before our time bleeds over into someone else's appointment."

He bit his lip as he tried to fight the grin forming. He counted it a win when she used her schoolteacher tone with him. "Let's jump to the end then. I'll tell you what I think happened to me. Then you'll say that's very enlightened of me. Then we won't really speak of *the guy* because I'm not open to exploring anything more with him. Sound like a plan?"

"Go on." Of course, she never agreed with him when he tried to control their sessions. She lifted a hand, encouraging him to continue.

"For a while now, there's a customer at the club who's been giving me the interested vibe. He's extremely nice to look at with a set of big brown eyes and full pouty lips." Julian instantly felt exposed and didn't like it one bit. He changed course, suddenly uncomfortable. "Actually, he's a cowboy and fucking gorgeous in that big, rugged, outdoors kind of way. His tight dress pants outlined his package like they were tailored to do that very thing…"

"Julian," she interrupted, not letting him change course with his outrageous sass. "We have ten minutes."

"You're such a buzzkill," Julian retorted. Beckett's nice-sized package had moved to the forefront of his mind. It took a second to readjust his thoughts before he could continue. "Anyway, I broke my rules—"

"Rules I've disagreed with, correct?"

"Omigod. Let me finish," he said with as much attitude as he could muster. "I broke my rules. I'm not ready to engage with a sexual partner or consider dating and a relationship. Nothing's changed there, but I got carried away on a superficial level by his aforementioned attributes, and I danced with him."

Sarah tilted her head as if trying to read more into his story, so he rushed on.

"Three dances. I enjoyed myself a little too much. For a few minutes, I felt normal again." Julian looked down at his trembling hands and curled them into fists.

He'd cherished those few minutes of letting his cares slide away on the dance floor and just enjoyed the feel of a strong, handsome man holding him close. When Sarah stayed quiet, her attention still fixed on him, Julian felt compelled to fill in the silence.

"Before you encourage me to open myself to his advances, he doesn't know my past. And I know his type. He's a good guy. Not the kind to entertain a relationship, let alone any kind of longevity, with a fucked-up former sex worker. He'd probably be willing to do me, but that's it. So please don't push me."

She wrote several lines of notes, nodding her head as he spoke. "We've talked about this many times. It's not fair of you to decide how others feel without asking them first." She lifted her gaze, staring pointedly at Julian, pinning him in his seat. "What's the breakthrough that's happened from this man?"

She had a way of cutting through his bullshit and finding the exact thing he didn't want to share. Sneaky.

Julian anxiously bounced his foot. He'd stalled long enough. "I think I'm beginning to feel emotion again. More than just the guilt and shame I've been living under since my accident. I've been thinking about this guy I mentioned. He's slipped past my barriers. My staff calls him the Marlboro Man. He's got the best eyes. They're really, sincerely caring eyes."

Julian paused, lifting a hand between them to stop her from butting in. Saying those words aloud had somehow given them a foundation. It wasn't the flashback that played through his head, but instead, Beckett. All the little memories he hadn't let himself consider came roaring to the forefront. The way Beckett quietly gave a single nod of his head spoke for so many of his answers. That tilt to his head showed appreciation, acceptance, greetings, and goodbyes. Warmth seeped over Julian as he leaned back into the comfortable seat, absorbing the emotional blow of his attraction to Beckett.

"But when I was outside with Woofer, I was thinking about his eyes when the sounds of a passing car grabbed my attention and I looked up. I don't know what happened. Maybe by letting my guard down with Beckett other memories were able to surface. I glanced over at the car and something about it triggered a rolling slideshow in my head. I was at the club the night of my accident, having a good time. There were a lot of drinks that I didn't remember before, but that wasn't all that unusual. I never paid for my own drinks. I remembered feeling woozy. My vision grew hazy, and all the faces around me became distorted. My dumb ass never saw it as a red flag. I liked the feeling of being out of control."

"Did you call your investigator?" she asked, showing no emotion as to what he revealed.

"That's your response to what happened?" he asked incredulously.

Her face never cracked from its patient, tolerant expression. He was convinced that if he fell to the floor with a seizure, she'd look exactly the same as she did right now.

"It's an important question, Julian. This is a first for you. Tell me what happened after you had these memories. You fell?"

Julian gave a harsh bark of a laugh. "I didn't fucking fall. I passed out. My neighbor saw it happen. He ran across our shared walkway but couldn't get to me fast enough. At least that's what he told me happened."

"And you went to the emergency room?" she asked in an open-ended tone as if to keep him talking.

"I did. I had to call Thane because the fucking emergency room took so goddamn long, and I was scheduled to work. I didn't tell him what happened, but it didn't keep him from overstepping. They kept me overnight for observation. They lied to me and told me my health insurance wouldn't pay if I took off without their consent. It took me a couple days to figure out that wasn't true. Fucking Thane got in my head and in the heads of the hospital staff. He asked them to keep me." Julian was spitting mad when he'd learned the truth about that dick move.

"Now he's back in town. I've been forced to take a few days off. His protectiveness has reached an all-time high, and he doesn't even know about the flashbacks. I told him I fainted, and it's still been fucking awful." Julian rolled his eyes, knowing the most likely culprit of all his disdain landed squarely on Levi's shoulders. The med student had shown up at the hospital and stayed huddled up with Julian's care team. They'd given him no say in his own treatment plan.

The frustration was back in waves, bringing Julian to his feet. A coffee table separated him from Sarah and gave Julian a bit of room to pace back and forth, needing to move to keep the aggravation from ruining his mood.

The most annoying part of it all? His missing nights of work had given Franklin the opportunity to talk his way back into the kitchen. The stupid douche claimed his recent divorce messed with his head, causing him depression. He'd given an oath to never let quality slip again. Julian didn't believe that lie for a second. More like Franklin's divorce caused the guy too many hangovers from all the carousing he'd been doing.

"What happened to Woofer when you passed out?"

Thankful for the change in topic, Julian gave a silent huff at both her weird questions and the dog's behavior. "They couldn't get Woofer to move away from me. I'm surprised they were able to hold him back from following the ambulance. He tried to get in there with me."

She nodded and smiled as if she had expected that answer. Julian had gotten Thane back for meddling in his care by sending Woofer to Escape to stay with the Walker-Silva clan for the night.

"This is good, Julian. I know it might not feel that way, but it is. You've been successfully coping, but not necessarily living. I want to see you again in the morning. We need to begin preparing you for more memories to surface."

Did he hear her wrong? He absolutely refused to restart daily sessions with her ever again. "You're too expensive, doc," Julian said, getting to his feet. "I can't afford to come here every day."

"Julian, your health insurance pays me now, not you. How about eight o'clock in the morning?" she asked, staying in her seat as he ran the palms of his hands over the wrinkles in his cheap pants. He hated those fucking wrinkles.

"It's too early. I don't get home until after two in the morning."

"Woofer will wake you. I'm not worried. And perhaps it's time for you to use him properly. Just a suggestion, but his purpose is to provide you with emotional support. It sounds like he's really doing his job."

"Now wait a second, don't give Woofer a hero of the year award just yet. He didn't break my fall..." Julian couldn't even continue that line of teasing, even if for humor's sake. Woofer had been next-level good to Julian.

Damn it, now he owed the dog his deep appreciation.

Julian gave an exaggerated roll of his eyes and twisted away as he headed for the office door. Fuck it if he wasn't going to have to keep that damn dog. The attachment he'd been trying to avoid settled over his heart, moving Woofer into the same category as Thane and the others for helping him through this awful ordeal.

Hell, he should be Catholic with as much guilt as he carried.

Sarah rose to her feet as the almost silent beep of the alarm went off, letting him know their session had come to an end.

"You've been through a lot, Julian, but I believe these are positive steps. I want you to consider, once again, that it may be time for you to stop making assumptions about what other people feel. Your eyes lit up with the way you spoke about the man you danced with. That's a first in all the time we've worked together. I'm not saying he's the one for you. I'm saying it may be time to reconsider the possibility of more."

The round and round of counseling had his jaw setting tighter. Julian had already made these decisions months ago. No matter his draw to Beckett, he didn't want to be beholden to another living creature. What he wanted was to have his old life back—a secret he'd not shared with anyone.

Julian shook his head, ready for his exit. At the door, right before he opened it, he turned back to Sarah. She had only ever tried to help him.

"Yeah. Yeah. I'll see you in the morning."

She gave her signature nod, telling him she'd let her topic go for now, but she never gave in. He'd hear about it later. He left the office through the back exit, assessing his current feelings. Sarah considered him hardheaded and assumed he didn't listen to her, but he did. She was always good at making him aware of the meaning behind his emotions, even when he refused to let himself dwell on what they might mean.

He stepped out into the bright sun of the parking lot, drawing in a deep breath. More than anything, he just wanted to feel normal again.

CHAPTER 5

Beckett stepped from the shower, reaching for a towel. He ran the soft terry cloth swiftly over his wet body, drying his heated skin. Then repeated the same fast scrubbing motion over his short, wet hair, sending the strands springing every which way. With a step toward the sink, he used the towel to wipe across the condensation covering the bathroom mirror before wrapping then knotting the towel around his waist.

Between the streaks of beaded moisture on the mirror, Beckett leaned in to check the skin underneath his eyes. Circles had formed from his lack of sleep. The brutal sun and wind during his three-day intensive training session turned out to be particularly rough, leaving his cheeks raw.

Beckett reached for his shaving gear, making quick work of removing his four-day-old growth. Not that it could be called a beard as thin and spotty as his facial hair grew. His ancestry was a good mix of Native American and French Canadian. By the look of his deeply tanned skin and splotchy beard, the Native

American genes had won out. But the rest of him? Well, except for the auburn highlights running through his brown hair, he'd say straight-up American mutt.

His cell phone rang before he could get the comb all the way through his hair. He tossed it aside and went for the phone charging on its docking station. His buyer had tried to call several times over the last three days to help better explain what shoes and shirts went with what slacks and suit coats. Of course, he'd had no cell signal while tucked away in the mountains.

"Hello," he answered on the fourth ring.

"Beck?" she asked, seeming surprised that he answered. "It's Taylor. I can't believe it's you. I've been trying to call you for *days*. I was afraid you didn't like what I'd sent."

With the phone to his ear, Beckett headed for the living room. "It's been crazy busy for me. I had a training group that kept me out of reach. But you know I trust you to work your magic. You've done great so far."

"Are you with the clothes I sent?" she asked, her worries apparently appeased as her tone changed to all business.

"I am." Drop him in a jungle somewhere with nothing more than the clothes on his back, and he wouldn't be as freaked out as having to navigate what went with what on those clothing racks.

He hadn't touched a single article of clothing since they arrived. How had he gotten so unlucky to be in a year where the suit was again considered stylish? Honestly, he didn't know that much about fashion trends; Taylor told him such.

"I'm going to put you on speaker so I can take pictures of what you say."

Her chuckle filled the room as Beckett pushed the speaker option. He narrowed his eyes at the screen. His thumb halted in midair over the camera button. He'd been totally serious. No way would he remember all this during his upcoming weeklong trip to Coronado. Especially with the way he'd been burning the candle at both ends lately. The schedule for the next week consisted of early mornings, all day training classes, and plans to spend each night at Reservations. He saw little sleep in his near future.

Shit, had he made his reservations?

His brow crinkled as he tried to remember. Surely, he had, right?

Beckett bypassed the camera and tapped the email icon to make sure he'd gotten the confirmation message from the club. Taylor dove right into her explanation.

"I sent pictures with all the mix and match apparel. You have several different looks there. I tried to get you some distance with these wears. After meeting you and checking out the Reservations' website, I feel sure you have some clothing that you'll feel comfortable in and still falls within their strict dress code. Your frame is perfect. It's a pleasure dressing you." She only paused to take a breath before she got down to details. "Find my instructions. They're attached to the navy Havana suit."

He found the navy suit and pulled the packet off the hanger, dumping the stapled papers into his hand. He flipped through the pages as she spoke, seeing her thorough instructions of all the different looks she'd sent him.

"Do you see the navy dress shirt? The suit and shirt are a perfect color match. That style of suit is considered an athletic cut. It's designed to fit your body type. I sent several in that same cut. All the colors this season really compliment your complexion. You might be sorry you gave me free rein. I added undergarments and cuff links. Oh, and each suit is tailored to your exact measurements so don't overeat all that delicious food they serve there…"

Beckett let Taylor drone on in the background as he refocused on finding the confirmation email from Reservations. His heart did a little pitter-patter when he found proof of his reserved table at the club for the next seven nights.

The striking blue-green eyes raced back into the forefront of his thoughts, and honestly, in his heart too. His boldness had paid off at their last encounter, and he planned to keep that luck going.

Beckett looked at the time on his screen then turned back to the clothing chart Taylor had sent. As if she'd sent an intricate blueprint, Beckett pieced together every item. She'd been clever to do it this way, obviously having worked with some left-brained clients in the past. The analytical approach allowed him to follow along easily. He had as many as fifteen unique looks for anything that might pop up, and boy, did he want something unexpected to happen.

He ignored the enormous price tag highlighted at the bottom of the eighth page. As far as he was concerned, she'd earned her commission. This collection of menswear was better than any before.

"Remember to expect everything to fit snugly and have Escape properties press your clothes. It's a service they offer. I'm super excited about how this turns out for you. You have to call and let me know."

Beckett barely said more than two words since she'd started her explanation. "Thank you for taking all this time to help me."

His phone chimed, drawing his attention to the alarm notification titled *Be Bold Initiative—make the call*. His heart drummed against his ribcage in anticipation.

"I need to make a call. Are we good here?"

"Of course. Send pictures of yourself dressed up. I can't wait. Ciao." She disconnected the call.

He searched his contacts, found the bar's telephone number, and pushed the call button before he had a chance to back down. His internal panic threatening to derail his intention.

He raised the phone to his ear and lifted his eyes to the ceiling. By the fourth ring, he was afraid he hadn't timed the call properly.

"Reservations." The greeting sounded more like a bark. Thane Walker. He'd know that voice anywhere. *Shit*. In a bitch move, Beckett thought about hanging up, but what if caller ID showed his name? "I said Reservations, can you hear me?"

"Yeah, can you hear me?" Beckett asked just as coldly. His eyelids slid closed while his heart dropped to his feet. In what world did the owner of all the Dishology restaurants around the world answer the phone at a bar? Obviously, in Beckett's world. "Is Julian around?"

"Why?" Thane asked, his tone clipped and unyielding. Beckett's restraint snapped. He glanced down at the phone in his hand and took a deep breath. His jaw set firm.

"You don't like me very much, do you?" Beckett tried harder than most to de-escalate any and every rocky situation, but he didn't like Thane Walker any more than the man appeared to like him. After three days in the mountains in rough conditions, he didn't have the energy or inclination to placate anyone.

"I don't know you," Thane fired back in a dismissive tone.

"Yet you speak to me in a tone I've never heard you speak to another person in that club." Beckett balled his free hand into a fist.

Silence held between them for several long seconds before Thane gave a harsh laugh. "You've never heard me talk to Julian then, but you're right, I don't like you. So why do you want to speak to Julian?"

"It's none of your damn business, Walker. Is he available?" His chest heaved from holding back all the insults he wanted to fling at this guy.

"I pulled your file. You're squeaky clean," Thane said with an edge of insult. What the hell was his problem? "You own some oil rights and have a survivalist camp. It's the premier in the country…"

Beckett decided against pointing out how he could kick Thane's ass seven different ways before the guy even knew what hit him. "Yeah, and I've spent a shit load of cash in your establishment. Do you take such an interest in every member's business, or is it just me?"

After a small patch of rustling, Beckett heard Levi's voice

say, "Thane, stop. Give me the phone." Levi sounded as irritated as both Beckett and Thane. Seconds later, Levi said into the phone, "Beckett?"

He had to take a quick breath to keep from barking at Levi. He liked Levi. Levi was the only one in the whole club to take pity on him and reveal bits and pieces about Julian.

"I'm here," Beckett finally said, trying for a lighter tone. "I thought you were moving to Maryland."

"I am, once Logan graduates. Listen, Julian's not here. He's had a… Well, he's taken a few days off. He should be back tonight. Can I give him a message for you?"

"I…" What did he say? Thane threw him off course. "Yeah. I'm coming into town for about a week. I'd like to…schedule some time with him." Oh holy hell, that sounded stupid as fuck. *End the call.* "Could you just have him call me?"

"Levi, hand me the phone," Thane demanded before Levi could respond.

"Why? You get angry when Julian oversteps, then you do this? This is none of your business," Levi countered.

"But it is my business." The jostling noises let Beckett know there was a struggle for control of the phone. One which Thane obviously won since his voice sounded loud and clear as he said, "St. Clair. We need to meet. Lunch tomorrow." Not a question, but a demand.

"Early dinner," Beckett countered, refusing to let go of the control.

He and Thane both said, "Away from the club," at the same time.

Beckett was still firmly in the kicking Thane's ass mode.

"Where?" Thane barked.

"You have my number." Over this conversation, Beckett clipped out, "Tell Julian I called."

Beckett started to lower the phone when Thane said, "I will

after we meet." Then that psycho control freak ended the call on Beckett.

He drew in a deep breath to release his irritation and lowered his cell. His good mood had plummeted. A while ago, he rationalized that he and Thane might have some tension because Beckett's normal table was in Levi's section, but that was Thane's fault too.

If Thane didn't like Levi having friends at the club, he should have thought about that before he'd hired his boyfriend to work there. Thane could financially take care of Levi. He didn't have to work in a place where he catered to so many men. If given the chance, Beckett would do that for Julian in a second...

Wait, slow down. He'd just taken a pole-vaulting jump into the stratosphere.

His already souring attitude took a full nosedive. He scrubbed a palm over his face while scolding himself. He needed to let it go and concentrate on his trip. There were a million things to get ready before he could head out in the morning.

Beckett went for his bedroom to dress, whipping the towel off his hips with more force than necessary. Man, he wanted to kick Walker's arrogant ass.

Julian quietly took each step up to the night club's office, listening to Levi and Thane. He couldn't tell if they were fighting or mating. An argument might intrigue him; them getting their sex on, not so much. At the top of the stairs, Julian paused, tucking his chin to his chest, concentrating on deciphering the unusual exchange. Julian tilted his ear toward the door to better hear the heated words.

Levi surprised Julian. Thane's forceful personality even had

Julian giving into that demanding side more often than he cared to admit. Levi never did, though. Thane had met his match in the young med student. Levi gave Thane the one, two punch over whatever they were fighting about.

Thane demonstrated a deep need to care for his boyfriend, but Levi was just as determined to take care of Thane. He could see how the two might butt heads while trying to balance one another out, but this disagreement sounded different.

Their voices grew louder, and Julian heard his name used.

Thane implied Levi held back some information… Julian raised his eyebrows at the mad respect he had for Levi, which grew by leaps and bounds as Levi refused to spill Julian's secret.

Then Beckett's name got tossed into the mix, and Julian straightened his spine as he edged closer to the door. Thane put his foot down about Julian dating someone they didn't know. Levi insisted it was none of their business.

Julian gave a curt nod of agreement. Damn straight. He was sick and tired of their merry-go-round with that topic. By God, he could date whomever the hell he wanted to.

He didn't wait another second to bust through the office door to see Thane putting the landline in the cradle as if he'd been talking on the phone moments ago instead of just arguing with Levi.

"What in the *WWE SmackDown* is going on here?" Julian asked in such a way that made it clear he'd been listening and knew exactly what happened.

A flushed Levi whirled around to face Julian. "Beckett called. He asked us to tell you." The words rushed out as Levi stalked past Julian toward the door. Then the sound of Levi's feet hitting the stair treads reverberated in the now quiet office.

"Levi," Thane called out and rushed after him. Julian put a hand on Thane's chest, stopping him from leaving the office.

"You have to stop making everyone crazy about St. Clair. It's nothing. Let it go." Julian aimed for a calm but forceful and decisive tone, wanting this discussion to end right there.

Pain mixed with perhaps anger flitted across Thane's face, his brows snapping down. "I'll never forget how you looked when I walked into your hospital room after I finally found you. I've never seen anyone as bruised and battered as you were. The weariness you had then is back in your eyes." Thane's strong hand clasped Julian's where it still rested on his chest. He gave a reassuring squeeze. "You're family to me. I watch your back like you watch mine." Thane cocked his head in Levi's direction. "But Levi knows something I don't. What is it?" He drew in a breath and shook his head as if clearing his thoughts. "You're right. I'm making everyone around us crazy, so I get why you've stopped confiding in me."

Julian had made Levi promise to keep the secret of the flashbacks from Thane. He opened his mouth to tell Thane as much, but no words came.

"I'll give in for right now. I'll try to butt out, but it hurts me that you're keeping secrets from me." Thane slowly let go of Julian's hand. He looked wounded and dejected as he started out of the office and down the steps.

Thane was more than right. Through this crazy road they had traveled together, Julian and Thane had become family—bound together as tightly as any modern-day family could be.

The secret flooded from Julian's lips, damn the overprotective consequences to come.

"Thane, look."

Thane took two additional stomping steps down before his shoulders squared, and he turned his hurt gaze back to Julian.

"I've remembered some things. That's what happened the other day. Levi caught me in a raw moment of openness. I begged him to keep my secret because I didn't want you to worry. The memories were fleeting but intense. I'm talking to my counselor. St. Clair isn't on my radar. I'm not ready to go down that path. Be done with the worry of his involvement. I am."

Thane's facial features ran through a range of emotions before he finally nodded. Julian could see Thane was torn but trying hard to roll with this new information.

"Go. Make things right with Levi," Julian said, nodding Thane away.

"We can get you personal security, Julian," Thane offered in a harsh whisper. Not the first time Thane had suggested such a thing and the very last thing Julian wanted.

"Oh lord, no." Julian shook his head and ventured further into the office, calling over his shoulder, "Go. I've got work to do. I can't imagine the mess I have to clean up after being gone so many days."

"I'll be back, and we can talk more," Thane offered.

"I hope not. That sounds awful," Julian said loudly to the echoing sound of Thane hightailing it down the rest of the steps. Julian scrubbed a hand over his face. This was too much introspection on a good day.

CHAPTER 6

With a row of bellhops pushing carts with Beckett's belongings behind him, he led the way down the length of the luxurious Escape Coronado lobby toward the front desk. He'd hit the mother lode with this military contract. One week a month, for the next twelve months, he was scheduled to spend time in this over-the-top resort, training SERE classroom courses before the trainees came to his mountaintop to put book lessons into real-world experience.

The military covered the costs of his stay while sending their soldiers from all over the world to take his training class. His chest swelled with pride at the accomplishment, but the hardest part yet would be to hide his complete lack of sophistication while inside all this opulence.

A young woman in a crisp blazer and matching skirt, both in hotel colors, stood in the middle of the large foyer, making eye contact with Beckett as he approached. It seemed odd to think anyone from Escape Coronado would be waiting for him.

"Mr. St. Clair, welcome. I'm Jeannie, your personal concierge." She extended her hand in greeting. "Have you been told which part of the conference center is yours this week?"

Beckett opened his mouth to speak the question he really wanted an answer to, which was how did they even know who he was? But he managed to keep that inside. Only after the briefest pause did he say, "No. The valet out front said for me to unload here. I've got my training manuals and supplies behind me." Beckett hooked a thumb over his shoulder to the bellhops behind him. "Is that correct?"

Out of his peripheral vision, he caught the bellhops pulling the carts loaded with boxes and equipment down a long hall, seemingly without being told where they needed to go.

"Yes. We'll have the conference room prepared to your specifications tonight. They'll secure your boxes until it's time to put them inside the room." She pivoted and turned to walk to the front desk. He looked over his shoulder at the single remaining bellhop who stood about four feet away with all his personal luggage. Beckett barely refrained from rolling his eyes at the sight of that cart loaded from top to bottom. Ridiculous. His normal luggage load consisted of a single duffel bag he tossed over his shoulders and that wasn't ever full.

Beckett's cheeks flushed as he followed her. He had to keep his goals in mind and remember the *Be Bold Initiative* was as important to him as the classes he planned to teach this week. Jeannie went around the front desk to check him in on a computer.

"Let's see, Mr. St. Clair. You have a salon appointment scheduled for a haircut in the next hour." She continued staring at the screen as she said, "It seems we have an opening for a massage. Would that interest you?"

Her gaze lifted to his, waiting for his answer.

"I'll pass on the massage." He reached for his wallet in his back pocket and pulled a credit card free, handing it over the desk.

"Not necessary, sir. We know how to find you." She grinned

broadly at the joke as she worked behind the desk, preparing a small folder of information. "We've arranged for you to have the same room every month when you come back for your training sessions at Escape. If there's something not quite to your liking, please let us know. We've given you a suite close to the meeting rooms at the conference center. It's a bit of a walk from here, but there's a valet at the southern entrance door, and that'll be a much closer walk for you."

An Escape Coronado logoed folder slid across the counter as she continued her introduction. "We've also assigned a personal assistant to you, available as you need. Their contact information is inside the folder. They'll be responsible for setting up the training rooms, for the lunch boxes you're providing your attendees, and whatever else you need. We're happy to help, day or night." She flipped open the folder to an attached card on the inside flap.

He reached for the access code to the room, tucking it inside his wallet. "Will this always be my room and entry code?"

"Yes, sir," she nodded happily, her ponytail bobbing behind her.

"This is an incredible place. I've never seen anything like it," Beckett said, taking the folder as he looked back around the lobby again.

"I agree. Escape's unique. It's a great place to work." She smiled as she came back around the counter, waiting at the end for him. She extended her hand to indicate the bellhop still waiting by the cart. "Tommy will show you the way to your room. If you need anything, call out the name Iris or assistant, and a hologram will lower from anywhere in your suite's living room."

"Thank you." Beckett walked toward the bellhop, who grinned big and cocked his head to the side as he led the way down the same hall the others had taken. He followed, taking in all the intricate details of the hotel as they went. The artwork alone looked designed specifically for the hotel and blended every inch of space together. At the first bank of elevators, Beckett turned in a complete circle, staring up at the detailed design of a dome.

"Beckett St. Clair?"

Tension automatically tightened his shoulders. He'd know that voice anywhere. He rolled his shoulders to help loosen the suddenly tight muscles and looked over to see Thane Walker taking long strides in his direction. Thane carried a superior attitude. Maybe not with everyone, but definitely with Beckett. Thane looked Beckett up and down as he approached. Judgment evident with the way he lingered over Beckett's scuffed work boots and well-worn blue jeans he'd chosen to travel in.

"I wasn't sure it was you."

Beckett had to force himself to stick out a hand to shake Thane's. "We're heading to my room. Good to see you."

He tilted his head toward the bellhop who came to a stop several feet away. Beckett went to the side of his cart, pushing the elevator call button again, wanting Thane to take the hint and move on.

Of course, he didn't leave, but Beckett never looked back.

"Did we finalize dinner plans?" Thane asked.

Fuck. He tried to decide whether they had enough distance between them that he could pretend he hadn't heard Thane's question.

There wasn't. Beckett rolled his shoulders again and turned, twisting his upper body only. He reached a hand around the pole of the cart, gripping it tight. Thane closed the gap between them as if Beckett had extended an invitation. He didn't move one solitary step toward Thane, making the other man cover the distance.

"I have a casual dining grill in the front lobby area. Can you meet me there in about an hour and a half?"

Beckett's salon appointment was at five. His reservation at Reservations wasn't until eight. So yeah, he technically had time to meet Thane.

Fuck. Why couldn't he be better at lying? "I'm just not

interested in a bunch of bullshit with you."

"Great. I agree." Thane clapped his hands together once as if Beckett had said yes to their dinner date. "Just you and me, and maybe another friend—the owner of Escape—if he's free."

Beckett's hand tightened around the pole. Just what he needed: two of them. He stared at Thane, who had dialed back the attitude he usually projected. That could have been a good sign. Or maybe Thane thought having the other man would give him a better chance at hiding a body—Beckett's. The macabre thought made him smile.

"Did you give Julian my message?" Beckett asked, only to know if Julian had purposefully ignored his phone call.

"Let's talk tonight." Thane nodded once as if Beckett responded favorably then turned away. "I'm late for a meeting. I'll see you at six thirty."

"Dog, you're not listening to me. I'm telling you that you must stay inside this conference room. Look, it has a soft chair you can curl up on. That's your favorite thing to do." Julian snapped his fingers then with a sweep of his arm through the doorway, pointed to the chair. Woofer took a seat on one of Julian's shoes—one he was wearing at the time—his big body knocking against Julian's leg. His tail gave a single wag as the big chocolate eyes stared up at him.

Julian scrubbed both hands down his face until his fingers rested on his cheeks. He stared down at the dog. Great, now they were in a staring competition. He wasn't an expert on emotional support anything, but the damn dogs he'd seen on television had always responded to verbal commands and never went off course of their master's directives.

Julian finally caved and brought Woofer to work with him tonight in the first place. He felt guilty for leaving Woofer at home alone all the time.

Ricco, the club's head bartender, came around the corner, carrying his pay stub in hand. The bartender stopped short at seeing the enormous German shepherd then looked at Julian, in obvious confusion. He took a giant step backward when Woofer gave the slightest growl.

Woofer had a naturally menacing look, one of the reasons Julian had chosen the dog in the first place, but he didn't have an aggressive bone in his body, not that Julian had witnessed. The growl could have been a rumble in his stomach for as sweet as the dog was.

"Whoa, what's that?"

"My dog, Woofer, and he's being a giant pain in the ass," Julian added for Woofer's benefit.

Ricco looked surprised as he shook his head as if trying to understand. "You don't strike me as a dog person." Ricco then gave Woofer a wide berth as he edged past the dog into the break room.

"You think? Of course, I'm not a dog person," Julian confirmed readily.

"Then what's he doing here?" Ricco dropped the paystub at one of the tables on top of Julian's portfolio.

"Aren't you full of questions, Mr. InMyBusiness?" Julian asked, eyeing the stub. Today was payday, which always meant something was wrong somewhere. "Why're you back here?"

"They didn't put my raise on this check. It was supposed to be there. You need to check it out for me," the bartender said while, again, skirting past Woofer, who stayed happily glued to Julian's leg.

The dog shed like crazy, and Julian looked down at the hair already covering his dress pants. He immediately reached down, swiping at the stray hair, remembering the deshedding appointment Woofer had missed during Julian's hospital stay.

"Woofer, get in the room," Julian barked. He had to find some tape or something to remove the hair from his dark-colored pants.

"Woofer, like Woof?" Ricco asked, lifting his brow and shaking his head as he spoke. "Of course, you would name him that."

Julian smiled at Ricco's statement. At least someone got the meaning behind Woofer without him having to explain it.

The buzzer and twirling red lights went off, alerting everyone in the kitchen that the back delivery door had been opened. Julian glanced up as a cool summer breeze blew through the open door, ruffling his hair.

A memory flashed seconds before the blinking lights dulled, taking Julian's sight with it. He was transported to a place with muted sounds of conversation, and the hum of fluorescent lights piercing his skull, sending pain vibrating over every inch of space inside his head.

His body hurt too badly to move. Everything was spinning, and he felt groggy. This wasn't right. Why was he hanging over a guy's broad shoulder? He couldn't see much from his position, only the back of a pair of cheap black jeans. The air around him filled with even cheaper aftershave. The breath rushed from Julian's lungs as he was tossed over something hard. Blinding pain shot through his ribcage. He could barely open his eyes and had no control over his movements. Three or four men surrounded him. He couldn't see their faces, but they called Julian by his name.

Where was he? Why was it so hard to breathe?

"Julian."

Woofer's heavy bark echoed in the background and the world swirled back into place. Julian staggered under the weight of what had just happened but managed to stay on his feet.

"Dude, are you all right?"

"Do I look all right?"

"You look green."

Not now. This couldn't be happening now. Julian had turned into a fucking headcase. Woofer's big noggin knocked into Julian's thigh, urging him toward the break room. Ricco took his arm and guided him to one of the chairs in the small space.

"Let me go get you some water and a wet rag."

Julian grabbed Ricco's arm. His grip was weak, but enough to stop Ricco from leaving. "No one needs to know about this."

Ricco shook his head in disagreement. "I don't know, boss. That was some weird shit you just did." Woofer's head came to Julian's lap as if he agreed with Ricco. His dog made a whining sound, his eyes focused on Julian's face. "Dude, you should probably go home. You look like hell. I should call Thane."

Julian tossed his head back, letting the chair's comforting squeak and plush cushions surround him with familiarity. Something he desperately needed right now.

His limbs were heavy and his mind still foggy from the memories that blindsided him. His hand went to Woofer's head when the dog whined again.

"Let's start with a glass of cold water. Then we'll see what happens before we freak out all my babysitters."

CHAPTER 7

Beckett finally understood the power of a well-cut suit.

He strode through the front doors of the grill Thane owned, past the line forming at the hostess stand, making his way to the bar. He felt like a million bucks. Maybe the new stylish haircut, with a few well-placed honey-colored highlights helped boost his confidence and build his resolve.

He hadn't chosen to wear the cowboy hat tonight. Hadn't even brought it with him to have something to do with his hands.

He'd left something else inside his suite, too: patience. He refused to take any shit from Thane Walker tonight.

Beckett's spine went ramrod straight when he thought about the arrogance of the man he was about to meet. Thane had had it out for him since day one. Even though he'd never so much as sneezed in the man's direction. Tonight, he was determined to find out exactly why Thane disliked him so much.

At thirty-three years old, Beckett had lost hope that he'd ever find his missing piece. He didn't know if Julian was the one, but he knew he'd never been this interested in anyone before. Whoever got in his way could kiss his ass. That included Thane Walker.

Images of taking Thane into the mountains and leaving his ass there tugged a smile from Beckett's lips as he looked around the restaurant. He liked that idea more than he cared to admit.

"Excuse me, sir. There's a wait for the bar. The lines that way." A fresh-faced young woman informed him.

"I'm meeting someone here," he started to explain, but she cut him off before he could say who.

"Parties aren't seated until everyone arrives," she said, pointing toward the front door. The direction she wanted him to go. "Our waiting overflow area is just outside the doors to the right."

"I've got him." Thane materialized out of nowhere, sticking out a hand to Beckett.

Thane the Difficult grinned ear to ear. His normal, super well-kept appearance had a tousled air about it this evening. He looked more relaxed than maybe Beckett had ever seen him before, at least when Beckett was in his vicinity.

"We're over here."

He could easily see over Thane's shoulder when he hitched a thumb that way. He expected to see Levi somewhere in the crowded, loud restaurant but didn't.

"I've invited Arik Layne to join us," Thane explained. The volume of the casual restaurant drowned out anything more he might have said as he turned away. Beckett had no choice but to follow.

He wound his way through the tables and chairs to the farthest corner of the restaurant. A waitress dressed in blue jeans and a restaurant logoed T-shirt placed many plates of different appetizers in front of a nice-looking blond guy who tilted a cocktail glass up to drain the contents.

"Arik Layne meet Beckett St. Clair."

Arik extended a hand across the table while using the other to hand the waitress his glass. Thane slid into the booth first. Beckett was thankful for that. He didn't want to be caged in between these two men.

"Would you like another?" the waitress asked.

"Absolutely." Arik's handshake was firm and friendly. When she took his empty glass, Arik pointed toward Beckett. "Hook him up. He has some catching up to do. And it's Thane's treat."

"*Pfft.*" Thane grunted. "Arik doesn't believe in moderation, so he spends three hours a night working out to burn off his meals."

A teasing, fun Thane had Beckett taking his seat, questioning what alternate universe he'd landed in.

"I'll take a Heineken," he said to the waitress. Thane pointed to his cocktail glass and nodded to the waitress who gave a single nod in reply before she turned away.

Arik didn't rest on any formality. He dug straight into the food, grabbing several crab balls off a plate. "Beckett, Thane was telling me you're interested in our Julian."

Thane cut a shocked gaze, his expression frustrated, toward Arik, throwing out a hand across the table in a clear *what the hell* motion. "We were supposed to ease into it, Layne."

"I never understood why," Arik said nonchalantly, picking up a small white plate and handing it across the table to Beckett. "Dig in. This grill has delicious food. Best crab cakes in California, and I've tried them all to know for sure."

"He's probably not lying about that," Thane muttered as he picked from one of the five plates of appetizers in front of them.

The *Be Bold Initiative* infusing Beckett's confidence took a solid hit at the direct confrontation. Uncomfortable, Beckett sat back in the seat, looking between the two men. In every conceivable way he'd planned for this meeting to go, it was nothing like this.

"He doesn't talk much," Arik said, then placed a nice-size bite of the crab ball in his mouth.

"No, he doesn't ever say much at all, except to Levi." Thane gave Beckett a menacing stare until the table jolted. Beckett liked assuming Arik had kicked Thane underneath the table. And Thane's actions—whipping his head toward Arik and giving him the same glare Beckett had received—confirmed his theory. "I bet that leaves a mark. You could have just told me I veered off course."

"But then that'd be less like a kick and more like a reasonable exchange," Arik said cheekily while chomping the food in his mouth. "You and I don't do reasonable."

At least Beckett knew now that he wasn't the only one Thane ever got pushy with.

"Right before you arrived, I was telling Layne that you owned a survival training company. It's highly respected." Thane's hand motioned toward Beckett as he continued to speak to Arik about Beckett as if he had some sort of insider information. "He's the owner, operator, and lead instructor, if my Google search is to be believed." Thane's penetrating gaze landed on Beckett. "Did I get it correct?"

Beckett confirmed with a nod.

The one thing that Beckett had struggled with since first seeing Julian was how the club and its employees were overly protective of the man. Maybe a tipsy Arik Layne, or Thane Walker for that matter, might loosen their lips enough to let something spill.

Thankfully, his beer was placed in front of him.

He nodded his appreciation to the waitress, grabbing a napkin and placing it in his lap for nothing more than to crush in his fist when needed.

"He's got manners, Walker," Arik said aloud as if defending Beckett. "He told me you were one of those outdoorsmen. You don't say much. They call you the Marlboro Man at the club." Arik squinted as if to assess Beckett from a different angle.

"Oh yeah, he's a perfect Marlboro Man," the waitress chimed in, giving Beckett a wink as she cleared the empty glasses from the table.

Beckett lifted the bottle and took a couple of hearty swallows, thinking about the nickname he'd been given. He had no real idea what it meant. When he'd first heard the name, he'd adamantly explained to Levi that he wasn't a smoker and never had been. Levi only laughed at him.

"I don't really know what that means," Beckett finally said when the waitress left the table, looking between Arik and Thane, who appeared to be waiting for his answer. Beckett nodded toward Thane. "He hasn't been my biggest fan."

In the middle of taking a drink, Thane began to choke at Beckett's directness. Arik laughed and reached over to casually pat his buddy's back. "He's protective of our Julian. We all are. Give him a break."

Beckett paused with the bottle halfway to his lips. "Why protective?"

He placed the beer bottle back on the table under the heavy weight of their stares. With how serious both Arik and Thane had become, it couldn't be good.

"He doesn't know?" Arik's brow lifted in question as he focused on Thane.

"No, I don't think so," Thane answered. Then both men turned expectant stares on Beckett again. He remained silent as his heart drummed with uncertainty.

Beckett tried not to overthink what could have happened to change Arik's happy-go-lucky expression. "Is Julian taken? Is that the deal here? You have Levi," Beckett said to Thane then turned his attention to Arik. "Are you and Julian together? Have I overstepped?"

Arik chuckled, lifting a glass of water, taking a long drink as he wiggled his ring finger for Beckett to see. "Married for a few years now. What's your backstory?"

Beckett trained men in the art of managing interrogation, yet he felt like he'd landed in the middle of the hot seat. He still hadn't gotten any clear answers. What did "married a few years" mean? Could Arik be married to Julian? The panic of such a thought had heat rising up his neck, flushing his cheeks even as everything inside him rejected the idea of Arik's marriage to Julian. Julian was single. He focused his attention on Arik. His brain still tried to connect the dots as he spoke. "I haven't been out very long if that's what you're asking."

"It wasn't, but why haven't you?" Arik asked, turning curious or perhaps concerned again.

Beckett tried hard to navigate any possible landmines being set out unseen in front of him. He let out a sigh and tightened his grip on his bottle in one hand and the napkin in the other.

"I wasn't comfortable with the idea of being gay." What a major understatement. Beckett took a long drink, draining the beer, washing away the bitter taste of his half-truth.

Arik made a motion to the waitress then pointed to Beckett's beer.

"Family issues?" Thane asked. Of course, the man would poke around for more.

"About me accepting myself?" Beckett asked. "Nah. It was all me. I was raised in an extremely masculine environment. The survival camp idea started from a hobby my father and I used to enjoy for fun. I struggled. Last year, I realized I was tired of being alone, tired of hiding." Beckett turned his full attention to Thane, not backing down. "Your club was my first venture into this world of being out openly."

Beckett sat back in the booth, feeling vulnerable about telling his story. It had taken a lot to get to this point, and just about anything could resurrect that old discomfort. He was a work in progress, to say the very least.

"So, you're saying your idea of a fun time is to be lost out in the wilderness with nothing but the clothes on your back." Arik's gaze slid down his body. "How does it feel to dress like that?" Arik asked. The man was intuitive. Beckett reached for his new beer bottle.

"It's not easy for me." Beckett chuckled at his truth then took a drink, watching as both men dug into their food again.

"You know, Layne, in all the years I've known Julian, I'm not sure I've seen him outside other than to move from point A to point B," Thane said.

"How do you two know Julian?" Beckett asked.

For the second time in the last few minutes, the uber-sophisticated Thane choked on the bite of food in his mouth. This time, Arik's whacks to Thane's back were done with a good-natured chuckle. Thane coughed, then took a long drink, draining his cocktail glass. Thane's discomfiture made Beckett wonder if Thane and Julian had dated before. He got the draw to the man. Julian was a gorgeous guy, next-level handsome. It might also explain the protectiveness that Thane had over Julian.

"That's a story for Julian to tell," Thane finally answered.

"Then tell me why I'm here." Beckett looked down at his new wristwatch. He had about twenty minutes before he was due at Reservations, and the conversation with these two men hadn't offered him any worthwhile insight.

"Did Julian call you back?" Thane asked.

That question struck a blow to the center of his chest. Beckett decided Thane hadn't told Julian about his call. If for no other reason than Beckett was a customer, he'd assumed Julian would have called him back.

"How old are you?" Arik asked. The volley of questions had Beckett turning to Arik.

"Thirty-three," he answered without hesitation.

Arik nodded at Thane. Something unspoken passed between the two men.

"So, I guess we're going to do this." Thane ran a napkin over his lips and pushed his plate a few inches away. "You've probably guessed Julian's been going through something. Those of us who care for him are worried. I'm not from here. I've only stayed in California because Levi's here. We're heading back to Maryland. Levi's going back to medical school."

"And I live in Dallas," Arik added.

"Julian's on the mend, but not quite where he should be, at least where I wish him to be. So, Layne and I put our heads together and decided Julian could use some self-defense training."

The picture being painted didn't look good. He had no idea what Julian might have gone through, but from the look on their faces and the tone in Walker's voice, the story was probably bleaker than he'd let himself imagine. His heart took a dip.

"Levi told me that Julian was being promoted within your company. That more of these clubs were going to be built," Beckett said. That being the main reason Beckett had agreed to do the training so close to the naval station instead of having the trainees sent to him for classroom instruction then straight into the field. He wanted to get his foot in Reservations' door and to be on Julian's radar before he took off.

"He was being promoted, but we've changed our minds," Thane said so casually that Beckett had to think about each word. Beckett's brows dropped in a hard V. His protectiveness for Julian came on strong, blowing off the charts. He didn't like Julian being handed something as big as a promotion, then having it idly taken away. Some friends these guys were.

"He's got it bad," Arik asserted, pushing his plate aside.

"You noticed that too?" Thane asked Arik, but Beckett held all his attention. "You aren't overly expressive, but you get that fierce look that I bet makes small children cry." Thane arched a brow Arik's way. "That look's been aimed at me for at least the last month."

Oh hell no. Thane was the motherfucker in this scenario, not Beckett. "Because you scowl at me all the damn time, Walker.

Does Julian know you're stripping him of his promotion? That doesn't seem right. And it's not right to be so casual about Julian's life in front of me."

Arik barked out a laugh and clapped his hands together. He had to have drawn every eye in the restaurant with the sheer volume of the outburst. One being the waitress who Arik instructed to serve another round.

"Calm down. No one's doing Julian wrong, but Julian doesn't know yet that the general manager over both the restaurant and club has given his notice. We've decided to ask Julian to take that position," Thane said.

"It's crazy how well he's done running the club," Arik added with enthusiasm that helped Beckett take the edge off his increasing ire.

"He has no management background or real training, but he's killed it," Thane continued, nodding at Arik. "I believe he'll accept the new position and be happy to have it. He loves Reservations. He's the whole reason for the concept, but it's not been enough to make him start living his life again. That's where Layne and I have decided you come in."

No matter how Thane made it sound, Beckett didn't believe Thane meant that he and Julian should shoot for a relationship. That somehow, magically, in the last twenty hours, Thane began to side with Beckett, encouraging him to make his move.

"How do you mean?" Beckett finally asked when nothing more was said.

Thane, who clearly thought of himself as a master negotiator, propped his elbows on the edge of the table as he leaned Beckett's direction. Sincerity slid over every part of his face.

"Julian needs to feel empowered again. We believe a private, intensive self-defense training program would do Julian very well. Something designed to help him regain his confidence."

Since Beckett knew nothing of Julian's problems, he couldn't agree or disagree with the plan. He nodded though; Beckett probably had a confidence that he might not have otherwise by knowing he could survive through any disaster while being able to kick every guy's ass in this room without breaking a sweat.

"I'm not sure what you're insinuating, but I don't teach self-defense, and ultimately that's Julian's decision, not yours."

As if Beckett hadn't said anything other than he didn't teach self-defense, Arik spoke up. "But you know it. I watched some of your combat training videos on YouTube. You can handle teaching Julian."

Beckett was as lost as ever. He barely knew how to work his cell phone. He had no social media and didn't own a computer other than what the secretary at the main lodge used. Of course, he didn't have videos on YouTube.

Thane added, "Julian will be against this because he's against everything I suggest."

"Like he's a damn out-of-control teenager," Arik confirmed with a commiserating nod.

"Like a bad teenager who needs to go to military school," Thane murmured and rolled his eyes, sitting back against the booth. His bluster disappeared, his shoulders slumping as his hands fell to his lap. "A pain in the ass teen."

Neither of these men made any sense. Beckett had to pull them back into the conversation before they spun off on some side topic about having kids. "Let's say I'd do it. How would you get Julian to agree? Would you tell him it was me? I'm not sure it would help if I were the one because, most of the time, I feel like he doesn't even know who I am."

"You caught that ignoring thing, huh?" Arik said, laughing. "Kellus did that to me. He made me work like I never worked before just to earn a simple glance. I fell hook, line, and sinker. I'm still hooked."

Beckett assumed Kellus must be the spouse Arik had referred to. He lifted his bottle, draining the beer, tilting it all the way back for every last drop.

"Julian struggles with trusting people," Thane started. "But I believe he trusts you enough that he'd open up for the first time in a long time. I haven't seen the real Julian for so long that I thought his current ways were his new normal. That was until he danced with you. Levi's helped me see." Thane shook his head. "If you can get Julian back to his old self, I'll owe you a huge debt of gratitude."

The emotion in Thane's words touched something inside Becket. "Would you tell him what we're doing?"

"No. Maybe. I don't know." Thane shook his head, likely seeing all the ways this could go wrong because who didn't appreciate people trying to control and manipulate them? "I think he'll be resistant. I feel like I'm going to have to trick him."

"Is that really a good idea?" Beckett asked. "I can't see Julian responding well to manipulation."

"It's the only way," Arik said, passing off his empty plate and glass to the waitress. "Julian's strong-willed."

"Julian's stubborn and hardheaded," Thane added.

Beckett didn't like the idea of lying to Julian, and he wouldn't if he ever got Julian in front of him again. "And what do you want me to teach him?"

"How to defend himself." Arik's hands flew out like that was a given.

Beckett gnawed on his lower lip and nodded at the waitress when she replenished his beer. "It sounds like something bad might have happened to Julian." Beckett let go of a deep sigh. He absolutely didn't like the idea of Julian being hurt or abused to the level that it changed him as a man.

Aggression surged inside of him. Just thinking of someone hurting Julian made his blood boil. The need to protect Julian overshadowed his desire to find out why these two were including him in the process.

"Repetitive combat training is the key to managing your head during a fight-or-flight response. I could teach him some things I've learned, work with him in the training room in the convention center after I finish classes. I'll be discreet, keep it private, and I'm here for the next week."

What did it say about Beckett that his heart did a little pitter-patter at the idea of spending any amount of time alone with Julian?

"Tell us your schedule, and we'll get Julian to you. Let us worry about getting him there," Arik said.

At a loss for words, Beckett had no clue if this was a good plan or terrible idea, but both men staring at him with such intensity felt like a good dose of solid peer pressure. He nodded into the silence as he tentatively committed to their plan. Still so unsure how this could do anything more than blow up in his face.

CHAPTER 8

More than anything, Julian didn't want to go home to the emptiness of his condo. Being alone gave him way too much time to think. If he'd had his choice, he'd continue with the night as if nothing had happened, managing the hell out of his shift to distract himself from himself. But Ricco had pulled a sneaky move and called Levi, who promptly pulled a dick move by saying he'd tell Thane about the newest "incident" if he didn't take it easy tonight.

It was probably the right thing to do. His nerves were fried. The fear sent his anxiety skyrocketing as he'd remembered the pieces of what had happened left him chilled to his core.

So rather than leave right away, he'd positioned himself at the edge of the bar with Woofer between his stool and the side of the bar as the guests began to arrive. From where he sat, he could easily field any problems while casually sipping on a cocktail that was more whiskey than sour. He'd pretend as if he didn't have a care in the world.

Julian couldn't help glancing over to table thirty-four. A move he'd made fifteen times already that evening. The reserved sign still sat on top, but its occupant hadn't yet arrived.

Since Julian's obsessive side could recall the moment-by-moment details of the man who had reserved that table, he understood how weird it was that the cowboy was late. Beckett hadn't arrived at the club on time nor had he called to ensure his late arrival. Maybe a first since Beckett had started regularly coming to the club.

Julian looked down at his wristwatch. Twenty-three minutes late, to be precise. Beckett made Reservations a prettier place to be. Julian lifted his cocktail glass to his lips, wondering if he should reach out to see if the table was still needed. Maybe that was why Beckett called last night.

Damn. He'd assumed Beckett's call had been personal, not business-related.

Ricco placed a salad in front of Julian with a hearty portion of his favorite raspberry vinaigrette coating the assorted greens and slices of vegetables. Plants became a large part of his clean-living diet. A change he'd made well over a year ago, and much like he did every time he dug into a plate of vegetables, Julian yearned for a thick, juicy steak. Someday he'd have better control over his moods, and he'd add meat back into his diet, he promised himself.

"He's doing great," Quinn, one of their waiters, said and nodded down to Woofer.

It went against Julian's personality to give the counselor the win on Woofer being actual emotional support. The damn dog that annoyed the shit out of him at home was almost unnoticeable, quiet and alert as he sat.

"I'm being asked if table thirty-three can incorporate thirty-four into their party."

Julian looked over to see a crowd of men gathered around the larger high-boy table. "No, give it some time. St. Clair's a good customer. Get some barstools from the back, and let's see if he arrives."

"Hey, Julian. Have we heard from thirty-four? Is he coming in tonight?" Remington, another waiter, asked from about the midway point down the bar where he loaded his tray with cocktail glasses. "One of my guests wants to know."

"Who wants to know?" Julian looked over to Remington's section of tables as if a large red arrow would point him out.

"The older guy at table twenty-seven."

Julian's gaze locked on that table. All the men looked older, sophisticated, well put together, and handsome. Damn.

"Which one?" Julian asked.

"The older one," Remington repeated, then turned with his tray full of drinks in his hand. "Is he coming tonight?"

So, the Marlboro Man had built a fan club involving more than just the club's waiters and bartenders. Julian's possessive side stood on guard. "We're holding the table for him, but he's late."

Julian dug into the salad with his fork, stuffing a big bite into his mouth, and reached for the untouched glass of water nearby. He chomped out his frustration that the big, tall cowboy hat wearing mystery man was building some possible hookups.

Julian had watched as Beckett sat alone for hours at his table until some of the waiters were cut from their shifts and ended up joining the guy. Beckett had become a welcome patron in the club and his table a safe place for most of the guys who worked for Reservations to gather.

No, Julian hadn't missed all the long lingering looks Beckett tossed his way. He liked the way Beckett watched him. Those intriguing brown eyes and that appealing gaze. Beckett was all man, every single inch of him. He knew that for a fact because he'd rubbed himself against all that masculinity when they'd danced.

An unexpected sensation had Julian dropping the fork in his hand to the plate, his gaze lowering to his slacks-covered cock. Holy hell, the way it plumped painfully against his zipper had his heart thumping wildly in his chest. The damn thing did, in fact, work. How long had it been since he'd grown hard? He couldn't remember. Tears of happiness sprung to his eyes, making him fight to swallow the lump forming in his throat. Damn, it felt good.

How much had he had to drink? Regardless of his actions over the last few days, Julian had given up alcohol. Should he have been drinking this whole time?

"Boss, you good?" Ricco tapped the edge of the bar to gain Julian's attention.

He paid the bartender no heed, not wanting to lose this moment. Julian only had two cocktails over the last couple of hours. That meant he was practically sober, yet his cock was working again for the first time in a long while.

Under Ricco's intense scrutiny, Julian's cock deflated. He closed his eyes, bringing forth images of Beckett sitting alone at his table, rarely speaking to anyone. Every single time Beckett showed up or planned to leave for the night, his gaze sought out Julian. No matter how hard Julian fought the urge to turn Beckett's way he eventually would turn, helpless to do anything but.

Beckett would smile and touch the brim of his hat. Fuck, what a sexy move. Beckett's strong jaw and full lips, his dark tanned skin… Julian's dick swelled at warp speed.

Hell yeah. Julian was helpless to stop the tear that built enough steam to trickle down his cheek. This had to mean he was healing, right?

"Julian. You good?"

He opened his eyes, prepared to share with Ricco exactly why he was great right now. His hand reached to wipe away the tear when the unique scent of outdoors, sunshine, and exotic spices hit his senses. Unmistakably Beckett. He looked over to see an expansive masculine chest and broad shoulders leaning into him as Beckett busted a move to avoid a collision with one of the busboys.

Julian lifted his gaze. Of course, he held all of Beckett's undivided attention. They locked gazes for one, maybe two long seconds, before Ricco's hand slapped down hard on the bar top, pulling Julian's gaze toward Ricco.

"What?" He said the word with maybe three syllables of frustration.

Ricco showed zero cares about Julian's obvious annoyance "Are. You. Goooda?"

"Mind your business. Concentrate on the job you're being paid to do." Julian motioned to the line of waiters standing at the bar, waiting for their drinks. But even that only held his attention for the briefest of moments before he happily lowered his gaze again to his dick. The damn thing was rigidly hard, straining against his form-hugging pants. Holy fuck. The relief was staggering.

Julian dropped his head between his shoulder blades, thanking the universe for this blessing.

"Mr. St. Clair, we were getting worried about you," Ricco said.

"Call me Beckett." The rich masculine timbre held hints of a deeply cultured southern accent, drawing Julian's gaze to Beckett once again.

"A guy at one of Remington's tables wants to buy your drinks tonight," Ricco said to Beckett as he started to pour again. "He asked me to see if you're interested when you came in."

Julian's head dropped forward; he couldn't help his astonished stare. He got caught up in Beckett's new look. Julian's gaze narrowed to Beckett, admiring how he wore the hugely popular suit with the athletic cut. Beckett looked fashionable in a style that accented every one of his masculine curves and edges. He was clean-shaven with his hair styled and pushed back off his forehead. No cowboy hat to be found anywhere.

"Which table?" Beckett asked and turned toward the grouping of tables. His body angled to look where Remington pointed to a group of three men. Julian looked down the length of Beckett's long body. He wasn't wearing boots tonight or a tie. Instead, his collar was unbuttoned with a small amount of fur peaking from the opening. The look suited him. Julian's fingers twitched to run over the man's exposed skin. He'd bet Beckett had the same dark tan all the way down that expansive chest.

Beckett was mouthwateringly gorgeous in this new look. Who would have known the man could be even more handsome than Julian remembered?

Tonight, the man held an air of confidence that he didn't usually have. Beckett lifted a hand to the men, grinned a sultry smile, and turned back to Ricco. "Buy his next round on me and tell him thank you, I'm flattered, but I've got my eye on someone else tonight."

More than the words spoken, something compelled Julian to look Beckett straight in his eyes. Julian was never at a loss for words, yet his brain blinked out on him. He sucked in a breath because more than just his cock appreciated all those good looks focused his way.

"What did I miss?" Julian finally asked, clearing his throat, forcing himself to act casual and hold Beckett's direct stare.

Damn, if Julian wasn't beginning to feel like his old self again. The emotion of it was almost too much. He fought the excitement building inside him as he reached for his napkin and wiped his mouth.

"My phone call," Beckett quipped in a teasing tone. "I heard you got my message. Why didn't you call a guy back?"

Ricco burst out with a loud laugh, his brows shooting up at Beckett as he grabbed a hand towel, wiping his hands, staring in disbelief.

Julian wondered if all that rugged manliness affected Ricco like it did him.

"Answer his question, boss man," Ricco teased. The towel in the bartender's hand whipped out, popping Julian's knuckles. What the hell was happening? Julian looked shocked over at the playful Ricco, especially as the line of waiters waiting for him to fill drinks grew.

"Worry about your damn self and fill the goddamn drinks. Why do I keep having to say that?" Julian slung out a hand to the waiters again gathering. Ricco's gaze followed. Then he jumped to work, pulling glasses as fast as Julian had ever seen.

Julian shifted his gaze back to Beckett, who hadn't turned away. It was a bit flattering. "You think because we shared a dance, I owe you a phone call?"

"No, not at all. I just enjoyed the dance and wanted to say as much," Beckett said lightheartedly and stood to his full height, looking past the end of the bar to where Woofer sat quietly. "What's he doing here?"

Julian instantly dropped his gaze to Woofer and his enormous paws. "Being a good boy."

Maybe the six bottles of beer Beckett had downed with Thane and Arik in a little over an hour on an empty stomach fueled this sudden burst of confidence, or maybe the new suit made him finally feel like he fit with the club's other patrons or maybe it was seeing Julian sitting casually at the end of the bar, eating his dinner, something Beckett had never seen before. Whatever the reason, Beckett grabbed the empty barstool close to where the dog sat and parked his ass right there, turning his body in Julian's direction as he anchored his loafers on the bottom rung of the stool.

"So, does the good boy have a name?" he quipped in the

same teasing tone he'd used before.

Julian's pouty mouth quirked up in one corner as the manager chided Beckett in a playful tone with all the expected sass that Julian was known for.

"Woofer. Were you invited to take a seat here with me? I see a perfectly good table, a coveted one, in a prime piece of real estate in this club, going unused."

Beckett turned, angling toward his empty table but made no move to head that direction.

"Then come have a drink with me over there," Beckett drawled, suddenly completely at ease with Julian. He wondered if all his preparations had worked. Could he dare hope that the enticing outline of Julian's cock in those snug-fitting pants was due to him? The tempting sight had caught his eye when he first arrived, and he had to lean into Julian's personal space to avoid a busboy with a tray full of dirty glasses. Julian's cock only grew more pronounced with each second Beckett spent in his company.

Beckett's own desire grew. A growing warmth seeped through every nerve ending in his body, but that was nothing new where Julian was concerned.

"You think because we danced together, that means what?" He watched Julian drop a cloth napkin on his lap, covering the bulge in his tailored pants. Beckett saw a slight hint of a flush on Julian's cheeks before he lowered his eyes, his hand going to the dog's head.

Maybe the beers gave Beckett courage. If he could break through Julian's resistance toward him, he wouldn't have to play a part in deceiving Julian into learning self-defense. Whatever the reason, Beckett couldn't find it in him to back off and give Julian space. Especially after all the half-discoveries he'd found out about Julian this evening. Beckett's new bottom line: if Julian needed a friend, then he'd allow Julian to friend-zone him. At the very least, he'd be closer to the man while providing the emotional support Julian needed.

Beckett lifted a brow, giving Julian a playful but knowing look. "You need some help with that?" He boldly tilted his chin to Julian's lap, hoping to ease the tension between them.

"Shit," Julian hissed and pushed the barely touched salad plate away as he slid off his seat. "You're definitely persistent. Trust me, Marlboro Man, you don't want to rope me. I'm not what you're looking for. Go find yourself another stud to lasso." Julian's hand flew out toward the table of men who'd just offered to buy Beckett's drinks for the night. "All you'll have to do is turn toward the room and give that swagger of yours, and you'll have so much ass backing up on your big guy you won't be able to shoo them away."

Instantly, Beckett lost all his bravado and pushed off his seat. "I was trying to tease you. I didn't mean anything by it. I'm not any good at flirting."

Julian stood to his full height, tucking his shirt neatly into his pants, eyeing Beckett closely until he burst out with a long laugh, definitely a laughing at Beckett kind of mockery. Julian gently slapped his thigh, and the dog got to his feet.

"Have a good night," Julian said and patronizingly patted Beckett's forearm.

No, this couldn't be happening. Beckett quickly dug his money clip from his pocket and tossed out a ten-dollar bill, then another, remembering he'd bought that dude a drink to impress Julian.

"Five more bucks," the bartender called out, forcing Beckett to pull his money clip back out as Julian slipped behind a curtain. He tossed a twenty on top of the bar, reeling at the idea that a drink and a tip cost him forty dollars, and started after Julian.

Beckett jogged up the steps to where Julian ducked behind a curtain. When he crossed that threshold, everything about the over-the-top elegant club disappeared as he hit a long sterile hallway with a swinging door at the end. Beckett pushed through and found himself at the edge of the Reservations kitchen with another door on the opposite side of the room swinging shut. Beckett took off that way, dodging the kitchen staff who were hard at work. Beckett kept going through the far door, spotting Julian as he turned a corner.

"Hey, Julian. Stop. Let me apologize," Beckett called out. Julian halted, his shoulders tightening, but he did stop and turn a surprised look Beckett's way.

"Good night, St. Clair. Go enjoy yourself with your much-deserved posse out there," Julian said, nodding him back toward the club, a brilliant smile hovering on his lips. One of his fake smiles, something designed to create a false sense of ease. Julian disappeared behind a service door without another word. Beckett closed the distance with long strides.

"What if I told you I'm here for you," he said, out of breath, turning the corner into what looked like a break room. Luckily, Julian was alone. "And if you're not here tonight, then there's no reason for me to stick around."

Julian bent over one of the tables in the middle of the room where a monitor sat on a table and began tapping the screen.

"I'd tell you that you're wrong," Julian said distractedly without looking at Beckett as he worked something on the screen. "I'm not interested in dating anyone, and as much as it pains me to say… I no longer just fuck guys for a good time."

It was nice to hear Julian wasn't taken. Beckett decided a long time ago if Julian spent so much time at work, he probably didn't have someone significant waiting for him at home. Still, Beckett also knew firsthand how lonely living without someone could be and decided to say it aloud. "Sounds lonely."

"Woofer is here," Julian said cheekily and reached for a leash Beckett hadn't seen before. Beckett wouldn't let himself be sidetracked no matter how much it sounded like Julian would rather be with the dog than him.

"Is he an emotional support animal?"

Julian slowly lifted his head to glance at Beckett even as he remained bent over to work the leash's clasp onto the dog's collar.

A rare moment of unguarded honesty tumbled from Julian's lips. "Is that your first thought when you see Woofer? I chose him because I didn't think he'd tip people off, but he's truly been awful. He's an emotional stress animal."

He looked down at the beautiful German shepherd, sitting on his hind legs close to Julian with his tongue hanging out the side of his mouth. The dog looked as if he might be a bit of a mischief-maker if left unattended. The missing pieces of Julian's life connected in new ways. The abuse Beckett had suspected became the forefront of his thoughts. It all began to make sense.

His heart gave an ache for a different reason now.

"How about some coffee?" Beckett blurted. "The strip has a couple of places I've seen going back and forth between the base and Reservations."

"Are you military?" Julian asked, his brow lifting in question as he stood, leash in hand. "I didn't pick that up from you."

Julian would know that answer from his application had he cared enough to take a look. If given the chance, he would have memorized every part of Julian's life.

"Briefly. Right out of high school, but my company has a contract with the naval base here. I've spent a lot of time in Coronado. That's how I found Reservations."

Beckett's nerves were beginning to get the best of him. The fleeting buzz of his earlier beers was wearing off, his courage evaporating with them. His palms were sweaty, and he rubbed them down his pants as he balled his fists then tucked them in his pockets.

"How about that coffee or even a quick bite to eat? You didn't touch your salad out there?"

Julian let out a huff and crossed his arms over his chest. He kept that speculative arch of the brow as if he tried to figure out Beckett's angle. Beckett was helpless to do more than wait for whatever might come next. Julian always kept him guessing.

What he could see clearly were those haunting eyes turning icy and calculating.

"What do you want from me, St. Clair?"

Beckett didn't hesitate. "I'd like to get to know you better."

"Why?" Julian asked curtly as if it were the most absurd thought.

"I'm attracted—"

Julian cut him off from finishing his sentence. "I told you, I'm not interested in dating or fucking. How does that fit into your attraction?"

Beckett kept his focus on finishing what he planned to say. "…to you. I want to get to know you better." He forced himself to continue into the uncomfortable territory of his disclosure. "I haven't been out all that long, and I've never met anyone like you. Have a drink with me somewhere outside of here. No pressure or expectation for anything more."

Julian stared at him for several long seconds, eyeing him with a critically arched brow as though in deep speculation. He was beautiful, such a stunning man. Julian took Beckett's breath, causing him to lower his gaze if he had any hope to appear convincing. He'd ruin the little bit of ground he'd manage to gain if Julian sensed the longing inside him.

"Can I pet him?" Beckett asked, changing the subject. He stepped forward with his hand extended but waited for Julian's permission. Woofer started a low-level whine, wanting the touch, but waiting for Julian to agree.

"Might as well. He's the worst emotional support animal on the planet."

Beckett reached for Woofer, who bent his head into his touch. "German shepherds usually shed pretty badly. He doesn't appear to."

"Yeah, he does. Don't get too close. Woofer's missed his deshedding appointment." Julian grabbed his suit coat off the back of the chair. "And wherever you're taking me, he needs to be able to come along with us. Is that a problem?"

"Not at all," Beckett said, relieved that he'd somehow talked Julian into going.

"Don't get a big head. Everyone could use a new friend." Julian nodded toward the door behind Beckett. "Turn to the right and go down that hall. It leads to an outside door. You can get us an Uber."

"It's only a mile or so down the road," Beckett said, hoping if they walked, he'd keep Julian with him a little longer.

Julian gave him a mocking side eye as he passed by. Other than the few moments they'd danced, Beckett hadn't been this close to Julian. He greedily took in everything about the man.

The heady scent of Julian's cologne caused Beckett's cock to punch against his zipper as all those tingly feelings raced along his nerve endings. Julian's striking gaze spoke directly to Beckett's heart. Julian was no more than a few inches shorter than Beckett.

"Those are new shoes you're wearing. Do you really want to risk it?"

Beckett looked down at his feet and shrugged as Woofer sauntered past, trailing his caretaker. Julian had a keen eye and a good point.

Lifting his gaze back up to Julian, he gave a soft chuckle. "I think I can tough it out."

Julian glanced back over his shoulder. "Shut the door behind you, tough guy. It locks automatically."

It made him crazy happy to know Julian noticed his new shoes. He'd deal with any possible blisters. Beckett reached for the door, drawing it closed, following Julian out.

CHAPTER 9

The hum of fluorescent lights inside Danny's Palm Bar & Grill added to the ambiance of the small, cozy outdated grill. The bar took up half the space, but on a Monday night, there was little action going on. Julian and Beckett sat at one of the booths lining the interior walls. They were the only ones left inside the dining area. Woofer strategically placed himself underneath the table, planting himself on Julian's feet. Besides an initial bout of whining when they first arrived, most likely due to the proximity of the pet groomer next door who regularly bathed and deshed Woofer, the massive dog had gone practically unnoticed.

Beckett got all the credit. Woofer responded well to Beckett's commanding presence and simply stated commands.

Woofer wasn't the only one to respond well to Beckett. Julian struggled to keep perspective. He'd never known anyone to be such a true gentleman. But more than just the gentle side of Beckett, Julian couldn't quite put his finger on the mystery surrounding the man. Beckett oozed sensuality in all his masculine, rugged swagger. From the way he walked to the way he talked, Beckett carried himself with class and pride. Combined with his attentive gentle nature, the man was a triple threat.

"We should have gone somewhere else," Beckett said before adding the last few fries to his mouth.

"And miss the chance of watching you inhale that burger? No way. We made the right decision. Who eats a burger in four bites?" Julian teased.

It might have actually taken five or six large bites. And he hadn't missed the way Beckett's eyes lit up from the second the waitress put the red plastic basket filled with a hamburger and fries on the table. Apparently, Beckett stopped here regularly while in town. He'd ordered without a menu and had peeled out of his suit coat and expertly rolled up his shirt sleeves as he prepared for his feast.

Honestly, watching Beckett undress was an unexpected treat. Julian had gotten a little lost in the tight cords of muscle on Beckett's forearms. They teased of something harder underneath all those clothes.

"Are you going to eat those fries?" Beckett asked, causing Julian to chuckle. He pushed the half-full basket toward Beckett.

"Have at 'em."

Beckett started to reach, then hesitated. "I don't want to take your food," he said in that considerate way he always seemed to have. Beckett's eyes, though, spoke of something else. He was still hungry and wanted the fries. Julian reached for the ketchup bottle and squirted across the top of the fries because Beckett had smothered his in ketchup when they'd first arrived.

"Go ahead. I don't usually eat greasy foods. I've got to watch my figure," Julian teased as he lifted his whiskey sour in the air, motioning to the bartender for another.

"I watch it enough for both of us. You're perfect," Beckett said, giving Julian a wink as he added salt and pepper to the top of the ketchup before digging in. Whatever had loosened Beckett up, probably the beer he steadily consumed, had shown Julian glimpses into the real man. Some he'd tagged early on, like those damn manners being innate. Others he hadn't realized…like Beckett was a fun, clever guy who Julian enjoyed spending time with.

"You're good with the compliments," Julian said halfheartedly.

"Sounds like it bothers you." Beckett paused on his first bite of fries long enough to get the words out, then stuffed three or four fries into his mouth.

"Let's just say there was a time I knew what it meant to shine. Not so much anymore." Julian lifted the glass, shaking the ice, trying to make enough liquid to help wash down the truth of his words.

"You keep saying things like that without any explanation, so I can't speak to your past. I do know you're quite possibly the most handsome man I've ever seen, and you're sharp as a tack. I don't know how you could be any more special." Beckett dragged another group of fries through the ketchup and took a bite.

Thankfully, the waitress showed up with a refill. Julian lifted his cocktail glass, taking a couple of long drinks before letting a few small ice cubes drop into his mouth. Julian chomped as he registered the warmth sliding over his body and resisted the urge to put the cold glass to his cheeks to help cool the flush heating his skin.

"You ready to explain the emotional support animal?" Beckett asked.

"Absolutely not. It's your turn anyway. Tell me about Beckett St. Clair." Julian pushed back in the booth's seat, leaning against the wall. He kicked one leg out to stretch across the seat, disrupting Woofer, who settled more fully against his leg. Julian flipped out his index finger encouraging Beckett to start talking.

"Then let's do a question for a question," Beckett countered, taking the last few bites of fries before reaching for the napkin again, rubbing it over his mouth, then his hands before tossing it in the basket and pushing it away.

"Maybe," Julian said, eyeing Beckett closely, wondering if he should admit now or later that he had no intention of opening up about his sordid past. Not that Julian was ashamed; everything was just really complicated. He wasn't in the same place he had been. Hell, what would he say? *I fucked guys for money, cars, and trips, and I loved my life. I want my life back…*

Instead, he steered the conversation away from Beckett's request and asked his own question, crossing all lines of decorum. "Don't get salty when I say I know you're financially loaded per the background check we did on you. You're a very admired man, and even though I've seen your files, you're still a mystery. You're putting off a far more comfortable vibe here in this outdated grill than you do at Reservations. What's up with that?"

Beckett's grin was immediate, and he reached for his beer, taking a drink as the waitress took the last empty basket of food off the table. "I haven't always had money. About six or seven years ago, an investment I made paid off in a really big way, and it's paid, and paid, and paid since then. I was in the right place at the right time."

"You own some sort of training camp, right?" Julian asked. Not only was Beckett more comfortable here, but the man also made Julian more comfortable, and he had practically lived in seedy dive bars when he was sixteen years old and off on his own.

"I do with my father. It's a survivalist training camp, but I get to ask the next question. How do you not have a boyfriend?"

"Down, boy." Julian laughed at such a question and gave Beckett a wide grin. Interest in wanting to fill that vacancy for Julian rolled off Beckett in waves. Julian shook his head. "I've never had a boyfriend. I didn't want to be pinned down in that way. I've never had the hang-up other people have about monogamy and relationships. For as long as I can remember, I've lived my life on my terms. My life was straight fire. I enjoyed the hell out of it."

"You lived your life in what way?" Beckett asked. Julian wondered if he had picked up on his smallest hint of his past lifestyle. "Never had a one-on-one relationship?" Beckett watched him, perhaps weighing his answer.

Julian lifted his brow and shook his head. "My turn to ask a question. Survivalist. Like what does that entail? You could be dropped in the middle of nowhere with nothing and survive?" Julian asked.

Beckett nodded before tilting the bottle back for a long drink. "I'd live and thrive. I could pull you through too."

"Oh lord, no. I have a firm rule. If we have a zombie apocalypse, save yourself, leave me behind, remember me as I was. I'm a concrete jungle kind of guy. I lived in LA for twelve years and loved every minute." Julian lifted his hand, sweeping it around the room. "I grew up in a small town with places like this. I wanted out so badly."

Beckett sat back in the seat, bringing a hand to his heart. "You should have said something. We didn't have to come here."

"Not the point, St. Clair." He didn't appease Beckett, who reached for his wallet as if preparing to get Julian out of there.

"We could've gone somewhere else. I was just starving. I missed dinner."

Julian tapped the top of the table, drawing Beckett's attention to him.

"I'm fine. Besides, nothing compares to seeing you wolf down that hamburger. This might be my new favorite place. I've never seen anyone eat like that before. When I bring meat back into my diet, I'll be trying one of those overpriced cheeseburgers. You can bet on it." Julian quirked his lips, drawing one side up, watching Beckett's eyes focus on his mouth. Old habits were hard to let go of.

He used to know every one of his clients' little turn-ons, and he'd used them to his advantage. The Marlboro Man liked Julian's mouth and his eyes, so he used that knowledge to draw

Beckett's attention there.

"What investment paid out so well that now you're wealthy?"

Beckett took the bait. A twinkle flashed in his eyes as he placed his wallet on the table in front of them. "I'm sharing secrets with you that very few people know."

Julian motioned with his finger of crossing his heart over his chest then gave a wink. He pretended to turn a key to lock his lips.

"To make a long story short…." Beckett stopped speaking and shook his head. His smile couldn't be contained. "I invested in a medical marijuana company—basically a pot farm. They bought a lot of land from me and my father. I flipped that cash around and reinvested in the larger company. It's paid out in a big way."

Out of all the stories Julian had contemplated, he couldn't have been more surprised. "I was expecting you to tell me you invented some sort of bougie tactical gear or weaponry that's made military life better." Julian leaned in across the table, truly shocked to his core. "You look like the last person I'd believe owned a pot farm. Are you messing with me?"

"No," Beckett chuckled, shaking his head.

"So, I've used the term Dudley Do-Right when talking about you, and you've made millions of dollars off pot?"

"Yeah. Just because I've been drinking, and I'm pretty relaxed, I'm going to throw in that my mother's a fortune teller in New Orleans."

Julian was rendered speechless. What the hell was he hearing? "No shit?" Julian almost couldn't get his next question out from laughing so hard. "Do you have the sight?"

As Julian hoped, Beckett burst out laughing and raised his hand to the waitress. "Check, please."

"We don't have to leave." Julian threw out a hand, palm side up. "Tell me about my love life."

Beckett only shook his head, dropping his hands in his lap.

"Maybe next time. Whatever caused you to bow out of work tonight and bring this guy along with you probably means you should get some rest."

Julian reared back as if offended. "Is that some kind of curve? Did you just brush me off?" The waitress laid the ticket down on the table, and Beckett reached out, swiping it as if Julian intended to pay. He guessed that trait hadn't moved forward with him into his new life. It never occurred to him to attempt to pay their bill.

"Absolutely not," Beckett said, still grinning, thumbing through the cash in his wallet. "As if you could get rid of me. I seem bound to follow wherever you lead." Beckett laid the cash on the table and looked up at Julian. "Did that sound stalkerish?"

"Probably, based on all the twisted things I've learned about you tonight." Julian laughed out loud again because the warmth of such a happy time seeped through him, making him feel good. It had been way too long since he'd felt this free. Maybe Beckett did have the sight because he knew exactly how to ease Julian's worries and make him feel good again.

Julian pushed from the booth. Woofer immediately got up to follow, bumping into the table with his big body. The dog pinned them both in their seats as he tried to navigate out of the small opening. The humor they shared had them both laughing at the silly dog. Julian grabbed the dog's leash, helping to guide him out backward.

CHAPTER 10

Beckett wasn't sure he'd had a better night in his life. Now that they were walking on the well-lit path back to the hotel and club, Beckett took a deep breath, committing every second of the night to memory. Sea salt hung heavy in the air, the ocean waves churned in the distance, and Woofer walked between them with the man of his dreams, keeping pace with each step… Beckett looked around, making sure he earmarked this exact moment as the ripple in time when his heart went from infatuation to the possibility of finding his one.

Did love always feel special like this?

He didn't know the answer, but the sheer romance of the moment had him wishing they were at the point of holding hands. Between Northern California and New Orleans, Beckett had always lived around large bodies of water. Still, the draw of the ocean had never enthralled him this way before.

"I'll be in town all week," Beckett started, wanting more

of this with Julian. "Are you working every night? I could take you somewhere you'll probably like better." Beckett gave Julian a side eye, but the man kept his gaze focused on the walkway ahead. The only sign Julian heard him was the cute little quirk he did with his lips right before he teased Beckett about something.

"I work. It's my thing, and remember, dating isn't my thing. We had that conversation before I was coerced into tagging along tonight."

"I'm not asking you out on a *date* date," Beckett lied and shook his head as if Julian weren't right on the mark. The playful slant of the blue gaze turned Beckett's way told him that Julian knew he'd fibbed. Beckett let the lie ride as he tucked his hands inside his pants pockets. "You have to eat. I have to eat. Woofer likes me."

Oh, so much for having game. Even repeating his words inside his head didn't make them come across as anything more than lame.

"I'm going to let you in on a little secret. One I wouldn't just admit to anyone. You don't want to date me. Not really," Julian said.

"Well, that's a leap. I just said I wasn't interested in dating you," Beckett teased.

"Exactly, but everybody's interested in fucking me," Julian chimed in, his sassiness on full display, but this time it came with some seriousness in its undertone. "And I know interest when I see it. I've decided with you, that you see something that's probably not real."

"What do you think I see?" Beckett asked, pleased that Julian finally allowed him past the walls he erected and wore like body armor in every other situation.

"You see someone like yourself," Julian answered with all certainty. Beckett burst out with a loud laugh at the ridiculousness of such a thought, causing Julian and Woofer to stumble, looking over at him.

"Right." Beckett came to a stop. "To set the record straight, I'm certain this is an opposite attracts deal. You're nothing like me."

Julian stopped, his spine snapping straight. He gave a slight tug on the leash to stop Woofer. Julian looked offended as he turned and squared off with Beckett. "Again with the curve. You think I'm *basic*?"

Shit. Whatever Julian thought was not what Beckett meant. Beckett ducked his head, looking over at Julian. What did he say now? Beckett's shoulders slumped from the weight of knowing his words came across wrong. He wasn't the player he might pretend to be.

"I didn't mean…" Beckett stopped speaking and bit his lower lip. His hands fisted in his pockets. "You're…dazzling, elegant, sophisticated. You walk into a room and take my breath away. I suspect you're right. Everybody's interested in being with you. Who wouldn't want your undivided attention?"

"If you see me like that, then how do you see yourself?" Julian asked, the sincere question lingering in his eyes.

"I'm the average guy," Beckett answered honestly. "I'm the basic one."

This time Julian laughed straight at Beckett. "You aren't the average guy, far from it." Julian pivoted around and started walking in the direction of the hotel again. Beckett followed.

Several steps were taken in silence, Beckett flattered in the way Julian said he wasn't average. The warmth was back. Becket's grin grew as he watched his feet move.

"You said you haven't been out long. Expand on that for me."

"I wasn't comfortable with all this," Beckett said. "It took me some time to reconcile it all. Then longer to go public. My friends and family were surprised. I hid it well."

"So, none of that NOLA wild free love inside you?"

Beckett chuckled. Julian had to be talking about his mother's side of the family. He never spoke of her. People didn't get and often judged him on her way of life, but he'd freely told Julian. "I guess not. When I was younger, we lived in New Orleans. I was exposed to quite a bit before my father and I moved to Northern California. I had no problem with others being gay. I just always figured I'd have a big family, a wife, kids of my own. I was an only child. I wanted a big family. Make sense?"

Julian barked out a laugh, startling Woofer who nudged Julian's leg as if to check that the man was okay. "No, I don't understand wanting that way of life at all. I was the oldest of a pack of kids and couldn't wait to get out of that intense, controlling family dynamic. I've always known I was into guys. I kissed my first boy in kindergarten. I set up my first orgy in third grade after Sunday school—at the time, I thought that meant three boys kissing each other. Which was hilarious now that I think about it. I charged a dollar for our friends to watch. I made twelve bucks that night. I smoked pot for the first time at church at eleven. Had sex for the first time with a boy at fourteen, in that same church." Julian looked over at Beckett and waggled his brows, completely comfortable with the outrageous truths he tossed out. "My point is, I've been out my whole life."

"Have you always been this open?" Beckett asked with a grin.

"You know, you've got that charming thing down with the way you duck your head and tilt your chin, grinning like that." Julian smiled too, shaking his head. "I see you. You aren't average."

"Thank you. I know it's painfully obvious, but I haven't dated too often. The art of flirting doesn't come easy for me," Beckett said.

"Couldn't tell. You're doing a fine job," Julian said, chuckling. "So, what makes tonight so different?"

Beckett enjoyed the connection they were building with one another. The comfort of talking. Exchanging the bits and pieces of their lives had him being honest now too. "I had six beers before

I showed up tonight."

"Ah. That explains it, then." Julian stayed with him as they strolled along the walkway leading up to the front lobby of Escape Coronado. He took the steps up, tightening his grip on Woofer's leash as they entered the building. Beckett reached out before the valet could get the door and opened it for Julian. He didn't want the evening to end. This had truly been one of the best nights of his life.

"Why don't you let me give you a ride home?" Beckett offered as Julian slid by instead of asking Julian to come up to his room like he wanted.

"My car's in the lot closer to Reservations." Woofer walked past Beckett as many of the heads in the lobby turned their way.

"Hey, Julian."

Julian kept going toward the bank of elevators as he reached out to fist tap the bellhop's extended knuckles.

"Hey, Julian," The same woman who had helped Beckett when he first arrived smiled down at Woofer.

Beckett kept pace, watching as the same thing happened over and over. Julian literally knew everyone they passed. He answered questions about the restaurant, about scheduled events, about Woofer. Beckett was impressed with his friendliness. He stayed silent as they walked down the long hallway toward the back of the building.

They were in their last few minutes. Beckett needed to be bolder, and he one hundred percent had to cancel Thane's harebrained scheme. He never wanted Julian to know about his reluctant involvement.

When they reached the doors leading to the parking lot that separated Reservations from the resort, Beckett pushed through, again holding it for Julian and Woofer. "About that dinner. We could make it breakfast or lunch."

"I think we should stick to Reservations," Julian answered and kept walking toward the lot.

No. Beckett could feel the special bond they'd created fray at the edges. He had to do something.

"Okay…" The word lasted until they fell into an awkward silence. Something they hadn't been all evening.

"Here's where we part ways." Julian pointed to an older model Tesla in a parking spot close to the front of the building. He dug a key fob from his pocket and tapped a button. The locks released with a click. Julian didn't pause as he reached for the backdoor and loaded Woofer inside. That door slammed shut, and Julian reached for the driver's side door handle without a backward glance toward Beckett.

"Hold up," Beckett said, reaching past Julian for the car door and shutting it. It seemed less final to have Julian on this side of the car. "I get there're things I don't know." Beckett took a step in closer with Julian arching a brow as he watched each move. "But can I just try something?"

Beckett moved slowly, lifting his hands to Julian's cheeks. He counted it a win when Julian let him run his fingers over his perfectly cropped scruff. Julian stayed utterly still, not pulling away, but also not moving any closer.

For a man who was kissing boys at church, Julian sure didn't make this easy for him. Julian left it to Beckett to do all the heavy lifting. The pad of his thumb crossed over the soft skin of Julian's cheek. "This is just an experiment."

Something uncertain crossed over Julian's face, drawing Beckett to focus on more than the most perfectly formed lips he'd ever seen. His gaze lifted and locked on Julian's eyes, causing him to pause midway to Julian's mouth. The uncertainty had Beckett pulling back a fraction of an inch, concerned.

One of Julian's hands reached out, tightly gripping Beckett's bicep. Not necessarily pulling him forward or away, more like a grip on a life preserver.

"What? Did I do something wrong?" Beckett whispered, watching the swirl of emotion crossing Julian's face.

Julian gave a quick shake of the head, dispelling whatever held him back. "Shh. If you're going to kiss me, then kiss me, Marlboro Man. I don't think I can initiate it."

He took the invitation. Beckett instinctively wrapped an arm around Julian's back, sliding his hand from Julian's shoulder to the small of his back, feeling all the muscular ridges of Julian's perfect body. Beckett stepped in, his body barely touching Julian's, still very aware of the fingers digging into his bicep.

Beckett leaned in and paused, hovering inches from Julian's lips. He felt compelled to promise, "I won't hurt you."

"I can't promise the same." Julian lifted on his tiptoes at the same time Beckett leaned in. A soft moan left Julian's throat as their lips touched. Fireworks exploded inside Beckett's head as electricity sizzled around them. He opened, sliding his tongue forward, meeting Julian's as tingles rippled throughout his body, setting his nerve endings on fire. Julian tasted like the sweetest nectar, everything Beckett had imagined and more. He was hooked. He'd never get enough.

He tightened his arm around the man and brought Julian up flush against his chest. Julian was made to be right there against him.

Julian.

His Julian.

Beckett's world shifted under his feet. He moved his hands up to Julian's head, his fingers sliding in the short strands at the base of his skull. Their mouths worked together in a sweet sampling of tongues. Julian's hand at Beckett's bicep relaxed and caressed its way around to Beckett's back as Julian fought for control of the kiss, which he gladly relinquished. They fit perfectly together, just like Beckett knew they would.

He never wanted this to end. Beckett eased Julian back against the car, his hand tightening in Julian's hair, angling him as Beckett sank deeper inside that delicious goodness. His heart slammed against his chest. Where their bodies pressed together, the thump of Julian's heart drummed wildly, acknowledging for Beckett that the experience wasn't one-sided. He couldn't seem to let Julian go as he worshipped the man's mouth. He could kiss Julian like that forever and die a happy man. They would be explosive together; Beckett would make sure they were.

He'd found his reason. All the pain and confusion, the decision to come out and be out, everything he'd feared he'd lose from life was all made better as his tongue slid languidly against Julian's before Julian pulled away, gasping for breath. Beckett tried to follow. He didn't want to be done, but Julian's ragged breath puffed against his face, dancing over his skin in all the right ways. Somehow Julian was even more gorgeous with thoroughly kissed lips and a flush coloring his face.

"That was really nice," Beckett murmured, wanting Julian to lean back again, offer his mouth for another kiss.

Instead, Julian's eyelids closed, and he grinned before blowing out a deep breath. He tucked his lip sweetly between his teeth. "Hush. Don't say another word." Julian's palm came to Beckett's chest and patted him, then caressed over Beckett's heart. "I've got to go. I'm going home."

Great. Beckett could ride along too.

The hand at his chest became unexpectedly forceful. Julian pushed Beckett back a couple of steps. Far enough away that Beckett lost hold of Julian, and his hands dropped away. Julian opened the car door, shooed Woofer to the passenger side, and dropped down into the seat. The door shut on Beckett, and the engine came to life. Beckett was helpless to do anything more than watch Julian leave.

Beckett never liked for things to come too easy for him. He thrived with a challenge. But, damn, it was hard to watch Julian leave. He stood in the parking lot until the taillights vanished. The grin that broke out across his face spoke to another side of his thoughts. He'd spent the entire evening with Julian. He'd kissed him, and Julian had kissed him back.

Oh fuck, he was in deep.

A silly smile spread across his face as he kicked at the gravel then started back for the hotel as he reached for his cell phone to text Thane. He didn't want anything to do with Thane's plotting. He refused to mess up what he'd shared with Julian.

CHAPTER 11

"Self-defense classes?" Julian couldn't have been more stunned. What the hell did that even mean? In fact… "How the fuck would that have helped anything? I was drugged." He almost dropped the landline receiver in its cradle without an answer out of nothing more than sheer exasperation. Thane's mother hen qualities had surged to the forefront again. The constant reminders of the attack made everything harder to get past.

Woofer's big, dark caring eyes stopped Julian from hanging up on Thane. How could a silly dog make Julian try to be a more compassionate, understanding man?

A dog.

Ridiculous.

He wasn't even an animal person. Julian did Julian.

So why had he brought the dog with him into the office again today?

Since Julian was being so honest with himself, were Woofer's big chocolate eyes motivating him to be a better person? Or rather Beckett's intense dark gaze pushing him not to hang up on his overly protective helicopter friend?

Julian's heart danced wildly against his ribcage as he thought about Beckett. His excitement caused him more concern than the flashbacks. Julian arched a single brow while scolding himself for his wayward thoughts and refocused on the floor-to-ceiling windows overlooking the club. He had to get a hold of this infatuation before he did something crazy, like give Beckett a chance.

"Look, I knew you'd be a dick about it," Thane said in his normal condescending tone.

"And, yet here we are," Julian countered as if it were a given, happy to call the conversation over. "What else do you need?"

Silence held between them.

Since Julian refused to allow himself another thought about the Marlboro Man, or their fun dinner, or their romantic walk, or their magnetic connection that ended in that fucking kiss— Beckett could kiss a man until his toes curled. The way Beckett had held Julian's face, his calloused palms so strong yet tender. The man was almost reverent in his actions. He let out a deep sigh and dropped a palm on the window, letting the cool glass ground him in the moment, and closed his eyes.

What started out as an experiment to see if Beckett was truly behind all of Julian's newfound feelings had ended in a rigid hard-on that still sought attention twelve hours later.

How would Thane feel if he learned Beckett was the catalyst to everything that had happened to Julian over the last week? The blissful numbness of the last year had been a blessing in disguise. Beckett had opened a floodgate of confusion and longing. Desires he'd thought were buried forever had risen to the surface and stirred that part of him that had been lost. The sensual tingles that lit Julian's body on fire were out of this world and—

You need to stop right there.

"Stop what?" Thane asked. *Shit*. Julian thought he said that in his head. "Look, I knew you'd be resistant because you always are. I'll table it for now, but I need you to meet us at Escape at three o'clock in the conference center room we always use. Arik and I need to talk with you."

"What about?" Julian asked, trying to decide whether the meeting had merit or if he needed to avoid it too.

"This isn't open for negotiations," Thane said with finality.

Julian strode back to his desk. "Business 101 taught to me by the irritatingly successful Thane Walker: Everything is a negotiation."

"I regret that class, and much like everything I've taught you, you've proven me resoundingly wrong. I'll meet you in the conference room at three. Come prepared to take notes."

Julian rolled his eyes. "I have thirty minutes available. I have interviews scheduled this afternoon," he explained truthfully.

"Get Ricco to take your interviews. I'll need you for a couple of hours."

"You're annoying," Julian said. He'd planned to be available for the liquor delivery this afternoon. The current inventory didn't add up. Either the liquor wasn't arriving properly, or they had someone with sticky fingers working there. Julian was determined to find the truth. "When do you go back to Maryland?

"Sooner than you realize." Thane ended the call. Julian slowly lowered the phone as his belly growled. Another result of the soul-destroying kiss last night was that his appetite had returned with a vengeance. He'd had breakfast twice this morning, a couple of snacks and now needed lunch. He'd also added meat back into his diet by way of bacon. Man, bacon tasted so damn good.

"Julian." Arik Layne greeted him as Julian peeked his head through the door. The man was always crazy aware of his surroundings. But somewhere between Julian's lunch and this three o'clock get-together, he grew skeptical that there was, in fact, a business meeting at all. Instead, the appointment was no doubt some sort of ruse to introduce him to a trainer or instructor for Thane's asinine idea of self-defense. Thane never gave in as easily as he had during their last phone conversation.

Relieved to see only the three of them in the room, Julian pushed open the door and stepped inside as Arik got to his feet and stuck out a hand. He gripped Arik's hand in greeting.

"Thank you for taking the time to see us this afternoon." Arik's words made him feel on equal footing. Julian appreciated the respect Layne always gave him. In Julian's life, he'd rarely ever earned anyone's respect.

"No problem. Why am I here?" Julian asked, nodding at Thane, who looked knee-deep in paperwork on the other side of the small table. Arik and Thane had joined forces on several different projects, the ownership and expansion of Reservations being one. When the two men got together, Thane regularly left with a list of tasks to accomplish. Arik, not so much. The man knew how to delegate without anyone realizing it.

"Take a seat," Thane said, setting a large, loaded file folder on his lap, flipping pages over from a stapled packet. "Regardless of what this says, I believe we should begin construction on the East Coast, Layne. We're ready to begin. Contracts, permits, and funding are ready to go. There's no reason to wait. DFW can come in next, maybe early next year."

Arik winked at Julian then grinned as he shook his head. Arik was the seasoned business mogul between the two men and had taken Thane under his wing, mentoring him. They hadn't gotten to the point of Thane having much of a say in the outcome of their decisions. "My legal team will have the permits ready by the end of day tomorrow. Dallas is our highest earning property. There's less competition for Reservations in DFW."

Thane looked up, his face contorted in question, his eyes

glazed from going through the enormous amount of paperwork in front of him. It took a second for him to fully focus on Arik. "How can they have the permits in twenty-four hours?"

"Alec Pierce," Arik said as if that answered everything. Thane nodded his understanding then shook his head.

"Who?"

"My new legal counsel," Arik explained.

"What happened to Reed Kensington?" Julian had to give it to Thane, he tried really hard to catch up but still looked utterly lost.

"Pierce works for Kensington but I'm going to steal him away. He's very good at what he does," Arik answered, reaching for a pen off the unused pad of paper in front of him. He stretched back in his seat.

Thane nodded again. Julian might not know Pierce, but he did recognize the intent behind Arik's claim. A gleam lit Thane's eyes. "I'm the one who needs a miracle worker. Have him come work with me. I pay better."

"Fuck no," Arik said without hesitation. "Pierce is extremely well connected in DC. He'll never leave me. He's given his blood oath, so look elsewhere, Walker." What a ridiculous statement that Arik made with all certainty.

As fun as all this was, watching Arik tease Thane, Julian had a schedule to follow. He cleared his throat, trying to refocus the conversation back to why they wanted him there in the first place. If he didn't get a hold on this back-and-forth banter, Arik and Thane would go off on a verbal volleyball match and wind up talking for the next two hours about something as inane as the coastline of Norway's fishing industry.

Julian should know. He'd sat through that very intensive debate once. He damn sure wasn't going to let that happen ever again. "So when would you be sending me to Dallas? Not my first choice in destinations, but it's good enough. I can hire my replacement here. It won't take long. I have someone in mind."

Thane's head shifted Julian's way, and he just stared. Arik did too. Julian's brows dropped together as Thane shut the folder on his lap and tossed it on the table. "Right. That's why you're here."

Thane's tone and Arik's tilt of the head, looking away from Julian, didn't seem like positives. His gut twisted.

"Why am I here?"

Were they letting him go?

"Julian..." Thane started. *Oh hell no.* Not that tone of disappointment.

Julian butted in, attempting to explain why he did what he did before Thane could justify taking his promotion away. "Franklin the fucker deserved to be fired, and guess what? He's magically doing a million times better." Julian pointed to his chest. "I did that. Standards are everything, and that's always what I'll bring to any leadership role I'm—"

"Calm down, Julian," Thane interrupted.

Julian sat up in his chair, snapped his spine ramrod straight, and clasped his hands together on the table. They were not taking his promotion away. It was all he had that made him feel whole. "And had you followed your own personnel training, you'd know to never start a disciplinary action with the words calm down—"

"This isn't a disciplinary action," Arik raised his voice over Julian to grab his attention. When Julian glanced at the man, the Cheshire cat grin had him snapping his mouth closed.

He was fucking glad to see how his dedicated hard work amused these two bastards. Julian's gaze shifted between the men. His heart drummed loudly in his ears.

"Julian, we've changed things up," Thane said quickly.

When Julian opened his mouth to respond, Arik added, "Your role with Reservations is valuable to us."

A single brow arched. Had he heard that right? "Then why does it feel like I'm being fired?" Julian shot out, wondering how he was still sitting in this seat and hadn't exploded like a firecracker.

Thane gave him an exaggerated roll of his eyes. "You're ridiculous. If you didn't make me second-guess every damn thing I ever plan to say to you to keep you from arguing with me all the damn time, I could just say it."

"I'm still waiting," Julian countered immediately.

"We're changing your role," Arik answered.

"Why? You know I would be perfect in a regional manager position over the clubs," Julian burst, jumping to his feet. "No one has this company's best interest at heart more than I do. My standards of excellence need to be the measure that every employee who works for this company strives to achieve. I'm the only one who pushes and pushes and puts the time in to make this company great."

"I agree," Thane said, slipping into an ultra-calm demeanor.

Julian couldn't breathe. What did *"I agree"* even mean? This company was his baby, his life. He needed this job. "Then don't take my job away from me."

"We've decided to manage Reservations in the same way I manage Escape properties," Arik explained. "Reservations Coronado will become the flagship property of the wider company. It will be the standard of excellence every other Reservations site will strive to achieve. It will be our official training hub and possibly the corporate office once we get that far along. We'd like you to become the general manager of the Coronado property, leading the future of all Reservations sites to come."

The air pushed from Julian's chest as he stared at Arik. He reached for the armchair to keep it steady as he took his seat because his knees went weak.

Well, Julian hadn't expected that at all, and he felt a little silly. He'd been seconds away from a full-blown breakdown. Honestly, he still might be a little on the hot mess side of things when he thought about all the responsibility these men were entrusting him with.

Julian turned to Thane, his savior and mentor. "What if I fail? You always say I don't have the experience to manage on a larger scale."

"You don't, Julian," Thane said, tossing his hands in the air in a *that's obvious* gesture. "But you're a quick study and you're right. No one cares more about this concept than you. The standard you demand needs to be held for the entire company. Of course, you'll have training, and you'll pick it up quickly. I don't doubt that for one second."

"I'll have the general manager over Escape mentoring you as well. You'll do fine, I'm certain," Arik nodded.

Excitement at such an opportunity edged out the uncertainty. "What about Joshua?" he asked about the current Reservations general manager.

"He's been hired by Bennigan's corporate office. They're trying to make a comeback and need some seasoned help," Thane explained. "We asked him to keep it quiet until we could speak with you. He's given a month's notice effective yesterday."

Reservations - Coronado would become the flagship entity of at least twenty planned restaurants and clubs that Julian knew about. He could stay in California and still keep an eye on other properties, while the flagship site became the company standard. His mind reeled at the possibilities. Julian sat back in his seat, staring at Thane, the man who'd become his hero. He'd thought introducing Thane to Levi had helped even out his tremendous debt to Thane. With this move, they were solidly back on an uneven playing field. Julian owed Thane a world of appreciation.

Julian didn't say any of that. Instead, he waved a hand, encouraging Thane to say more. "Go on."

Arik chuckled.

"We believe it's the best option for you and for the future of Reservations," Thane said, his voice growing softer. Thane wasn't fooled. He could read Julian better than anyone. "You could put down some roots here. If it doesn't work out, then we'll transition you into Dishology, you can be a greeter in one of my restaurants somewhere, but I think it's the right move."

"What's the money like?" Julian asked, hiding his deep inhale by crossing his arms over his chest as he tried to settle his frazzled nerves.

"I'm having the paperwork drawn up now. You should have it in email by the time we end this meeting. You won't be disappointed, but it's also not open for negotiations," Thane explained.

Julian rolled his eyes and crossed his arms tighter over his chest. "Sure it is. You always lowball me."

"No, I don't," Thane shot back. "We have a salary structure that needs to be adhered to."

Let the negotiations begin. "But we're a new company. Who set the salary standard?"

"Julian, take a couple of days or even longer and think hard about this," Arik interjected. "The benefits are that it will keep you here in California, which might also be the disadvantage. I want you to really decide if you're ready to take on such a large job."

Arik was right. The new regional training position they previously offered him had been an inviting break from the monotony of his nonexistent life, but all that had changed. How far down the rabbit hole would these flashbacks and new stirrings of emotion take him? Was he emotionally ready for such a big job with everything else happening inside his head?

As much as Julian hated to, he caved and nodded in agreement. "How long do I have?"

"We've both dedicated resources to this spin-off company. My HR department will handle the offer and hiring paperwork—" Arik abruptly stopped speaking and both his and Thane's gazes shifted past Julian to whatever was behind him. Julian looked back over his shoulder to see the blinds were open on the small window looking out over the larger conference center. A string of buff rough-and-tumble men dressed in military fatigues were leaving another sectioned off room. They were probably part of some sort of special teams based on their look.

Living in Coronado had its benefits. The sheer volume of physically fit men was a plus to staying in the area. Thane shoved his chair away from the table and got to his feet. Julian watched him move around the table, his gaze focused out the window. That was strange for the new Thane Walker. As a reformed rake, Thane rarely let his eyes wander to anyone other than Levi.

The scraping of Arik's chair against the floor had Julian looking his way. Arik's gaze was transfixed on the men too. And Arik's new husband held all of the man's attention generally.

Julian found himself automatically rising too, lost to the bizarre behavior of the two men. Arik wrapped his arm around Julian's shoulder, guiding him out of the office to follow Thane. Something was off, but he'd play along until he could figure it out.

"Have you seen the rooms surrounding the conference center? They're newly decorated. Kellus designed the theme. It's a first for us. He's charging me a ton of money. You'd think I'd get a family discount." Arik kept up the inane chitchat as he urged Julian out the door. Arik only paused, still holding on to Julian as he reached back to shut the door behind him.

"Why do I need to see the rooms?"

Thane's stride had purpose as he went for the door the pack of military men just exited from.

"Moving a little slow there, Cullen?" Arik teased, ushering Julian through the door Thane had just entered. Julian wasn't prepared for the heart-stopping scene he encountered. The muscular thighs and ass had him catching his breath. Beckett was bent over a box of supplies, his hard, suntanned body on full display in a tight-fitting T-shirt. His broad expansive chest stretched the material to its limit. But those tight clingy shorts— short shorts—gave his imagination a workout.

Beckett looked back over his shoulder, spotting him, and rose, letting the supplies in his hands fall into the box. Sweat dotted his brow, and he wiped it away with an arm while standing to his full height, concern marring those handsome features. The man was fucking breath-taking. Bowed chest, broad shoulders, thick arms. Julian's mouth watered. Why would Beckett ever hide that body underneath a jacket? Reservations' dress code was a menace if it covered the likes of Beckett St. Clair.

Beckett's surprise morphed into something more serious as his brow furrowed. "Did you not get my text, Walker?"

Although Beckett stared at Julian, he spoke directly to Thane.

Since when did Beckett get on texting terms with Thane? Julian scowled in Thane's direction, waiting for an explanation of why he'd been dragged in here. Thane was clearly up to something again.

CHAPTER 12

Though caught completely off guard by the sight of the three men standing in the doorway, only one drew all of Beckett's attention. Julian always looked like a million bucks with his sharply dressed good looks, and today was no different. Beckett shifted his gaze to Thane then to Arik before cutting back to Julian.

"Thank you for agreeing to work with Julian," Arik Layne said, removing his arm from around Julian's shoulders to step forward, his hand extended for a shake. Beckett reached for a hand towel nearby and wiped his sweaty palms before shaking Arik's hand, not happy with this ambush at all.

Beckett saw the exact moment Julian realized what was going on. Outrage and disappointment flashed across Julian's handsome face. "You're in on this?"

"No." Beckett shook his head, running the towel over his sweat-damp hair. "Well, I was approached, I guess. It's hard to tell them no, but I backed out after we talked last night."

Julian's brow arched as he crossed his arms over his chest and shifted his accusatory stare from Beckett to Thane. "You've gone too far."

"Julian, this is what he does for a living," Thane explained. "He's got your best interest at heart, and he's given his promise to be discreet."

"Oh no. Absolutely not." The words held finality. Julian whirled around in both elegant grace and fury, exiting the room in three long strides, leaving the three of them standing there in stunned silence.

Without any real plan, Beckett started out of the room to go after Julian. At the door, he spared a glance at Thane. "Dude, what are you doing? I told you now wasn't the time. He's not ready."

Beckett didn't wait for an answer. Instead, he took off after Julian, who was hurrying out the main doors of the conference hall. At the entrance, Beckett looked this way and that, but Julian was already on the last step of the stairwell on the right, then rushing across the parking lot toward Reservations. Beckett took the steps down two at a time, wiping at the sweat on his face as he went.

"Julian, wait."

Julian's long stride ate up the distance to the parking lot separating Escape from Reservations. The man's frustration could be heard with every step that pounded against the concrete.

"Hey, hang on."

He didn't. If it were possible, he picked up the pace.

"Julian. Please. Stop."

Julian whirled around on him and unexpectedly stepped in his path at the same time, causing him to reach for Julian, so he didn't bowl him over.

"Do you think you're the first person to be infatuated with me?"

The words lost some of their bite as Julian's arms flung out. Beckett busted a move, his arms tightened around Julian's waist, bringing the smaller man flush against his body, steadying himself to keep them both on their feet.

"Listen to me, Julian. They set me up yesterday. Walker asked me to dinner and Layne was there. You have to know they don't take no for an answer. Hell, they never shut up. It's hard to say anything."

Julian pushed out of Beckett's arms, backing several feet away from him. "I'm so fucking sick of this bullshit." Julian's fist shot out, punching at the air before he searched the area and started back toward the restaurant. Right as Beckett started to follow, Julian spun around, pointing a finger at him in warning to stay where he stood.

His heart broke, begging him to make this right. Julian's anger crackled in the air around them, his icy glare piercing Beckett's heart as if cupid had shot a wayward arrow.

"St. Clair, this isn't going to happen between us. You need to understand that I'm not someone you want." Julian gave a dramatic tilt of his head as if what he said were more than obvious. "You have no idea how I'm so not for you."

Beckett's heart refused to accept those words. He fought the urge to caveman out on Julian by tossing him over his shoulder and taking him far, far away from this crazy shit show they'd somehow fallen into. Beckett forced himself to concentrate on the steady rise and fall of his chest to fight the building panic.

"We're not talking about that right now." Beckett cast his eyes down, trying to think of anything to diffuse this situation. He'd never meant for any of this to happen. Honesty was always the best answer. Inspiration struck, and he lifted his gaze to Julian who looked fierce as hell, his blue-green eyes blazing with indignation. "I know something happened to you. I figure it was something life-altering considering the way those two men want to protect you. Put their concern aside." Beckett lifted a hand, motioning toward Escape where they'd left Thane and Arik. "Whatever happened, you haven't gotten past it, and people are worried for you. I get where their heart is, and I get your frustration. Put that aside. Self-defense training can help build confidence."

Julian's hands flew in the air as if that was the last thing he wanted to hear from Beckett. "I don't appreciate *you* talking behind my back."

"I didn't. I drank a few beers. They did all the talking." Beckett took several timid steps forward while Julian gave a harsh blast of a laugh before closing his eyes and lifting his face toward the sky. The sun cast Julian in a warm glow, making him even more mesmerizing.

Beckett waited until Julian released his breath in what seemed like a calming technique. Julian barely spared a glance Beckett's way before making a beeline back to the club.

"Don't follow me." The words were said with command and finality, making Beckett stay where he stood. Whatever had happened to Julian was bad—worse than he had wanted to admit.

Julian pushed through the side door of the club. The contrast between the bright sun and the natural darkness of the club made it hard to see. Somehow the lack of clarity felt comforting as Julian sent the door flying shut behind him. He bypassed the employees setting up the club for the night and made his way straight to the stairwell leading to the office above. Past sick of being treated as if he was helpless.

"Woofer is up there. I took him out about fifteen minutes ago," Ricco called out. Julian absently lifted a hand in acknowledgment but never turned back as he took the well-worn steps up two at a time. So goddamned tired of people interfering in his life.

Julian pushed through the office door with much of the same ire as he used with the door below, and Woofer bolted toward him. He braced himself for the damn dog's exuberant greeting.

One thing he knew with certainty, what he was doing right now wasn't working for him. Woofer jumped up and licked across his neck. It would have been Julian's lips had he not lifted his chin out of the way. Woofer stood on his back legs, his big paws on Julian's chest, keeping them close together.

"Get down, boy," Julian said, taking Woofer's front legs and dropping them toward the floor. Julian edged around the big dog, on a mission to get to the wet bar. He poured a double shot of whiskey and swallowed it down in two large gulps.

Maybe he'd been wrong to stick around California like he had. Perhaps he'd needed a fresh start. Maybe he still did. Julian poured himself another shot, this time adding ice to the glass.

Julian's head ached. He just wanted it all to go away. Never in his life had he felt so helpless, so embarrassed, angry, and— Hell, Julian didn't know what he felt anymore. But he damn sure wasn't happy about Thane and Arik going to Beckett behind his back. This shit had to stop.

He chugged the amber liquid, hoping it eased the pounding in his head. The room swirled, his thoughts frantic and disjointed until a dizzying loop of flashbacks from that night began to play like a slideshow in his head.

Confusion and fear rushed like icy water through his body and buckled his knees. He reached out to clutch the edge of the bar, determined to stay on his feet.

Darkness and men's voices surrounded him. Julian couldn't see any faces, but he definitely heard voices. His eyes were covered with something, a cloth of some sort. He struggled against the arms holding him in place, causing the covering on his eyes to rise just enough to see some shadows against the cheap orange and brown carpet.

The smell of stale cigarettes and cheap whiskey flooded his

senses, making him nauseous. Forceful hands pulled at him, groped him, as he tried to remember where he was.

Desperation consumed him as deep laughter echoed in the room. Julian tried to fight. His arms didn't work. His shoulders ached. Even as he tried to kick at the hands holding him in place, his limbs were just too heavy to cooperate.

Terror seized his soul, sending his heart racing when he realized he was bound. His arms were tied behind him at an uncomfortable angle, his wrists burned, his fingers numb.

He couldn't remember how he ended up on his knees on the floor. Someone yanked his head back, fingers digging into his skin. The coppery taste of blood exploded across his tongue when a fist struck his face. A dick was then shoved down his throat. Julian tried to turn away; he couldn't fight. He couldn't move, held in place by his captors. He was choking, trying to breathe, he couldn't draw air into his lungs.

The office in Reservations and its surroundings snapped into focus, forcing him back into reality. He felt sick and weak. His brain felt fuzzy. He really needed time to sort out everything he'd just remembered.

It wasn't the first time he'd been bound and on his knees, but it was the first time he'd not given consent. This memory of the attack was violent and filled with hate. No one in that room seemed to care whether he lived or died.

Not knowing what happened to him was just as bad as knowing. He could still feel the ice-cold fingers of terror wrapped around his neck. Julian struggled to draw air into his lungs. His heart continued to race, and his body shook uncontrollably. He extended his hands, watching them tremble before he fisted both and willed himself to calm down while he tried to process what he'd learned from his latest virtual trip back through hell.

The blindfold explained a lot…

"Julian."

Startled, Julian jerked around, yelping for help, but no sound came as he swung a fist at the stern voice right over his shoulder. Beckett easily dodged Julian's uncontrolled punch in a *Matrix*-worthy move.

Woofer growled, but Beckett's commanding voice had the dog staying rooted in his spot. "Woofer, place."

"You shouldn't sneak up on people. What the fuck are you doing here?" Julian asked, his heart racing out of control, his breathing still erratic from the extreme fear elicited from his flashback.

"I wasn't quiet. I didn't sneak up on you," Beckett said, taking a step backward to give Julian room. "I said your name twice when I entered." Beckett's worried tone mixed with the forceful look on his face. "What's happened to you?"

Julian turned away as his body absorbed the aftershock of the fear running through him. He raked his fingers over his face then through his hair, fisting them as they dropped to his sides. Julian reveled in the sharp scrape of his blunt fingernails against his palm. If he didn't calm down, he risked a heart attack with as badly as his heart pounded against his ribcage.

Mere seconds ago, Julian experienced some pride that he stayed on his feet during a flashback. Still, the fear Beckett evoked from being so unexpectedly close had him reaching out for the sofa. Beckett's strong arm wrapped around Julian's waist to guide him down to the soft seat. The crystal cocktail glass he'd poured whiskey into entered his line of sight.

"Tell me what's happening to you, Julian." Beckett's voice grew softer as he sat beside him. His tone and proximity were comforting, as was the strong palm that came to rest on the middle of his back before moving up and caressing Julian's shoulder as he rested his elbows on his thighs.

Julian was tired and growing more weary by the second. A helpless feeling that engulfed him. He hated not knowing about that night, but if he were to be completely honest with himself, he was absolutely terrified at the thought of discovering what had actually happened.

He swirled the ice around in the glass and sighed, trying to make sense of it all. Why couldn't things go back to the way they were? He took a long drink of the whiskey, letting the familiar burn blaze a trail down his throat, warm his belly, and dull his frazzled nerves.

Julian placed the glass on the coffee table and scrubbed his hands over his face again as he tried hard to gain some perspective. Other than explaining his story during a physical therapy session with Levi, Julian wasn't sure he'd ever said these words aloud. Even in counseling, because she had known his situation before he ever got to her.

"I was kidnapped, beaten, and gang-raped well over a year ago. Two years now. Over the last week or so, the memories have started sliding back in. I just had another flashback."

The shaking of his hands had him reaching for the cocktail glass, needing anything left inside to squelch the angst building inside him. He tipped the drink back. Beckett took it from him, going for the bar. "Is there anyone I can call for you?"

"Fuck no," Julian said, dropping back against the soft cushion. "Those mother hens out there seriously make everything worse."

"So, both Walker and Layne know? It seemed like they probably did with what they said at that dinner. They never told me the specifics," Beckett explained as he walked back to the edge of the sofa and handed Julian the drink. Beckett stayed on his feet, and Julian couldn't muster the nerve to look up. No matter what Julian said to Beckett, he couldn't stand the idea of the man's deep interest and desire turning to sympathy and pity. Somehow the thought made Julian feel worse, and he lifted the glass to his lips, taking a smaller sip this time. "It makes sense they know. I guess it was a dumb question."

"Thane found me in a hospital. I missed a scheduled…date." Julian stopped speaking, knowing that a good guy like Beckett would never understand how Julian had previously lived. A life

Julian missed more than he could ever admit.

"You dated Thane?" Beckett asked in more of a way to keep him talking than hinting to any sort of jealousy.

"Not like what you're thinking." Julian took another sip as he decided to lay it all out.

The Marlboro Man represented a reprieve for Julian, more of a hopeful distraction. One he would always appreciate. Sadly, there wouldn't be a future for them, and it was time Julian explained to Beckett exactly why.

"Back then, I was an escort on retainer. I missed a scheduled date with Thane. I was supposed to be his date for the opening of Escape Coronado," Julian explained, possibly oversharing. He took a longer drink of the whiskey this time which tasted more like acid scorching his throat. Julian forced himself back into his old perspective, refusing to acknowledge the heavy shame he'd carried since the accident. He pushed to his feet, starting for the glass wall overlooking the club.

The disgrace wasn't new but damn hard to rebuff, and that was fucking Beckett's fault. The man brought all this uncharted emotion forward for him. Julian had never felt uncomfortable admitting anything in his life. Honestly, Beckett just needed to leave. Hope and kindness were not for men like Julian. He knew firsthand what the world was made of and exactly what people thought about men like him.

"I should have told you a long time ago. I just liked the way you made me feel. I miss the attention I used to get."

Julian tilted his head and looked out over the empty club below so he didn't have to see Beckett when he said, "I used to know what it meant to shine. I was on retainer for dozens of wealthy men when they came into town. I thought I had it all and I did. Money, cars, trips to the most exotic places. The best of everything. After the attack… I stopped living. Then you come along and make me think I could live again, you make me feel alive."

The vulnerability caused Julian to pause as he placed a palm on the window and took another drink. "I've always been proud of the man I was, proud of the life I made for myself. That is until I laid eyes on you."

"What did I do to make you think less of yourself?" Beckett asked in a little above a whisper from a closer position than where he'd stood before. "I certainly don't think less of you, Julian. Why would I?"

Julian didn't know how to feel. That wasn't the reaction he'd expected. What was wrong with this guy? Julian swung his head around, and his body followed, looking at Beckett as if he were the craziest man on the planet.

What Julian saw reflected in those chocolate eyes and handsome face melted away any lingering ice that had frozen around his heart. He didn't see the rejection he'd feared, but instead, the look reflected at him let him know Beckett genuinely cared. Beckett reached for him, his big palm caressing from his elbow to his bicep. The warm touch was meant to provide comfort, and it did, like a soothing balm easing over his soul.

"I'm not the man I was," Julian confessed truthfully. "I've wished I could go back in time, be the up for anything, full of life guy that I used to be, but I can't get there. I can't trust my instincts." He shook his head and lowered his gaze in regretful shame. "I haven't been with a man since the assault. I fucking hate that I can't get there. I loved sex. I loved everything about it. I miss it. I miss my life."

"Are you talking to a counselor?" Beckett asked, drawing Julian's gaze back to Beckett as the sweet man moved a step closer. "You need one. I can refer you to the guy I used when I was tired of fighting with myself over my sexuality."

Julian smiled. His friends had truly kept his secrets. "That's how I met Levi. He's the one who found my counselor for me."

Beckett's grip tightened around Julian's arm, drawing him in for an embrace. Julian allowed it, needing this man's touch like he needed his next breath. Beckett's big, muscular arms circled him, bringing him flush against Beckett's expansive chest. The heady scent of all man mixed with that spicy cologne reminded him of a pine forest after a spring storm, muddling Julian's senses, easing the tension.

It felt good to be touched so tenderly. Julian allowed the indulgence, resting his cheek on Beckett's collarbone, nestling his nose in the crook of Beckett's neck. Julian breathed in Beckett's amazing scent and closed his eyes. Everything he'd been fighting against settled. Julian felt safe with Beckett, and the knowledge rushed over him like a comforting blanket.

CHAPTER 13

Lost to the abuse Julian had suffered and the clinging way Julian held on to him, Beckett could do little more than tighten his hold and rest his cheek on the top of Julian's hair, committing everything about this moment to memory. Maybe not necessarily in the way he might have wanted, but nevertheless, the man of his dreams was in his arms, clutching onto the back of his shirt as if Julian's life depended on being right there.

Julian had been badly abused, so badly, in fact, it had altered everything about his life. The rush of sympathy had Beckett tightening his hold, and Julian responded by doing the same.

"Why did you kiss me last night?" Beckett murmured, wondering why Julian had chosen him to break such a long drought of connection. He let his lips ghost over Julian's dark silky strands.

"You make me feel." Julian spoke softly while trying to pull away, but Beckett wouldn't let him go. Not yet.

"Let me comfort you the only way I know how," Beckett offered, wanting to take any pain away from the man in his arms. Julian relented and settled back against his chest.

"I've somehow blocked everything about that night. I only remembered waking up with Thane by my hospital bed. We had a good relationship, but he'd only really ever been a client. I didn't have insurance, and he paid for my care. I never expected such devotion from him. No matter what a fucker he pretends to be, he's a good guy." Julian's voice was low. Beckett had to concentrate to hear. "Sorry. I'm struggling to stay on point with everything in my life right now." Julian's fist tightened into Beckett's shirt. "When you and I danced— You need to know, I haven't danced with anyone like I did with you since before my…assault. You've drawn me out of myself. It started a chain reaction. I've had three flashbacks since the first night. The one you just walked in on was the most vivid."

"Do you want to tell me about it?" he asked.

"No," Julian said with finality, in direct contrast to the verbal tumble he'd been doing and seemed to want to continue to do. "I was blindfolded. I don't remember much. It's coming in bits and pieces. They haven't caught the guys."

"Have you spoken with your investigator?" Beckett asked, not entirely sure what drove him to ask, but maybe something Julian remembered might trigger something in the investigation. "You do have an investigator, right?"

"I did, but I haven't talked to them in a year or more. Whoever did this was a pro—their words, not mine." Julian released a shaky breath. "This wasn't an isolated event. The LAPD had a serial abuser on record, targeting escorts for many years. Had I known, I might have been more careful, but back then, I thought of myself as invincible."

"You still should tell them what's happening," Beckett said, ticking over the list of police officers he may know in Los Angeles. "Maybe something you say will help point them in a direction."

Julian was riding on a thin line no matter what he tried to project to the world. Beckett wasn't sure how long Julian could continue traveling down this path alone. He hadn't tried to hang on to his heart where Julian was concerned, but right now, at this moment, he found himself willing to give his all to help Julian. He felt connected to Julian in every possible way. He saw how Julian wasn't in a place to give himself to anyone. Julian had to figure out who he was again and what he wanted out of life.

A deep feeling of loss cooled the empty space between them as Julian slowly pushed out of Beckett's arms. With the way the man's hands slid from his back to his chest, Julian seemed hesitant to leave the embrace, maybe because Beckett had a hold of Julian's waist, keeping him close. He held on as long as he could, watching Julian place his palms on Beckett's pecs until he felt the weight of them on his heart. Julian's eyes lifted to Beckett's with so much vulnerability in their depths.

"I couldn't help but notice you. I never ignored you, not really. I knew you were there. What I tried to ignore was this stirring inside me. Now you know why it's not the best time for me to explore anything personally. I had thought you might be the one to help me get back into my old life, but I don't think it's going to happen." Julian fully pushed out of Beckett's arms. A quirky grin split Julian's lips as he started to turn away.

Beckett wasn't entirely sure he understood Julian's meaning about leading him back into his former life, but that didn't really matter because he was on the exact opposite plane of everything else Julian said. More so, Julian wasn't getting rid of him. Even if they were destined to be nothing more than friends, Beckett was all in.

"Your old life, like back to escorting?"

"Yeah, I guess." Julian dropped down on the sofa, patting his thigh. Woofer didn't budge. The dog acted as if he wanted to move, muscles rippling as he looked to Beckett for instruction. "So, Thane and Arik cornered you at dinner last night to trick you into training me in self-defense?" He patted his thigh again, but Woofer stayed still. Julian followed Woofer's gaze, landing on Beckett. "That's why you were so loose last night. You'd been drinking with them. Probably to get through that meeting. They're a handful individually. Together, they'll plow right over a person. What did you do to my dog?"

He grinned. They weren't over speaking of what happened or how Beckett could help, but he did let Julian veer off course. "There are commands he understands. It's in his training. Didn't they tell you?"

"Maybe they did. I don't know. Woofer, come." The dog didn't budge.

"Break." Beckett gave the command and the German shepherd jumped up from his spot and sauntered over, ducking his head under Julian's touch. "Walker and Layne are two weird dudes. I didn't eat even though they had a table full of food—"

"Right? Arik can eat his way through a cookbook, and he won't really share," Julian interrupted, leaning back on the sofa, his hand staying on Woofer's head. "Arik Layne's a fatty at heart. He eats more food in a single meal than I eat over an entire week. Thane isn't too far behind him. The way they eat is shocking to me."

"Me too," Beckett agreed, walking around the small table to take a seat close to Julian. "Between the little bits of information you dropped and what they said, I knew something bad had to have happened. My nerves were tested while I was sitting there. I drank about a six-pack before I saw you last night. Maybe I should always have a few drinks before I come to the club. I was able to get my flirt on." Beckett gave Julian a big grin.

"Oh Lord no. You're hard to resist when you're all reserved. I might not have been able to stand it," Julian teased.

Beckett angled himself and reached over, taking Julian's hand in his. "You know, I'm not as good a guy as you keep giving me credit for." Beckett threaded their hands together. "Remember how I've made my money."

"Medical marijuana isn't bad, Dudley." Julian squeezed his hand and smiled, probably making sure Beckett knew he was joking.

"I like you thinking I'm such a good guy though, so I'm not going to dissuade you anymore…" Beckett waggled his brows, making Julian bark out a laugh.

"Yeah, okay…"

"What I want is to encourage you to train with me." Beckett held Julian's gaze. "Nothing intensive, just some self-defense." He lifted a finger, stopping Julian from saying anything more. "Because defense training is confidence enhancing. I feel certain you would benefit if for nothing more than building back your sense of security."

"I'm a lover, not a fighter," Julian quipped, letting Beckett play with his fingers.

"Are you, though?" The point hit its mark. Julian lifted a single challenging brow. That inner sass was back like the protective shield it had always been. "I suspect you're in survival mode, which isn't a bad place to be. The will to survive and the attitude to stay alive will keep you going. You'll survive. It's the crazy lesson that companies pay me hundreds of thousands of dollars to teach their people. You're naturally figuring it all out."

"I don't think so," Julian said, and Woofer settled at Julian's feet.

"I want to help." He came at it from a different angle. "You've given me so much. This is something I could give you."

"How long are you here for this time?" Julian asked. Beckett tucked his chin to his chest, hiding his grin. He loved the idea of Julian knowing that he came and went regularly.

"I can be here more. I generally drive to carry our materials back and forth, but I can fly. It's a pretty easy trip." Logistically, Randy and his other senior instructors could handle the trainees out in the field. Beckett could stick around Coronado indefinitely.

"You say fly like you're a pilot?" Julian asked. Of course very little got past him. Probably the reason he was such a good choice to manage all of Reservations.

"Yeah," Beckett said, not letting Julian stray off course this time. "We can work a schedule that fits both our calendars. It won't be difficult."

Julian finally nodded. He clasped his hand tighter around Beckett's. Beckett held on just as firmly, giving his promise to do his best by this man. He couldn't get past the weariness still lingering in Julian's eyes even as he teased, "I knew the infamous Marlboro Man was going to be a complication. You didn't bat an eye over my past."

Beckett laughed, deciding to remind Julian he had his own links to a creative past. "You're a good man. Besides, you ain't got nothing on my mother's side of the family. They might send you running far away from me."

Julian lifted his brow as if Beckett might have a point and finally let go of his hand, getting to his feet. Woofer looked at Beckett for his instruction, and he again cocked his head toward Julian. The dog followed Julian to the desk. "I miss the cowboy hat."

"I have it. Don't worry." Silence held between them as he watched Julian aimlessly riffle through some mail on his desk before the blue eyes lifted to his.

"Thank you," Julian whispered. A peace settled over Beckett as he nodded.

CHAPTER 14

Julian used both hands to lift himself onto the edge of the table Beckett used as a desk. He settled on top of the polished wood as he continued to watch Beckett pace in small, three-step intervals while continuing his instruction as if Julian were still right there on the mat with him.

He reached for his nearby water bottle, appreciating the view of Beckett's hard body in the tight-fitting logoed workout gear. Absolutely spectacular. A life of hard physical work had molded his physique. He could watch Beckett all day and never get bored by the masculine beauty.

A testament to that thought came from the last forty-five minutes of their session. Beckett's presence was just too damn distracting to get much done. He'd finally thrown in the towel. Beckett's heady, alluring scent was as much man as it was cologne. Having those big strong arms and legs wrap around him to teach him real-world techniques and the husky tone Beckett used to give the instructions set Julian's world upside down. Of course, he couldn't pay attention. Not with that hard body rubbing against him.

Beckett animatedly expressed his words as he spoke, waving his calloused hands to make his points. If Beckett knew he had bailed on the lesson and left him standing there, the man never let on.

The crux of this first lesson concentrated on the importance of repetition. Of doing the self-defense moves so many times they became second nature. Julian got it loud and clear. The lesson had made an impression and imprinted into his brain. He saw no reason to continue trying to drum it into his head, even if that was the definition of repetitive behavior.

Truth be told, Julian had learned these concepts well through his counseling. He understood how his brain might freeze if he ever had to put these techniques to use in reality. In the privacy of his condo, he'd watched countless YouTube videos. So many, Julian could probably become an instructor himself.

But Beckett had committed to Julian's training. He made a strong effort to drive his points home, to instill the muscle memory needed so that Julian wouldn't freeze. They focused on the handful of super-effective self-defense counter moves that were proven successful when used to fend off a would-be attacker. He and Beckett went over each one several times now. With enough practice, they would become second nature.

Julian's problem right now, though, didn't stem from the boredom born of repetitive tasks. But instead, if he were truly going to cement these practices into his subconscious, it probably wouldn't come from Beckett St. Clair being his teacher.

It took at least ninety percent of Julian's concentration to ignore all the tingly feelings Beckett brought out in him. His body sprung to life in anticipation whenever Beckett touched him, technically the exact opposite of the response they were trying to accomplish.

How could he push the man away when all he wanted in the

world was to bring Beckett closer?

He was hyperaware of the man. Too much so.

Maybe the whole problem stemmed from having to do these exercises over and over with Beckett's big, hard cock—the very one outlined so enticingly in those shorts—pressed snugly against Julian's back and ass. Yeah, way too distracting to pay attention to anything else. His body hummed excitedly, and his imagination ran wild under the pressure of all the sexual chemistry simmering between them.

Honestly, what right-minded person would expect Julian to push Beckett away when every single one of his instincts wanted those brawny arms wrapped tightly around him. The idea that Beckett was attracted to him for something more than sex… Well, it just made everything in his life feel a little bit easier.

If Beckett genuinely wanted Julian to feel safe, then he'd stay right by his side, guarding him against any future danger. It didn't seem like that would be too much of a hardship at all.

Other than that, this exercise in self-defense was turning into a giant motherfucking nightmare. He suspected the enormous cock in Beckett's shorts might be causing him a bit of trouble too. Especially since Beckett still hadn't realized Julian had walked away. Odd, since Beckett had always tracked all of Julian's comings and goings.

To his utter delight, Beckett busted a move, slinging his arm and foot forward as he circled around. When it didn't make contact, he gave such a look of confusion while executing the perfect three-quarter turn by pivoting on the ball of his foot to stay upright. When he landed, he dropped into a combat stance, making an almost silent chuckle slip from Julian's lips.

When Beckett's surprised gaze finally found him, Julian grinned, leisurely kicking his feet, teasing Beckett. Both Beckett's hands lifted in the air in a what-the-hell gesture as he said, "What're you doing? We're supposed to be working."

Julian didn't immediately reply, because it seemed answer

enough that he was now sitting on the table. When Beckett's hands fisted on his hips in frustration, Julian reached for his cell phone lying nearby. He tapped the side button and took a picture of the beautifully rugged man. He quickly glanced down at the screen to make sure the picture turned out correctly. Then he adjusted the phone as if Beckett could see the screen from so many feet away. "Can you pose again? It's a little blurry."

When Julian turned his cell for the new picture, Beckett had to fight a grin as he playfully stalked toward Julian. "What the hell, Cullen?"

"What the hell, Cullen," Julian mimicked, snapping another picture even though it would most certainly turn out blurry. "Can you guess how many times I've heard those exact same words in my life?" He lifted a hand, stopping Beckett from answering as if he'd planned a guess. "It's too many to count."

Beckett's easygoing nature persisted. His patience seemed worthy of sainthood. Beckett teasingly shook his head as if Julian amused him by failing to understand why they were there. He came to a stop within two feet of Julian, business still on his mind.

"We have fifteen minutes left. You're doing great. Let's go over it again…"

Julian interrupted with a raised hand to finish his sentence. "Preparation and repetition are the ways to compensate for the fear and flight response…"

Beckett cutely pressed his lips together, showing hints of exasperation. Julian really liked that look a lot and decided he had it in him to bring that look forward many times over.

"I never said that—" Beckett started, wrinkling his brow in confusion.

"Yeah, you did, but my counselor says it more succinctly than you." Julian gave a knowing wink for emphasis.

"You had an appointment with her this morning, correct?" Beckett asked.

"Yeah." Julian nodded. "How old are you?"

Beckett's face went through a range of expressions as if trying to follow Julian's train of thought. Julian lifted his water bottle and squirted a good portion directly into his mouth as he gave Beckett the time he needed to shift gears. Beckett's single-minded focus on the business of training Julian was respectable, but Julian scored master-level good at evading topics he'd rather not discuss. His counselor topped the list of unapproved topics.

Beckett finally relented. Julian liked a man who could weigh his options and come out on the winning side. Beckett stepped forward, using a hand to lift himself onto the table beside him as Julian said, "If we're going to continue this, I think we should find somewhere else to practice."

"Why?" Beckett asked as he scooted back on the tabletop and spread his legs to get more comfortable. The slight adjustment had his thigh touching Julian's.

"We're being spied on." Not that Beckett would have noticed once he got going on his topic. But Julian did. "Thane's been sticking his head in to see what's going on. Some of my staff keep walking by as if they have any reason to be in this part of the resort. It's distracting," Julian explained, watching Beckett pause from squirting water into his mouth.

"Are you sure? I never saw anything," Beckett said, jerking his head toward the open door. He lowered the bottle absently, his brow furrowed. "Walker seriously came by?"

"He's trying to be sly, but he's not good at it." Julian chuckled, not even angry at Thane's blatant snooping. The shit-eating grin on Thane's face as he stealthily poked his head around the corner showed the pride he held in helping to make this happen for Julian.

Beckett's infectious good nature was hard to get past. Julian placed his water bottle and cell phone on the table, gripping the edge with his hands. He angled his head toward Beckett to better see his face and asked again, "How old are you?"

"Wow, that's kind of an ego killer to learn you didn't look that closely at my file," Beckett quipped, turning his full attention back to Julian. Beckett leaned to the side, bumping his shoulder into Julian's. "I'm thirty-three."

"I wouldn't want to mess with your ego, so I'll come clean. I thought it might be a typo. You seem older," Julian teased, getting the dig in with that last line. He didn't know one single gay man who accepted Father Time's insistence in growing older.

The tease hit its mark. Beckett looked crestfallen.

Julian's immediate giggle surprised even him. He barely got the next words out with how hard he failed at trying not to laugh. "Don't look so butthurt. As I've gotten to know you, I suspected you were younger than we originally thought."

The bubble of laughter couldn't be contained. It spilled over, tumbling out of Julian's mouth as Beckett again knocked him in the shoulder with a little more force this time.

"Man, my ego's reeling from the compliments. Keep 'em coming. I might have to make an extra trip to my therapist after this. Really. How old did you think I was?" Beckett asked, his palm going to his heart, pretending to rub out the sting of Julian's words.

"Calm down," Julian managed, giving Beckett his genuine side grin. He couldn't resist Beckett; the man was too damn adorable. "It's not by the way you look, but the way you carry yourself. And you always had that brim of your cowboy hat covering your face. You were relentless with that thing." Julian's words appeared to instantly appease Beckett. His hurt expression morphed into a wide grin. "Now, don't get the big head that I was looking at your information. I have to be careful who I'm spending time with."

"He gives," Beckett teased, his palm resting back on his heart. "And he takes away."

"You lied on your application. I can't believe the background check came back approved," Julian shot out and returned the shoulder bump, knocking Beckett hard enough he lowered his hand to the table to keep himself upright. "That's grounds for an immediate termination of your membership. What's up with that?"

"How did I lie?" Beckett asked after a long, confused pregnant pause.

"You said your money came from oil." Julian cocked his head, arching his brow as he stared pointedly at Beckett.

Beckett's bark of laughter had Julian grinning too. He just wasn't sure why. "It's technically not a lie. We get a residual check from an oil company in Texas who leased some land on my mother's side of the family. Once it's divided up, I make about five hundred dollars off it every year."

Beckett looked so proud of those five hundred dollars that Julian nodded and lifted his brows, Julian's giant grin spreading across his face. He hadn't felt this light and carefree in years. "Oh, big spender."

"I didn't lie. I did make money in oil. I figured it sounded better than a pot farm investor," Beckett explained and looked toward the door. This time, Chase stuck his head through the doorway and interrupted them.

"Hey, boss, it's four thirty."

Julian gave the waiter a hard stare.

Before he ever arrived, Julian had preplanned. He paid Chase twenty bucks to come save his ass, just in case this training session had turned into a terrible idea. By his best estimation, Chase should have bailed him out about forty minutes ago. Some good that turned out to be.

When Chase didn't take the hint from the hard stare, Julian gave the guy an exaggerated eye roll and tossed out a thumbs up when Chase didn't immediately leave.

"Okay…" Chase said. "So that means you're good?"

Oh my God, what the hell was with this guy? Julian made a mental note to never use Chase as a wingman.

"Yes, we're good," he answered, tilting his head to the side to get the waiter moving. Finally, Chase tipped his chin up in acknowledgment. He took off, letting the door's kickstand flip up and the door swing shut with a hard thump.

"What was that about?" Beckett asked, staring at the closed door before shifting his gaze to Julian.

"It's time to get ready for work." The lie slipped free on a sigh. He hopped off the table and ran his fingers through his hair, looking down the front of his clothing. He'd chosen something loose and comfortable to wear.

Satisfied that all probable problem areas were well covered, he turned toward Beckett who stayed planted on the table.

"I didn't think about you needing a place to get ready for work. I've got a room upstairs…"

Julian burst out with a harsh laugh, interrupting Beckett again. Yeah right, like he'd ever go to Beckett's hotel room. That would create all sorts of new emotional issues for Julian.

"Going to your room is not going to happen, but how about we do this tomorrow at my place? My condo has a large workout room that's empty every time I pass by," he suggested, hoping for a little more privacy—at least from the people in Julian's life who mattered. He gathered his backpack and garment bag with his clothing for tonight's shift. Beckett may not have thought about his need to dress for work, but Julian had. He'd made plans to change in Escape's men's locker room but decided the employee bathroom at the club might be a better choice. At least it offered more distance away from Beckett.

"Sure. Text me the address. Let's do it at about this same time," Beckett said, hopping off the table in a fluid, agile motion. So smooth, much like everything the guy did. He reached for Julian's water bottle and cell phone, meeting him with both. "But you can use my suite to dress. I'll stay down here. I won't interfere. I promise."

Julian rolled his eyes again while tucking his phone in the front pocket of his sling style backpack. "Do you truly believe your privacy is respected around here? Especially with that big guy on full display." He pointed to the hard-on in Beckett's shorts, then took his water bottle from Beckett's hand when the man looked down. "I come out of your room, and I promise, the gossip mill that is my life will go into full blown—"

"I'm sorry. I can't help it when I'm around you. I try to ignore it," Beckett chimed in before he could finish. "Does it bother you? Is that why you called it off early today?" Embarrassment and sincerity rang in his voice as Beckett tried to cover the impressive bulge in his shorts.

The look on Beckett's face made Julian instantly wish he hadn't said anything. He didn't like that he'd caused this man, who went out of his way to help him, such worry.

In a rare move of honesty, which Julian seemed to do a lot of with Beckett, he slung the backpack over his shoulder then lifted his oversized T-shirt. Julian had prepared for his attraction by trapping his cock inside a pair of binding underwear, but his baggy sweats still showed exactly what was going on underneath. No doubt, Julian was as hard as Beckett.

A flush of color shot up Beckett's neck as he stared down at Julian's cock.

"Never apologize. You don't see me apologizing for being into you." Julian dropped the hem of his T-shirt. "Shit, I'll even go so far as to thank you. This is rare for me since my accident." Julian reached for Beckett's bicep, staying far away from the palm pressing against his cock, trying to make the hard-on go away. He gave a solid tug, dislodging Beckett's hand from his cock. "I take it as a compliment. At a different time in my life, I would have been all over that."

Julian took a final look at Beckett's hard cock and reached for the strap of his garment bag. Beckett didn't say a word as Julian left. A few steps from the door, Julian looked back over his shoulder to see Beckett still watching him leave. He always watched. Julian winked.

"I swaggered out of here because I knew you'd be looking."

He walked the rest of the way to the door, then he turned again.

"Thank you for this today. Drinks on me tonight."

"No worries. You don't owe me anything, Julian," Beckett said, his voice deeper and huskier. "I'm happy to do this with you. I'm getting something out of it too."

Julian doubted that very seriously. Most likely those words came from Beckett's deep sense of manners. God, Beckett epitomized seduction. Had Julian ever truly been this affected by another human being? Beckett was so damn irresistible. Julian kept all his brazen thoughts inside his head and winked again before leaving.

CHAPTER 15

The beat of the music combined with the subtle light show bouncing off the walls had a hypnotic effect on Beckett. He had been vibing at his regular table for a little over an hour and a half now. The long days and longer nights were causing cracks in his best-laid plans. Overwhelming fatigue had hit him hard while walking over to the club tonight, but much like the magic of Reservations, he'd settled into a comfortable relaxation and began to really enjoy his surroundings.

Reservations had become Beckett's safe place to just be himself. He didn't know what happened to shift things for him. Certainly, nothing changed in his feelings for Julian, but for some reason, he'd evolved past this being the place where he got to see the man. He truly appreciated Julian's ability to hire the perfect staff. Every single one of the waiters was hotter than he ever realized before.

Now that Levi had resigned, Chase became his regular waiter. Chase had a killer grin, and tonight, he wore a metallic jockstrap as his uniform. His naked ass swayed on full display. The perfect bubble butt flexing seductively with each step he took.

Beckett found out tonight that Chase had also given his two-week notice to the nightclub. He had just been hired as a full-time Andrew Christian model. He fit that world perfectly.

But the most likely culprit for Beckett's newfound recognition of the sexy scenery was all the alcohol Julian kept plying him with since he'd crawled on top of this stool tonight. The drinks kept coming in an endless supply. Once the other customers started noticing Chase always had a fresh drink available for Beckett, way before he emptied the old one, he had become a crowd favorite by the others who tried hard to get in on the free-drink action.

"Julian said he's switching you to water for a while and wants you to eat this," Levi said, placing a plate with what looked like a wrapped burger and a large order of fries on top. His belly grumbled its appreciation, and his mouth watered. He suspected the food came from Danny's grill. His gaze automatically lifted to the main bar then down its line until he spotted Julian, who paid him no attention as he worked to pour drinks, helping the bar staff catch up on the long line of servers awaiting orders.

"Up for company?"

"Yeah, sure." Beckett motioned to the coveted empty stool he always kept by his side in case Julian might want to take a load off. Of course, it never happened. "Take the seat before someone manages to get it away from me. They try to grab it when I'm not paying attention."

Beckett unwrapped the hamburger that was, in fact, a burger from Danny's. The rumble in his stomach grew in both volume and force.

"You know he can't have outside food in here," Chase said to Levi, dropping a coaster onto the table and placing a glass of ice water within easy reach of Beckett.

"Julian told me to tell anyone who says anything, *waa.*

His words, not mine," Levi teased, clearly getting a kick out of repeating Julian's catchphrase with his staff.

"Yep, that sounds like a Julian reply. I'll repeat it to anyone who asks," Chase said, dropping another coaster in front of Levi. "You staying for a drink?"

"Yeah. Give me a Sidecar on Beckett's tab," Levi teased, nodding in Julian's direction. "I'm hearing there's an endless supply tonight of whatever he wants."

"That's what everyone's saying as I keep bringing all these drinks up." Chase's thumb hooked over toward Beckett. "He's gonna feel all this tomorrow if Julian doesn't slow it down."

Beckett let the exchange happen as if he wasn't sitting right there listening. He reached for the glass of water, taking a hearty gulp to cleanse his palette before he bit into the delicious burger. It made his mouth water—made exactly the way he liked it with lettuce, tomato, pickles, and mustard. It only needed one thing.

"Can you bring me some ketchup?"

"I got it." Quinn, another waiter, came by with a bottle of ketchup just as Beckett asked, and slid it across the table with a stack of napkins before making his way to his own section of tables.

"Thanks," Beckett called out, reaching for the bottle, dumping a good amount of the ketchup directly onto his fries then on to the inside bun of his hamburger. Right as he lifted the burger, his gaze absently landed on Julian who had his hands moving, mixing drinks like a pro at the bar, but this time, he looked up, catching Beckett's stare.

The moment their gazes connected, a shock wave rushed through his system, setting his heart thumping wildly against his ribcage. How many times had he wished for this very moment when he had sat in this seat for hours, even days, lusting after that man? Beckett lifted the burger a few inches, giving a small grin while nodding his appreciation.

"You know, I'm really interested in what's changed here,"

Levi said, looking over his shoulder toward Julian who had turned his focus back on his work.

Beckett dug into the burger.

"Does Thane know you're here?" Beckett asked before taking another bite.

"Ha!" The question had managed to gain Levi's undivided attention. "Yes, he knows. Why has Julian changed his tune toward you?" Levi narrowed his eyes in speculation like the answers were written on Beckett's face as he continued to eat. "You've been busy since you got back. All Thane said is that you're good for Julian. He asked me to come over here tonight and be nice to you until he can get here. And before you answer, I'm going on record to say: You and Thane sitting down to talk is technically what I've suggested for months now. So I get the win."

Beckett nodded, swallowing his bite, listening to the undertone of Levi's uncertainty. He had rationalized a long time ago that even though Thane Walker was an absolute dick, what Thane and Levi had was now his own goal for a relationship. They were so into each other and fit together so well that he likened them to peanut butter and jelly. It just didn't get any better than that.

Once Beckett had made that decision, he recognized how being friendly with Levi might have made Thane uncomfortable. But, fuck, Thane never stopped with all his intensity. It always rolled off him in waves. Maybe Thane's jealousy pointed more toward being Levi's fault. Levi had made Thane work awful hard to build their relationship. Levi drove Thane crazy, and Beckett was certain he didn't even know the half of it.

"That's what you ordered at Danny's, right?" Julian asked, sliding stealthily up to the table from out of nowhere. With one hand, Julian hurriedly deposited a small set of salt and pepper shakers and a few more napkins.

"Yeah, and it's great," Beckett started when Julian used his other hand to bring a second plate forward with another wrapped burger on top. Beckett had always heard the way to a man's heart was through his stomach, which meant Julian dazzled right about now. "Thank you."

"I felt like you would have eaten two if I hadn't been there, so I ordered you another. It came separately," Julian explained, working at cleaning their table the whole time he spoke. He used a napkin to wipe away the beads of condensation gathered from the cocktail glass that Julian pushed toward Beckett. "Drink this so I can take the glass."

Beckett was nothing if not obedient, at least to Julian. He took the cocktail glass and downed the swallow or two left inside.

"What?" Julian asked with attitude. As Beckett drank with his head dropping backward, making sure he got every last drop, his eyes slid sideways toward Levi, whose mouth gaped wide open.

"I'm really out of the loop," Levi finally said, stunned, looking between Beckett and Julian. His confusion showed on his face as his finger swept back and forth between Beckett and Julian. "What's happened here?"

"Thanks to the love of your life, the Marlboro Man here knows what's going on with me." Julian cocked his pretty head in Beckett's direction. "He trained me this afternoon in some self-defense techniques, per Thane's request." In a classic Julian kind of move, he reached across the table to tap Levi's chin, encouraging his mouth closed when he opened it again, but no words came out. "Be careful. You'll collect flies."

Julian took the cocktail glass from Beckett's outstretched hand, his gaze scanning the tabletop one last time for anything left behind before turning away. Beckett committed fully to watching Julian's ass as he walked away, preparing for the visual treat of Julian's swagger in the tight-fitting slacks he always wore. Beckett quickly adjusted his gaze up when Julian turned back to the table in mid-step. He wasn't near fast enough in his inebriated state. Julian caught him red-handed and gave Beckett a knowing smirk as he spoke to Levi.

"You can tell your boy here how you and I met. I think that's the only part of my story he doesn't know. He hasn't seen the scars." Julian's demeanor grew darker with those words as he shifted his gaze to Beckett. "So now you know about those."

Something heavy and emotional crossed Julian's troubled brow. Beckett had seen those glimpses of pain over the last couple of days but had no real idea what Julian tried so hard to hide from the rest of the world. Like a mask dropping in place, Julian's carefree attitude returned just like that. Now Beckett knew differently. It never occurred to him that Julian's insecurities might be both mental and physical. His heart connected as he watched Julian busily handle the small things that arose as he went by the other tables, heading back to the bar.

Some of Beckett's hunger took a hit with Julian's last words bouncing around in his head. He wiped a napkin over his mouth before he asked, "Scars?"

"My mind is officially blown…"

Beckett stared down at the plate of food. His hamburger was almost gone, but his appetite waned under the anxious swirl in his gut. Julian's consideration for Beckett had him scowling at the food on his plate. He'd gone out of his way to order him this dinner, and Beckett needed to eat it.

Besides, with all that insecurity emanating from Julian's expression, he was probably watching for what came next once Beckett fully learned Julian's secrets.

He reached for several of the fries as Levi drew in a breath and revealed the story. "I haven't shared this with anyone. Thane probably knows because it's before I started working here at Reservations, but we've never talked about it. Julian and I met at an outpatient physical rehabilitation center where I worked."

"How did you wind up here?" Beckett asked. Julian had hinted about PT, so that wasn't new information.

"It was all about the need to make more money. I was a physical therapy assistant, and Julian was our patient. I didn't have him as a patient for long. Julian wasn't progressing as he should. He'd been through hell. Back then, he could barely walk without a cane and not that well with one. He's always been outrageous but also very private. It took me a few weeks to get past his audacious stories to learn what had happened to him. When I did, I worked behind the scenes to help find him counseling," Levi explained as he reached over for one of the fries.

Beckett let that information resonate inside his head. He wished he hadn't had so much to drink as he tried to commit the explanation to memory to consider later. The idea of Julian being unable to walk bothered Beckett more than he could process.

Lost in the thought of Julian with a cane, Beckett took another hearty bite of the burger. It didn't taste near as good under the weight of Julian's ordeal. What must that have been like for Julian?

"What about the scarring?" he finally asked, not entirely sure he wanted to hear anymore.

"What do you know about what happened?" Levi asked, his elbows coming to the edge of the table. He leaned in to better hear Beckett's answer as the music changed, growing louder.

"Just that he was drugged, abducted, and abused." Beckett summarized the facts he'd learned, leaving out the extent of the severe trauma Julian had suffered; it was damn hard to say out loud. "And that Thane found him in the hospital."

Levi nodded. "Julian's a prideful guy. He had multiple surgeries and spent several weeks in the hospital. He paid as much as he could toward his medical bills, but it still wiped him out financially. Thane jumped in and covered the rest of them."

"Thane paid for his medical care?" Beckett asked, taking the last bite of his burger. It tasted like sawdust now. He didn't take his eyes off Levi.

"Yeah. No matter what you've seen, Thane's a real good man. He's selflessly helped me more than I can ever repay. Julian, though, hasn't coped well with Thane paying his way."

"I thought Julian was an escort back then?" Beckett picked up the plates, stacking them together. Chase popped out of nowhere before he could push them to the edge, dropping Levi's drink off and ready to take the dishes away. Beckett quickly grabbed the second burger before Chase could take off with it. If nothing else, he'd eat it in his hotel room later. When Chase walked away, he continued, "I heard that Thane used to hire Julian on a regular basis?" Beckett spoke quietly, not wanting others to hear Julian's private pain, causing Levi to lean further into the table as he sipped from his cocktail.

Levi nodded, his voice going even lower than Beckett's. He had to really concentrate to hear each of the words over the increasing volume of the music. "So, you *do* know what's happened. Julian apparently ran his business differently than others. He had many men like Thane on retainer. He was said to be exceptionally good at what he did and had the reputation to prove it. Julian lived his life on his own terms. And with the stories I've heard, I can say that was true, until the assault. It's taken a lot for him to feel aligned and centered in this new life. I'm not a hundred percent sure he really feels that way."

Beckett's gaze left Levi's and searched out Julian. Of course, Julian paid him no attention. Now though, he recognized that wasn't necessarily the truth. His heart ached for the pain such a vibrant man had suffered. "I think he's pulled himself together really well."

Levi turned, following Beckett's line of sight. "He gives his all to Thane and Reservations, but I think it's out of appreciation. The concept of the club was made with Julian in mind. Thane wanted a safe place for gay men to meet and hookup."

Beckett's head jerked toward Levi. "Are you saying guys are meeting here then exchanging money for more?"

Levi stared at Beckett in astonishment then gave a knowing smirk. "When I first started working here, I struggled with the concept of money exchanging hands for sex. I didn't want to go there even though I needed money in a bad way for my brothers. But it's not the majority. Still, there's a decent size group of wealthy men finding happy endings here. You didn't know?"

Beckett shook his head a little harder than necessary and reached for the glass of ice water. He took a drink, wondering why no one ever approached him to buy or be bought for the night. His feelings were a little hurt.

"Stop looking like that. It's a very private exchange, and everybody here thinks you're Dudley Do-Right. You have to know that. You're relationship material, not looking for an escort. Besides, you only have eyes for Julian. Everyone knows that too."

Beckett let himself be distracted away from the pain of Julian's past. It seemed too upsetting to explore too much deeper.

"You're wearing new clothes, and where's the cowboy hat? You're looking young and metro. We might have to change your nickname."

Beckett looked down at the tieless suit he chose tonight based on the schematic his buyer sent. "I like my new clothes."

Levi laughed at his uncertainty. "So do I."

"You do what?" Thane asked. He carried his own stool and placed it close to Levi before leaning in with a ready pucker on his lips. These public displays of affection weren't something Beckett had been exposed to during his life, but they seemed important in building the connection Thane and Levi shared. Levi rose enough to accept Thane's kiss. Levi's actions seemed a gift to Thane who grinned as if the man gave him an extraordinary prize in that quick peck.

For Beckett, the Reservations VIP treatment continued. Chase stopped by the table with three cocktails on his tray. He guessed his alcohol timeout had come to an end. Without a word, Chase placed a drink in front of each man.

"We were talking about Beckett's new clothes," Levi said, filling Thane in. "I asked where the cowboy hat was."

"What's the answer?" Thane asked, nodding at Chase as he reached for his glass.

The relaxation brought on from too many drinks and food in his belly had Beckett chuckling at the waiting stares and shaking his head at their silliness. "It's not far away. I promise."

CHAPTER 16

Minutes from midnight, the night was finally coming to an end. Only a few stragglers remained. Last call had been made well over ten minutes ago.

As Julian watched the revenue totals appear on the screen, he mentally tallied the take for the week, pleased with the money they had made so far. Considering it was only Wednesday night, they would easily exceed their weekly goal.

The continued success of Reservations made his heart swell with pride. Both the club and the restaurant consistently turned a profit. Julian reached for his cocktail glass, taking a drink of the straight whiskey as he let his mind wander.

Almost half his life ago, at the young age of sixteen, he'd run away from his strict Christian home. By running away, he really meant he'd been forced out after being caught inside the family church having sex with the pastor's son, Micah. The memory always made him grin, remembering the noises he'd made when

Micah had shoved his fat cock down Julian's throat, cutting off all oxygen.

Man, he'd always been a sucker for that move.

Julian tucked his lip between his teeth, lost in the mental visual of the way the lack of oxygen had the edges of his vision darkening and shooting stars sprinkled his line of sight. Fuck, that turned Julian on. Why he'd panicked, he didn't know, but the noise he'd made had brought the entire congregation down on their heads.

Of course, he'd had to drop out of high school. For a troubled youth, he'd learned his own form of survival by doing whatever it took to earn a few dollars to keep a roof over his head. Not one time had he ever bemoaned his past. Julian had pride over the road he'd carved for himself, and those first few years out on his own held some fond memories. Julian's mom had correctly labeled him a reprobate. He had always loved to immerse himself in the seedier side of life.

While he craved having his old life back, earning a more respectable living had shaped up to be almost as good. General Manager of Reservations - Coronado. Wow.

But did he have what it took to run a multi-million-dollar establishment? Even with as much money as he made as an escort, he regularly found his bank accounts in the red. So, the answer was no, he didn't have what it took, but if effort and dedication counted, he'd figure it out.

Besides, he'd stress about it all later, or never, whichever was fine.

Warmth bloomed up Julian's chest to his shoulders, rising to his neck. All the little tingles flittered over his nerve endings as an unexpected pride swelled in his chest. Who would have ever thought he could make a respectable living in the business world?

Without even thinking about it, he cast a quick look over his shoulder toward the dance floor.

The few lingering couples danced provocatively with their

partners, drawing out the anticipation of unspoken promises the night held. Thane had somehow talked Levi into staying until closing time. Watching Thane and Levi dance felt almost voyeuristic. The chemistry between them sparked and sizzled, by far the most X-rated pair on the floor.

Thane's sexual magnetism shone like a beacon whenever he had Levi nearby. Their combined heat even had him reaching for a fan. Witnessing the two together left no doubt in his mind that Levi just did it for Thane. His boss's newfound happiness helped settle something inside Julian, glad his friend had found the one who completed him.

Julian's stare traveled to Beckett; the man he seemed to want to share all his good news with. Beckett had moved from his regular table down to one closer to the dance floor. Their gazes met and locked for one, maybe two, long moments. Julian couldn't help the smile breaking out across his lips. The handsome Marlboro Man transformed into a sleek, modern young professional. Whoever had helped him with his new wardrobe had done an excellent job. Like last night, Beckett's tieless state drew Julian's eye to that collar with two buttons open. Beckett had a hint of dark hair on his tanned chest, enough for a man to run his fingers through.

Julian liked Beckett this way, with the hints of the Marlboro Man shining through. Beckett had his long sleeves carelessly rolled to his elbows. His shirt and slacks snugged to his hard body, his suit jacket carelessly tossed across the small round-top table. Beckett was an extremely attractive guy, but he'd seen that the minute the shy man had walked through the front doors of Reservations on that very first night.

He had little doubt that if he got a closer look, he'd see a worldly intelligence reflected in Beckett's dark stare that Julian found alluring. He'd also spotted the rigid lines of Beckett's thick cock outlined nicely in his new, crisp pants.

There was a time that Julian would have been all over that guy. Even if he couldn't have talked Beckett into becoming one of his regulars, Julian would have happily crawled up that muscular body and fucked the shit out of Beckett's firm ass. Beckett thought he had a thing for Julian now; he had no clue. Julian would have fucked him so good he'd have the man desperately panting for more.

He broke their stare, turning away while tucking his chin to his chest. The warmth of knowing someone cared for him for no other reason than being drawn to him settled over Julian like a protective blanket, easing his worry.

He took the cash drawer before starting for the office. Months ago, honestly from the first moment Beckett had entered the club, Julian had trained himself to keep his eyes forward. To not look back at the man who bore holes through his body with that laser beam focus. Beckett made Julian feel special and genuinely appreciated. Both those qualities had been in short supply for him for longer than he cared to admit.

At the base of the steps to the office, he couldn't resist another moment. He looked back in the direction of the dance floor before disappearing as he took the first steps up. Beckett still stared after him. The coy, shy man disappeared from his gaze, though. Beckett blatantly made his interest known, not caring in the least that he might appear a bit stalkerish. He liked that more than he'd admit.

Julian let his inner smile beam. You couldn't stalk the willing. He picked up his steps, taking the stairs up two at a time. With everything that had happened over the last several weeks, he wasn't sure why he couldn't wipe the grin off his heart.

Julian pushed through the office door and took the cash drawer to the desk, discarding it absently there. He'd been making cash drops into their safe all night. It wouldn't take much to finish his nightly duties, but instead, he went to the one-sided mirrored glass to look down over the club. Beckett still sat there, looking up toward the office. The man never relented. Beckett couldn't see Julian, but that didn't seem to matter. Beckett stared up at the darkened glass as if he knew Julian was looking down upon him.

A drunk Beckett had been a fun guy. Beckett had been more

open to the possibility tonight, and the club responded in kind. Julian had enjoyed watching Beckett dance with Quinn. When Quinn made a blatant advance, Beckett, in his kind nature, gently rebuked him before the waiter ever got his offer fully out of his mouth. Julian had wondered if Beckett had even realized Quinn was making a play. He suspected so. He was just a one-man kind of guy, and at the present, his sights were set on Julian. The sincerity of such a thought hugged him like a warm blanket.

"He's not for you, dipshit." And he wasn't. Beckett wasn't for him.

Julian couldn't think of any scenario where he and Beckett could cohabitate together as anything more than friends. Relationships got complicated. Beckett seemed like a really nice guy. And nice guys didn't take escorts home to meet the parents. Beckett deserved more than what Julian could offer, and his future plans were a tossup at the moment. Julian wanted his old life back. More than anything, Julian wanted to be the man he used to be. If he were half as good a man as Beckett, he'd be actively searching for the perfect guy to set Beckett up with and stop leading the man on.

Beckett stood, drawing Julian's focus back to him. He lifted his cocktail glass, draining the last of his drink before he absently discarded it to the small tabletop and grabbed his suit coat. His long stride ate up the distance to the private staircase. No matter how much Julian feigned disinterest, his heart gave an excited lurch as Beckett came for him. By God, Beckett was hellbent on becoming Julian's knight in shining armor, and damn, if he wasn't doing a great job.

When Beckett took the turn toward the staircase, Julian listened to the clomp of each step coming toward the office. Out of anxious necessity, Julian went behind the desk where Woofer lay sleeping. The dog opened one eye and wagged his tail one time, acknowledging Julian, but didn't move another inch.

As Beckett turned the doorknob, Julian's gaze riveted there. Beckett first stuck his head inside. His rumpled look, with that longer piece of hair dropping down over his forehead, and his glassy, intoxicated eyes landing on Julian, instantly eased Julian's anxiety. He had gotten Beckett drunk. Even when Beckett had tried to scale back his drinks, Julian kept them coming, and he really liked the results. Beckett looked ten years younger and was a happy drunk.

"I wanted to walk you out," Beckett said, pushing open the door. His southern drawl had become more pronounced as the alcohol consumption increased throughout the night.

He looked down at the thumping noise hitting against the floor at his feet. Woofer's tail kept a steady beat, wagging after hearing Beckett's arrival. His eyes narrowed at the animal who rarely got that excited to see Julian anymore, kind of hurting his feelings.

Julian swung his head back toward Beckett still at the door. "Go to the hotel, St. Clair. I'm good." He had to steel his heart against Beckett's kind gesture. In response, he did what he did best, ignored Beckett. He started counting the remainder of the cash as the overhead announcement called the club officially closed. Seconds later, bright overhead lighting lit the large main club room, ending the evening. The glare pushed into the office via the large glass panels along the far wall.

"While I'm in town, it would make me feel better if I saw you to your vehicle," Beckett said, doing the exact opposite of what Julian had requested. He came fully into the office, closer to the desk where Julian worked.

When Beckett came to a stop, he swayed heavily on his heels. Having a drunk knight fit Julian's life to a tee. Woofer finally lifted his head, his tail picking up its excited patter until he finally gave up on sleep and stood, shaking off the fatigue with a long yawn as he slowly trotted around the desk to see his new best friend. Beckett turned more endearing when his face lit up, seeing Woofer coming toward him. Beckett instantly bent, giving a gentle, simple command to draw the dog closer to his side—as if Woofer weren't already headed there. Beckett reached down to give a full-body petting.

Of course, the dog was in heaven, becoming as attached to Beckett as Julian.

Julian kept counting the cash. He didn't stop until he went through the register twice and bagged the money to make the deposit. He logged the totals and put the cash bundles inside the safe. For some reason, he trusted Beckett more than reason should allow. It never occurred to him to hide any of it from Beckett.

"Hey, boss, the bar's closed," Ricco said, busting through the door without knocking, stopping short when he saw Beckett who had taken a seat, his head lying against the back edge of the sofa.

Woofer lay sprawled out on the sofa too—another firm rule broken; but Woofer hadn't wanted to lose the hand stroking his fur. Beckett's hand rested on Woofer's belly. His arm now circled around the dog.

"I thought he'd left. Want me to go get his hamburger?"

"No. I'll get it on the way out." Julian had to fight a yawn of his own and rubbed the back of his neck where his anxiety usually built after such a long night. The tension was absent tonight; his gaze skimmed the sleeping man, knowing Beckett's presence was responsible for all these feelings of security. He relished the idea of getting some real sleep tonight.

"They're cleaning the floors tonight, right?" Julian asked, forcing his mind and stare back to Ricco and their business.

"Yeah, they already buzzed in. They're setting up the equipment," Ricco said. He moved inside the office, crossing his arms over his chest, staring down at Beckett.

"Good," Julian muttered, racking his brain for anything else that might be scheduled overnight. He went for the hooks on the back of the door where his suit coat and dog leash hung.

"He's a good guy, Jules," Ricco said, casting a quick look Julian's way.

"Yup," Julian agreed and shrugged on his jacket. "We need

to find someone worthy of him and push him in that direction. Maybe that Jason Hammer, Thane's attorney." The thought turned Julian's stomach, leaving a bitter taste behind the words.

"Yeah," Ricco said, not very convincingly, as he shrugged and ambled back toward the door. He paused before leaving, looking back at Beckett who gave a gentle snore, drawing Julian's attention there too. "He's got a single-minded focus, boss, and that's all on you. You should tell him if you aren't interested. He's too good a guy. He'll get over it and be snatched up pretty quick."

Ricco wasn't wrong, but Julian was a selfish bastard and not near ready to lose Beckett's devotion. He knew what he should do but just couldn't bring himself to let the man go just yet. Julian said nothing more as Ricco left, letting his words be enough.

With the leash in his hand, he went for the sofa. Woofer leaped down and onto his feet, stretching out his long body. He instinctively understood when the time came to leave. He jostled Beckett as he jumped off the sofa.

Even inebriated, Beckett woke with no sleep confusion. He knew exactly where he was as he rolled to his feet, instantly wide awake. "I'm sorry. I think I've had too much to drink."

"I should walk you to your room. Make sure you get there safely," Julian teased, clasping the leash to the collar.

"Nah, I'll be fine. Let's go." Beckett nodded to drive his point home and strode toward the door, taking the leash from Julian's hold.

"Well, aren't you helpful?" Julian taunted at such a take-charge move, then pivoted on the balls of his feet to follow Beckett out with an almost silent chuckle. "I've got to make a pit stop before we leave."

"That's fine. I'll take him outside to do his business. Take your time. We'll be waiting outside the employee entrance for you." Beckett was just so damn straightforward as he trotted down the stairs, Woofer keeping his pace right beside the man. The dog never looked back to check on Julian.

Beckett's ass bounced as he went. Julian watched and recognized the deep sense of attraction drawing him to the man. He genuinely liked everything about Beckett. He loved learning all the layers Beckett slowly revealed of himself.

When had the tables so completely turned? He appreciated Thane. He owed Levi. But Beckett had somehow wormed his way inside Julian's caged heart. How had that happened?

Maybe he was finally growing up. No, most likely, the restraints of such a normal life were dulling his senses, making him think in terms of relationships…and possible monogamy… Oh lord, no.

On that odd note, Julian let out a sarcastic laugh and left the office, locking the door behind him.

All this overthinking would mess with the sleep he intended to get in exactly twelve minutes when he walked inside his condo door and went straight to bed.

CHAPTER 17

"You gonna go, boy?" Beckett asked as Woofer walked him all around the small patch of grass nearby. Between the lights of Reservations and Escape, the whole area was lit bright against the encroaching pitch-dark of the late hour. The cool salty breeze of the ocean helped clear his fuzzy brain. Exhaustion weighed down on him. Beckett needed some serious sleep. His five o'clock in the morning wake-up call creeped closer with every passing second.

As if Julian read his thoughts, he pushed through the employee entrance door, letting it bang off the brick wall. The rattle interrupted the quiet of the middle of the night. "St. Clair, you should be in bed, not waiting around here for me."

"I'll get there," he muttered, turning toward Julian, stopping in his tracks to watch the swagger Julian used as he walked toward him. His grip tightened as Woofer tugged on the leash. "Place," he commanded the dog, never turning away from Julian.

What Beckett wouldn't give to have Julian sauntering toward

him in just this way with that seductive sway of those hips only for his benefit. Where Beckett would have a right to reach out and kiss those pouty lips or gather Julian's hand in his as they walked to the parking lot to leave together. Where he could take his man home and take care of him after his long shift at work.

Beckett knew his life would be complete if Julian were in it.

Julian's gaze went to the dog, who instantly settled and came to stand close to Beckett's side, awaiting further instruction.

"How do you do that?" Julian asked.

"They're universal commands. He's a support animal. He should be trained to adhere to the commands. They didn't give you any instructions when you got him? They should have at least sent you to a special class so you could learn together."

Julian came to a stop in front of him. So close, the spicy scent of Julian's cologne mixed with the sea breeze and fresh night air.

Julian burst out in laughter, reaching for the leash. "Of course, you would know something like that." The teasing tone drew a smile from Beckett. Not offended at the nice-guy image Julian always had about him.

"You're thinking along the lines of Dudley Do-Right again, right?"

"Not much gets past you." Julian took the leash and handed Beckett the burger they'd saved for him hours ago. All those sweet feelings resurfaced as he took the food, pleased Julian had remembered something so trivial.

"Buying me dinner was thoughtful of you. I hadn't eaten," he said as Julian circled around him and started for the parking lot. He easily fell into step beside Julian. His exhaustion fled; being near Julian always made him feel energized. He wished they would slow down, take their time. He loved these unguarded moments.

"You're starving every time I see you. When do you eat?" Julian asked.

"Escape has a huge breakfast buffet. I hit it before class starts. I eat like it's a horse trough," Beckett said teasingly as they walked. "We provide a box lunch for our classes. I eat that as I prepare for the afternoon session. It's the sleeping I'm not doing very much of."

"We don't have to continue with the training." Julian's steps slowed as he turned his concerned gaze toward Beckett.

He chuckled and kept going, slowing his steps for Julian to catch up. "That's the thing I want to do the most."

Julian gave an exasperated sigh. The same one Beckett had heard several times from the man. "You know, I'd decided you had a mental illness or something else just as concerning until it hit me; you're doing all this because you feel sorry for me."

"What?" Had Beckett heard Julian correctly? He stopped dead in his tracks. "Of course, I don't feel sorry for you."

Julian continued another few steps, shoulders tense until he finally faced him. The briefest hint of insecurity lurked behind those vibrant blue-green eyes. He fought the urge to pull Julian against him and chase that doubt away.

"I'm sincerely sorry for what happened to you. I hate it and wish I knew you back then so I could have been there for you. I'm hurt and angry for what you've been through, but I'm in awe of you."

Julian's face went through a range of emotions until landing on a familiar look Beckett knew well. Julian's smirk always gave him away. They were back to Beckett being mentally ill. He disagreed. Still incredibly tipsy, his brain misfired on several cylinders, but insanity wasn't in his top one hundred most prevailing issues. His deepening desires for this man took all the top spots.

Luckily, Julian didn't say what was so clearly on his face. They walked together toward Julian's car. If he read the sudden silence correctly, he suspected Julian had resurrected some of those walls between them.

From the minute he'd decided to pursue Julian, he'd considered their destiny to be more a journey than a moment. Never more true than right then, but damn, panic edged in at the idea of losing any ground he'd gained.

Julian unlocked his sedan, opening the back door for Woofer to jump inside. When the door firmly shut, Julian reached for the driver's door and turned back to Beckett, giving him the Boy Scouts hand gesture. "You did your duty."

Instinct more than reason guided Beckett into action. This could either change the dynamic of their relationship again or cause Julian to fully back away from him. He didn't know the right thing to do, but he couldn't let Julian leave without saying something. He placed his palm against Julian's door, gently closing it. Julian's perfectly arch brow raised.

If Beckett were, in fact, going to make his move, then he'd have to do it slowly. Give Julian enough time to feel like he had a say in what happened.

"We need to move past you saying all those things to push me away." Beckett took a step closer to Julian, setting the burger on top of the car in a very purposeful movement. "Nothing's changed for me except that I'm finally breaking through your barriers. I'm getting to know you, and I really like learning about the complexity of the man you are."

"Beckett," Julian said, his voice a little louder than a whisper as his blue eyes tracked every one of Beckett's movements. "I'm not good enough for you. I'm not saying I'm a bad guy, but you deserve so much more than me."

Beckett took the final step in, stopping a hairsbreadth from being chest to chest. He looked over Julian's handsome face, memorizing every angle like he had done so many times before. Julian wouldn't look him in the eyes. The uncertainty came as a surprise from a man who appeared to own the world around him. Beckett slid a finger along Julian's perfect jawline, the tip catching him under the chin. He slowly lifted Julian's face until those haunting eyes met his.

"I know what I want. I'm just waiting for you to catch up."

Resignation crossed Julian's face as he opened his mouth to speak. His sweet breath puffed across Beckett's face and neck. Julian's warm hand slid inside Beckett's suit coat and fisted into the side of his dress shirt. Seconds passed before Julian finally spoke.

"I'm not into monogamy. I have no interest in the confines of a relationship."

Beckett grinned and stepped closer, brushing against Julian's chest, bringing his palms to Julian's cheeks. That was such a strong relationship boundary statement that Beckett's heart clung to the hope. His palms skimmed across Julian's stubble. He couldn't help the way his fingers ended up tangling in Julian's short, silky strands. The pads of his thumbs swept across the soft skin of Julian's cheek. He committed it all to memory as he registered Julian's heart wildly thumping against his own.

"Julian, I'll never ask you to change. When we get there, we'll deal with it."

Julian opened his mouth to say more, probably another argument as to why this would never work. Beckett wasn't interested and shifted his thumbs to cover Julian's lips, stopping him from saying more.

"I'm going to kiss you. Are you good?"

Turmoil swirled in Julian's vibrant eyes, but he gave a single small nod as he pushed his other hand into Beckett's jacket, his arms circling Beckett's waist, sliding up his back. Beckett dipped his head at the clear invitation. Julian lifted on his tiptoes, meeting him halfway.

Beckett palmed Julian's face as their mouths met, hot and greedy. Those lips were soft but firm and oh so fucking pliant against his. When they parted, and he slid inside, the sugar and cinnamon of Julian's taste drove him to chase after the intriguing flavor with his tongue.

Licking into Julian's mouth, soft and slow, Beckett savored every second, every brush of Julian's tongue against his. The fact that Julian had wanted to kiss him meant everything. He'd kept to his word and allowed Julian as much time as he needed.

Their tongues tangled as the kiss deepened, and the intensity grew tenfold in a matter of seconds. Beckett couldn't get enough of this man. He moved his hands from Julian's face to the back of his neck, holding him in place as he explored his mouth, swallowing Julian's soft moans as he clung tighter to Beckett. He didn't ever want to let Julian go either. He had lost himself in this beautiful man. Beckett wanted nothing more than to hold Julian in his arms forever.

The sheer romance of the moment had Julian clinging to Beckett, begging for more until the need to breathe and gain perspective had him pulling back from the intimate kiss. Julian's insides shook. Not for the reason he might expect but from passionately kissing a man again. The unbridled desire running rampant through every nerve ending in his body had set off the trembling. He had a hard time thinking straight. Impossible to put his thoughts in any sort of succinct order. The kiss had affected him.

Beckett tightened his arms as Julian lifted his eyes, staring into Beckett's compassion-filled dark gaze. Their soft puffs of breath hit and mingled together as Julian's heart drummed wildly in his chest. He couldn't hold the stare. The moment was too intense. He dropped his chin to his chest, his forehead knocking against Beckett's collarbone.

The barrage of emotions had completely caught him off guard, fueling the desire. Julian didn't want to close his eyes, because he didn't want to miss a single second of what happened.

And something significant was happening.

"Are you good?" Beckett had angled his head, trying to get a glance at Julian's face.

He should try to ease the concern of the man who had just kissed the fuck out of him. But he couldn't find it in him to do anything more than tighten his own hold and purr like a damn cat against the opening of Beckett's dress shirt. "I'm good. It was a… good kiss."

A deep laugh rumbled through Beckett's chest, vibrating against Julian's rapidly beating heart. "That's an understatement."

Yeah, a big one. When had a kiss ever affected him so much?

Julian sighed, wishing life could be just like this forever.

"We should get you inside the car so you can go home." Beckett's hands traveled up Julian's back, caressing and massaging until Beckett pushed past Julian's shoulders and tangled his fingers inside Julian's hair. Beckett gave a subtle, enjoyable yank, forcing Julian's head backward. Julian's cock liked it a whole lot as Beckett's pelvis rolled against Julian's, grinding an equally hard arousal against his. It seemed to surprise even Beckett. "I'm sorry about that. I don't want to make you nervous. I'm just really into you."

Beckett's hands, still tangled in Julian's hair, tugged gently, lifting Julian's head until he looked Beckett in the eyes. Beckett searched his face. Whatever he saw softened the fine lines around his warm eyes, and the smallest of smiles lifted the corner of his mouth.

"You have stunning lips. I dream about your lips." The light puffs of Beckett's breath felt like tender caresses against his heated skin as Beckett's words wrapped around Julian's heart, giving a little squeeze.

Julian spoke his own truth. "So do you. I knew you'd be a good kisser. I could tell by the way you care for people that you'd make it good for me."

Julian forced himself to loosen his grip. He was reasonably

sure his legs would hold him upright. If he were going to have a flashback episode, surely it would have happened by now. Beckett surprised him by caging his cheeks between those strong palms and placing a simple kiss on his lips. He kissed Beckett back, following Beckett as he pulled away to kiss him again.

He had no idea what his future held. Honestly, he guessed nothing had really changed for him or between them, but he wanted Beckett to know that if nothing else, this moment had mattered. He'd take these nice feelings and the memory of their time together with him for the rest of his life.

The chaste kiss held until Beckett's mouth opened. His tongue swept forward, and Julian instantly lost himself to the velvet plunge. All seduction and romance, then he found himself sucking air as Beckett fully lifted and unwound himself from Julian's embrace.

Julian's eyes fluttered open as Beckett's hands came to his biceps, dislodging Julian's grip. He blinked wildly and had to force his mouth shut. "Why did you stop?"

"Because this needs to go slow, and because you need to get home and get some rest. You were in the hospital just a few nights ago."

Julian's brow dropped into a scowl. Maybe it hadn't been such a good idea to give Levi free rein to say whatever he wanted.

"I need your address for tomorrow's class."

When Beckett decided Julian was steady enough on his feet, he let him go. He took a firm step backward while he gathered the lapels of his suit coat and buttoned the single button together. The modern-cut jacket, of course, didn't hide the solid erection outlined in Beckett's slacks. Julian didn't mind the visual and suspected several bellhops waiting by the back entrance wouldn't mind either.

"I live in a condo complex nearby," Julian said, watching everything about Beckett as he spoke. "I'll text you the address. Will you come after you finish your class?"

The neurons in Julian's head finally pulled together. Julian would be back at the club in the morning, but he could shoot home at any time.

"I finish around three, so three thirty works the best for me."

Julian nodded.

The loss of Beckett's warm body and tender hold sent an unreasonably cold shiver racing over him. It made no sense. When Beckett reached past him for the burger on top of the car, Julian had mistaken the move for another attempt to get closer. If Beckett realized Julian had wanted more, he didn't act on it. He curled his hands into fists, digging the blunt tips of his nails into his palms to keep from reaching out. He craved the satisfyingly comfortable warmth that was all Beckett.

"Get in the car, so I can take off." The warm southern drawl ghosted over Julian, and he nodded absently. He opened the door and shooed Woofer to the backseat.

"He takes good care of you," Beckett said, nodding to the dog.

"Yeah. I chose him because he was so big and fierce." Julian stuck his loafer-covered foot inside the car and lowered to the seat. "Maybe I should have just chosen you. You're bigger and fiercer."

Beckett laughed, a throaty sound, and finally came forward to the edge of the open door. He stared down at Julian, who couldn't seem to make himself shut the door. He'd only been partly teasing. He'd bet Beckett could keep him safe.

"I'm going to shut this door," Beckett drawled, "before you finish that thought with something that dashes the image of me you just built. Text me your address. I'll see you tomorrow." Beckett lowered his head far enough to see inside the car. "Woofer, take care of our guy for me."

The dog's tail thumped wildly against the seat whenever he heard his name. Woofer was a damn traitor, much like Julian's fucking heart.

Julian situated himself inside the car and let Beckett shut the door. Beckett waited. His finger twirling, instructing Julian to start the engine when he paused. He did as directed, and Beckett gave him a thumbs up.

He watched Beckett and all his rugged swagger cut across the parking lot to the back door of the club. Julian had the same ridiculous urge of wanting Beckett safely inside the hotel before he left. He wanted nothing to happen to the only light inside his life.

A sigh slipped free as his shoulders slumped and his back hit the seat. How long had it been since he'd kissed a man and not ended up in their bed?

Never, that was how long. Yet, he sat there watching after Beckett, content as hell, looking forward to seeing him tomorrow. Nothing else mattered. He actually felt hopeful for the first time in forever.

Beckett turned at the door and threw out both hands in a what-the-hell-are-you-doing-Julian pose, before motioning for him to leave. Julian put the car in drive and started out of the parking lot as happiness swirled all around him.

CHAPTER 18

"Yup," Julian said, distracted, momentarily blinded by the bright sun as he pushed through the Reservations employee exit with his cell phone stuck to his ear.

Thane was on his way to the airport again. This time he planned to leave Coronado for good, moving back home to Maryland full time to prepare for the Silva guys to follow. Julian could hear Logan and Luke, Levi's younger brothers, talking excitedly in the background, which probably meant Thane had rented a limo for the special ride. He could tell the boys were blown away by all the cool features. The confusing part was why Thane chose to talk to him during the ride instead of focusing on being with his new family.

"The corporate management training team will be in touch with you today. Be on the lookout for their call. I want you to shadow Joshua immediately. You'll also begin protocol and policy training. It's your biggest weakness. Pay close attention; there'll be a test afterward. They'll also work you through all the service areas of Reservations. It'll be rushed training but intensive, and I need you to focus. Let the club take care of itself. You've accepted a big job, Julian."

The sun was way too bright. He reached for his sunglasses resting on top of his head, dropping them over his eyes. "I've been thinking about who should take my position at the club. I believe Ricco would be the best fit. He's a self-starter and I like him. He's become my right-hand man."

"I was going to ask you what you thought about him. I've instructed HR to post the position. It's our company policy that it must be posted before we fill, but I want you to encourage Ricco to apply. Feel him out tonight, but don't offer him the job." Thane's voice turned stern, all business. "Professionalism is critical now that you're in the role…"

A light honk drew Julian's attention toward the parking lot as he fished the key fob out of his pocket to unlock his car doors. He looked up to see Beckett's big black truck coming to a stop behind his car.

Julian lowered the phone as an age-old fantasy played out inside his head. Man, he loved a guy and his truck and started in that direction as the passenger side window lowered.

"You haven't left yet. I was afraid I was late," Beckett called out.

"Nah, I'm late. Thane's giving me a list of things to do—" Shit. Julian quickly lifted the phone to his ear, praying Thane hadn't realized he had stopped listening. He was so damn long-winded when he talked business.

"Are you there?"

Julian quickly ducked his head, lifting a single finger in the air for Beckett to see he needed a minute, and schooled his voice, trying for something sedate, as if he were contemplating Thane's directive.

"I'm listening. I'll talk to Ricco, and I'll be vague. I'll follow the management training. On Britney's honor," he said, trying to sound convincing when all he really wanted was to offer Ricco the nightclub management position and start transitioning into the new job. All the red tape made everything harder than it had to be.

"Julian, think bigger picture than this moment. I want Coronado to be the premiere Reservations property. I want you to set the standard and train all the management teams that run the other properties. If you don't follow the rules, they won't either. Then chaos ensues."

Julian executed a spectacular eye roll at the reprimand. "Got it, Papi. I promise."

"How many times do I have to tell you to stop calling me that?"

"Apparently, one more," Julian quipped like he always did, then looked up at the truck. "I gotta go. Stop working and spend this time with Levi. I'm worried about what he's gonna do without you around all the time."

Thane's silence meant Julian's diversionary tactic had worked. Thane and Levi had less than three weeks before all three Silva brothers left California to join Thane in Maryland full time. It wasn't Levi who worried Julian the most. Thane loved his new family to pieces. Julian could already hear all the bellyaching to come from Thane missing Levi.

Julian took the silence as his chance to end the call. "I'll work with Joshua in the morning. Have the management team call me."

He didn't wait for an answer before disconnecting. Julian went to the edge of the window, barely able to see inside the truck. The lift kit made the truck and its driver that much more intriguing. He tucked his lip between his teeth as he implied the exact opposite of what he was thinking. "You know what they say about men and their trucks, right?"

Beckett chuckled, a sound Julian seriously enjoyed. The man was so damn sexy. The aviators he wore today fit the shape of his face perfectly.

"Yeah, I've heard. Many times, in fact. I'm not compensating for anything, don't worry. You heading home? Want a ride?"

Julian looked back at his vehicle then reached inside his pants pocket, unsure how far he'd gotten in the unlocking process. He clicked the key fob and reached for the truck's doorhandle, having to hoist himself up into the seat. The dashboard was a thing of beauty and lit up with all the special LED light kits. He'd been in some nice cars, owned a used Tesla himself, but this might rival the best of the best he'd seen. He could see how the drive to Coronado from so far in Northern California was made a million times easier.

"Nice ride, St. Clair," Julian quipped, shutting the door then strapping his seatbelt in place.

"I spend a lot of time in my vehicle." Beckett was a humble guy. He didn't flaunt his wealth, but this truck was a big fucking flaunt. He wished he could have been there to witness the inner turmoil that had to have played out before he'd bought this thing. Julian could see Beckett really agonizing and justifying his decision to buy something so extravagant.

The truck rolled forward as the GPS voice guided them toward Julian's condo.

"I know a faster way. Go to the light." Julian pointed to the streetlight at the end of the long drive leading into the resort. "Keep going straight through the intersection—"

Beckett cut Julian off as he stared in that direction, trying to see what Julian saw. "Go through the neighborhood?"

"Yeah. My place is at the end of the street. There's a side entrance we could use that leads to my parking area." Beckett nodded and worked the buttons of his navigational system, turning it off before giving the pedal some gas.

"I got a call from Thane." Beckett gave him a side eye stare. Julian could only guess what Thane might have to say, and none of it pleased him. He swung his head in Beckett's direction. He was instantly irritated, but Beckett's handsome profile and enormous bicep on the arm casually draped over the steering wheel helped ease his sudden ire. The only sign that he enjoyed Julian's annoyance was the small smile quirking the edge of his lips. "He told me to watch out for you."

"The motherfucker needs to stay out of my personal life. I'm hiring Ricco tonight." Julian crossed his arms over his chest, arching up one brow. The other brow lowered in anger as he stared unseeing out the window. What did he have to do to get Thane to back the fuck off?

"Hey now. I had your back and told him you were doing a fine job looking out for yourself," Beckett explained, the truck coming to a stop at the streetlight.

Julian had to force himself to let his aggravation go. He'd been looking forward to this afternoon all day. Beckett represented a different prospect, and Julian was loving the hell out of it.

"Where's Woofer?"

He took a deep breath and slowly released it before he felt his shoulders lose some of the tension. "He's at home. And before you say anything, I know he should be with me."

"I wasn't going to say anything," Beckett said, lifting his hands in surrender, showing Julian that his words might have had more bite than he'd intended.

"Full disclosure, and because you're literally the only person on the planet who inspires me to be honest, I only chose Woofer because he was the least emotionally supportive animal presented to me. He has a hard time following the rules, which technically makes him my spirit animal, and he's so fucking huge. That first day when I visited the center, he barked at me, getting my attention before I could look at any other dogs. I think he picked me as much as I picked him. But I see him as more of a guard dog. He's so loud and looks fierce as hell."

"So, you got him for the protection aspect?" Beckett asked as the light turned green.

"Yeah," Julian said, trying to explain his decision. "Sounds lame when you say it, but I'm a lover, not a fighter."

"Yeah? You put me on my ass several times yesterday," Beckett teased as he drove through the neighborhood.

"I never planned to keep Woofer. I'm not sure it's fair to him if I keep him. And he's costing me a ton of money with dog walkers, groomers, his expensive food. I'm going home over and over during the day and night to check on him."

"He doesn't normally come to the office with you?" Beckett asked.

"No, just this week."

Beckett pointed toward the condo community. Julian had to look around to realize what he was asking. They had made it to his complex, and he hadn't even noticed.

"The code is my condo number, A121. Then pull into one of the front parking spaces. It's a short walk."

So close, in fact, that Woofer must have spotted them through the living room window. Julian could hear his deep, resonating bark as he rounded the hood of Beckett's truck to the walkway leading to his unit.

"That's Woofer?"

"Oh yeah," Julian answered. "We're close to my place." He led the way through the common areas. He saw Woofer leap from the window toward the door. He was always so excited to see Julian. "Let me change. I was going to suggest you wait in the gym, but the dog probably wants to see you."

He walked past the gym's floor-to-ceiling windows and absently looked inside. He stopped dead in his tracks, causing Beckett to bump into him so hard that he was forced to take a step forward as he stared at the senior citizens working out inside the facility.

"This is the first time I've ever seen anyone inside there," he said, counting each person. There were twelve men and women in workout attire following the direction of the class instructor.

"The note on the door says senior cardio class followed by

CPR training," Beckett said from over Julian's shoulder.

"Well, I hope those are two different classes," Julian quipped, grinning as he looked back at Beckett.

"Woofer is going nuts," Beckett said, motioning to his front door and starting that direction. "We could train in your condo."

Julian followed before Woofer managed to break through either the window or the door. He kept going back and forth between the two to get to them. "I don't think we can train inside my condo."

"I'll keep my hands to myself." Beckett casually threw the remark over his shoulder as if that should be a given. Julian agreed it was; he utterly trusted Beckett.

"That's not the problem. I'll let you see for yourself." Julian edged past Beckett to unlock the door. He tried to push the door open, but Woofer crowded against it in his excitement.

"Your neighbors don't mind this barking?"

"This is the first time it's been this bad. Brace yourself." Julian looked back over his shoulder to make sure Beckett was ready when Woofer bounded out.

Woofer launched past Julian, aiming for Beckett who instantly implemented his Jedi mind trick and said, "No. Sit."

Woofer stopped dead in his tracks and dropped to his ass. His tongue slipped to the side of his mouth as he panted his excitement. His tail swung wildly. Beckett fisted a hand in the air, his eyes trained on Woofer who stayed quiet and waiting.

Beckett needed this dog. Maybe that was why Julian was so drawn to Woofer. He was the conduit to match these two beasts together.

"Good boy," Beckett said, bending to pet the top of Woofer's head and neck. He loved every single stroke.

"Come inside, you two."

Beckett patted his thigh, and the super calm German shepherd trotted alongside Beckett, completely oblivious to Julian's presence. Julian didn't even feel slighted with as happy as Woofer was to be with Beckett. He might even have to agree with the contentment of the moment.

"My God, what's going on in here?" Beckett asked.

Julian chuckled, looking over his packed living room. "I lived in a loft in LA. It was a nice size with those high ceilings. The furniture fit my loft very well, but not so much here. I have a storage unit that has most of my things, but I thought if I brought some of my furniture in here that it would motivate me to not stay too long."

He had gotten used to the snug fit but tried to see the room from Beckett's point of view. There might be a foot of space between his sofa, coffee table, and side chair. His large television and stand took up the entire area of where a kitchenette might fit. His two barstools occupied the remaining space, pushed snuggly against the kitchen island separating the two rooms.

"How big is that TV?"

"Stop making fun of my shit," Julian said, tossing his keys on the center island.

"I'm serious. It's gotta be the movie-screen size. Does it hurt your eyes being so close?"

Julian didn't look back at the comedian as he started for his bedroom.

"I call the look *bougie* garage sale. I'm going to change clothes, but we can call the training off too."

"No," Beckett said with that instructor voice he used. "Repetition is critical. We can move the coffee table like this…"

Julian was certain anyone else would have taken the out he had just offered. Of course, not Beckett. He left Beckett to do his thing and shut his bedroom door behind him.

Beckett surveyed the cozy living room, witnessing much of the struggle of Julian's life played out in the belongings piled into this condo. Even as packed as the condo was, it held all the beauty of Julian. All the furnishings looked expensive and well kept. It represented both sides of the man. The old and the new. But it also held a certain amount of conflict.

He ran his hand over the length of the expensive cloth of Julian's sofa. This furniture didn't come cheap and spoke of a past life Beckett had no real understanding of and didn't fit the look of the condo.

The biggest purchase he ever made was the pickup truck he was driving. Outside of that, maybe the clothes he'd bought to woo Julian could be considered extravagant. Other than that, Beckett lived a modest, simple life.

He carefully moved the decorations before he lifted the coffee table high in the air and gave a huff at the weight. Beckett decided the sofa was the best place to move it out of the way and keep it safe. He looked around, trying to find a way to make more room. The barstools were next. He reached behind the sofa and had to exert more muscle power. They were damn heavy too. He put the barstools in the middle of the kitchen and shoved the sofa to the edge of the island.

As he pushed the side chair toward Julian's bedroom door, it opened. Julian's brows lifted as he blocked Julian's entrance to his room. Woofer jumped on the chair's cushion as if he owned the thing. "Is he allowed up there?"

"Of course not," Julian said and lifted a leg to climb over the chair, not putting a foot on the fine fabric.

"Woofer…" Beckett started, but Julian cut him off.

"He's fine. I let him on this chair. I have another two in storage and more of that fabric saved," Julian said, hoisting himself over the oversized chair. "He spends lots of time in this tiny condo. If I ever get out of here, we can train him to behave properly, and by we, I mean you. He responds to you."

Beckett lifted a hand to help Julian, surprised at how long and limber Julian actually was. No part of him touched the expensive furniture, which spoke to how much he valued Woofer if he worked so hard to care for the furniture but allowed the dog to sit on it.

Julian's long fingers clasped his hand, sending tingles instantly shooting up his arm and over his skin. Beckett felt reasonably sure he'd managed to keep things casual between the two of them since the moment he rolled down his truck window. Holy hell, his insides were in straight-up freak-out mode.

"You make me laugh. Your neck gets flushed. It's the only way I can tell what's going on with you," Julian teased, letting go of his hand and walking into the open space of the living room.

"What's going on with me?" Beckett asked, then instantly wished he could take those words back.

Julian stretched his body with bends and lunges but stopped to give him a look over his shoulder that he interpreted to mean he'd made the joke too easy for Julian. *Whatever.* Beckett knew exactly how Julian had responded to him last night. Julian also had to know that wasn't going to be their last kiss, but he wisely kept all that to himself.

"What's that grin mean?" Julian asked, his eyes narrowing.

"Nothing," he replied, grinning broadly at Julian as he moved closer. "Do you remember the break and escape?" Beckett didn't give Julian a second to consider his answer because Julian's would-be attacker wouldn't give him a second's notice before an attack. Reaching out with his left hand, Beckett grabbed Julian's T-shirt in the middle of his chest. His grip was tight, and Julian did as he'd been taught, immediately implementing his counterattack. The seconds required to think through each move would have cost him if this had happened out on the street. But today, the student became the aggressor.

Julian reached for Beckett's free right hand while covering Beckett's fist with his other, doing exactly what Beckett had taught him to do. Peeling away Beckett's firm grip, Julian used Beckett's pinkie finger to twist him away with such force that it surprised Beckett. Julian had a solid hold on Beckett, bending his arm while never letting go of his hand. He remembered to rotate his body around, too, completely dislodging Beckett from his attack stance.

Then he only gave the slightest hesitation before shoving his left hand into the back of Beckett's arm and shoulder, pushing him away as Julian jumped backward several steps, bouncing on his tiptoes until he bumped into the wall.

Beckett flipped all the way around to see Julian up on his toes with his fists ready to fight. "Excellent. Julian, that was excellent. But you paused on my arm and shoulder."

"Goddamn it! I was hoping you didn't notice." Those balled fists that were ready to throw down at whatever was coming next, dropped to his hips as his feet landed on the ground, and his heels planted there. Julian looked ready to fight Beckett with his words, not his hands.

"You surprised me, which is what we want, and you also gave a slight hesitation with the roll of your left shoulder when you disengaged my fist."

"It pisses me off that you know that." Julian's disgust with his first attempt was clear as he came into the middle of the room. "Let's do it again."

Beckett grinned and moved forward. "This time I'm going to hit you with my right fist. What do you do?"

Julian started to say whatever he planned, but Beckett went for the element of surprise. Julian didn't disappoint. Even going so far as to tilt his head out of the line of his fist before grabbing and twisting the shit out of Beckett's arm. This time Julian's palm hit his shoulder, and Beckett dropped to his knee.

That gorgeous grin was even bigger this time, making the sudden burst of pain bearable.

Much of the time it felt like Julian just gave everyone around him lip service, especially Beckett, but the man had obviously paid attention to his instruction, which increased the value of this whole self-defense training. Instead of saying any of that, Beckett twisted around and implemented his next controlled lunge. Again, there was a minuscule pause before Julian executed the perfect countermove to bring Beckett back to his knee.

The slight pauses and hesitations would end with more practice. Beckett pressed forward, this time grabbing Julian's neck. Woofer gave a low growl until Julian used maximum effort to come down on Beckett's elbow. Beckett let go and twisted away. If not, Julian might have actually broken his arm. He wasn't able to block Julian's knee to his gut that landed between his thighs. Beckett dropped to both knees, riding out the burst of pain as he tried to catch his breath. Julian followed his instruction and bounced backward, disengaging the would-be threat.

Beckett lifted his gaze to Julian who immediately stopped preparing for the next blow and quickly stepped forward. "I'm so sorry. I didn't mean to hurt you."

"Yeah, you did," Beckett said through gritted teeth. "Exactly like you were supposed to do. You learn fast."

"I've been hearing that a lot lately," Julian replied. His palm rested on Beckett's shoulder, giving a gentle squeeze of apology. "I'm not sure any of my schoolteachers would have agreed with you."

Beckett forced himself to rise to his feet. He still had to bend at the waist, breathing in and out through his nose. The pain washed over him in rolling waves. This time, Julian's tender touch slid over his back, massaging up his neck.

"I'll be more careful."

"No, you keep doing what you're doing. You would have

stopped anyone in their tracks with that move. This was my fault. I should have gotten out of the way." Beckett finally pushed backward, squaring his shoulders as he rose to his full height and stared down at the caring eyes. "Let's keep going. I came at you with one hand. Do you know what to do if I come for you with two hands?"

"I'd say drive my hands on the inside of your arms to break them away?" The answer came by way of a question, making Beckett smile and nod.

"Correct. You use force, because you're knocking both my hands and arms away." Beckett demonstrated the move, steepling his hands and lifting upward before spreading them open. Julian nodded. "Let's try."

Beckett had no idea how much time passed or when Woofer stopped growling every time Beckett went after Julian. Sweat trickled down the side of his face and Julian had brought him to his knees for about the millionth time since they started.

This time, Beckett let his body fall fully to the ground. He lay on his back, looking up at the ceiling, panting. He'd be bruised by morning. "How are you not tired?"

Julian bent over Beckett, his face coming directly in Beckett's line of vision. Julian had his ever ready mocking stare in place. "It's the H in my ADHD. My head keeps me going ninety to nothing all the time. It's why I'm so good in the bedroom and why I kicked your ass today. Maybe you need some of my training."

"Ha," Beckett managed half-heartedly and caught a hint of challenge in Julian's eyes. He'd show him a challenge. In a swift move that caught Julian completely off guard, Beckett knocked Julian's feet out from underneath him. Beckett bolted forward, reaching for Julian's body to cushion his fall. Julian gave a surprised yelp, his arms and legs flailing, grasping for the air to help protect his fall. Beckett got a slap to the face and a knee to his thigh as he took all of Julian's weight onto his body.

"Ugh," Julian said, releasing a breath. Their faces less than two inches apart. "What's wrong with you? You should be praising me."

"For kicking my ass?" Beckett teased.

Julian used Beckett's body to launch himself to his feet. "Yeah, exactly. Star student award today."

CHAPTER 19

As Beckett stood in Julian's kitchen, finishing a glass of water, Beckett took inventory of his body's pain level and what was going to hurt tomorrow. Julian hadn't held back in today's training session, and he'd encouraged him not to. His muscles ached and he suspected the spots on his legs and the few tender places along his ribcage were already turning blue. Julian was stronger than he gave himself credit for. Beckett glanced over at the bedroom door when he thought he heard Julian calling out to him.

No matter how Beckett tried, he couldn't make sense of the rest of Julian's words. Absently, he set the empty water glass on the countertop and moved closer to Julian's bedroom door.

All Beckett could make out from Julian's reply was the word *suggestion.*

"Are you talking to me?" Beckett called out, tilting his head closer to the door, concentrating on Julian's words.

"Open the door!" Julian yelled. That command came through loud and clear. Beckett pushed open the door with his foot.

He wasn't prepared for the open design of the bedroom and bathroom. The adjoining bathroom doors were wide open. Julian stood in the shower, his sculpted nude body glistening under the spray of the water. Julian didn't look away, his bold gaze issuing a challenge.

Beckett's heart sprinted in his chest. Desire raced over him in the most visceral of ways, sending his thoughts spiraling at the glimpse of the most beautiful man he had ever seen.

Heat inflamed his body. Beckett tried to control his reaction, but he'd lost that battle long ago when it came to Julian. His dick rammed against the tight constraints of his underwear, straining the material as he fought for breath and rational thought.

An instinctual sense of decorum had Beckett shifting his gaze to the floor as his manners propelled him backward, stepping completely out of the doorway.

Goddamn... Motherfucker... Shit.

If he and Julian were dating, nothing would have stopped him from joining Julian in that shower.

The sound of blood rushing to his head echoed loudly in his ears, drowning out everything else around him. All Beckett could see in his head was Julian's long, chiseled, sexy as hell body. Of course, Julian was perfect with toned legs that would feel so good wrapped around him, a lean waist, and a muscular torso. Jeez, he wanted to map those with his palms.

He'd tried not to stare, but he couldn't help himself. God, he hoped Julian hadn't noticed.

Julian's laughter rang loudly through the small condo.

Fuck. Julian's laugh had Beckett's cheeks burning. He'd noticed his indecision. What the hell was wrong with him? Beckett had to get control of his body's reaction to Julian before he faced him again. It was just so damn hard.

The image of Julian's naked physique played behind his eyes. He'd caught a glimpse of the scar running the length of Julian's left thigh, from the bottom of his hip bone to his knee.

Why had he drunk so much last night? He should have been paying better attention when Levi had given him the rundown about Julian's past. Even now, Beckett wasn't entirely certain of what he saw because his attention had gone straight to the cock hanging enticingly between Julian's thighs.

Beckett strained to remember everything. Other scars had also marred Julian's perfect body. Some might have come from incisions. Others, like the cigarette burns, were more likely a result of his assault. Those made sense with the hints of the faint scars Beckett has seen on the edge of Julian's cheek, right above his scruff.

Beckett's heart broke as the abuse Julian had suffered took shape in his mind.

Julian was always in control of his surroundings. He had to have known what he was doing by calling Beckett to the door. Maybe Julian had wanted him to see the scars. Perhaps to scare him away? It made sense with the way he was posed. Julian's thigh being so prominently positioned front and center.

Fire licked its way up Beckett's spine, turning his desire into anger and sending it shooting through the stratosphere. What he wouldn't give to find the motherfucker who did that to Julian. The person who had caused so much damage, both mentally and physically, to that beautiful man.

Beckett fisted his hand as his body tightened with rage. Goddamn, Beckett didn't like getting so angry. Every fucking day Beckett made a solid effort to be positive and happy in his life, but right now, he promised himself if he ever got the chance, the fucker who hurt Julian would hurt in return. Such an oath helped take the edge off the intensity of his mounting fury.

He took a deep cleansing breath, clearing his erratic thoughts. Julian had been through enough; he didn't want to freak him out any further.

"I'm gonna be honest, there aren't too many men who've turned away from me like you did," Julian said from the threshold of his bedroom door. Beckett kept his gaze averted, not sure he could handle another fully nude display.

"It wasn't easy," Beckett replied truthfully, hearing the desperate roughness of his voice.

"You've got that I'm-a-gentleman thing down." Julian's voice faded back into the bedroom. "I have a crazy idea. What about I buy your dinner tonight?"

Beckett had to swallow the lump in his throat as the back of his head hit the wall before he corralled his scattered thoughts. "Yeah. Dinner. Okay. Don't you have to work tonight?"

"Not really the response I expected," Julian said, peeking back around the corner. Beckett allowed himself a look at Julian. This time, he caught the guarded hesitancy in Julian's expression. "Be honest. Did you see something you didn't like? We're good if you'd rather take off."

The insecurity from such a vibrant man confirmed his earlier thoughts. If Beckett ever got the chance, he would destroy with his bare hands the motherfucker who'd hurt Julian. Julian was beautiful, and nothing Beckett saw would make him feel any differently.

He took a deep breath and answered on the exhale. "I haven't been shy in pursuing you. Seeing you in the shower only confirmed what I've known all along. You're the most beautiful man I've ever seen." Beckett shook his head as the truth tumbled from his lips. "Who could have thought you'd be any more gorgeous out of your clothes than you are in them?" He dropped his head hard against the wall, wanting to knock away the images flashing through his brain. "I'm so fucked over you, Julian."

Julian almost preened under the praise. Holy hell, Julian moved enough to have his bare chest exposed, his silky robe lapel dropping open. Beckett closed his eyes, praying Julian wasn't truly the exhibitionist he proclaimed himself to be.

"I'm transitioning out of my current position to begin training for general manager. You could help me celebrate by staying in and watching something on that big ol' screen I haven't turned on since I've been here."

"I don't think I've ever known you to take a day off," Beckett managed, unsure if committing to being alone with Julian was a good idea.

Thankfully, Julian ducked back behind the door and spoke louder as he moved about the bedroom. "Thursdays are my scheduled days off, but I never take off. If you'd rather keep your reservation, we're good. I can go in."

This time, Julian didn't sound pained. It relieved Beckett.

"I'm into staying in tonight," he said, and finally pushed off the wall, glad his feet held him upright. "I have a change of clothes in the truck…"

"Be prepared. Boy Scout rule number one," Julian called out mockingly, back to his normal self. Beckett grinned, at ease again. "You can shower if you want. I'll call the restaurant and order us something to be delivered. Sound good?"

"Perfect," Beckett answered and started for his truck. Maybe he could regroup before he got back to the condo.

The warmth and comfort of being held by another was finally seeping through Julian's well-constructed barriers. No matter how indifferent he acted, having Beckett's muscular arms around him while they lay sprawled out on top of his oversized sofa, watching Netflix, was an important step in the right direction for his mental health. Julian wouldn't ever admit it out loud, but he enjoyed the domesticated bliss he was feeling at the moment.

His head lay cushioned on Beckett's thick shoulder and chest. He slowly trailed his palm down Beckett's soft T-shirt as he stared at the screen, feigning interest in whatever show they'd chosen. Beckett's other brawny arm was pushed behind his head, keeping him at an angle to better see the television.

The arm wrapped around Julian tightened its hold. A show of appreciation for his simple caress. Beckett's consideration ran so deep. He never failed to show Julian exactly how thankful he was to be there with him. How did that make him feel so damn special?

What an utterly normal night to have shared a pizza together, along with a fifteen-dollar bottle of wine. Laughing and just enjoying the other's company. Beckett was so intuitive. A true gentleman, giving Julian the space he needed even though he could tell Beckett was really into him. The man was a saint. So utterly classy.

Had Julian ever done something this basic in his life? And enjoyed it so much? He couldn't remember a time if he had. As a younger person, Julian was too rebellious to relish a moment like this. He grew up way too fast, but it sure as hell hadn't felt wrong at the time.

Once he'd gotten out on his own, lived his life on his terms, he'd been content in his life, perhaps as content as he felt right now. What did that mean? Julian's mind raced. He couldn't quite process the confusion of such conflicting thoughts, bringing on a newfound uncertainty, but what the fuck was he unsure about?

Today was a good day. Julian had conquered one of his biggest fears. The grin he tried hard to hide couldn't be contained, and he bent his head, not wanting Beckett to see he wasn't fully paying attention to the show. If Beckett thought Julian wasn't interested, he'd insist on turning off the movie. Then there'd be a thirty-minute discussion about watching something Julian would rather see. No one had time for that. It would disrupt their snuggling time—the part of this whole night that Julian liked the most.

Beckett was right. The one thing Julian didn't have any control over was his own desire. He hadn't lied about that. An aroused Beckett wasn't some big accomplishment on Julian's part. He had never failed to entice a potential lover. Most men had thought of him as attractive, and he'd always used that along with his clever wit to get what he wanted.

The value Julian had placed on his looks was solely based on making a living. Julian was as comfortable in his clothes as he was out of them. Well, at least before the accident. He had happily coasted through life on something as superficial as his good looks. Life had been made much easier before all this scarring littered his body.

Based on Beckett's reaction, he'd worried about that for nothing. Maybe he couldn't entice the top one percent to take him on as an escort, but wealthy men of Beckett's stature could easily be added to his list of clients.

His smile faded as he realized the direction of his thoughts.

Julian had never wanted his current life. His most secret desire was to be the man he used to be.

"What's going on?" Beckett asked, moving the shoulder Julian rested his head on to help gain his attention. Julian let his hand trail back up those tight stomach muscles and schooled his features, trying for passive interest in the television show before he looked up at Beckett.

"What do you mean?" Julian asked, lifting an eyebrow. "I'm watching this entertaining show you chose."

The teasing worked. But Beckett lifted a challenging brow of his own. "Then what just happened?"

Of course, Julian had no idea. He'd stopped paying attention during the introduction. Instead of admitting he'd lied, he aimed for super vague. "There's this one dude that was talking to another dude."

Beckett's lips quirked up in the corners. "Just so you know, you're a terrible liar. I meant, why did your body tense?"

Of course, the survivalist picked up all the minuscule details of every increase in heartbeat and shift of Julian's body. Julian raised one brow higher as the other lowered. He stared at the man, taking everything about Beckett into his heart. Beckett was such a handsome man. How he'd ever thought him old was beyond Julian. He made Julian feel whole and safe again. Beckett allowed him to let go of his fear and live.

The realization added another layer to Julian's deep self-awakening. Julian hadn't been nude in front of anyone for so long. He hadn't even considered the risk involved. That's how safe Beckett made him feel. With little thought to the consequences, Julian had disrobed, positioned himself under the spray of warm water, and posed with the most prominent scars on the left side of his body on full display. Then he'd coaxed Beckett into the room.

"What's going on, Julian?" Beckett asked, his look turning serious. He reached for the remote control to pause the show.

"Did you notice the scars on my body when you saw me naked?" Julian asked directly, all pretenses gone. If this weren't so important, Julian might have laughed at the comical display of Beckett's facial features as he searched for his answer and settled on a single nod. "What did you really think of them?"

That answer seemed easier for Beckett. "Your scars prove just how strong you truly are. I don't like what caused them. I hate that you were physically hurt. But what I hate even more is the insecurity and doubt you're living with because of those scars. You're more than your looks, Julian."

Julian nodded, unsure what to do with that answer and again lowered his head to Beckett's shoulder and reached for the remote. "Can we turn the television back on?"

"You don't like that answer?" Beckett asked, his cheek resting against Julian's head.

"No, it's fine," Julian said, stopping short of actually turning the television back on. They lay there several long seconds. Maybe Julian had been wrong. He couldn't attract the right men back into his bed.

Beckett knocked his shoulder again, lifting Julian's head up as Beckett moved to his side, edging Julian down beside him until Julian had no choice but to look Beckett in the eyes. "When I looked at you in the shower, your scars weren't the first thing I saw. I wasn't lying when I said you're beautiful, Julian. You're desirable. If I didn't know what you'd been through, I would have taken it as an invitation and been all over you."

The sincerity in Beckett's eyes eased Julian's heart, but he still rolled his eyes for dramatic effect. "You and I both know you aren't the kind of guy to jump someone. I'd have to do a whole lot more to coerce you into the shower with me."

"I'm not going to force myself on anyone, but I've been known to work pretty hard at talking someone into sex," Beckett admitted, his warm palm coming to Julian's cheek, caressing over his beard.

Julian gave a small shake of his head at the simplicity of Beckett's words. He was so fucking endearing. "I don't believe you."

"You bring out something in me that I haven't experienced before." Beckett caressed the skin on Julian's neck with the tips of his fingers before tracking back up to trace his lips. The intimate touch had Julian's cock taking notice as currents of arousal rushed through his veins. Beckett's eyes held his as he spoke. "You matter to me more than I matter to myself. I looked away from you because I had such a primal reaction I didn't want to scare you. Only when I looked back up did I notice the scars." Those sensual fingers rose to Julian's cheek, where he'd spent time and a considerable amount of money to laser the scars away. "I've seen the lines on your cheek. I knew something had happened, but the ones on your thigh and chest sent rage through me I haven't experienced in a long time."

The glimpses of who Beckett insisted he was compared to the man Julian had gotten to know showed the true depth of his character. Julian nodded and let Beckett trace the scars on his cheek, the gesture healing the wounds from the outside in. He had to look away from the intense stare. The honesty he found there was much too alluring to allow him to think properly.

"I'm not going to hurt you. Not ever. I've never been that kind of man, but I haven't always considered other people first. You inspire something inside me that makes me want to take care of you. I've never experienced anything like it before."

Julian connected with those words. Beckett accepted him for who he was, whoever that was, something he was still trying to figure out since the assault. Everything he'd ever believed or enjoyed had been tainted since that night. Had anyone ever appreciated him for anything more than being on his knees, swallowing cock? He didn't think so. Which took his thoughts in a different direction.

Yes, Julian was attracted to Beckett. Clearly very much so, but could he have sex with Beckett? That he didn't know. Not only did Julian have to deal with all his own mental shit, but he also wasn't certain he could keep from hurting Beckett emotionally. A deep sigh of uncertainty resonated as he lifted his gaze back to Beckett's.

"Your face is so expressive, but I have no idea what you're thinking," Beckett said tenderly, running his fingers through Julian's hair.

Beckett didn't seem to mind being his temptation or his salvation. Even though Julian knew he shouldn't, his willpower crumbled in the face of Beckett's allure. Julian eagerly pushed his hand under the hem of Beckett's T-shirt, his palm grazing across the warm skin of Beckett's tight stomach muscles. The gentle touch made everything inside him feel right. Julian craved closer contact as he slid his palm higher, touching every part of Beckett he could reach.

Over the top of his T-shirt, Beckett's hand came to rest on his, stopping his trek upward. "What are you doing? I don't expect…"

"I don't know how far this can go, but I need you to kiss me." The words rushed out of him as he lifted his mouth. Beckett eased off his hand even as the confused look on his face remained. It was the most natural thing in the world to capture Beckett's mouth with his. Julian lifted himself, thrusting his tongue forward while pushing at the T-shirt until Beckett was forced to break from the kiss and sit up enough to let Julian pull it over his head.

Julian lost interest in helping Beckett remove the shirt as he stared at the wonderland that was Beckett's muscular chest. Oh fuck, his cock was definitely on board, straining against his pants, urging him on as he splayed his hands over Beckett's pecs and lowered his lips to the warm strip of skin underneath Beckett's collarbone.

The rapid rise and fall of Beckett's chest had Julian lifting his head to seal the moment with another kiss. It had been so long since he'd kissed a man like this. Julian was blindsided with a desire he'd thought had been stolen from him. So many feelings rushed over him, filling his mind with questions he'd have to confront sooner or later. But not right now. One thing he knew for certain was that Beckett's mouth moving with his was just about the best thing he'd experienced in forever.

Beckett wrapped him in his arms, his firm hand cupping the back of Julian's head. As much as he'd planned to control their moment, Beckett beat him to it and angled his head, driving his tongue forward. Julian surrendered to Beckett's kiss, opening for him, allowing his sweet taste to chase away the last bit of uncertainty that held him back. This felt good, too good. He deepened the kiss. Beckett's moan sent thrills echoing through his body. Julian wanted more.

Julian went straight for the button on Beckett's pants. The need to watch Beckett come drove his every move. He worked the button free then slid the zipper down. Beckett didn't resist; his hands rushed to help push the material away, then he drew back, questions written all over his face.

"Stroke yourself for me, Beckett." He held Beckett's dark

gaze. "Please. I need to watch." For a split second, Julian wasn't certain his cowboy would give in to his request.

Beckett didn't say a word. He only nodded as his big hand circled that gorgeous cock and stroked. At first, he moved his fist slowly up and down on that thick shaft as if he were drawing out the pleasure. The broad tip leaked with each pass of Beckett's hand.

The smell of arousal hung heavy in the air. Beckett twisted his hand before sliding back down and up again. His breaths deepened as he picked up the pace, mesmerizing Julian with the uninhibited movements.

Julian's dick pressed against the front of his pants, aching to be freed as he watched Beckett work himself. The man was magnificent, his muscles flexing with every downward motion of his fist.

"That's it," Julian praised, encouraging Beckett to let go. Need bloomed along his spine and fervent desire churned in his balls. His intention was merely to watch, but that wasn't going to be enough for him. The sight of Beckett fucking his fist was sexy as hell. "So beautiful." Julian choked out his words, their syllables thick with lust.

As hard as he'd tried, Julian couldn't resist. He quickly undid his own pants, shoving them down as he gripped himself and stroked in time with Beckett.

"Oh, hell," Beckett hissed, that whiskey gaze dropping to his cock, watching his hand move over his dick. Fuck if that didn't make every stroke that much more satisfying.

Julian could guess by Beckett's breathing that he was close; so was Julian. He snuggled closer. Julian placed his hand over the man's fist, letting it ride Beckett's a few strokes before moving away.

"Let me do this for both of us." Julian urged Beckett to change positions and lie with his back down on the oversized sofa. Julian stretched out along Beckett's body. He wrapped his fingers around them both, pressing their cocks together.

"Oh fuck, Julian." Beckett's intake of breath made him smile as he slid his palm back and forth over them.

The heat of Beckett against him had his head spinning and his body going on overload at the feel of that hard cock, hot and perfect, against his. He stroked them long and slow. Beckett's mouth found his and his tongue pushed between his lips. Julian moaned into the kiss as Beckett's hand joined his.

Heavy breathing and quick pants were the only sounds filling the room. Julian tightened his grip and used his thumb to tease the head of Beckett's cock. "Come for me, Beck."

"Yes." Beckett groaned. His big body trembled as liquid heat coated Julian's fingers.

Julian wasn't prepared for the orgasm that slammed into him, taking him over the edge with such intensity that he cried out from the sudden burst of pleasure. Beckett kept his hand moving, working Julian through a release that seemed to go on forever. He was wrung out in such a good way. Floating in total bliss as he tried to catch his breath. It took everything inside him not to fall flat against Beckett's body.

Julian had ended his dry streak in such a tantalizing way. He was energized to his core, happier than he ever remembered being. What a fan-fucking-tastic orgasm. It might have been the best of his life. His head wasn't even the least bit fucked about it all.

Beckett kissed his forehead then the tip of his nose. "Thank you," he murmured, his voice heavy and thick.

"I should be the one thanking you," Julian replied and gave Beckett a quick kiss before he rolled from the couch and headed for the small powder room off the entryway. His body hummed with excitement.

He was actively finding his way back to normal after worrying he'd never fully recover. He owed Beckett everything.

Julian cleaned himself then grabbed a small hand towel,

wetting it under the warm spray of the faucet for Beckett before returning to the living room.

His hot savior hadn't moved a single one of those big muscles. Julian's vigor was met with overly exhausted eyes.

"Thanks." Beckett groggily smiled up at him as he reached for the towel and wiped at his stomach and hands.

"You're very welcome."

He took the towel as Beckett closed his eyes. His grin couldn't be contained.

CHAPTER 20

An overwhelming sense of contentment flowed through Julian like a healing balm. Funny how the buzz of his sexually sated body pulsed radiantly through his veins. Had he ever noticed how reinvigorated he felt after such a basic release? Probably not.

Julian lifted his chin. His direct stare focused on the silk tie in the mirror as he executed an expert Windsor knot at his neck, lost in thought over the way Beckett had given him courage in his moment of self-doubt. He wrapped a hand around Julian's, anchoring Julian in the moment, allowing him to guide their climax.

How had something so simple been so fucking hot?

That was another new side he'd discovered. When sex was his job, he rarely delighted in the pleasure. Instead, he'd reveled in a job well done. Satisfied customers always came back for more, and Julian had made the big bucks.

Many of those times came by way of a partner with some

serious fetish inclinations. Julian had tied up countless men and had been strapped down in return. He'd let his clients play daddy, where Julian starred spectacularly in both roles. He'd organized more orgies than he could remember. But he'd enjoyed the simplicity tonight, more than he'd ever thought possible.

Tonight had been so fucking tame compared to what he was used to but much more satisfying. He and Beckett had shared what some people would call normal or even boring. They hadn't even attempted penetration, yet it was fantastic. He'd actually orgasmed with Beckett. That hadn't been his intent, but once he'd caught sight of Beckett stroking his own cock, something in him flipped.

It wouldn't be long before Julian was back in the game. He felt it in his bones. Maybe even by the end of the weekend if Beckett planned to stick around. Julian racked his brain, trying to remember Beckett's schedule.

Beckett. The name fit the man spectacularly. How had he gotten so lucky to meet such a genuinely tender, caring man? No question, it was Beckett's goodness bringing Julian's sexual side to the forefront. Did he believe Beckett's claim that Julian didn't see him clearly? Those do-gooders always saw their tiny flaws that no one else could see.

What did it say about him that Beckett's goodness brought out his raunchy side? Julian gave a silent chuckle. His Marlboro Man had no idea what he was getting into. Maybe he was Beckett's exact opposite. Julian was the darkness in direct contrast to Beckett's lightness.

His grin tipped the corners of his lips as he gave an amused chuckle. Fuck, it felt good to be getting back to his old self. Julian critically assessed his clothing, twisting to check all sides. He had always liked to look his best. Most of the measly income he made went to his appearance. Tonight, Julian wanted to walk out of this bedroom and be as mouthwateringly gorgeous as he could for the man waiting for him in the living room. He liked Beckett's tongue wagging after him.

Beckett had made several comments about Julian's eyes. He liked their color. The soft blue dress shirt he wore tonight made his eyes and naturally tanned skin pop. It added a vibrance to his dark, almost black hair. His fitted black slacks left nothing to the imagination. They were expensive and designed to impress. A throwback to his old life. The fit of his pants could be considered X-rated in many circles.

Julian did another half turn, running a hand down his ass, thinking about Beckett peeling him from the tight fit.

Fuck yeah.

He was back.

Julian fisted his hands. The thought sent his excitement to the stratosphere.

Hold your horses, hot stuff.

It wasn't right to taunt Saint Beckett, especially since Julian wasn't ready to go all the way, but he couldn't tamp down his anticipation. The way Beckett pursued him and wanted him to be happy filled his heart with joy. The thought of Beckett seeing enough value in Julian that he still wanted him by his side made him walk from his bedroom with a bit more swagger than necessary.

The scene that greeted him was again far too normal for anything he fully understood, especially to be so damn endearingly sexy. It touched a newly dominant place inside Julian's heart, a section he didn't know was there until meeting Beckett.

Beckett had made it as far as pulling his jeans up. His T-shirt was haphazardly on, and that was as far as he had gotten before passing out on the sofa. The moment was made complete with his German shepherd stretched out on the floor under Beckett's arm where his hand lay on the dog's back. Woofer would totally sell Julian out for a good rubdown by Beckett.

No matter how hard Julian tried to keep Beckett compartmentalized, he repeatedly lost the battle, and Beckett kept trekking around inside his head.

Julian went to the edge of the sofa to stare down at the sleeping beauty. When Beckett slept, he looked younger. Now Julian understood the true benefit of keeping his furniture. If he hadn't, he wouldn't have this moment. The slow, steady rise and fall of Beckett's chest drew Julian's eyes from his perfectly formed lips to his sweet sleep-time expression.

Maybe bending over for a kiss might wake Beckett in the best possible way.

Beckett had to be exhausted. Julian should let him sleep.

He looked over at the time display on the oven. It was already past eleven o'clock. He could Uber to the club, close everything down, and talk with Ricco about becoming a temporary night manager. If Beckett hadn't awakened before Julian returned, he'd wake him and send him back to the hotel. It seemed reasonable, and Julian bent to run a hand over Woofer's head.

"I'll be back."

Those words usually sent Woofer into a tailspin, knowing he was being left behind. Not this time. Woofer had attached himself to Beckett, apparently leaving Julian in the rearview mirror. Julian knew it. Woofer did too. Beckett was the one who needed to catch up with the dog's plan.

Two hours later

Unlocking the front door, Julian walked in and was met with utter silence. The television had timed out, the room was dark, the quiet briefly interrupted by the sound of a slow, heavy exhale, making Julian smile.

What neither he nor Beckett had thought to do was to cancel Beckett's reservation at the club tonight. The questions Julian had had to field from both his staff and the clientele spoke to the friendship and community Beckett had built at Reservations in such a short time.

Julian had apologized to Chase for not calling and canceling. Beckett's absence caused his table to be empty for the evening. Julian pulled money from his own pocket to cover the tips Chase had missed by keeping Beckett's table open. What a mistake that had been. Chase, and Ricco who eavesdropped on their conversation, spread the knowledge that Julian had some secret intel about Beckett's MIA status. The gossip took wings, making the speculation, from literally everyone, the topic of conversation for the rest of the night.

The amount of flak he took at the idea of he and Beckett spending time together outside the club was crazy. Even when Julian had tried to patiently explain the wild concept of *meeting* people being the whole idea behind Reservations nightclub, he still got all sorts of kissy face expressions and mentions.

What Julian hoped he had accomplished was hiding how happy he'd been tonight. It seemed hard to contain. Maybe he hadn't hidden it as well as he'd wanted.

One emotion that refused to be held at bay was that he'd never felt safer in his life.

Fear had guided Julian's every move since his assault. He regularly had to make himself man-up to walk alone from his designated parking spot to his condo, despite all the complex's safety and privacy features. Hell, Woofer sounded like the meanest guard dog on the planet when he went nuts at a stranger's approach. But tonight, Julian knew nothing could get to him if they had to go through Beckett first.

Julian walked to the edge of the sofa. Beckett had changed his sleeping position. Probably the only reason Woofer sleepily got to his feet and shook off his tiredness as he walked to the back door. Beckett laid on his side, knees drawn up with his hands tucked underneath his cheek. He slept like a baby.

As quietly as he could, Julian gathered and attached the leash to take Woofer out before bed. He made quick work of that task. Woofer seemed right on board with the idea of getting back inside the condo as fast as possible. Julian didn't even feel slighted in the least. Woofer took his place on the rug at the base of the sofa while Julian carefully covered Beckett with a throw before going to his bedroom. He left the bedroom door open.

On the way home, Julian recalled Beckett saying he had a five o'clock wake-up call. He set the alarm on his cell phone, hoping he wasn't making a mistake by not waking Beckett earlier.

Julian gave a big, long yawn as he undressed and slid under the sheet, bare assed. The cool Egyptian blend felt amazing, sliding over his skin. How long had it been since he'd slept with no clothes on?

Fuck, he felt good and safe and nodded off to sleep.

Julian's scent wafted over Beckett like a seductive wave, eagerly drawing him from sleep. The beautiful bright smile and forever teasing glint in Julian's gaze blocked the bright sun, showcasing his handsome face. Beckett woke happy and didn't hesitate to reach for Julian, drawing him down for a tender kiss. Julian obliged, opening before their mouths ever met.

The sun shone brightly in Beckett's face as Julian lowered his head. Beckett closed his eyes, kissing Julian. Damn the consequences of anyone who might see.

Beckett could feel the gentle breeze of the sunny afternoon. The scent of wildflowers mingled with Julian's enticing cologne. How he'd gotten Julian to go camping with him, he didn't know. Surprisingly, Julian wasn't whining. He had figured camping was something he'd have to do by himself.

Julian's palms roamed Beckett's chest, teasing his nipples and clawing at Beckett's T-shirt. His lover was a self-proclaimed bad boy leaving Beckett torn on how best to proceed in this situation.

Should he let Julian continue? More than anything, he wanted to give Julian what he wanted, what Beckett wanted too, but he could hear his father snoring heavily nearby.

"We shouldn't," Beckett whispered against Julian's mouth.

When Beckett opened his mouth, Julian took the opportunity to dip his tongue inside, priming him for what was to come. Julian knew how to kiss, and it turned Beckett on. Julian licked a trail to his ear.

"Let me fuck you, Beck," Julian's husky voice whispered against his ear before tracing the outer shell and sliding inside. Fuck he loved that, and Julian knew it. The man didn't play fair. Beckett gave a full-body shiver at the thought of Julian's suggestion. He fucking loved to bottom and rarely had been given the chance. The men in his life had always considered him the alpha.

His dick punched against his camo trousers as Julian rose above him, tugging his dress shirt over his head. His guy was elegant and classy even while out in the rugged wilderness.

"Beckett," Julian exclaimed.

His body shook, not of his own accord.

"Shh, you'll wake my dad." The hoarse sounds of his voice dragged through his brain. Something wasn't right.

"Did you just mention your father?" Julian asked, and the shaking on his arm took on a fevered force until it landed heavily on his chest. "It's five thirty. I slept through my alarm. Do you need to wake up early or do you want to keep dreaming of your dad?"

Beckett opened his eyes, startled to find Julian standing over him, dressed in a blue satin robe. He looked around the dark living room, trying to gather his bearings. He was on the sofa in Julian's condo. Beckett immediately sat up. Julian pushed upward to his full height to avoid a possible collision with how fast Beckett rose. "What happened?"

A second or two passed before Julian gave him that cute little eye roll. "It's weird how you just wake up to be wide awake."

Not the first time he'd heard such a thing, and he chose not to dash Julian's perception. This time he'd struggled with as soundly as he'd slept. Beckett's cell phone vibrated. Julian went for the kitchen island, grabbed his phone, and handed it over the sofa while grabbing the leash.

"You got off then slept like a baby. So much better than Ambien," Julian chuckled, coming back around the edge of the sofa toward Woofer who stood ready by the back door.

"I'll take him out," Beckett offered, reaching for his runners.

"I got it," Julian said, attaching the hook to Woofer's collar. "You were sleeping so hard."

Beckett scrubbed his hands down his face, willing away the haze in his brain. "I was tired. I am tired. I could sleep for a week."

"If you'll take him out," Julian said, changing his mind as Beckett shoved each foot into his shoes. "I can make you a cup of coffee for the road."

"You've got a deal," Beckett said, his gaze traveling the length of Julian's body. He reached for the leash, marveling at the sheer beauty before him. Even disheveled from sleep, Julian looked stunning. Beckett took the leash in one hand and circled Julian's waist with the other, drawing him to his body. "I'm sorry about crashing on you last night."

"I'm not," Julian teased. His expression conveyed that signature you're-being-silly look as he lifted up and lightly pressed a kiss to Beckett's lips. "I left you sleeping and went to the club to close. When I got back, you didn't hear me come in. I decided you had to be exhausted."

"You left me here?" Beckett asked. He must have been seriously conked out to have missed all that.

"I did." Julian squirmed out of his hold and headed to the kitchen. "Go. Let me start the coffee. There's a small patch of grass he prefers. He'll drag you over there."

As he watched Julian walk away, his body stirred as the memories from last night rushed forward. No one on the planet compared to that man. Beckett had never experienced such a profound emotion with sex. Just having Julian's hands on his body had made his orgasm next level. Who knew how mind-blowing it all could be? Especially watching as his orgasm triggered Julian's. It had been magnificent to witness Julian's release and feel his body shudder while riding out the pleasure together.

He followed Julian's instructions, letting Woofer lead the way. His cell phone chimed again. Generally, he'd push the snooze button a couple of times before dragging his ass from bed. He fished the phone from his pocket, muting the thing. He always built time into his morning. So, he didn't necessarily need to hurry away. He watched Woofer until he decided to give the poor pup some privacy—performance anxiety and all that.

There was always something special about being outside in the early morning, but this morning was extra special. Beckett's head swam with everything he and Julian had done. What a difference a few weeks had made. He owed Thane for finally pulling him into their inner circle. Funny how the man he'd sworn to hate became his biggest advocate.

A satisfying warmth that was all Julian Cullen seeped over Beckett as Woofer finished his business and they headed back inside. He barely had the leash on the hook before Julian started toward him.

"I have an idea," Julian announced, stepping into Beckett. He loved they were past the stage of keeping a respectable distance. Beckett took the travel cup of coffee and reached for Julian, running the pad of his thumb across Julian's unshaven cheek. He needed the simple caress before he was sent away to face the day on his own.

"Yeah?" Beckett asked, barely paying attention to anything more than the way the dark navy silk robe brought a different dimension to Julian's blue gaze. He was tumbling off the edge of his boundaries, falling hard for this man. He had tried to control all this emotion—fuck, he'd tried—but waking to Julian was something unique. His day made right before it ever got off the ground.

"When do you go home?" Julian asked, bringing Beckett's musing to a crashing halt. Home. This was Friday. If he followed his plan, he'd need to leave tonight. He had the group he'd just taught heading for the training camp early next week to practice real-time simulation.

The thought of leaving weighed heavily on him. His shoulders slumped and his hand dropped away. In the best-case scenario, he didn't see himself coming back to Coronado for a while. His heart didn't like that at all and showed its frustration with a piercing ache.

"I planned to hang out at Reservations tonight then drive home afterward. It's an easier drive at night, and I've got a haul to get home," Beckett said against the intense sadness enveloping him. If he left and came back, how much ground would he lose with Julian?

"Well, I was thinking that maybe you could stay through the weekend." Julian's palm slid enticingly across Beckett's chest, teasing a trail over one pec. "You've been burning it at both ends. I'm transitioning into a new position. The current GM had the weekend scheduled off and can't start officially training me until Monday. I have some unexpected time off."

Emotions were fucking hell. Hope instantly sprang forward, edging off the rising melancholy of having to leave Julian. "I'd have to see if I can keep my room at Escape."

"Or you could stay here." Julian nodded toward his sofa. "You slept good there. I only slept a few hours, but it was solid sleep. We enjoy each other's company. Stay."

"I'd have to take off early Sunday…"

Julian's index finger popped in front of Beckett's face, stopping him from saying anything more.

"Or you could fly home and leave your truck here. It seems

a monster of a drive to only come back in a few days…" Both Julian's brows rose as Beckett nodded yes. How could he refuse such a request?

Julian had put some thought into the idea, which caused Beckett's heart to swell with promise. Hell, he'd fly back every few days just to spend a couple of hours with Julian to see that hopeful look on his face.

He tucked his lip between his teeth. When would they ever get another chance at a free weekend again? Especially once Julian started as the general manager of Reservations.

The idea took root. He could get Randy to pick him up from the airport Sunday night, or maybe Monday morning. They could pay the instructors to get the field training session ready to his specifications. He could scan and email the profile information he'd gathered on each participant so his team would be ready when they arrived Tuesday. There was no reason this couldn't work.

"You'd keep an eye on the truck?" Beckett teased, lifting a brow at Julian, letting his lips quirk into a smile before taking a hearty drink of the black coffee. "I love my truck."

"One eye always fixed on it," Julian replied, lifting three fingers on his right hand, giving the Scout oath hand sign. He was always ready to give a lighthearted joke. "I'll check the flights today. Keep your phone on so I can book whatever I find," Julian offered.

Before Beckett could respond, Julian stepped away, sweeping an arm toward the front door.

"You need to leave so I can go back to sleep."

The directness Julian exhibited in every part of his life was much appreciated. No awkward goodbyes. Beckett had to go or risk being late, which he never allowed himself to be. He quickly leaned in, stealing a kiss from a surprised Julian before he started toward the door.

Julian countered by reaching out and swatting Beckett's ass

as he turned away. Of course, Julian got the last word.

At the door, Beckett looked back over his shoulder. "Was that a promise of something special you have planned for the weekend?"

A challenging glint lit Julian's face as he reached down to Woofer's collar, keeping him from following Beckett out. "Be mindful of what you ask for." Julian's sexy grin grew in both promise and challenge. "The rush of anticipation is fucking intoxicating."

No doubt he was getting a glimpse of Julian's former self. Beckett let that be enough, chuckling as he left the condo.

CHAPTER 21

"Thane says it's corporate policy; we have to post my position before we can officially offer it to you. What I'm going to suggest is for you to really take the next week and see what you think about the job. I'll fight for a good salary, but it'll be a decrease in pay for you," Julian said, watching Ricco as he entered the daily liquor inventory into the Reservations proprietary software.

Ricco never looked up at Julian. His fingers continue to furiously fly over the keyboard, typing in the totals from the back of a small cocktail napkin. Damn, Ricco was faster than even him. "I need to get my foot in the door at Dishology. It's not the money that's the problem, it's these damn pants. I haven't had to wear real clothes since I started working here."

Julian chuckled at the observation, one with which he secretly agreed. He'd rather be wearing the Reservations designated underwear uniform too.

His cell phone vibrated in his pocket. Beckett had been all

over his text messages today, and Julian couldn't seem to wait even thirty seconds to answer whatever was sent. This incoming text had to be alerting him of Beckett's arrival to get the key to his condo. This new weirdly endearing pitter-patter in Julian's heart had a small smile forming as he fished the phone from his pants.

"I usually get to this point then let you check what I entered. I went over the numbers three times like your control issues require. Do I just sign it and hit enter?" Ricco asked.

Julian ignored Ricco, lost in his haste to see Beckett. All his thoughts, all day long, had focused on his roommate for the next couple of days. He couldn't stop thinking about Beckett and pivoted, taking long strides down the hall toward the employee entrance door. At the same time, his staff began arriving for the impromptu mandatory employee meeting he had called to explain the upcoming changes.

"Your cowboy's out there," Chase announced, hooking a thumb over his shoulder. Julian had to do a sidestep, then duck to get past the flood of men moving in the opposite direction from him.

"Nah, he's coming in," Quinn called out from the door. Julian looked up to see Beckett a few feet away, holding the door for each employee to enter ahead of him. His gentleman.

Julian knew the ribbing he was destined to receive over Beckett coming to see him in the middle of the day like this. It couldn't be any worse than all the kissy faces he'd endured over the last week. After all this time of Reservations being the most important thing in Julian's life, it felt damned odd to have Beckett taking the top spot of his concentration. Julian got close enough to reach for Beckett's waist, pushing him back several steps toward his truck to do the key exchange as privately as possible.

Beckett followed his lead, except the cowboy didn't seem to understand his privacy goal. Beckett wrapped his arms around Julian's waist, drawing him into a tight embrace against that muscular chest as the heavy door swung closed behind them.

"You smell amazing," Beckett said, lifting Julian's chin to look in his eyes. Julian couldn't seem to make himself pull away no matter how hard he had lectured himself for doing just that. He had to find his professionalism while on work property like Thane had literally begged him to do. "This is a nice greeting."

The employee entrance door squeaked open behind him. Somewhere in the back of his mind, he registered the whooping as he lifted on his toes and met Beckett for a sweet, chaste press of lips. Beckett stayed in his face, looking all doe-eyed, melting Julian's heart and his resistance.

"Hi," Julian whispered hoarsely. His voice momentarily stolen by the man holding him in such a powerful embrace.

"It was a long thirty minutes since we talked last," Beckett murmured. With a calloused palm, he brushed away the strands of hair blowing in his face. The tender care Beckett used any time they were together never faltered and always managed to make Julian feel special and worthy.

"You were supposed to stay in the car." Julian cocked his head toward the entrance of the club before he turned that way. Beckett's gaze followed. He seemed surprised to see all twenty-five of his waiters spilling from the open doorway. Even Ricco was there. All the guys needed was the recognition they were being seen to ratchet their hollering up a notch.

Beckett's gaze came back to Julian; his arms tightening their hold for a split second before releasing him. "I can't imagine that has to do with me. I've been pretty damn transparent about running after you all these months."

"It's not you; it's me. I should be nominated for an Academy Award with how indifferent I must have seemed toward you. They can't help but give me hell." Julian edged them toward Beckett's truck as he dug the key to his condo out of his front pocket.

"Yeah, you didn't give me much hope either. Made the prize better in the end," Beckett said cheekily, wrapping an arm around Julian, keeping him close as he took the key and shoved it in his jeans pocket. "I'll take Woofer out then shower and change and be back here in a few hours."

"You'll probably want to stop and get something to eat. I don't have much food at the condo," Julian said as Beckett opened the door to his truck's cab. He looked through the window then turned his back to the door, blocking the view before drawing Julian to him again.

"You're something special, Cullen," Beckett whispered. "I liked texting with you all day. We need to keep that up after I leave."

"I was worried I was interrupting your class," Julian confessed, lost in the hypnotic effects of Beckett's dark gaze. Those eyes drew an honesty from Julian.

"Who the fuck cares about that? Now kiss me like you mean it. They can't see past me." Julian knew his staff would find a way, but he no longer cared. He wanted nothing more than to follow Beckett's command. Julian lifted an inch or so to meet Beckett. His lips parted at the same time Beckett's tongue swept inside his mouth. Their kisses were fluid and made of something otherworldly. He couldn't recall a single time he'd ever been obsessed with someone's lips. Beckett's were soft and fleshy and felt so right pressed against his. All the tingles and goose bumps did Julian in, drowning out everything else but the wonderful man literally sweeping him off his feet.

It had been a while since Beckett had left Reservations without being drunk off his ass. Tonight was different. He was completely sober with countless bags of groceries in his hands as he pushed past an excited Woofer blocking his entrance into the condo.

"Place, boy."

The dog instantly lowered to the floor, wagging his tail, that tongue hanging out the side of his mouth as he watched Beckett with eager eyes. He was such a sweet boy.

"We have an hour before Julian gets home," he explained to Woofer, hoisting the heavy bags onto the countertop.

He left them there while shrugging out of his suit coat and tossing it over his suitcase at the edge of the kitchen's island. He'd downsized his luggage, leaving most of his things in the truck, knowing Julian's condo could only handle so much more.

"We're gonna cook Julian a dinner. You in to help?"

The dog tilted his head as if he understood. Maybe he did. That tail picked up time at the mention of Julian's name. The loyalty was astounding. Beckett removed his cuff links, dropped them into his suit coat pocket, and started rolling up the sleeves to his dress shirt.

"Can you hold it a minute more so I can start marinating the meat and mushrooms?"

Since Woofer wasn't standing next to the back door, Beckett figured he could wait. He quickly unpacked the grocery sacks, mentally ticking off the recipe he'd found online while in the store. He opened the refrigerator and tossed the few things that needed refrigerating inside. Again surprised at the complete lack of food inside this condo. Food was always such a motivator for Beckett. Clearly not for Julian. He didn't even have a ketchup bottle sitting on the shelves. He wasn't all too certain he could date a man that didn't like ketchup.

Beckett laughed at the thought as he worked quickly to prepare the marinade, digging through all the drawers to find the knives and other utensils he needed. Five minutes later, he tossed the marinade into the refrigerator and reached for the leash.

"Come on, boy. We gotta work fast. No dawdling out there."

As he took long strides toward his condo, Julian ignored the inner voice chastising him for how easily he'd brushed off his closing duties, leaving it all to Ricco. Usually, Woofer parked himself by the window so he could watch the squirrels and easily see Julian pulling into his designated parking spot. His fierce bark could be heard for what seemed like miles away. The dog was always so damned excited to see him, but he wasn't there tonight.

Through the blinds, he could see the lights were on, and something unknown had him moving a little faster in anticipation of the homey vibe just mere feet away. He felt the gentle tug pulling at his heartstrings. All fresh and new, and one hundred percent Beckett-induced.

He opened the front door as Beckett opened the back door. Woofer noticed him first. The dog's tail wagged uncontrollably, and the stick he held in his mouth dropped to the ground. Beckett must have done the Jedi mind trick on Woofer, who stayed in place until Beckett gave another command, encouraging him through the door he held open.

"What are you guys doing outside this late?" Julian asked, stepping fully inside, bending to pet Woofer, noticing the foil-wrapped plate in Beckett's hand.

"I was starving, and I didn't see you eat anything tonight," Beckett said as he moved through the maze of furniture toward the small kitchen. "I stopped by a grocery store and got some fajita meat and mushrooms, the shiitake ones. I figured you'd like those and used the grill outside in the park."

Julian rose from his crouch, his stomach growling at the delicious smell. He made a beeline toward the sink to wash his hands so they could dig in. Beckett kept surprising him. Anyone who could create a heavenly aroma like that needed to be in his life.

"How did that go? The grill's close at nine."

"Yeah, I found that out when the police came," Beckett said, pulling some pico de gallo and sour cream from the refrigerator. "You ready to eat?"

"The police came? Like someone called in a complaint?" He had heard the complex was vigilant in the safety of its tenants but had never seen it taken quite so far.

"Yeah. Apparently, Woofer needs to be on a leash all the time too." Beckett cocked his head toward Julian while covering the tortillas he'd grilled. "Are you ready to eat now?"

"Wait, go back to the police. What happened?" he asked, pulling several towels off the paper towel roll to dry his hands. Resting his hip against the counter, he wondered how big a citation Beckett got.

"The officer asked me who I was. The complaint said I was a stranger, which is true. When he heard I owned the survival camp doing the training here, that's really all we talked about after that. I think he was supposed to ticket me about Woofer, but I explained I've never lived anywhere where a dog had to be on a leash. Woofer is just so damned well behaved..."

Julian gave a bark of laughter. "He's only well behaved with you. And, of course, the Marlboro Man could talk his way out of a ticket. Some secure complex this is," Julian teased, lifting the side of the tin foil, looking at the grilled meat and mushrooms. His mouth watered at the sizzling fajita blend. Lost in the idea of eating this delicious food that Beckett's descent, as he came in for a kiss, surprised him. His gaze riveted to Beckett's dark stare. Beckett paused seconds before their lips touched.

"Am I crossing a line?" Beckett asked, confused.

"No." Julian snaked a hand around Beckett's neck and lifted the inch or so to reach Beckett's fleshy pout for a quick press of the lips. "You've made me reconsider my dietary restrictions. This food smells incredible. The steak looks so tender."

Beckett chuckled and leaned against the counter's edge,

turning fully to Julian. One of the things Beckett did astoundingly well was giving Julian his full attention in every damn moment they shared. "I saw a citywide margarita tour scheduled for tomorrow. I bought two tickets at the grocery store. It's supposed to be spectacular with all different kinds of foods and drinks."

Julian couldn't help himself. He reached for a plate and teasingly hip-bumped Beckett to move out of the way. Beckett took Julian's indication of a different direction as an invitation and circled around to stand flush against Julian's back, wrapping his arms around his waist while he filled his plate.

"Margarita tour, huh? Do I look like a man who strolls around drinking margaritas?" Julian teased, casting a quick look over his shoulder.

"Kind of you do," Beckett murmured, his lips pressing against the skin right above Julian's collar. "You like a good cocktail. It's a walking tour. It's supposed to be nice weather, sun shining, lots of vitamin D. And if you decide to go then everybody gets a chance to see you as we walk by, making Coronado a prettier place. It's a win all the way around…"

Julian gave a side smirk over his shoulder at the ridiculousness of Beckett's attempt to talk him into going. "It's a walking tour if you mean we'll walk miles and miles. Reservations dining club is taking part. I completely forgot."

Some of the tight hold Beckett held Julian with loosened. "Do you need to work it?" He could hear the dejection in Beckett's voice.

Julian reached for another plate, handing it over his shoulder. His answer fell solidly in this weird, unfamiliar territory where Reservations had taken the second spot of importance in Julian's life. Of course, he *had* planned to work the margarita tour until he got the harebrained idea to keep Beckett around through the weekend.

"I'm off until Monday morning when I drive you to the airport. It wouldn't be my responsibility anyway even though I regularly stick my nose in everybody's business, regardless if it's the club or the restaurant."

"You're so bossy," Beckett teased, easily slipping back into his good mood. He kissed Julian one last time on the neck before following behind him to make his own plate. "Boundaries must be awful hard on you."

"You think you know me?" Julian angled his head, looking over at Beckett.

Beckett's playful grin showed he'd easily blown off the quick rebuke. "I've been watching you for months. I know you, Julian Cullen, but I want to know more."

The warmth that only Beckett brought to Julian's life seeped through him like a constantly healing balm, instantly disarming his automatic comebacks that lay like an arsenal ready to fire when literally anyone in his life said something like that.

"Huh. Good thing you're cute and can cook, but can you do the dishes afterward?" Julian winked when Beckett's brow lifted. "Don't worry, I'll tell you that you did a good job when you finish."

"Thanks," Beckett said and chuckled. "Such a sweet guy."

Julian took his plate and reached for a bottle of water in the door of his refrigerator before proceeding to the barstool on the other side of the kitchen island. "That's me. Sweet guy. Hear it all the time."

CHAPTER 22

Maybe Julian wasn't the only one who purposefully broke the rules. He and Beckett sat on the edge of the complex's swimming pool well past closing time, relaxing on two loungers they had pushed close together, enjoying the warmth of the night. Beckett lifted the bottle of wine they'd brought along, topping off Julian's red Solo cup before filling his own and draining the bottle.

"Let's see," Beckett said, his husky voice a little above a whisper. "What else do I need to know? You left your home at sixteen and came to California. You were top of the game in the escort business. Like how much money did you actually make a night?"

Julian gave Beckett a skeptical side eye, still waiting for the Dudley Do-Right to pop out and judge him. It never happened, no matter how long Julian waited. Everyone had judged him for both the good and the bad of his previous profession, but Beckett did neither. It made no sense at all. Julian lifted the cup to his lips, hiding the sudden bout of skepticism.

"How much do you think I made?"

"Well, I know what I've paid, but I've never had the good fortune of being with anyone who could ever compare to you," Beckett said, lifting the glass to his lips, his full unabashed focus trained on Julian. In a tender, all Beckett style move, he reached his hand across the lounger, taking Julian's, making everything right in his world.

"How much did you pay?" The question wasn't a hard one, but the complexity of the math showed on Beckett's semi-intoxicated face, causing Julian to chuckle quietly. "Don't hurt yourself there."

Beckett's expression instantly morphed into humor, grinning at Julian. "I haven't spent very much. I usually swipe right, but I think I've spent a few hundred dollars."

"What?" Julian acted offended for those being paid so little in his past profession. The back of his lounger flipped forward when he sat up in faux outrage. "Are you serious? Poor broke guys. You give clients a bad fucking name…"

"Shh, you'll get us kicked out." Beckett grinned, and his hand tightened, giving a gentle squeeze. His laughing, sweet expression was so damn enchanting. Julian wished he could climb on top of the man and let him know exactly how much he liked that sexy grin. "I'd guess you'd probably make five hundred dollars a date. I honestly don't know how it works."

Enchanting just turned to wildly naive, and that was damn sweet too. "I haven't worked for five hundred dollars a *date* since I was seventeen years old, but I got paid differently. I worked my business on retainer and was selective with who I worked with. I averaged about three thousand dollars a night."

Beckett's head whipped toward Julian. "You made more than a million dollars a year? No shit? I feel intimidated now." Beckett dropped his head on the back of the hard recliner with a thump. A defeated sigh slipped free as he released Julian's hand.

"Hey now," Julian started, turning fully toward Beckett. He

shouldn't laugh at such a genuine reaction, but Beckett was so damned cute in his insecurity. "I made a million and a half dollars my last year in business. I was such a dumbass shit though. Not focused on saving a dime. I never thought it would end."

Beckett watched him. "No wonder it was so hard to get your attention. You must've thought I was a joke."

The simplistic way Beckett had pursued Julian, the idea of wanting a man and doing what it took to be noticed, was something Julian had never experienced before. He'd never consider Beckett a joke. His sweet and sincere ways endeared Beckett to him, making the man shine brighter than any other.

"We're talking about me, not you, but I can't imagine anyone saying Beckett-the-beast is a joke." Julian playfully slapped at Beckett's arm when he didn't readily respond. "You're the one that brought up the topic. Stop pouting and pay attention. My problem was that I spent as much as I made. When everything came to a crashing halt, I was in quite a bit of debt. I rented a badass penthouse and leased a badass sports car. I never owned anything. I was always trading up. The adjustment in my income has taken a lot to get used to."

Beckett's hand came back to Julian's as he turned, so they were face to face. "Why did you give it up?"

Julian rolled his eyes and let the words he never said aloud tumble from his lips. "Honestly, I know I got by on my looks. Now I'm damaged. My body's not the same. It's not personal, it's business. When everything went south, Thane was the only one who stood by me." Julian let the painful words sit there as he turned the other direction to get to his feet. Beckett wouldn't release his hand, stretching his arm across the lounger. "It's two thirty in the morning. We have margaritas to drink tomorrow."

"Babe." Beckett started with an endearment. The first Julian remembered hearing from him. He braced himself, squaring his shoulders as he turned back. The warmth of Beckett's stare soothed the sadness that always enveloped him when he thought about everything he'd lost.

Beckett finally let go and fluidly rolled to his feet. He gave Julian a perfectly executed dramatic eye roll. Technically, that was Julian's go-to move.

"You keep mentioning the scars. I'm telling you straight up, they take nothing away from your beauty. You're gorgeous, Julian. You star in all my dreams. I wish you'd believe me." Beckett came around the loungers to circle his arms around Julian's waist. His deep concern touched a hard-to-reach place inside Julian. The emotion caused him to glance away, unable to hold Beckett's caring stare.

The raw vulnerability was too damn much to process.

"I don't know if you're right. It seems insurmountable. Thane was the only one who continued paying me. Everyone else cut me off before I ever made it out of the hospital. I can't explain how proud I was of who I used to be and what I made of my life." Julian shook his head and tried to leave the embrace and head toward the gate. "I don't want to keep talking about it. Stop bringing it up."

"Did I bring it up?" Beckett asked, using his tight hold to draw Julian back flush against his chest. His strong fingers nudged Julian's chin up to look him in the eyes. Maybe Beckett hadn't been the one to take the conversation in this direction. Perhaps the blame did rest on Julian. He'd struggled to get past his body issues for a long time now.

"Of course, you brought it up. Why would I?" Julian teased, taking a sideways turn in the conversation as he tugged free. He went for Beckett's glass and the empty bottle of wine. "I was thinking my California king is more comfortable than the sofa. If you promise to keep your hands to yourself, you can sleep with me." Julian took a steadying breath as he digested his intentions at such an invitation.

The undeniable trust he had in Beckett was about to be tested. Silence held between them until he lifted and looked back.

Skepticism tugged that tough brow down.

"In this offer, do you have to keep your hands to yourself?" Beckett finally asked, bringing an instant playful joy to Julian's heart.

"Of course not. Regardless of having the authorities called on you tonight then watching you easily break into the locked swimming pool…" He spread his arms out wide to encompass the entire pool area. "I'm the rule breaker. The reckless one. Not you. I play with fire, you don't."

Beckett burst out with a loud laugh. Within seconds several window lights around the common area flipped on. They'd been caught. Julian took off in a sprint toward the gate. The latch that Beckett had managed to spring free had fallen back in place, locking them in from the inside.

Beckett passed Julian in a dead run, hopping the gate in one skilled move, causing Julian to stop in his tracks and just stare at the man. "I can't do that."

"Sure, you can. Hand me the bottle, and I'll catch you on this side." Beckett's hands went out as if Julian were ready to jump.

Right. Like he was Sporty Spice…

The manager's front door opened. She stepped out, doing her best Damien from *The Omen* impression, full of frightening promises of reprimand and homeowner association citations. Julian all but threw the bottle and cups at Beckett, quickly doing a weird half climb jumping thing. He knew what he had to look like; athletics had never been his thing.

"Julian Cullen, is that you?" the manager called out.

He answered with the first thing that came to mind. "No. It's his next-door neighbor on the east side. The one who loves carbs." Damn, he wished he remembered the nosey woman's name.

As promised, Beckett caught Julian even with the bottle and glasses in his hands. Julian's bright smile and heaving chest slammed into Beckett, who absorbed all his body weight. Julian's inner laughter bubbled in his throat. Beckett barely had him on his feet before he grabbed Julian's hand, taking off in a dead run toward his condo.

Beckett stood in front of the mirror in the guest bathroom, staring at his reflection. He always traveled with a pair of pajama pants and a T-shirt for just-in-case situations, but he'd never had to use them before. He usually wore underwear to sleep in. Tonight though, he felt fully clothed. His gaze lowered to his annoyingly rigid hard-on. His fucking cock was relentless. Beckett stuck his hand in the waistband, trying to do anything to hide the obvious.

He sighed in failure. Julian had to be used to his arousal by now, and he reached for his toothbrush, quickly brushing his teeth before running a hairbrush over his short strands. The style he wore made for the perfect morning bedhead. Nothing to be done about that either.

All these worries were superficial to the anxiety he had about sleeping with Julian. He kept telling Julian that he gave him too much credit for being a decent guy. Of course, he would never force Julian into anything, but the wet dreams he'd quite possibly have while lying next to the man of his dreams… *Fuck.*

"Stop *thinking about it*," Beckett hissed to his reflection quietly.

Maybe he should quickly rub one-off.

He shrugged and reached for the knot in his drawstring. It didn't seem like a bad idea.

"I feel as if I should wait for you to go to bed, but you're taking a really long time in there…" Julian's teasing tone was yelled from a distance but still made him jump, drawing Beckett's eyes to the closed bathroom door. Why did he feel like a horny teen that just got caught jacking off? He took a deep breath, trying to control his libido.

Julian had to be in bed already. He should just go out there.

He'd stalled long enough and left the knot alone, lifting his finger to point at himself in the mirror. The stern look he gave said everything that needed to be said: *Control all your urges. No wet dreams. Watch the hair and breath.* He should probably sleep on his back to keep his hair from standing on end.

Decision made and confirmed with a nod. He quickly packed his belongings together and tucked them away.

When Beckett opened the door, the only light came from a small lamp on the nightstand on Julian's side of the bed. Julian rested against the headboard. Woofer snored quietly from his nearby bed.

Julian hadn't lied when he spoke about the actual size of his mattress. The mattress was huge. Julian took the right side, so Beckett went to the left.

"I didn't expect you to be a pajama pants guy," Julian said, eyeing him up and down like he was a grade A piece of meat. "You should always wear your shirts that tight. You're built."

Beckett smiled at Julian, intentionally ignoring the last comment. "I don't normally sleep in clothes," Beckett said, stopping at the edge of the mattress. "You sure you're good with this?"

Julian nodded without hesitation. His lower lips tucked between his teeth.

Beckett had barely settled his ass on the edge of the mattress before Julian moved toward him. He tracked each of Julian's moves. His heart slammed madly against his ribcage as the duvet whipped away and Julian's hands reached for him. Julian wore nothing more than a tight pair of sexy black underwear.

"Motherfucker." His cock burst free of his mental control, tenting his pajama pants. So much for hiding his erection. How could anyone concentrate with something so beautiful coming at them? *Jesus.* Beckett had to force his hand to his side as he slid into his spot on the bed.

"Get comfortable. I told you I wouldn't be keeping my hands to myself…" Julian purred, helping to push Beckett to his back. "Scoot to the center. I haven't slept with anyone in my bed for years. I like you here. I'm exhausted, and my protector's here to keep me safe."

"Julian…" Beckett hesitated. He was shit to do anything more than follow Julian's exact instructions. He watched Julian's tantalizing palm travel over his T-shirt from his navel to his pec, caressing and massaging the muscle rippling and twitching from his touch. "I want you. You know that. I…"

"I trust you. You give me courage. You've changed something in me," Julian confessed as he anchored the length of his lithe body against Beckett's side. Julian's hand burned the same trail, this time going lower until his warm fingers slid under the hem of Beckett's shirt and pushed the material up. Every one of Beckett's senses leaped to high alert in instant overdrive. Julian moved his hand over the bare skin of Beckett's chest while easing a long leg over his body.

"Lose the shirt." Julian's voice held full authority.

He was helpless to do anything more than let Julian guide the shirt over his head as Beckett reached for Julian, drawing him closer for a kiss. Seconds before their lips met, Julian whispered something that caused Beckett's dick to punch against his pants. "I want you, too. You're sexy as hell, Beckett St. Clair. Let me take care of you tonight."

Julian's hips rolled against Beckett, driving his rigid cock against his thigh. Julian was just as hard for him as he was for Julian.

Beckett's stuttering heart took flight. He fought his most basic urge, driving him to take charge, to allow Julian to guide their way tonight. Every one of Julian's actions showed how hard he was trying to find his way back. Beckett walked a tight rope of his desire. Too many months of wanting Julian in just this way made it hard to balance the give and take.

As gently as he could, he pulled Julian down for a kiss and somehow managed to keep it light. A consuming desire pumped through his veins as he nipped at those fleshy lips, tracing them lightly with his tongue before pressing in. Julian's lips parted, and their tongues met, sweet and slow.

Just like always between them, the kiss shot to hot and heavy in record time. God, their chemistry soared off the charts. He wondered if Julian could feel the energy surging around them. He sucked Julian's lip into his mouth then drove his tongue back inside as Julian rutted against his thigh.

Breaking from the heated kiss, Julian pushed at his pajama pants.

"Off," Julian demanded then helped tug the dark gray bottoms down his legs before tossing them to the floor. Julian seductively crawled down Beckett's body, teasing a path of kisses from his nipples to his hip bone, before long slender fingers circled his cock. Beckett's body hummed, vibrating under the tender assault. Having Julian's fingers on him felt so fucking good.

"Julian, are you sure?" he managed. The rise and fall of his chest revealed his steady pant for oxygen. He shifted his position on the bed to get a better view, tucking the pillow under his neck. This was what dreams were made of, and all his were coming true. He didn't want to miss any part of what Julian Cullen had in store.

After two sultry tip to base tugs, Julian's heated gaze lifted to his. He grinned as he gripped the base of Beckett's cock. Wet, velvet heat engulfed him, pulling a gasp from his lips as Julian swallowed him down with a dip of his head. Julian's head bobbed a few times before easing off his cock to work him, alternating between his hand and mouth.

Julian's mouth was fucking sinful. Amazingly sinful. His eyes nearly rolled back in his head as Julian's clever tongue curled around his sensitive head and toyed with his reserve. He gripped the sheets with such force the tips of his fingers hurt.

The way Julian worked his cock with his mouth then his hand made Beckett's insides quiver with erotic intensity. He couldn't take his eyes off the man nestled between his legs. Not with the way Julian worshipped his cock. He was held spellbound by Julian Cullen.

He spread his legs a little wider as he hoarsely whispered, "Turn around and let me taste you, Julian."

The suction on his dick stopped, and he almost groaned from the loss as Julian lifted his head. Beckett lost his breath at the sight. Wet lips parted, cheeks flushed with color as the tip of Julian's tongue darted out to dip in Beckett's slit, sending a searing rush of heat straight to his balls.

Julian's hooded eyes slowly lifted to his. Their unusual blue/green color peeked from behind a fringe of dark lashes. "I love sucking your cock, B. I need you to lie back and let me do this."

When the meaning of Julian's words seeped into him, he understood. Beckett wanted nothing more than to please Julian, but tonight had to be on Julian's terms. There would be many more times to taste Julian in their future; he'd make sure of it.

He smiled down at Julian and softly traced his flushed cheek with the pad of his thumb. Julian's confident gaze changed as if searching for understanding and approval. Beckett nodded as his heart fully connected. Julian took him back into his mouth, driving him to the edge with each dip of his head and stroke of his tongue.

Beckett's toes curled, and his eyes slammed shut when Julian's warm palm cupped his balls and caressed them. Need coursed through Beckett as he rode the sensation of the moment. He thrust up into that tight wet mouth, urging Julian to handle him a little rougher. Julian did exactly that and then some.

Beckett pumped his hips as he drove his fingernails across Julian's scalp then tangled his fingers in all that silky hair. Those warm lips slid up and down his shaft, sending chills all over his body. Fire raced through his veins. He forced his eyes open, intent on memorizing everything about this moment.

"So pretty with your lips wrapped around me," he hissed, watching Julian's head bob as the suction on his cock increased and had him approaching the point of no return quicker than he'd like. He tightened his fingers against the man's scalp as he fought the release building within him.

"So close," he said through gritted teeth. Julian's tongue traveled around his sensitive tip as he spoke. Fuck, that skilled tongue was talented.

He thrust into Julian's mouth harder, needing more. The heat of Julian's palm retreated from his balls, and deft fingers moved tantalizingly down his perineum. His body tensed and his legs shook with anticipation when Julian's finger found his hole and pushed inside. The combination of Julian's mouth and tongue were maddening as he rode the finger in his ass. His stomach muscles hurt from the intensity of it all.

Julian swallowed around him, sending shock waves vibrating down his shaft. It was all too much. He tried to warn Julian the only way he could, by pushing him away. The overwhelming pleasure stole his voice.

Julian clung to him tighter, swallowing around him, curling that finger against his prostate, rendering him blind with pleasure. He succumbed to the ecstasy and emptied his balls down that hot, slick throat.

"Fuck, yes, Julian," he gasped, clenching around the finger in his ass as he held Julian's hair and continued bucking into that glorious mouth even though his balls had been wrung dry. After the last shudder echoed through his body and his muscles quit seizing, he relaxed against the bed.

His heart raced, his eyes heavy with bliss as he glanced down at Julian and caressed his hair with the tips of his fingers. A triumphant smile widened on Julian's beautiful face. It took Beckett a few calming breaths to get his body back under control before he could speak.

"Come here," he huskily growled while reaching for Julian, drawing him up his body. He took those pouty lips in a hard kiss. The bitter, salty taste of his own seed exploded across his palate as Julian's tongue tangled with his.

After years of giving and receiving hundreds, maybe a thousand blow jobs, Julian instinctively knew this one had mattered the most. *Beckett*. Such a ravishing, vibrant, gentle man who methodically showed Julian his value at every opportunity.

"Do you have anything to say?" Julian teased, preening under his own self-satisfaction.

"Best of my life." Beckett didn't hesitate except to yawn in the middle of his praise.

"Well, of course, it was," Julian quipped as if that were a given. His body hummed with excitement even as Beckett's big body softened with fatigue. Julian's long sexual drought had come to an end, and he couldn't be more pleased.

There wasn't a light at the end of his dark, lonely tunnel but a vivid disco ball of color, luring Julian out of his fog.

"How are you?" Beckett murmured.

"I think I need a T-shirt to commemorate the resurgence of my oral proficiency. Maybe pose nude for it?" Julian asked, unable to squelch his chuckle. "I'm good. Real good. Thank you."

"Me too. Everything you just said." Beckett yawned again, this time bigger than before. "Stay right here with me?"

Julian was wired. Wide awake, but he couldn't think of moving a single inch. "Outside of a possible bathroom run, just try to peel me away."

Beckett nodded and closed his eyes.

He rested his head on Beckett's shoulder, staring off into his dark bedroom. It wouldn't be much longer; his old self was moving to the forefront.

He owed Beckett the world.

CHAPTER 23

Noiselessly, Woofer knocked his head against Beckett's bicep, causing his eyes to open wide, instantly awake. There wasn't a single moment of confusion as to where he was or who slept directly on top of him. The darkened room spoke to the quality of the blackout curtains lining Julian's window. Beckett had slept like a baby on the side of the bed he'd been assigned. Julian though knew no boundaries, with his mouthwatering body draped over Beckett, caging him in place.

Julian stirred, his stubble scraping against Beckett's shoulder and pec, sending a shiver of excitement racing over his skin. Beckett tightened his hold when Julian reached for the edge of his pillow, angling his body to the side of Beckett's, pulling the soft duvet to his chin as he snuggled deeper into the comfortable mattress.

"Five minutes, boy."

"I'll take him," Beckett whispered against the heated skin of

Julian's neck. He pressed his lips there, giving a soft kiss.

He paused a second or two, worried that the decisions of last night might come with a rebuke this morning. Julian moved just enough to allow Beckett to withdraw the arm still wrapped underneath him. The heavy exhale of sleep confirmed Julian's deep exhaustion.

Beckett rolled from the bed and reached for his underwear and pajama pants, a reminder that he was the only one not wearing them.

Julian was a complicated man.

His desires ran deeper than anything Beckett had ever known before, and he suspected they had only broken the surface of the real Julian. The idea of getting to know all those different facets fueled Beckett to move a little faster to lessen his time away from Julian and that insanely comfortable bed. As he went for the leash, he caught a glimpse of the time. Eight o'clock in the morning. How long had it been since he'd slept to such a late hour?

Instead of adding the leash, Beckett took a risk and opened the back door. Woofer bolted out to do his business. A dog needed a chance to run. Besides, Woofer was a boss at following his commands. As if he and Woofer were on the same wavelength, the dog did his thing and ran back to Beckett's side before he reached the edge of the small porch.

"Good boy." He gave Woofer a solid rubdown as he started back inside the condo. He tossed the leash on the sofa and dropped his clothes to the floor as he went. From the second he entered the bedroom, Beckett kept his eyes on Julian. Julian turned onto his other side, drawing the covers with him as he cracked a single tired eye open.

"What time is it?" Julian murmured.

"Early," Beckett said noncommittally, crawling back into bed. Julian automatically lifted, letting Beckett back in his spot. Julian didn't hesitate to stretch out over his body, burying his face in the crook of Beckett's neck. Damn, it felt good to be right here.

Beckett drew the duvet over both their bodies as Julian's soft lips kissed the skin on his neck as he settled in.

"Did you take him out?" Julian's breath caressed the skin he'd just made wet as he nodded. "I'm gonna sleep a little while longer. You good?"

"Very." Beckett let his fingers graze Julian's back, taking a deep breath, loving the way Julian's scent filled his soul. Heaven. Quite possibly the second-best moment of his life. Last night still reigned as number one.

Two hours later, Beckett stopped the gentle caress of his fingertips up and down Julian's back when he moved with more purpose than merely adjusting his body in sleep. Beckett couldn't remember a time he'd ever been motivated enough to lay idly in bed with another person, let alone give his time to help another man sleep.

An absurd silent laugh rumbled from him as he brought his lips down to the top of Julian's head, kissing the silky strands. Beckett was so in love with Julian. Head over heels, sickeningly sweet in love with this beauty in his arms. This over-the-top physical attraction had morphed into a solid, everlasting love. Julian had turned out to be someone he could see himself settling down with. Fun, engaging, and so unintentionally loving.

Beckett knew with all certainty that he'd give up everything to forge a new life with Julian. This week had sealed Beckett's fate. Julian just needed time to get on board, and if actions did indeed speak louder than words, it sure seemed like Julian was right there with him.

Julian's head moved. His full lips lightly brushed across Beckett's pec. Beckett wanted to believe Julian placed a kiss there as he stretched out his long body and opened his eyes. He blinked then blinked again before his eyelids slid closed.

"It seems like it might be later than I think."

"Ten seventeen," Beckett murmured, angling his chin to keep an eye on Julian who bolted straight up. "Sleepyhead."

"Are you serious?" Julian whipped his head toward the small clock on his dresser before jerking the duvet away. He used Beckett's body as a launching point to crawl to the edge of the mattress, his knees and elbows hitting all the wrong spots as he went. "Woofer has to go outside, or he'll have an accident, and nobody wants that."

"I took him out," Beckett said, grabbing his stomach from the pain of the elbow landing there.

Julian stopped midmotion of shrugging Beckett's pajama pants on, letting them drop again to the floor. Woofer leisurely strolled around the corner into the bedroom, coming to Julian's side. Like both men, Woofer had slept the morning away. The dog seemed to relish everyone being home together.

Julian's hand automatically reached for the dog as his critical gaze went back to Beckett's body, turning to admire him as it ran the length from toe to head. "Your body's incredible. There's not an inch of fat on you. You never go to the gym?"

The praise made Beckett grin as he recognized again that he was the only nude one between them. His dick didn't seem to mind as it firmed under Julian's speculative gaze.

As much as he might want those lips back on his cock, his way of carefully handling Julian came roaring to the forefront. Julian needed to be the one to set their pace. So, instead of trying to entice Julian back to his cock, he made a show of the pain of Julian's elbow hitting him in the stomach and reached for the duvet, tossing it over his lap to hide his arousal.

"Yeah, yeah. Stop trying to distract me. You could've been a little more careful."

The diversion tactic worked. Julian reached down to toss his pants on the end of the bed and pivoted toward his bathroom, taking long strides that direction. He spoke, even as he closed the door behind him. "I never sleep this long. Not ever. I'm not really a sleeper…"

Beckett regretfully left the bed. He reached for his underwear and pajama pants as he lifted an armpit to do a quick sniff test. Seemed good, so he gathered his clothes and toiletries from the suitcase. He chose to dress in the small half bath off the entry. Maybe they could go for a bite of lunch before the margarita tour.

Getting them out of the condo, enjoying the day outside of these walls might be their best bet against pushing Julian sexually before he was ready. The guy hadn't lied when he said he was skilled at sex. That blow job fucking blew his mind.

A life filled with sexually charged episode after episode filled Beckett's mind as well as his cock as he brushed his teeth. Holding back his desire was getting harder and harder to do.

"Did you hear me?"

Beckett looked at the wall separating the two bathrooms when he heard Julian's voice. "Maybe. What did you say?" Beckett called through the sheetrock.

"Lunch or back to bed?"

"Lunch," he answered firmly. Mind over matter and all that mess.

"Good choice. I'm starving."

Beckett smiled at Julian's reply. His mind jumped to other thoughts as soon as he heard the shower turn on. He had to force his mind from the imprinted picture of Julian standing nude in the shower a few days ago.

Think coffee… Making room inside his truck for Julian to sit… Think steps, walking many, many steps on the tour. He needed comfortable shoes. With another heavier sigh, Beckett focused on dressing as Julian's shower continued.

The day's anthem, "Margaritaville" by Jimmy Buffett, played from every bar they hit throughout the afternoon. If Julian didn't know the words by now, he'd have to be an idiot, but that wasn't what had him transfixed, not by a long shot. Instead, his cowboy held all his attention, standing at the edge of the bar, a shot of tequila being pushed into his resistant hands.

"Drink, drink, drink, drink!" Julian happily chanted alone, drawing every eye in the bar and on the street their direction as he tried his damnedest to peer pressure Beckett into drinking another shot of tequila.

Beckett's brow furrowed as he lifted the small glass and looked over at Julian as if he were crazy. "Now, why am I drinking this and you're not?"

That same question had been asked at their last three stops on the margarita tour. The answer never changed. Things that applied to Beckett didn't apply to Julian. It seemed reasonable enough to understand.

"I had to pull strings to get you that shot," Julian said, winking at the bartender in question. A person he'd never met before but made a big production of knowing only moments ago when he ordered the shot in the first place. "I can't use my connections to benefit me. What would that say about me?"

Beckett lowered the glass as he wobbled on his feet. Julian just barely kept the word *timber* in his mouth as he wondered if this was the time Beckett might actually fall over and pass out. Beckett held his liquor well, but countless different flavored margaritas, and three hearty shots of potent tequila, proved to be Beckett's tipping point. Good intel to file away in the back of his brain for later.

"Here, you do it," Beckett said, handing the glass to Julian. "I need to switch to water, or I'm not gonna make it through the night," he said with a slight slur to his words.

Julian playfully shook his head *no*.

Instead of rising to the challenge, Julian rose on his tiptoes, circled his arms around Beckett's waist, and settled in underneath his muscular arm. He beamed up at Beckett as he whispered against his ear. "I have plans for you tonight. One of us probably needs to be drunk to get through them."

He saw the moment curiosity changed to understanding for Beckett. His drunk date's grin turned sexy and seductive.

"Plans like you or me top?" Beckett's voice was a little louder than it should have been for such a personal question. Julian could hear the bartender chuckle as he motioned the customer behind them in line around to be served.

Julian didn't care in the least.

"Like me on your hot ass," Julian whispered, blowing against Beckett's ear as he said the words.

"You ready for something like that?" Beckett asked, his gaze growing darker.

"After last night? Oh yeah," Julian replied. Beckett nodded and lifted the shot glass, but Julian threw out a hand to stop him.

What was he thinking? If one of them needed to be drunk, it needed to be him. Hell, if for nothing more than liquid courage, Julian took the glass and slammed its contents back in one long swallow. Everyone around him cheered as he dropped the glass on the bar top and didn't wince as the tequila blazed a path to his stomach. Even Beckett cheered for him. Woofer, at their feet, barked loudly to get in on the action.

What a silly, fun day. It had been so long since he'd felt this free. He was getting his groove back. Julian shook his head and threw his arm out at the crowd.

"Yeah, yeah. Come on, hoss. A new adventure awaits!"

CHAPTER 24

"I think you got me drunk," Beckett said, loving the weight of Julian's hand in his where it had been for most of the day. The salty breeze, the moon rising high in the sky, and the lapping waves hitting his ankles as they walked together on the beach made for a perfect end to a perfect day.

"Me too, which is surprising with the amount of food we've eaten today." Julian's hand tightened around Beckett's, giving him a gentle squeeze of reassurance. "You know, he's gonna do great back at your place. He needs a place to run."

Beckett's brain had a hard time connecting Julian's words. He looked down the beach at Woofer, who'd been off the leash for several minutes now, running and playing in the surf. The city had done very well with its margarita tour. Most of the residents and tourists were at the street party, listening and dancing to the live music that had been playing for hours now. He and Julian were virtually alone on this section of the beach.

"What do you mean, back at my place?" Beckett cocked his head, watching Julian's lips quirk in the corner, a devious smile forming.

"You have a way of making an honest man out of me." Julian never looked at Beckett who struggled to understand what in the heck they were even talking about.

"Are you planning for Woofer to come home with me at some point?" No, that didn't make any sense.

He couldn't remember having a conversation where Woofer didn't stay here in Coronado with Julian. Once he left, surely Julian needed Woofer to help him feel safe.

"Why aren't you answering me?"

Julian rolled his eyes and pivoted his body around, letting go of Beckett's hand. His fists went to his hips as he came to a stop to confront Beckett. "I think you got me drunk on purpose. Tequila gives me loose lips. I didn't plan to tell you until tomorrow."

Beckett nodded and waited, his gaze switching between Julian and Woofer, keeping an eye on both.

"Come on." Julian urged Beckett to keep walking, and he did, because he'd follow Julian anywhere, especially with the way Julian took possession of his hand, tightly clasping it to pull him walking again. "I bought Woofer a ticket to fly home with you. I should've asked, but I was afraid you'd say *no*. He's not the kind of dog to be cooped up like he is. He needs to run and be free. You know how to speak his language, and the airline approved his flight."

Julian stopped him again, this time drawing Beckett into his arms.

"I'm doing far better than before. I'm beginning to feel like my old self again, and I never thought that would happen. The credit goes to you and that crazy dog. Woofer deserves a good life."

All Beckett's attention focused on Julian's upturned face and the honesty pouring from those perfect lips. His heart connected to the happiness and truth he saw on Julian's face. Then Julian gave a hard eye roll, and he pushed out of Beckett's arms as if he had accused Julian of something. His hard stare turned to a glare.

"Goddamn it. You make me want to be a better man. *I* didn't pay for the ticket; you did when you gave me your credit card to book your flight. I planned to buy Woofer's ticket myself, but my credit card is maxed out because of the new colors in the fall collection at Nordstrom. They suit my complexion very well. There're also some extra fees to accommodate for Woofer. Just take the money off the top of the weed you plan to give me."

What in the world was this crazy man talking about?

When Julian shrugged as if his explanation solved everything and turned away, Beckett had to reach out, take his hand, and draw him back. "I've tried to explain that I'm not the grower. I just invested in the company. I have nothing to do with the actual pot."

"Don't tell me you didn't work free pot into your investment. I won't believe you," Julian said, shaking his head as if that were obvious. Julian's shoulders lifted, and his hand extended in a what-gives motion. "Hook me up."

Beckett could only stare at Julian's audacity as Woofer bounded forward, drawing their attention. The seriousness of taking Woofer away, of removing the small amount of protection Julian had, caused Beckett to worry. "I think he needs to stay here with you. He's here to give you a sense of security."

Julian reached for Woofer's head, rubbing until the dog moved enough to have Julian scratch behind his ear. A particularly favorite place for Woofer who wildly thumped his foot. "The next few weeks will be sunup to sundown for me. He'll do better with you if you have a place for him. We can see how it goes, but he deserves the best person caring for him just like you've cared for me." Julian's hands reached around Beckett's, tilting his serious face up. "Thank you for what you've done for me."

"I don't want your thanks, Julian," Beckett started, and he

didn't, he wanted so much more.

"Shh. Not now. I'm not ready to go there," Julian confessed and dropped his chin to his chest, his forehead resting against Beckett's shoulder. "I've enjoyed this week. The connection we share is unlike anything I've ever experienced before. I usually feel so guilty when people try to help me, but I don't with you. I feel like it's a give and take between us. Honestly, you might be the most functional relationship I've ever had. I know what you want from me…"

Beckett unwound one hand and brought his palm to the nape of Julian's neck. His thumb caressed along Julian's unshaven jaw before it pressed against his lips, stopping Julian from saying more. "I'm not asking for anything except for you to heal. Let me be here for you." He wouldn't push Julian. Not now. They'd made such good strides at building a relationship together. His thumb slid underneath Julian's chin, lifting his face.

Julian released a heavy sigh as he said, "You deserve better than me, Beckett. I know you want more…" The deep anguish and hurt in Julian's gaze made every other worry flee. They had tonight and tomorrow. The rest would take care of itself.

"Stop." Beckett scanned Julian's handsome face, memorizing how the moon's glow turned those vibrant eyes into a slate gray. The light reflecting off Julian's dark strands resembled a halo. Julian looked like some kind of exotic angel standing beneath the stars.

No matter how many times Julian tried to dissuade Beckett or to warn him off, it only made him want more. No, he didn't expect a commitment from Julian, but Beckett hoped someday Julian would give him the chance to make him happy. When that day came, he'd do everything in his power to give Julian the world. They would find their way, soul connections this deep always found their way together. Surely, they did.

"If he goes with me, will you come see him?"

Julian smiled as relief eased the tension building on his

brow. "You know, I'm not really a camping guy. I couldn't find a glamping option on your website. I'm afraid I need more amenities than your current packages offer."

"You looked at my website?" Beckett asked, grinning broadly. Julian's sexy smile grew bigger. His eyes lit up as he casually shrugged his shoulders.

Yeah, Julian was into him. No question.

"*Pfft*," Julian added and flipped his hand in the air, waving it dismissively before turning and drawing Beckett from the ocean, back up the beach. "Let's go home, Romeo. My feet hurt."

Julian turned in the direction of his complex, patting his leg for Woofer to follow. Beckett's grin held as he watched that perfect bubble butt sway as he took purposeful strides through the sand.

"You mean home for you to have your way with me?" Beckett called out once he reached for his shoes and Woofer's leash laying in the sand.

Julian glanced back with his chin tilted over his shoulder, those piercing eyes caught Beckett in a wicked promise of what was to come. "Fuck yeah. And it'll be the best you ever had…" He gave a confident wink to the truth of his words and turned away.

Oh hell, Beckett's heart steadily drummed in his chest as he fished his phone from his pocket. They'd be Ubering to the condo. He wasn't wasting any more time before holding Julian to that promise.

Beckett's strong arms slid around Julian, drawing them together as he stepped up behind him, Beckett's wide chest flush against his back. Julian's heart thumped wildly against his rib cage. The alcohol amplified every tantalizing sensation.

"The ride's four minutes away," Beckett said against his ear. "I've been thinking about what you said today."

Julian thought about those words and couldn't help the laughter that welled. "I bet." He looked over his shoulder, catching Beckett's eye as he winked. "I feel like a virgin on prom night…"

"We don't have to…" Beckett obviously didn't find the humor. The thing about alcohol and Beckett was that it caused his chivalrous side to really shine. His demeanor took on an old-fashioned quality.

Julian pressed his ass against Beckett's hard-on, trying for a different reaction. His cowboy remained silent. He needed to change the course of this conversation.

"Of all the beach-friendly fashion choices out there, Ricco chose a three-piece suit to manage the margarita tour." He lifted his hands to the warm night air as if to prove his point. "While we're in Coronado, in the middle of a heat wave. I've got to talk with the boy."

"Ricco seemed so eager to do a good job. He was working himself into the ground. Maybe his mentor taught him that." Beckett's hold tightened around Julian's arms, driving the point home. Funny how those words were once true, even as soon as last week, but not so much now. Julian hadn't felt compelled to jump in and help like he always had before…and he stopped thinking about that too. No need to dig any deeper into the ease with which he'd walked away from Reservations this afternoon as they worked hard to stay caught up with the crowd of locals and tourists participating in the margarita tour.

"Don't blame me," Julian teased and lifted his hands to run a finger around his armpits. "The sweat stains showed. I'll have to take him shopping next week. He really needs to learn how to pick a uniform more fitting for the environment."

Beckett chuckled and bent down to kiss his cheek. Beckett continued kissing up between his ear and hairline before he whispered, "You got me drunk today. Don't you know by now, I'm a sure bet?"

"Yeah, I know."

CHAPTER 25

When had an Uber ride been so full of romance? Something about the day they shared, the allure of a midnight walk on the beach, strolling hand in hand had cemented Julian's fate. Maybe it was the big dog that had forced Julian to the middle seat, pressing him firmly against Beckett's warm body that had Julian's heart connecting so solidly with his plan to seduce his cowboy tonight.

Beckett's heavy palm landed on his thigh, giving a gentle squeeze. He looked over at Beckett who smiled at him. "I had a good day."

"Me too." Beckett angled his body and lifted a hand to Julian's chin—such a sweet, simple gesture that curled his toes—to better angle him for a soft, lingering press of the lips.

The more Julian thought about what he and Beckett were about to do, the more excitement fueled his rising confidence. After so long without sex, it was strange to have zero apprehensions, only a desire to push him to act.

Sexual energy buzzed between them and made it hard to concentrate on any small talk with the driver. It wouldn't surprise him at all if the poor Uber driver feared that he and Beckett might get it on right there in the backseat with all the electricity zinging between them.

Yeah, he needed to behave himself. Beckett was way too classy to give the driver a free show, and Woofer didn't need to witness such debauchery either. But damn, it was fucking hard to do when the heat of Beckett's palm blazed a trail from his knee to his thigh, the sizzle of the touch running straight to his balls.

Now that his desire had returned, keeping such a tight rein on his actions might have been the hardest thing he'd done in a long time. All he could fantasize about was guiding Beckett's palm to his cock to quickly bring him to completion before they made it home. He might fucking burst if Beckett didn't put his hands on him.

All the things he planned on doing to the gorgeous cowboy filled his head. The mere thought of a naked Beckett in his bed made the quick ride to his condo feel like hours long instead of mere minutes.

"We're here." Beckett's deep voice pulled him from his depraved fantasies as the car door opened. He glanced over at Beckett and his heart picked up a beat. "Are you okay?" Beckett asked as he helped him from the car.

No, not really. All of Julian's blood had rushed from his brain and had headed south. He wondered if this was how a virgin felt on their wedding night. The air sizzled and popped around him, making Julian hyperaware of every moment he and Beckett shared. Woofer leaped from the backseat and smartly took a seat on the pavement next to Beckett's feet.

"I've been thinking about all the things I'm going to do to you, Marlboro Man," he purred in Beckett's ear as they stood on the curb in front of his condo, finalizing the ride. Julian glanced down at his swollen cock trapped behind the expensive material of his tight pants, making sure Beckett's eyes followed his as the car drove away.

He knew exactly what he wanted to do and loved the reaction when Beckett realized what he had drawn attention to. "Look what you've done to me."

Woofer took off to do his business on his favorite patch of grass. Julian grabbed Beckett's hand and led him through the complex, practically racing to get to his unit and get the door opened. Woofer rushed past them as soon as he opened the door, his nails clicking on the tile as he ran to the kitchen.

Needy anticipation vibrated through Julian. The moment they stepped fully inside, Julian reached for Beckett, needing to drown himself in the other man. It had been so long since he'd been intimate with anyone in this way. And the level with which he craved Beckett blew that desire off the charts.

Right now, he wasn't going to analyze any of the intensity pushing him to take Beckett; his counselor would cover all those bases. Instead, he planned to enjoy every minute of this moment.

Oblivious to all Julian's intentions, Beckett took Julian's face between his warm palms and placed a sweet kiss on his lips before entering the small hallway. "We don't have to rush. I'm not going anywhere. I'm all yours, Julian."

He stared at Beckett and narrowed his eyes as he assessed those words, which sounded more like a promise than a statement. Did the man even know what was about to hit him?

Julian shut the door behind him, his heart still hammering against his chest as he took a deep breath to calm himself. He didn't bother to turn on a light. The small lamp on the side table gave off just enough illumination for what he had in mind.

After the door lock clicked into place, he turned and stalked to where Beckett had come to a stop. Beckett gave him the control. Julian's eyes never left Beckett's as he backed him against the wall and took his mouth in a demanding kiss.

Beckett gasped as Julian ground his rigid hard-on against

his equally hard cock. Julian took advantage of the situation and pushed his tongue between Beckett's surprised parted lips. It took a fraction of a second for Beckett to catch on to his intention. Their tongues met in a frenzy of pent-up desire and growing hunger. Julian pinned Beckett's larger body against the wall holding him hostage as they kissed.

An excited woof echoed in the hallway, making Beckett tear away from the kiss.

"Woofer, bed," Beckett commanded huskily. His desire-filled gaze never strayed from Julian. Woofer turned and went straight to his kennel and lay down with a sigh.

Julian lifted his brows at Beckett and looked over at Woofer, then back to Beckett. "Impressive."

"Thanks." Beckett nipped at his lips. "Now, show me where we were?" The growl in Beckett's voice sent tingles shooting up his spine. He bet under normal circumstances that Beckett liked to dominate his men. The efforts he used with Julian seemed right on the edge of forced control, showing the genuine care Beckett took with him.

Julian reached out and unfastened the buttons on Beckett's shirt. "We were headed to the bedroom where you were going to let me have my way with you." Julian pushed Beckett's shirt off his shoulders and down his arms, exposing the dark hair on his chest and the flat brown nipples he couldn't wait to get his mouth on. Julian stepped back and slowly unbuttoned his own shirt then dropped it on the floor next to Beckett's. He fought against the unease that his body wasn't as perfect as it had been. But seeing the desire in Beckett's eyes helped to drive away the moment of insecurity.

Beckett reached for him, pulling him against that hard chest. "I can't get enough of you, Julian. I want to feel your beautiful body against mine."

Beckett lowered his head and caught his mouth in a sultry kiss. Their lips collided hot and heavy as he let himself get lost in the Marlboro Man's arms. Beckett made him dizzy with need in the way he kissed. The soft but demanding nips and devilish probing tongue had Julian moaning for more. He slid his fingers through Beckett's hair, deepening the kiss as he ground against that large frame.

Julian had always been the one to seduce his clients. He'd never been seduced, but that was quickly changing with every flick of Beckett's tongue. The emotions connecting him to Beckett startled him.

Being with Beckett was way too easy. It felt natural. He didn't have to pretend. The chemistry drawing him to his cowboy soared off the charts. Strong hands cupped his ass as Beckett rocked against him. Their hard cocks pressed together with each thrust of his hips. He could come from the friction alone, it felt so damn good.

Breaking from the kiss, Julian sucked his way down Beckett's neck, enjoying the taste of his salty skin on the tip of his tongue. When he got to Beckett's nipple, he slowly slid his tongue over the flattened disk, then sucked it into his mouth, using the tip of his tongue to toy with the hard nub before taking it between his teeth. Beckett groaned. Strong fingers slid up Julian's neck and into his hair. Beckett tugged his head up and kissed him, rough and demanding, leaving Julian breathless when he pulled away.

"Take me to your bedroom." Julian didn't hesitate to take Beckett's outstretched hand and lead him to his room. Julian quickly kicked off his shoes and wiggled out of his pants then turned, reaching for Beckett to help with his.

"I could stare at you all day," Julian said and stepped back after he finished ridding Beckett of his clothes to take in the entire tableau. Julian hadn't exaggerated one little bit when he'd confessed that truth. Not even close. He tucked his bottom lip between his lips as he absorbed the image of the muscled beauty. Beckett stood naked. His cock, hard and thick with arousal, jutted rigidly from his body.

Julian's own cock jerked with excitement as he watched Beckett stroke that gorgeous cock a few times as lust filled the cowboy's gaze.

Beckett finally chuckled. "Is that so?" His Marlboro Man didn't seem a bit shy as he worked his fist up and down his shaft. "I could get off watching you watch me. You're so fucking beautiful, Julian. I couldn't wait to get started."

The sultry timbre of Beckett's voice had his dick not only taking notice but leaking like a fucking broken faucet. Damn, he was caught in Beckett's spell. The sight of that beautiful man pleasuring himself had his mouth watering for a taste of his own. He'd never witnessed something so mesmerizing as watching Beckett St. Clair taking himself in hand. The man was beyond gorgeous; his muscular body looked as if Michelangelo himself had chiseled it. Strong muscles and deep valleys invited him to explore all that flesh with his tongue… Julian swallowed the groan rising up his throat.

"Let me help you out," Julian purred. He took a step forward, dropping to his knees in front of Beckett. His fingers curled around Beckett's hard cock and stroked. He used his other hand to cup one of Beckett's firm ass cheeks and draw him closer.

He kissed his way down Beckett's lower stomach and hip bone then buried his nose in Beckett's thatch of short hair. Julian breathed him in while tightening his fist to work the thick shaft in his palm. God, he loved the musky scent of this man.

He pulled back enough to lift his head, meeting Beckett's gaze as he opened his mouth and took Beckett inside, circling that sensitive tip with his tongue. Beckett's legs shook as his sweet essence burst across Julian's palate, making his own dick weep with delight.

He swallowed Beckett down to his root then drew back and did it again and again. Strong fingers tightened in his hair, gently tugging his head back and his face up.

"You're amazing, but you have to stop, Julian. I'll come. It's honestly too much right now. I want you in me when I come, Julian." Beckett's eyes locked on his, their dark depths penetrating straight through to Julian's soul. "Please don't make us wait any longer."

He kept his gaze locked with Beckett's as he leaned in and kissed the tip of that enticing cock one last time before standing.

"Isn't having patience a virtue or something like that?" Julian teased. But he didn't want to delay a second longer, and he wouldn't keep Beckett waiting either.

"That saying is overrated, and I'm not feeling very virtuous at the moment." Beckett slid his palms down Julian's back and over the swell of his ass. Then he bent to kiss the scars on his neck and chest. "You're so perfect, Julian. Every part of you is beautiful." Beckett slid his hand around his hip and curled around his cock.

Julian's body lurched at the touch; it had been so long.

"In me now." Beckett's tentative rough palm felt amazing on his cock.

He couldn't help but thrust his hips, fucking into that calloused fist. His balls drew tight against his body as he fought to keep his sanity.

"Get on the bed." Julian tried to hide the urgency in his command.

Beckett seemed reluctant to let go of Julian. Pausing for only a second before he threw the comforter back and dropped down on the ice blue sheets, situating himself on his back. He bent his thick muscular legs at the knees, then allowed them to butterfly out as he spread his legs wide. Heat rushed through Julian's body at the sight of Beckett's blatant invitation.

Beckett made it so damned easy on him.

Need churned within Julian as he leaned down to kiss Beckett's full lips before he then crawled his way onto the bed, kissing a trail down the man's body as he went. He licked a wet path down the thick cock then nosed the soft skin of Beckett's balls, taking his time to enjoy the intoxicating scent that he was forming an addiction to.

He reached up to take Beckett's cock in his mouth.

"Julian." Beckett's warning helped to keep him on track. Hell, it wasn't his fault Beckett's body was so fucking tempting.

With a sigh, Julian sat up and grabbed the lube from the nightstand along with a condom. He got back on his knees and scooted between Beckett's parted thighs. He ripped open the foil package with his teeth then rolled the condom on. Using his thumb, he flipped the lid of the lube open and drizzled the oil on his fingers before tossing the bottle aside.

His movements were sure, his craving so damned strong.

Julian slid his fingers over Beckett's perineum and dropped down to follow their path with his tongue. Beckett's moans grew desperate as Julian took the time to lick across the tender flesh and pressed his slick thumb into Beckett's tightness. Beckett's quick intake of breath had Julian's body vibrating with an urgency that he'd believed had been stolen from him the night of the attack.

He used his fingers and tongue to work Beckett open. Beckett grabbed his knees, lifting his ass, giving Julian the best possible angle as he added two fingers, pumping them in and out of the other man's body, enjoying the tight heat gripping him. He curled his fingers to find the tight bundle of nerves.

"Please." Beckett's breathless plea drew his attention.

"You're tight, Beck. I don't want to hurt you." Julian gently removed his fingers.

"You won't. You can't. I need you," Beckett begged.

He'd remember this night for the rest of his life. He had to make sure Beckett was primed and ready for him. He quickly reached for the lube again and slicked the condom this time. Situating himself as he gripped his own cock, locking eyes with Beckett, who easily held his stare. Julian panted. His heart raced as he gathered confidence from the sweet gaze urging him on. He pushed the tip of his cock past the tight ring of muscle he'd worked to relax.

The ecstasy of Beckett's body took Julian's breath.

Home.

He was finally home.

Beckett's pleasure-filled moan sent tingles dancing along his spine as white-hot heat engulfed Julian.

His vision dimmed, and the breath he'd held rushed out of him as he sank into all that scorching mind-numbing tightness. Julian had always prided himself on being able to last forever, to please a client before himself, but this was different. So *fucking* different.

"God, you're tight." He held still as Beckett's body stretched to accommodate him. It fit him so perfectly as if made just for him. Overwhelmed with a barrage of unfamiliar feelings and sensations, he fought to push the thoughts aside. He was seriously in danger of coming if he moved.

"Fuck me, Julian." Beckett's dark eyes searched his. Julian felt as if Beckett were his foundation in this moment, grounding him. Showing Julian that he had this. Beckett reached up, grasped Julian's head, and pulled him down, welding their mouths together in a rough, satisfying kiss. Julian opened for Beckett, their tongues tangling and teeth clashing as he slowly moved in and out of Beckett.

Beckett's body clenched around his. Julian immersed himself in an inferno of gripping heat. He canted his hips, thrusting harder as he plundered Beckett's mouth with his tongue. Their bodies strained as they moved as one. He caught Beckett's hands in his as Beckett wrapped his long legs around Julian's hips, his heels digging into Julian's ass.

He stretched those long arms over his lover's head, keeping him trapped for his amusement. Julian was caught up in the pleasure of Beckett's body. Nothing else in the world mattered.

Beckett's deep moans were damned addicting. He loved drawing the guttural sounds from the man beneath him. Beckett freed his hands, those warm palms settling on either side of his face as they held him long enough for a deep kiss.

Julian pulled out and slammed back into his lover over and over as Beckett clawed at his back. His legs trembled from exertion. He was close. His balls ached to be emptied, and the liquid fire rushing through his veins threatened to incinerate him on the spot.

Their groans mingled as he grabbed Beckett's cock and stroked him in time with his thrusts. Nothing had ever felt as good as being balls deep in Beckett. He struggled to keep moving, so afraid he was going to come. He fought the fire licking up his spine. Sweat beaded his brow as he fucked Beckett with hard, demanding thrusts.

"Ahh fuck yes! I'm close, Julian." Beckett's husky and ragged words underscored how close he was to the edge.

"Come, B." As soon as the command left his mouth, he plunged in one last time. Beckett's ass clamped down on him and ropes of come painted the ridges of Beckett's stomach. The sight of Beckett giving in to his release took Julian over the edge and had him erupting in the condom. His body shook with pleasure as he rode out his orgasm.

Lost to his release, he collapsed face down on Beckett, fighting to draw air into his burning lungs even as the edges of his vision dimmed.

Beckett's firm lips pressed against his temple. "That was amazing, Julian."

He lifted his head, pushing himself up on shaky arms to gaze down at a blissed-out Beckett. "I believe you meant to say mind-blowing. Thank you."

He slanted his lips over Beckett's and kissed his Marlboro Man for all he was worth.

CHAPTER 26

"Guys, come on!" a very impatient airport attendant called from several feet away, causing Beckett to lift his head from the beauty in his arms to give the woman a nod. She gestured wildly with her hands in the air, her frustration clear. "You're killing me. You gotta get movin' or I'll get in trouble."

The problem with her request was that Julian had his mesmerizing hard body pressed enticingly flush against Beckett, his arms wrapped around Beckett's neck. Julian wouldn't release his tight hold. Their long goodbye was on display for the entire world to see.

Well, for anyone in the world who might be awake and at the airport by five forty-five on a Monday morning. Beckett's always impeccably dressed boyfriend—*please let Julian see himself as my boyfriend*—had dressed down this morning. Julian wore a slouchy beanie, designer sunglasses and an equally designer pair of formfitting joggers. He looked sophisticatedly rumpled in the sexiest of ways, always in the sexiest of ways. What made it all that much better was that Julian had opted to stay cuddled up with him in bed until the very last possible moment for them to leave.

Beckett's whole heart connected with Julian in a complete and everlasting way.

"She's not wrong. We need to get going." Beckett nodded toward the attendant. He had forty minutes to navigate the airport before boarding his flight with Woofer in tow.

Beckett bent his head for a final press of the lips when Julian met him with another soul-destroying kiss. They'd been coming one right after another for the last ten or so minutes that they had been parked outside the departure entrance.

Julian's strong fingers tightened their grip on Beckett's T-shirt as he backed away from the passion of the kiss. Julian's bright blue eyes fluttered open as he whispered against Beckett's lips. "I owe you everything."

"You owe me nothing. This has been the best week of my life." Beckett shook his head and tightened his hold around Julian's waist, doing the exact opposite of what the attendant had instructed them to do. He didn't want gratitude to come from what they had shared with one another. He wanted a long-lasting coupling and nothing less. "I should be thanking you for finally letting me in. I was beginning to think it would never happen."

Julian's palms pushed upward and out of Beckett's firm hold to take his cheeks, stopping him from saying or doing anything more than looking Julian in the eyes. "Come back as soon as you can and plan to stay with me. We got along pretty well together except that you take more than your share of the bed."

Beckett's silly grin instantly widened at the allegation. "That's on you, and you know it."

"Well, I knew one of us did." Julian cheekily quipped and stepped away. Beckett begrudgingly let him go.

All the things Beckett wished he could say left a burning trail of unspoken regret… *Come home with me… Let me be the one to take care of you… Can't you see how right we are together… I'll keep you safe for the rest of our lives… I love you.*

His and Julian's little bubble, hiding them from the world, was about to pop. The sun moved overhead. The noise of increasing traffic picked up around them. The attendant blew her whistle then threw out her frustrated hands, done with the lovers having to say their goodbyes.

"I should go. We're gonna be late." Woofer had patiently waited by their sides for the length of the emotional goodbye. Beckett reached down, taking Woofer's leash, then he took the strap of one of his suitcases and tossed it over his shoulder before taking the other's handle in hand. Only then did Julian take a decent size step away from Beckett. "Watch my truck?"

"I decided if you don't hurry back, I'll start driving it myself. That should be a warning," Julian teased and shut the trunk of his car. He reached out, giving Woofer a good rub to the head. "Call me when you get home."

Beckett's heart gave a painful thump as he nodded and took small steps backward toward the sidewalk. "Go learn how to manage Reservations."

"*Pfft,*" Julian said, tossing a careless hand in the air. "I need to go show them how Reservations is going to be run from here on out."

Beckett didn't doubt Julian's declaration. They stood there, six or seven feet apart, staring at one another. None of the connection they'd shared was lost.

I love you. I've never loved anyone like I love you… Please love me.

A quick exhale burst from Beckett's parted lips. He meant every one of those words and wished he was brave enough to say them out loud.

His racing thoughts focused on the private security company he'd hired yesterday. Marc was a longtime friend. A member of Beckett's inaugural training course—the group of men who began his and his father's company. He and Marc had become fast friends. So much so that Beckett hadn't thought twice about asking Marc to watch over Julian in his absence. Luckily, Marc was semi-retired and able to start immediately, but he hadn't offered any friends or family discounts. Twenty-four seven secret personal protection details didn't come cheap.

"Go. And take care of my dog," Julian said, tossing out another hand toward the airport's entrance. Woofer took the motion as a command and turned, giving a tug to the leash in Beckett's tight hold.

Something raw and vulnerable crossed Julian's brow before he ducked his head and started for the driver's side door. Beckett had given his oath to Julian, swearing Woofer would have the best possible care, while in return, Julian promised Woofer he'd see him again soon.

Julian never looked back. Beckett knew that with all certainty because he kept his eyes on Julian until he pulled away. He let their non-goodbye be enough for now since he'd be back in Coronado soon. This wasn't a goodbye. Not by a long shot.

Hopefully, this was the beginning of their forever.

Somewhere along the way, Julian's fake it till you make it attitude had paid off. His faux sense of confidence in his job performance had somehow become a reality. Who knew that he had it in him to be anything more than a reprobate? Certainly not his parents. Nor the church nor the private school clergy who had hesitantly agreed to mentor him in his childhood.

This morning, all his lifelong doubts had changed. After several grueling and intensive hours of meetings with the Reservations general manager and the Dishology transition team, Julian truly believed he could handle his new position. He had even engaged enough to add value in his ideas of streamlining certain techniques to help the current processes flow a little easier. Based on the reactions of those in attendance—including Thane—Julian had clearly impressed his peers, which went a long way to boosting Julian's confidence in his business acumen.

"Thanks for fighting for me," Ricco said quietly as he walked stride for stride beside Julian down the sidewalk leading from Escape to the front doors of Reservations. "It sounds like I'll get an offer for the manager position."

"You will," Julian said confidently, never breaking his hurried gait as he mentally ticked off his to-do list before he could leave Reservations for the night. He cast a quick glance over at Ricco who was grinning ear to ear. This bartender had come to the interview with his A-game today, dressed to impress.

Julian had wrangled Ricco's first interview into the day's packed training schedule. Ricco had taken the opportunity to heart. The sexy, hot bartender, who could easily pull in a thousand dollars in tips on a Saturday night by doing little more than bouncing his perfect ass, looked like a young Wall Street professional.

His gaze moved past Ricco to the midsize sedan still parked in the furthest lot, directly in front of the Reservations employee entrance door. The tan four-door had similarities to an older model Toyota. The outline of a single head could be seen in the driver's side seat. It was too far away to make out any other details of the driver.

"He's been parked there all morning. Shortly after you arrived," Ricco said and started to turn to look at the car. "I checked the security video."

"Don't look!" Julian hissed, startling Ricco but managing to keep his face and eyes focused forward in a hilariously frantic swivel of his head. Julian would have laughed at Ricco had his heart not completely connected to Beckett's obviously protective move. "I had Aaron Stuart run his plates this morning. The car belongs to an ex-navy officer who retired from San Diego PD. I'm certain Beckett hired him to watch out for me."

Ricco nodded and threw out an awkward elbow bump while staring woodenly straight ahead. Good thing Ricco wanted a life in business because his acting skills were shit. "I told you so."

Ricco's superior, all-knowing tone had Julian's brows lowering, annoyance instantly building. He stopped just short of returning the elbow bump. "You told me what?"

"You and Beck being a thing. I called it first. I might have even won the betting pool," Ricco said, slowing Julian's step as his cell phone vibrated in his slacks pocket.

"I keep telling you dumbasses that Beckett and I aren't like that."

Ricco was a dumbass, and Julian's tone reeked the sentiment as he fished the phone from his pocket.

"I'm passing the time with him, because I literally have no friends anymore..." The words ran dry in Julian's mouth. He couldn't finish the lie as Beckett's handsome, smiling face illuminated his cell's screen for a video call. "Go on without me and stop spilling your junior high tea. I have to take this." Julian tried for a professional tone even when giving his final dig before pivoting around, walking several fast-paced steps in the other direction, trying to create distance between him and Ricco before he answered.

"You made it home?" Julian said as he accepted the call.

The happiness of the day was made better by the man whose profile was partially on the screen, with Woofer in the distance, leaping around, chasing after something unseen in the air. There was nothing more than utter wilderness for as far as the eye could see with both the males in his life looking joyful, fresh, and content in their forever environment.

Julian's happy heart lifted several notches. He grinned as he struggled with whether to pay attention to Woofer or the handsome cowboy. It was reminiscent of the very first time he had laid eyes on Beckett as he'd walked through the front entrance of Reservations. Beckett wore a pair of Oakley sunglasses with a ball cap positioned backward on his head. The sun accentuated his suntan. He wasn't certain Beckett could be more alluring than he was right then.

All the deep feeling that only Beckett had ever reached inside Julian burst free, drawing a grin from him. More than anything, he wished he was right there with his two guys, which was all sorts of weird. He'd never been an outdoorsman. Flushable toilets always superseded the idea of wide-open spaces of the wilderness.

"We're here. I planned to call you at the airport, but Woofer didn't handle the flight very well. He was skittish when we got off the plane. He didn't seem to understand what was happening to him. When we pulled in, he saw a squirrel and practically jumped out of the truck to play. The squirrels here aren't as friendly as in your neighborhood, but a butterfly caught his attention. That's what he's doing now." Beckett moved completely out of the screen to let Julian see Woofer joyfully jumping in the air, trying to catch and eat his new friend. Julian's heart swelled. He hadn't made the wrong decision in sending Woofer to his new home. Beckett's face came partially back into view. "I think he'll do okay here."

Julian gave into his desire to stare at the rugged Beckett. "I like that look with your ball cap on backward."

Beckett's handsome face filled the frame, stealing the remainder of Julian's words. "I'm casual when I'm home. This is pretty much how I always look. I flip the brim around when I need it. You know I always like how you look. I had to hire a personal shopper, so I could try better to fit into your world," Beckett confessed the obvious, making a little noise out of the corner of his mouth. "The calendar on my phone somehow synced with your calendar. I'm not sure how it happened, but I saw you were in a meeting all morning. How'd it go? You ready to jump in and take over Reservations?"

Julian wondered how long it would take for Beckett to figure out what he had done. "Remember when you were in the shower, and I asked for your passcode?" He waited until Beckett nodded, and his brows slid together under his Oakley's. "I synced our calendars. I decided you probably thought we were that far into our relationship to join our calendars."

The syncing had been a spontaneous choice. Designed to confuse and tease Beckett. The added benefit for Julian was that he'd already started to miss Beckett and Woofer. It helped his swinging emotional states to see Beckett's scheduled activities for the day.

"Ah..." Beckett started, grinning like a Cheshire cat—a sweet, smiling kitty cat. "We're in a relationship?"

The doe-eyed expression had Julian giving a dramatic eye roll. "I'm standing in the middle of the parking lot, letting the sun's violent rays touch my skin without sunscreen... This has to be bad for my complexion. I'm risking a wrinkle and dark spots to talk to you privately. So yeah, we're in some sort of an *it's complicated* relationship." Julian wasn't even freaked out by confirming their status out loud. "By the way, know anything about the tan sedan sitting in the back parking lot?"

Some of Beckett's excitement faded as he pulled the sunglasses off his face. He squinted as if he could see past Julian to the vehicle in the furthest lot. Beckett clearly wasn't sure if Julian was testing him or asking a legit question, so he turned the phone's screen to show the evidence parked in the distance.

"Julian..." Beckett started, giving a wince.

"*Julian*..." Julian mimicked, loving the way Beckett squirmed.

When no excuse readily came, Beckett's shoulders slumped as a heavy sigh escaped. His gaze lowered to his feet. "Look, I like the idea of someone keeping an eye on you when I can't. He's a good friend. He'll take this job seriously."

"Beck!" A booming masculine voice stopped Beckett's explanation midsentence. It gained all of Beckett's attention as he swung his head to the right. Julian did, too, as if he could see the man with such a commanding tone. "We need you, son!"

"Turn the phone so I can see him," Julian instructed.

Beckett did as he asked.

"I'll be there in a minute." Beckett's sweet-hearted tone changed. A tough voice barreled from his chest. Julian couldn't see Beckett's father clearly. He stood on a large wraparound porch with his fists resting on his hips and a round belly sticking out. Beckett and his father shared similar features, showing hints of what Beckett might look like as he aged.

"I should go." Beckett turned to face the screen. "Don't send Marc packing until you and I talk more. He'll stay out of your way, I promise, but if something goes wrong, he's right there to help."

"We'll see." Julian never gave in prematurely and didn't want to start now. "Call me later."

Beckett gave a two-finger whistle over his shoulder, drawing Woofer's attention. The dog bounded forward as Beckett started in the direction of his father.

"Don't do anything until we talk again. Promise me," Beckett pleaded. It seemed Julian was shit to go against what Beckett wanted and gave a nod before disconnecting the call. Julian felt so damn good he closed his eyes and lifted his face to the sun, grinning. In the measures of his life, he'd reached another milestone. His happiness was back. Damn, it felt good.

CHAPTER 27

The reclining chair had a comforting, familiar squeak as Beckett leaned back, taking his cell phone with him. Randy's instant irritated gaze shot toward Beckett. They were three hours into their preparations, and every single time Beckett pushed back in the seat, the noise seemed to grate on Randy's last nerve, drawing his immediate ire.

"My God-*da*," Randy declared, shifting his angry gaze toward Beckett again. "Stay off the fucking phone. You're making this take so much longer than it has to. You're killing me."

The papers in Randy's hand went flying as he tossed them in the air. Beckett didn't care in the least. He was proud he'd made it a full fifteen minutes before responding to Julian's latest text. His thumbs worked furiously on the small screen until his text messages app opened.

"What are you gonna do when you can't talk to this guy for three days?" Randy asked, pushing out of his seat.

"I'll have the satellite phone," Beckett answered absently as he read Julian's latest message.

If Beckett read between the lines properly, Julian seemed genuinely happy. The tone of the lighthearted texts and the way Julian consistently carved out time to talk to Beckett during his busy day was far different from the cynical, sarcastic persona Julian used as a shield against the world.

His heart warmed, all the Julian-induced tingles ran up and down his arms, leaving a trail of goose bumps as if Julian were right there with him, touching him in that tender way he had. The things Julian shared might be superficial—he'd sent the details of his management training—but it didn't matter. Julian was blooming right in front of Beckett's eyes. A surprising change.

Maybe Beckett was way off base. He didn't know Julian well enough to make such a bold claim. But he was happy to be the one Julian shared his day with.

"The dog's sitting by the front door. Do I let him out?"

Beckett lifted his gaze at the sound and smell of cooking oil spray as Randy used a can of Pam to grease the cogs of Beckett's chair.

"Mom swears that'll draw ants," Beckett murmured, cocking his head to see Woofer sitting at the door. Beckett had worried about all the wild animals he had heard roaming last night and had kept Woofer close this morning. He decided a normal German shepherd could handle himself against coyotes or wild cats, but Woofer had been raised as a city dog.

As much as it was likely to piss Randy off further, Beckett rose from his seat. Damn, the Pam worked. The squeak was now completely gone. He could have this conversation with Julian while sitting on the porch to let Woofer outside for a while.

"I got you, boy. I wanna be out there too." Beckett barely had the front door open before Woofer pushed through, shoving it the rest of the way. A fresh breeze riffled through the opening as Woofer took off, running toward then leaping from the porch steps. Another text message from Julian arrived as Beckett followed the dog out, sitting on the porch steps to keep an eye on Woofer.

Well, one eye. The other was on the text message Julian sent. This one had a selfie of Julian with a stack of paperwork on his desk. All Beckett saw was the crystal aqua eyes slanted into Julian's bright smile. Those pleasure-inducing lips had Beckett growing plump. Julian was beautiful and somehow always looked crisp and pristine, never fatigued.

"I'm heading into the kitchen for prep training. I'll be away for a few hours. Wish me luck. They expect me to help with dinner prep tonight. Not my forte. I think I'm better at setting the standard than creating the standard."

So taken with Julian's handsome face, Beckett had somehow missed the apron Julian wore. Beckett would have to see how Julian held up his appearance after spending time in the steamy kitchen. He hurriedly typed a message. *"Good luck. Have I told you I like a man who can cook? Take a picture when you're done. I'm always a messy chef."*

"I watched Ratatouille. It's all in the elbow placement. Signing off. Look out for my dog."

The back door opened and slammed carelessly shut with a loud whack. Randy's heavy booted footsteps came toward Beckett.

"Here." A cup of coffee appeared over his shoulder. He took the offering as Randy thumped down several steps before landing on his ass beside him. "You know you gotta get your head in the game. The trainees arrive in a few hours."

No shit. His headspace had been a problem for the last twenty-four hours. Every thought he had revolved around Julian. If he wasn't wondering what Julian might be doing, he was reliving some special moment in their last week together. Every thought was Julian.

"I know," Beckett said, inhaling the enticing aroma before

lifting the mug to take a hearty sip of the steaming coffee.

"Wanna talk about him?" Randy asked, cutting his gaze toward Beckett. "It might help to get whatever it is off your chest."

Beckett barked out a harsh laugh, jostling the coffee. He had to spread his legs and absorb the sting of the hot liquid as it sloshed out of the cup onto his hand and down to the porch step. "No, I don't want to talk about him, and at the same time, he's all I want to talk about. I'm so fucked over this guy."

"No shit?" The kind of jeering that came from a lifelong friendship readily slipped from Randy as he knocked Beckett on the shoulder. "I couldn't tell… It's literally all anyone is talking about—you being fucked."

Beckett cut his steely gaze toward Randy, judging the sincerity of those possibly vulgar words. His Julian-induced protective side leaped forward. He didn't like the idea of his and Julian's relationship being trivialized in such a derogatory way.

"Watch yourself…" Beckett warned.

"*Pfft*," Randy scoffed as if Beckett was nothing more than an annoying gnat. "Calm yourself." He tapped the side of his temple. "I meant happy and distracted. I have your back. Don't worry."

Beckett let that be enough of an explanation as he turned his gaze to the pasture in front of them, checking on Woofer, who ran at full speed back toward the house. He swore the dog had some Forrest Gump in his veins. How had Woofer ever made it as an indoor dog?

As he stared at Woofer, he took a breath and broke through another of his barriers to talk about a man in his life. "He's the general manager of a restaurant and nightclub I belong to. His name is Julian, and he does it for me in every possible way."

"Hmm," Randy murmured with absolutely no judgment or malice hidden in his tone. "So, he'll be sticking around?"

The fear Beckett hadn't let himself face came rushing to the forefront. He was happily immersed in the idea of his and Julian's forever, but he honestly didn't know if Julian was there with him.

"If I can swing it," Beckett managed to say.

Randy's side eye, drawing Beckett to look at his friend. "I'm not into guys but I'd put money on you being a good catch."

The compliment helped ease the building worry as he spoke of the true obstacle between them. "He's a city-boy through and through."

"How's that gonna work?" Randy asked, brow furrowed as if contemplating the options.

Beckett lifted his head to stare at the miles of blue sky, which only reminded him of the depth of Julian's unusual eyes. He took a deep inhale of the fresh air. The crisp, exotic woodsy scent reminded him of Julian's unique cologne. The majestic view of the mountain range sitting in the distance could only be topped by an ocean view, if Beckett did, in fact, buy a place in Coronado for him and Julian to live.

Damn. The heavy whoosh of an exhale escaped. He'd done more than one search on Zillow, looking for homes for sale in the Coronado area. All the primal, protective feels laced each of his breaths. Julian was his; they were perfect together.

"I love him," Beckett said in a whisper.

"Clearly. But did that answer my question?" Randy asked.

Beckett stayed quiet for a second or two, not truly comfortable explaining his new outlook on his rapidly changing life.

"We're not to the point of making any sort of decision about a future. I've known how I feel for a while now, but I only managed any sort of real connection over the last few weeks." Beckett finally looked over at Randy as he told his confidant the truth. "He was kidnapped and assaulted. He's got trust issues."

Randy's eyes widened, his brow wrinkling, as he mumbled, "I'm sorry to hear that."

"I was too," Beckett said. His heart showed its cracks in the wild thumping that came from thinking of Julian's abduction. "Everything in me wants to be with him. It's as strong as the need to breathe. He and I fit remarkably well together. He pulls a contentment out of me that I really like." Beckett shook his head, lost in everything he'd confessed. "Does that make any sense? My world's turned singular. I want to be the one to care for Julian. I want to be his person, you know?"

Randy nodded. They'd been best friends for a long, long time, but they rarely went into a deep dive over anything. "I do know. I feel the same way about Marly."

Beckett nodded, happy Randy understood. "So, I'll go to him," Beckett said, officially placing Julian first in his life. "He can't come here as easily as I can go there. He'd have to give up everything where I have you to oversee things here."

Randy's lips pressed together as if he'd figured out a complicated math problem then nodded again. "That's why you've been pushing the new hires so hard. I wondered if it was something like that."

"Does my dad know yet?" Beckett asked.

Randy lifted a shoulder in a one-sided shrug. "He hasn't said anything to me, but I know he's got your back too. We'll make it work."

"I thought you might want to be a partner," Beckett said, jumping way ahead of himself. Not that he hadn't thought through it all. His brain was always working through any potential barriers or problems that might block him from achieving his goals. "You know me, I'm always thinking through how to make it work with Julian. To do that, I should probably be there more. I don't think he's the kind of guy to leave alone for long periods, but I won't ever fully leave here. You know that."

Randy's heavy palm landed on Beckett's shoulder, giving a gentle squeeze. "My advice is not to get too far ahead of yourself. What's supposed to happen will happen." Randy then used Beckett's shoulder as a crutch to help get to his feet, toppling Beckett and the rest of his coffee over. "You know I'm here when you want to talk, right? You listened to enough of my falling in love bullshit over the years."

The vulnerability that caused the layers of doubt to form began to ease as he shifted around to avoid the spilled liquid.

"Whistle for your dog," Randy said, taking the coffee cup. "We have to go inspect the gear. They're waiting on us."

Beckett whistled while shaking any lingering drips from his hand. Woofer had plopped down contentedly in the patch of wildflowers they allowed to grow freely on the property. The dog loved that spot and only lifted his head, trying to judge the seriousness of Beckett's command.

"He's smart and well trained."

Beckett whistled again and patted the side of his leg, not giving any explanation as to Woofer's training.

The darkness of the night sky let Julian know he'd put in another exceptionally long day. He balanced a to-go container in one hand and stuck a finger into the knot of his silk necktie, loosening its tight grip. His brain rattled in overload as the mounds of information he'd digested today ran like a loop inside his head.

The one thing he learned with all certainty, his tenure with Reservations had been a major pain in the ass for the old general manager. Julian's constant need to challenge the rules had created more work for the old GM than was necessary. He should have been fired and might carry some guilt if his desire for change wasn't the exact reason he'd been promoted in the first place.

An exhausted jaw-cracking yawn that he didn't fight against tore free as he walked the length of the crowded parking lot. Julian didn't know if Beckett had told the personal security guard that he knew about him. Still, every time Julian checked the cameras, he saw the sedan. The man had to be working around the clock to look after him—which Julian really did appreciate. So much so that he'd taken a minute to grill a fresh burger for the guy before he'd left tonight.

As Julian drew closer, he must have caught the guard's eye. Because he immediately ducked his head away, causing Julian to chuckle. Apparently, Beckett hadn't told the guy. Julian happily walked straight up to the car as the guy looked every which way, even turning his head toward the passenger side to avoid Julian who used his knuckles to rap on the driver's side window.

After a good long pregnant pause, the guy's shoulders slumped as he rolled down the window and looked up at Julian. "Can I help you?"

"Here," Julian said, shoving the to-go container through the window. "If you're going to sit here all day, the least I can do is feed you."

"I'm not sure what you're talking about." The deep masculine voice had Julian grinning. He almost sounded convincing.

"Yeah, you do. For the next three days, I have this same schedule. I'll commit to waiting for you before I drive home if you'll stop sitting out here all day." The guard opened his mouth, but no words came as his brow lowered and he took the to-go container. "The burger's medium well and the baked potato is loaded. What do you say to my suggestion?"

"How did you figure it out?" he said, putting the to-go container in the passenger seat.

How did he tell this guy that he had a big red target on his back? Of course, anyone with eyes could see what was going on. "I saw you yesterday morning. I keep one eye open these days. So what do you say?"

"I need to talk to Beck. He's paying, but I don't mind doing it that way," the guy said, reaching for his phone. "I have someone helping me. They're at your apartment now."

All right, he'd give the guard a point. He had only spotted one tail. Julian pulled his business card free and jotted his cell phone number on the back. "I appreciate what Beckett's doing, but it's overkill. I've been through enough that I take extra precautions, like the cameras pointed at you. Text me and we can work out a schedule. All I do is come to work and go home to sleep. I'm Julian by the way."

"I'm Marc." A big beefy hand stuck out the window. He took the card then reached out a hand again. Julian easily accepted the handshake.

"Nice to meet you." Julian turned away but pivoted back around. "If it turns out you're back tomorrow, come in the restaurant and wait."

Marc was a friend of Beckett's, which meant he was a friend to Julian too. Julian shook his head hard as he started back toward his car. What was happening to him?

CHAPTER 28

"Hang on!" Julian shouted into the other end of the line, causing Beckett to yank the satellite phone from his ear. The volume pierced his brain like a red-hot poker. He swore he heard an echo of Julian's voice bouncing around the mountaintop where he stood.

When the echo quieted, Beckett hesitantly brought the phone back to his ear. At the same time, he scanned the top of the mountain, searching for any threats before he put the shotgun he held in one hand at his feet and shrugged his backpack off each shoulder.

A steady beat of music played in the background of the call as Beckett dropped to his ass. He landed unceremoniously on the hard rock with a thump, not even caring about any discomfort he might have to deal with. The fatigue of the last few days had finally set in, catching up to him with a long wide-open yawn.

"Are you still there?" The music was muted in the background until he heard nothing more than Julian's sultry voice. Both Beckett's exhaustion and anxiousness eased as he concentrated on Julian's tenor that had a way of caressing his heart. Beckett had grown to relish the gentle squeeze in his chest that only Julian had a way of reaching.

"I am. You're at the club?" Beckett asked, letting his head drop back between his shoulder blades to look up at the million twinkling stars above.

"Yup," Julian started. "I stopped in after work for a drink and to check on Ricco. My apartment feels lonely without my dog and you there. You still in the mountains?"

"I am." A gentle breeze ruffled over Beckett, sending a refreshing note racing along his spine. "I don't like the sound of you being lonely."

"It's better now that you called. It's weird not talking to you. How's training going?"

Beckett nodded, feeling exactly the same way until Julian mentioned the training.

He rolled his eyes and reached for his backpack, dropping it a couple of feet away before he laid back on it. "These are harder training excursions because the guys are so alpha. There's a constant challenge by some member of the group over everything."

"Oh…" Julian cooed. "I'd like to see that battle with my own eyes. I bet my big ole teddy bear has his own alpha, testosterone-driven side." Julian's words dripped with suggestion, as if he were licking his lips in anticipation. "My money's on you. I've seen those big biceps flex."

Beckett gave a low rumbled laugh, thinking over how well Julian had already gotten to know him. He absolutely didn't like dominating anyone but had resigned himself a long time ago that sometimes he had to be the biggest ass in the group to make the others fall in line. A trait necessary when dealing with all these leader types of men and women. Being dropped in the middle of nowhere to survive on his own—even knowing these mountains like he did—wasn't a time for an ego to flair in anyone.

"Probably wouldn't be a bad bet on your part," Beckett finally said.

"Oh! Look at you. Does my gentleman have an ego he's hiding?" Julian quipped with all his usual sass and vinegar.

Beckett continued to chuckle, loving the way Julian teased him. "I come from parents who are very much their own people. I had to navigate their strong personalities while learning to hold my own when I needed to. Change of subject. It's really a clear sky tonight. There's a million stars for as far as I can see. It's beautiful. I wish you could see it."

This time when Julian spoke, he had a pensive tone to his voice. "I remember all the stars when I was a kid. I'd sneak out of my house and roam my entire town. It was always so dark, but the twinkle of the stars in that night sky lit my path, taking me wherever I was going. Then, when I got old enough, I'd take my parents' car. That didn't go over so well."

The normal cynicism Julian used when speaking about the struggles of his childhood wasn't there this time. He sounded ruminative, not aggravated, as if reliving a good memory.

Beckett didn't want to risk any sort of downward spiraling topic, so he changed course. "Here's something honest for me to say. I can't stop thinking about you. I swear to God, you're consuming me… I've been jonesing for the last few hours, trying to bide my time before I could climb this hill to call you."

"Mmm…" Julian murmured, growing unusually quiet. Dare Beckett hope Julian felt the same way about him? Could Julian be willing to say the same words aloud to him? "I've been fielding questions about you all night. The regulars want to know if we're dating and if it's exclusive. If I don't answer with a *yes* to both, then they want to know if they have a chance at you. If I wasn't so secure with myself, I might be jealous over all the attention you're getting."

Not really the declaration his heart had hoped for but still a really good answer. "How do you respond?"

Julian gave a *tsk* before saying, "I told them I'd like to see them try. And I would. You're hilarious when you're so nice to all these guys panting after you."

"Nobody pants after me," Beckett shot back, regretting the curve Julian took in the conversation.

Julian instantly gave a cackle of laughter. "That's the best part. You genuinely have no idea it's happening around you. You've only ever seen me, not all the beautiful men partying all around you."

A smile begrudgingly tugged at Beckett's lips. Julian's teasing was always so damn infectious. "What're you doing right now?"

"St. Clair, you crack me up."

Beckett could hear the crackle of soft leather as Julian continued.

"I just dropped my ass on the sofa in the office at the club. I'm tired. I could probably sleep for a week if given the chance, but when I try to sleep, I think about you and that silly dog, wondering if you two are snuggled up together while I'm alone in bed. You got in my head, Beckett."

"Mmm…" Oh yeah, there they went. The warmth that was all Julian roamed suggestively over his body as he thought of Julian in his bed. "I was thinking of flying back to Coronado Saturday afternoon. I couldn't stay more than a night."

"I'd like that. You're always welcome. Sundays are slower days at the restaurant. I'll have to be available for brunch, but that's all. The restaurant closes Sunday night," Julian said, making Beckett's heart stutter with hope.

"Maybe if I left in the middle of the night, like at three in the morning, I could stay all day Sunday."

"Or you could fly back Monday morning and pick your truck up the next weekend when you come back…" Julian countered.

Beckett closed his eyes, his small smile turning into something more content as the understanding of Julian's suggestion excited him. Julian wanted him there as much as Beckett wished to be there with him.

"I could do that." If he stayed two nights, it would cause a bit of a hardship for Randy. He'd have to carry the weight of the next training class again. Beckett should have some guilt, but he didn't. Not in the least.

"Is anyone around you?" Julian asked, his voice growing huskier with his next words. "Want to get off?"

Beckett's dick took instant notice, going from aroused to a hard and unyielding force in a matter of two seconds flat. Of course, he wanted Julian to help him rub one off, and he *was* quite a distance away from the rest of the camp. He couldn't be seen, even with the best nighttime equipment.

"Are you already touching yourself?" Julian purred.

"Are you?" he countered, working his belt free.

"I will be as soon as I get my pants out of the way," Julian answered.

"Same here," he chuckled, propping the phone on his chest so he could work his pants down far enough that nothing got in his way, consequences be damned. Beckett's dick was hard as stone and leaking by the time he got comfortable. The thrill of being out in the open and vulnerable made it all the more erotic. Beckett curled his fingers around his cock and gave himself a few eager tugs. "I'm stroking myself, Julian. I'm imagining it's your fist sliding up and down my cock."

"You're not as innocent as you pretend to be, are you, Mr. St. Clair?" Julian teased. "Unfortunately, we're hundreds of miles apart. Otherwise, it would be my mouth sliding down your shaft. I can almost taste you. Is that what you want? Me licking, sucking, and teasing every drop of come from your balls?"

Beckett groaned and tightened his grip. "God…yes, Julian. I'd like that." Fuck, he wanted everything Julian offered. He closed his eyes, thinking of Julian's mouth on him. Using his thumb, he made circles around the tip of his cock, spreading the moisture leaking from his slit as he applied the perfect amount of pressure.

"Oh, I guarantee you'd more than like it. I'd take you between my lips and swallow you down over and over until I had you begging to come," Julian growled.

"Yes…keep talking, Julian. Tell me more." With every pass of his fist, his pleasure grew. He imagined Julian's throat constricting around him. Julian's velvety tongue lapping at his cock. The soft strands of Julian's hair sliding between his fingers as he guided Julian's head with gentle pressure.

"I'd fondle your balls, first rolling them in my palms, teasing you, making sure to pay special attention to every inch of your skin with my tongue."

Beckett listened to the sexy cadence of Julian's husky voice. The cool night air swept across the mountainside, kissing his exposed skin. Beckett was so caught up in Julian, and in the heat of the moment, the world around him melted away. His heart raced, and his brain short-circuited with obscene desire as he clung onto Julian's every word.

"Then I'd get on my hands and knees for you, Beckett, spread my legs and finger my pretty pink hole while you watched. I'd beg you to fill me with that big thick cock of yours and you would." Julian's voice, low and breathy, had become its own aphrodisiac. "Mmm…you'd feel so fucking good in me."

"Yes," Beckett moaned and bit his bottom lip, speeding his strokes as he chased his pleasure. Spellbound by the scene playing out in his mind and the tone in Julian's voice.

"Fuck your fist, B. Pretend it's my ass squeezing you. Pound me hard and fast." Julian's lewd instructions sent a barrage of images flooding his brain. His body couldn't take much more. He was already so close to coming.

"Jesus fucking Christ, Julian." He thrust his hips, letting

Julian's words and his imagination carry him away. As his fist slid up and down his cock, fire rushed through his veins. His orgasm built with every word coming from Julian's filthy mouth.

"Give it all to me, B." Julian's breathy command had him groaning as he thrust faster into his fist.

"Harder, spread me open with your big cock. I'm so close. I want to come hard on your dick."

"Holy fuck." The hot friction of his fist and Julian's words had Beckett's muscles tensing as his balls drew tight against his body.

"Come for me, B. Let me hear my name on your lips." Julian's command, husky and raw, unleashed a torrent of animalistic desire pulsing through his veins.

"Julian," he cried out as the fire building in his core suddenly rushed to his balls with such force his toes curled inside his boots as his release slammed into him hard and fast. Hot jets of come shot across his stomach and chest. His body bowed off the ground as he continued to stroke his cock, lost in the vision of Julian filling his head.

Julian's breaths were heavy and coming faster. "Yes, Beck… *Augh*…" Julian groaned, long and deep, sending a wave of aftershocks throughout Beckett's body.

"Damn, that was…" Words refused to form in his head. He was so fucking blissed out he didn't give a shit that his team had probably heard him cry out and could be searching for him at that very moment. He didn't move. He couldn't. He just lay there, staring at the sky full of beautiful stars, enjoying the sound of Julian's breathing.

As come trailed into Julian's belly button, he realized he

hadn't given a thought to the consequences before getting them started. Julian looked down at his lower chest and stomach, both splattered in his come and nothing in reach to help wipe it away. He'd been too focused on Beckett to think things through, and now he was going to have to do some fancy maneuvering if he planned on keeping it off his clothes.

"I'm putting the phone down for a second."

"Me too. I didn't think this through before we started." The sated drawl in Beckett's voice slid over Julian, making him smile. He put the phone on the sofa's cushion and reached for the tissues on the coffee table, giving his best attempt at keeping his body concave to avoid any drippage.

He quickly swiped at the release on his belly. Lost in Beckett's urgent tone, he'd painted every direction of his chest. With no warning at all, the edges of his vision began to fade.

Fuck, not again. This time, he didn't lose complete sight of his surroundings. His belly became a screen for the projector of images in his head. Julian was covered in come, both wet and dried. Based on the sharp pain at his wrists and ankles, he'd been tied down. Memories filled his vision of a man's hand aggressively rubbing a scratchy cloth over his belly and chest. No, not a cloth. It was the ugly outdated bedspread under him.

Julian tried to catalog every detail about the full sleeve of tattoos covering the hand and arm in his field of vision. That was the first concrete memory of anything associated with his abductor. He tried to hold on to the memory. The come on his chest appeared to be from multiple directions. A fat cock shoved into his mouth. They'd used him. He recognized the memory of his own fear, the taste of it bitter in his mouth. By this point in the abduction, he'd feared for his own life. Floating in and out of consciousness provided his only relief from the dread of what would happen next.

Bile rose in his throat as he relived the moment. He'd opened his eyes to see a hard fist with a silver skull ring coming at his face, and darkness swallowed him again. Julian pushed at his memory, anxiously grasping for more details. He was blocked with nothing but blackness.

"You there?" Beckett asked, his voice muted by the placement of the phone.

"Just a minute," Julian called out, drawing in a deep breath. He finished cleaning himself while taking inventory of his body's reactions to the memory. Julian was taking them in easier, processing what he saw. Maybe he could focus on the tattoos, find something familiar that might generate a lead.

A deep sigh escaped his lips as he welcomed the possibility of finding the guy who had caused so much damage. If they could catch this guy, Julian would be free to walk around without fear, without looking over his shoulder at every unexpected noise.

"Babe, you there?" Beckett's voice held more concern this time. The seriousness in his tone made Julian pick up the phone.

"I'm here, but I made a mess. I gotta run downstairs," he said, tucking the hem of his dress shirt inside his slacks. His emotions were all over the place. He'd careened from one extreme to the other in a span of minutes. His gaze landed on the whiskey bottle at the wet bar. He needed a fucking drink, and he couldn't stand the thought of being alone right now. He wanted to go downstairs and lose himself to the relaxation of such a powerful release.

"You always get me off so fast," Beckett murmured, the sexy slur in his voice thickening and deepening those husky tones.

Julian understood Beckett's attempt to cuddle together by way of a phone call. Hell, as much as he wished Beckett was there, he wasn't. Julian pivoted around for the bar, needing that drink.

"Julian, I know I'm pushing, probably harder than I should, but you need to know I'm so fucking into you I can't think straight. I don't have to be here all the time. I'm training some new instructors next week. It'll free me up to just run the classes in Coronado. I could be there so we can see what this is between us."

Julian listened to the sweetly muttered declaration, Beckett laying out his intentions as if he didn't already know. Beckett recognized he stood at a crossroads in his life.

Julian could see a visual picture of Beckett's words. Him and Beckett building a long-lasting, monogamous relationship, and it didn't freak Julian out near as much as it should…until right then.

He stayed quiet as he poured himself a shot of the straight whiskey, tossing it back in one stinging swallow.

"I freaked you out…" Beckett said. "Forget I said anything."

Yeah, if only he could. Julian closed his eyes. What was happening to him? For years, all he'd wanted was to return to his old life. His heart leaped at his most basic desires. If he ever got the chance, he wouldn't squander his opportunity or fortune again.

There was no doubt Beckett had been responsible for Julian's progress on his road to recovery. No question Julian had also firmly attached himself to Beckett, but he was navigating two different roads. One, the respectable manager of a fine-dining restaurant and nightclub. That path made Julian equal to men like Beckett. They would be a great match. The other way had Julian ditching it all for his old life. The two paths that he let blur were beginning to come into focus. Julian couldn't be both men. At some point, when he was fully back to himself, would he need or want more than to run this restaurant? Would Beckett truly support his decision?

He wasn't ready to let go of his hopes and dreams, even with the reality of his scarred body telling him a different story. With time, Julian's self-destructive side would purposefully come out and ruin anything he'd built with Beckett. He was a reprobate at heart.

If he was half the man Beckett thought him to be, Julian would let Beckett go right now. Quit straddling the line, leading Beckett on—leading himself on.

The thought of Beckett's eventual rejection slashed over Julian's heart with such a stinging blow he'd looked down to see if there were blood pouring from the wound.

"Julian, I can hear you breathing. Let it go. It was the release talking." This time Beckett's tone held that alpha quality. Beckett hurt even now.

"No, it wasn't the release talking," Julian said, tucking his chin to his chest. His voice lowered to little more than a whisper. "Honestly. I'm torn. My head says I need to keep things light between us. My heart says something different. I don't know who I am anymore. I feel like I'm being torn apart from the inside out. All of it is so damn confusing. But I'm certain I know that I'm not a man worthy of you."

"Am I doing something to cause you to feel that way?" Beckett asked, his concern evident in each syllable uttered.

Julian gave a humorless laugh. "You're the whole reason I question everything now." He inhaled deeply and anchored the cell phone on his shoulder, holding it there while he poured another shot. "Look, I need whatever's happening to us to continue. You make me stronger. Let's not label it. Instead, let's go with it. I don't want to hurt you, and I've been honest with you; I'm not the man you think I am."

"You always doubt yourself," Beckett finally said, and maybe that was true. "And I think you doubt me. I don't want anything to change about you, Julian. I can face whatever comes, I promise. We can take it easy, go with the flow. I'm sorry I said anything."

The alcohol warmed his chest and dulled Julian's senses, exactly what he'd hoped would happen. With a shake of his head, Julian turned to the full-length mirror so he could check his appearance. He could smell his release and suspected other's might be able to as well. His own blue gaze stared back at him. Perhaps he was changing, maybe for the better. Who knew for sure?

"Goodnight, Beckett," Julian said, turning for the door. "Text me your flight plans. However you decide to fly, I'll pick you up at whatever airport."

"You good?" Beckett asked quietly.

He nodded as he said, "Goodnight. Be safe out there." Julian ended the call as he opened the office door, the music loud enough to dissolve his wayward thoughts as he trotted down the stairs.

CHAPTER 29

Luke Silva sat in an empty chair in Julian's office. His complete attention focused solely on the new iPhone in his hands. Luke had shown up unexpectedly this afternoon, about fifteen minutes ago, looking for food while the resort had housekeeping cleaning Thane's suite. The skinny kid had wolfed down the double-decker sandwich Julian had prepared and an entire midsize bag of potato chips in two minutes flat.

No matter how busy Julian was, he never minded Luke's interruptions. Right after Julian had met the Silva brothers, Luke had boldly declared Julian the coolest guy he'd ever met. Since Luke wasn't wrong, as Julian had tried to explain to an offended Thane, Julian had decided Luke was probably the coolest teenager he'd ever met before too.

That declaration also supported Julian's goal of living a life designed to give Thane the utmost hell. When Luke had innocently made his pronouncement, and in turn wounded Thane deeply, Julian and Luke had become fast friends. Well, not "friendly" friends. Julian regularly had to watch his mouth whenever Luke pinned himself to his side. It was such a challenge to keep his ready arsenal of snarky comebacks to himself.

Speaking of Thane…

"You're distracted and I have things to do. Can we end this call?" Julian had too much to do and didn't have the extra second to spare to have this corded landline telephone stuck to his ear while Thane spoke to everyone around him but Julian.

"Did Thane tell you about the bar he wants to buy in Baltimore?" Luke asked absently, drawing Julian's gaze to the dark-haired young man.

Julian continued to wait, now drumming the blunt tips of his freshly manicured fingernails on the desktop. "I think that might be what he's talking about. What club is it?"

Luke never looked up or stopped the movement of his thumbs as he played his game on the small screen. "Not sure. He was telling Levi about it last night. I think the owners turned him down, which makes Thane more competitive. You know all that."

Julian silently nodded. Thane had an enormous competitive drive, made far worse with words like *no*. Julian had to rack his brain, trying to understand why he might need to be involved in some random acquisition in the first place.

"Julian, listen to me. I've got to run." Thane's harsh tone insinuated Julian had somehow been the one creating the extended phone conversation. "Thomas Peterson's a member of the club. He has a reservation for next Tuesday night. You know him, right?"

All Julian could do was give a humorless shrug as one brow lifted and a shit-eating grin spread over his face.

"Yes, I know him," Julian finally replied, limiting his response. It seemed the simplest answer, especially with Luke in the room. Tom was a longtime client of Julian's who had seriously been giving Julian the eye his last few visits to the bar.

Did he know Thomas? *Pfft.* Intimately. Even down to the

small incision scar on his right ball sac. Julian also knew Thomas liked to bottom in public settings. Julian had had to fuck the shit out of the man at every gathering and gala they had ever attended together, while they both stayed utterly silent. If Thomas didn't have trouble walking afterward, then Julian hadn't done his job properly. Try being dominant while silence was paramount.

"Good. Peterson has a connection to Pat's Pub here in Baltimore. I want to make an offer on the place, and I can't get past the owner's son. I need Peterson to help pave my way in. I'll make it worth his while."

"Sure." Julian could most certainly make that happen for Thane. "What's the place?" He couldn't understand Thane's interest in a random business. There had to be more to that story.

"Remember a few years ago, maybe four, when you were in town and we went out. Remember we went to Pat's Pub?"

Julian had to squint under the strain he put his brain through while trying to remember one place through a sea of hot spots he had attended. "Maybe. Who owns it?"

"The Collins family. The patriarch, Pat, is retired, but he still holds court at the bar, and no one in the family will sell without his permission," Thane confirmed. "He's Irish through and through. It's an Irish pub and the attached restaurant is called Sunday's. I understand Peterson's friendly with Pat. What else do you need?"

Julian pushed back in his seat at such a dumb question. He didn't need anything. Thane had made the call and crashed Julian's day, not the other way around. "You called me, Papi."

A huff of breath hit the earpiece before Thane lectured, "I've asked you numerous times to stop calling me that, Julian. It's unprofessional…"

Honestly, Julian used the old endearment just to get underneath Thane's skin. If Thane would just realize Julian's tactics instead of getting all riled up, it would take the fun out of it and he'd maybe quit using the name. But alas, Thane started on his angry roll, making Julian smile as he rose to his feet, extending the landline telephone across the desk to Luke.

"He wants to talk to you," Julian whispered.

It took Luke a second to finish before he reached for the phone, never looking up from the screen. "Hey," Luke said.

No matter how hard Julian tried, he couldn't contain the laughter that welled inside him as he left the office, knowing Thane's head just exploded. Julian lived for giving Thane shit. He glanced down at his watch, making a mental note of his daily calendar. He had scheduled an impromptu counseling session to discuss two things. First, Beckett and this attachment Julian was beginning to feel for the man. Second, the ease with which Julian had handled last night's flashback.

Those were Julian's discussion topics. His counselor wanted to do a deep dive into the new details he'd learned about his abduction. Something resonated within Julian. He sensed the time crept closer for all the scattered memories to connect. He should probably ask about some coping techniques to help get him through what he learned when the pieces finally came crashing together.

The abduction felt personal. Julian's eyes narrowed as he stared down at the polished concrete while he headed out the door. He forced a sigh through his lips. What if his abductor was someone he knew? Someone still in his life today? How would all that go down?

Julian shook the anxiety-building thought from his head and focused on the good in his life. After the counseling appointment, he planned to head straight to the airport to pick up Beckett.

In an attempt to calm his frazzled nerves and make sense of the conflicting feelings surrounding him, Julian had gotten himself good and drunk last night. He rationalized that whatever was happening between him and Beckett was always going to be this way. This morning, between loads of Advil and hearty gulps of water to help hydrate his depleted body, his world with Beckett in the lead role had shifted forward once again.

He and Beckett both knew the score.

Julian had let himself be distracted all day long. Everything reminded him of the man. Reservations' new chocolate fountain had brought Beckett's brown stare to mind. The salty sea breeze between the restaurant and the hotel had Julian reminiscing about the handhold they had shared while walking along the beach with Beckett's laughter filling the night. He loved Beckett's laugh. Julian mentally prepared ways to make Beckett laugh.

He felt good actually. He was excited and couldn't wait for Beckett to arrive.

Beckett stood in front of the airport bathroom mirror, quickly working his fingers through his short strands, trying to make his hair look the best he could. He tapped away the seconds with his booted foot as he checked his teeth for anything lingering then did a breath test with the palm of his hand. The mints he'd been chopping on while leaving the plane had done their job. He leaned in closer to the mirror and slapped his cheeks, trying to lose some of the tired lurking under his eyes. His dry skin from his time spent in the sun and wind made the fatigue appear even more pronounced.

It was dusk outside. Julian wouldn't be able to see him well anyway. Beckett grabbed the leather duffle bag at his feet and tossed the strap over his shoulder as he started out of the bathroom, taking long strides toward the exit. His heart drummed with anticipation as the sliding glass doors opened on his approach. This over-the-top excitement about seeing Julian was hard to contain.

Beckett came to an abrupt halt just outside the double doors, scanning down the length of the waiting cars. He'd chosen to fly commercial in hopes of getting some shut eye on the flight, but the excitement of seeing Julian had ruined his chances at sleep. His heart picked up a beat, fluttering wildly when he saw Julian's beautiful smiling face and waving arms as he tried to garner his attention. Julian was double-parked, so Beckett jogged the few steps in Julian's direction.

Only now did Beckett allow himself to admit that last night had been hard on him. Worry had soured his mood all day, fear about having overstepped in a way that might push Julian away. He hadn't known what to expect when arriving tonight, but there Julian was, rounding the trunk, acting just as excited to get to him as he was to get to Julian.

As Beckett took the step off the curb, Julian came for him with open arms. Beckett barely had time to drop the bag to the pavement before Julian launched himself at Beckett. Julian wrapped his long arms around Beckett's neck as he leaped forward. Then he wrapped his legs tightly around Beckett's waist, locking them together. Julian's sweet lips found his as he pushed his tongue inside Beckett's mouth.

Oh man, was he all in. Beckett gripped Julian's thighs, pulling him snuggly against his body while sliding his tongue over Julian's. What a fucking greeting. The passion radiating from the kiss blew Beckett's mind. He was so lost the whistle piercing the air around them barely affected him as he kissed the shit out of Julian.

"Not doing this with you two again! Get *moving*!" The voice was close, and Julian broke away, making Beckett try to follow those lips, wanting to draw Julian back into the kiss. Screw whatever fine they may receive. He'd gladly pay it ten times over just to keep Julian in his arms.

Julian brought his palms to Beckett's cheeks, pushing his face back as Julian dropped his legs, severing contact as his body slid down Beckett's. "You're stronger than I thought. I wasn't sure you could hold me."

"I've always got you," Beckett murmured his truth and

finally let Julian lower his feet to the ground. "I really liked your greeting."

"I'm glad you're here." Julian beamed. "I spent the last hour talking to my counselor about you." He slapped Beckett's ass as he waggled his brows suggestively. "I've got plans for you tonight."

Fuck, Beckett's hard as stone cock liked the promise in Julian's tone. It took everything for Beckett to release Julian, and even then, he kept one arm wrapped around Julian's waist as he bent for the bag he'd dropped. "Plans I'm going to like?"

"Plans *I'm* going to like." Julian's laughter was infectious. Beckett gave a side eye as Julian pulled away and started for the driver's side door. Unable to hold Julian any longer, a sense of loss crashed over him. He never wanted to let go of Julian.

"Are you going to tell me?" Beckett said, moving to the passenger side, watching Julian open the driver's side door.

"You'll see." Julian nodded. "Get in so we can get there."

Beckett didn't have to be told twice. He dumped the bag in the backseat and jumped into his side of the car, ready to go wherever Julian took him.

CHAPTER 30

How did his small bathroom feel so damned cozy when Beckett was around? Perhaps because that big man with the terrific smelling cologne made it feel that way, staying within feet of Julian with every step he took.

Perhaps the warm feelings had more to do with the mad, passionate kisses he'd received over and again. Beckett had the science of romance down to a fine art. The fact that he did so unintentionally only added to his allure.

That invisible connection they shared had reasserted itself from the second they saw one another at the airport and had lasted through the night into today. Beckett had a special way of gently using his strong, calloused palm around Julian's bicep to give him a playful tug, forcing him against Beckett's hard chest. Fuck, the move made him feel wanted and desired—it made him feel loved and whole. It didn't matter where they were, the grocery store, the beach or even the quick run to The Home Depot Julian had made for the restaurant, Beckett's arm would lock around him then he'd be shamelessly kissed for the world to see.

A familiar thrill shot up Julian's spine at the audacity of such a bold move. Julian was a showman at heart and Beckett continually showed the world how he felt about him. Those sweet, soul-searing kisses made his toes curl and his naughty side leap to the forefront. They may have been the best kisses of his entire life.

Julian had demonstrated his appreciation while in the parking lot of the local hardware store. He had pushed Beckett back against the truck's seat and instructed Beckett to lift the steering wheel while Julian tore open Beckett's jeans. Julian had sucked the frantic, uncertain man off right there for anyone to see.

Beckett did finally give in to the moment, tangling his fingers in Julian's hair and rolling his hips, shoving that hard cock further down Julian's throat. In the end, Julian had teased Beckett until his sweet blush had come from his certainty that they had been seen, not from the extraordinary blow job he had given.

Whatever the cause, the heat had stained those bright cheeks for the entirety of their trip home. Julian had been struck with an overwhelming boost of confidence since then, both proud of his actions and of the man who had chosen to stay by his side.

It sure hadn't been a hardship to have Beckett lingering nearby. Not by a longshot. His Marlboro Man was just so damn endearing. Beckett was a natural gentleman through and through. Maybe more so than any other man Julian had ever known.

Julian reached for the bottle of wine chilling in a bucket on top of his bathroom vanity as Beckett's heavy palm circled around Julian's waist. "I look silly."

That chocolate stare boring a hole through Julian had him chuckling as he topped off his glass of wine. "I wouldn't say silly…" Julian teased, turning between the sink and the chair he had pushed inside the bathroom to give Beckett a facial. "Okay, I'm not a liar. You look a tiny bit silly, but it doesn't matter. You're destroying your skin. No wonder we thought you were older than you are, Mr. Marlboro Man."

Beckett gave an irritated shake of his head and tried to arch a brow. The tight multi-purpose hydrating facial mask Julian had applied to Beckett's skin made it hard for Beckett to do anything more than look super passive, which cracked Julian up too. "My survival camp isn't a resort. Sunscreen doesn't just fall from the sky."

"Obviously…" Julian shot back without missing a beat then took three long gulps of the wine, draining the glass. When he turned away, reaching for the wine bottle again, Beckett caressed a trail up the outside seam of Julian's shorts, his only garment at the moment. How long had it been since he had willingly and comfortably shown this much skin around another man?

The always ready tingles zipped along the path Beckett made as both his firm hands circled Julian's thighs, right underneath the hem on Julian's shorts. His heart did little flips and flops in his chest with each stroke of Beckett's teasing thumb. Julian reached for the wine bottle, filling his glass again as his cock plumped under the tantalizing rub.

The timer buzzed, and the moment vanished. Beckett dropped his hold and stood, making the small space in Julian's bathroom even smaller. His guy wasn't into being pampered. He'd only gone along with the idea of a facial because Julian had insisted. Beckett grabbed the hand towel and reached around Julian to turn the faucet on, warming the water.

"Hey now. Calm down. It's not a race," Julian teased, trying to shimmy to the side out of Beckett's way.

Beckett's eyes twinkled with a sharp look aimed at Julian. He should have been prepared. Julian was the playful one between the two of them, but he wasn't ready when Beckett busted a move by snaking out an arm, circling Julian's waist. Their bodies locked together. Julian's wine sloshed out of the glass, leaving a trail running down their chests.

"You like it so much, you wear it." Beckett bent to mash the gooey, drying mess on Julian's cheek. He squealed and fought to get away. Beckett's strength kept him wedged right there between the sink's counter and Beckett's powerful body. Yet Julian experienced no fear at the forced confinement. In the few seconds of Beckett making a mess on Julian's face, excitement pumped through his veins as he dumped the rest of his wine in the sink to use both hands on Beckett's chest to keep him at bay.

The last thing Julian wanted was to push Beckett away. His palms rested against the warm skin of Beckett's expansive chest. Everything seemed to settle as Beckett's beautiful face lifted inches away from his. Beckett's genuine grin made him look as if he were the happiest man in the world to be in this tiny bathroom, roughhousing with Julian.

"You sure look proud of yourself," Julian murmured, feigning a small degree of frustration. It only made Beckett's grin brighter before he turned away, letting Julian go so completely that he stumbled backward against the counter.

Julian's decision cemented in that moment. Made even better because Beckett had no idea what was about to hit him.

Beckett aggressively scrubbed the hand towel over his face, knocking water droplets this way and that as Julian reached for a hand towel. His face still dripping water, Beckett stepped aside, giving Julian room at the sink while reaching for a dry towel. His considerate guy dried his face then draped it over Julian's head with a laugh.

"Are we done in here?" Beckett asked.

"Not by a long shot," Julian muttered, tugging the towel off his head so he could continue cleaning his face. He nodded his chin toward the chair while he hung the towel on a nearby hook, and he reached for the moisturizer. "Take a seat. I'm beginning to think you don't appreciate my efforts."

Beckett sat, using both his hands to grip Julian's hips, drawing him down to straddle Beckett's thick thighs as he took the seat. Julian let it all happen. It was where he wanted to be. He wiggled on Beckett's lap then squirted a liberal amount of the lotion onto his open palm.

"We've got to really spend some time working on your skin to stop the aging. Otherwise, someone might think you're my daddy."

"I'll show you daddy." Beckett's barked reply told Julian he had hit the mark and rubbed his hands together before bringing them to Beckett's cheeks.

"Yeah, promises, promises…" The astute Beckett picked up on the subtle offer in his voice. Beckett's gaze collided with his as he worked the moisturizer against the fresh, pink skin. No one in their right mind would ever think of Beckett as old.

Julian tucked his bottom lip between his teeth as teasing fingers edged underneath the hem of Julian's shorts. Beckett tentatively caressed and roamed his hands the tops of Julian's thighs, always moving slowly and methodically.

As his heavy palms explored, Beckett's moves grew bolder until they trailed a seductive line up Julian's hard cock, trapped behind the material of his shorts. Julian's lotion-covered hands fell to Beckett's pecs as his breathing shallowed with excitement.

It only took a single touch from Beckett to cause Julian's cock to weep with need. Their gazes stayed glued to one another. A wicked smile tugged at Julian's lips. Beckett removed his hands to push the elastic waistband of Julian's athletic shorts down to free his straining length. When Beckett released his own hard cock, Julian involuntarily rolled his hips, shoving his cock forward as Beckett gripped them both together.

Beckett's touch felt so damned good. Julian drew in a slow, steady breath, absorbing his body's crazy visceral reaction to this man. Beckett guided Julian's hands down, scooping at any remaining lotion to smooth down the length of their cocks. Beckett gave a firm tug that practically curled his toes. Pleasure took control of Julian's body, forcing him to roll his hips again. Julian was a visual guy. He loved watching almost as much as he loved participating. He fought to watch Beckett work them together, but that calloused palm sliding up and down his dick felt too fucking amazing, and his eyes closed under the pleasure.

"I want to make you feel good, Julian," Beckett cooed in a soothing, seductive voice.

The overload of feels happened all at once. Beckett, the seducer, jacked them off with a steady purpose.

Man, he really liked when Beckett took matters into his own hands—literally.

"You good with this?" Beckett asked, using the arm around Julian's back to encourage Julian closer, their hips fusing together as they moved in unison. Julian draped his arm casually over Beckett's shoulders, his hips moving back and forth.

"Oh yeah," Julian responded, closing his eyes, letting his head drop between his shoulders. Reality vanished. Beckett took every inch of Julian's headspace, silencing the crowded thoughts always plaguing Julian's sanity.

He slid his fingers wantonly into Beckett's silky hair, tightening them as Beckett leaned in and those warm lips pressed against Julian's neck.

"I don't want to push you into something you're not ready for." Beckett's tone had Julian prying open his eyes, staring at the man through the small slits he'd managed.

The chaos of Julian's life had settled into a blissful peace from the second he'd spotted Beckett at the airport. Julian felt empowered and sure of himself. He also felt so damn safe. He continued to roll his hips, letting Beckett keep him aroused as he questioned his own intentions one last time.

Was he truly ready?

Oh yeah. Way past fucking ready.

Beckett's kind nature and firm, gentle steadiness would do Julian right, and if Julian said stop, Beckett would, no questions asked. There was literally no risk for Julian to try this last step in bringing himself back.

He hadn't needed the liquid courage buzzing through his head right now. He was ready.

Julian tightened his hold, giving a tug to the short hairs on the back of Beckett's head. He stared at his lover as he said, "I want you to fuck me, Beck." Julian's voice was sexy, strong, and assured, showing Beckett exactly how he felt on the inside. "Something gentle and easy and everything my Marlboro Man has shown himself to be…"

Beckett's Adam's apple bobbed. The only readable sign Beckett had given, showing he was ready for the job.

"Show me how much I mean to you."

Beckett parted his lips before closing them again. His hand on their cocks came to a stop, but the tight grip on their dicks remained. Beckett's sudden show of indecision reaffirmed Julian's choice in partner to help him get his life back together.

Julian lifted his fingertips to Beckett's cheeks, his palms encasing Beckett's firm jaw. They were inches apart as he stared directly into Beckett's uncertain gaze. He spoke a truth he hadn't let himself consider before this moment. "I can't get to where you are emotionally about us until I tackle my insecurities. This isn't just about sex. We care about each other. I feel something different with you, and I know I'm safe with you. I trust you, Beckett. I want you. I want to explore what this is between us. Make love to me. Say *yes*."

CHAPTER 31

"Julian…" Beckett said seconds before firm, sexy lips captured his. Beckett stood, taking Julian up with him. Beckett's scent and masculinity surrounded him. Those strong muscles accepted his weight with ease. Julian wrapped his legs around Beckett's hips, grinding himself against the man as Beckett carried him to the bed then slowly lowered him to the soft cool bedding.

"I want you so fucking bad, Julian." Beckett tugged Julian's shorts down his legs. Those gorgeous dark eyes never left his. He stretched out naked against the comforter and crooked his finger, enticing Beckett to join him. He spread his legs and took hold of his throbbing cock, stroking to ease the need coiling in his balls.

"Damn, Julian, I swear you're going to make me come if you don't stop looking at me like that."

"Isn't that the goal? Lose the shorts and join me, B," Julian purred, running his finger around the tip of his leaking cock, spreading the wetness with the pad of his finger. The immediate tremble that shook Beckett's body as the words left Julian's mouth had him licking the pre-come from his finger just to taunt the man. He was feeling more like himself with Beckett than he had in an exceedingly long time, and he had no intention of scaling back his desire.

He'd convinced himself he'd never have these feelings again. He had even tried to fool himself into believing he didn't need them. He'd been wrong. Heat infused with raw need rushed through his body and had his dick leaking like a dripping faucet on his stomach.

Beckett's gorgeous dick jutted out from his body, hard and thick. His mouth watered to taste Beckett. More than that, he wanted to feel every inch of that wet-tipped cock inside of him.

He watched with bated breath as Beckett pushed his own shorts completely down his legs, stepping out of them as he inched forward.

"That's more like it," Julian praised as he took in the beauty of the man in front of him. Reaching out, he teased a finger along the side of Beckett's engorged cock.

Beckett was a dream, a mix of naughty and nice. Rugged and refined, honest, kind, celestial, and carnal. Everything about Beckett was a huge turn-on. "I know I told you to take it slow. I've changed my mind. I don't want to wait." Anything to quench the need coursing through his veins. It had been too long. Way too long.

"We can skip right to the sweaty part," Julian teased as he rolled to his stomach and crawled toward the middle of the bed. A hand on his ankle stopped him. Beckett easily pulled him back.

"Not so fast," Beckett growled, sending tingles along his spine. God, he loved that commanding tone. He slowly turned, allowing Beckett to pull him toward the edge of the bed. Beckett placed a knee between his thighs. "There's no need to rush it; I'm going to take care of you, Julian."

He gave Beckett a soft smile as he reached up and ran his

fingers across Beckett's full lips. "Yeah, I want that. I want it so much, Beckett."

Beckett's mouth crashed against his in a claiming kiss that caught Julian off guard and sent an excited thrill rushing down his spine. The soft mattress cradled him as Beckett's weight settled on top. Julian lifted his hips, grinding them into Beckett as they kissed. He grasped Beckett's firm shoulders as Beckett's tongue moved against his in a dance of sweet exploration. God, he might come from the friction alone. Beckett deepened their kiss, his hand moving to Julian's jaw, keeping him firmly in place. Julian moaned into Beckett's mouth, overtaken by a flood of new and compelling feelings—devotion and reverence all mingled together.

The kiss had his head spinning and his body on the verge of exploding from the electricity arcing between them. Never had he ever experienced such an overwhelming flood of desire racing through his veins from a kiss alone. He thrust his hips, seeking some kind of resistance to tame the ache in his balls. Beckett's strong fingers circled his cock and squeezed.

"*Mmmm*, so fucking hard. I know exactly what you need." Beckett's warm breath teased his skin as Beckett's mouth moved down the line of his neck as he spoke. Julian sucked in a breath and shut his eyes when Beckett licked a wet trail across his collarbone. Yes, he could get used to being worshipped by this man. His Marlboro Man was right… They didn't need to rush.

Julian pushed up into Beckett's firm grip and reveled in the tightness as Beckett stroked him slowly. The flick of Beckett's tongue across his nipple had Julian sliding his fingers into Beckett's hair, holding him right there against his chest. Beckett's teeth scraped over that nub, sending a jolt of electricity straight to his balls and sparkles of lights flashing behind his closed lids.

"More," he begged.

"In time… Been dreaming about this since I first saw you." Beckett chuckled as he kissed a trail down Julian's stomach before pressing warm kisses over his hip bone. The grip on his dick flexed just before Beckett's warm lips slid over Julian, drawing a moan from his throat. Hot wet heat burned along his shaft as Beckett swallowed him down. He squeezed his eyes together and tightened his fingers in Beckett's thick hair to urge him on. He never wanted this feeling to end as he thrust into Beckett's welcoming mouth.

"God, so fucking good," Julian groaned and twisted his fingers against Beckett's scalp. Beckett's throat constricted around him. Intense pleasure built with every dip and bob of Beckett's head. "I want you in me."

Beckett lifted his gaze. Desire swam in the deep whiskey stare as he licked up the length of his cock.

"And I want to be in you," Beckett whispered. He slid strong hands under Julian's thighs and guided his knees to his chest. "I'm gonna get you ready."

Julian was helpless to protest when Beckett's tongue circled his hole, and he was transported to nirvana.

Beckett held his legs with one hand while exploring and caressing Julian's balls with the other. Then his fingers joined that clever tongue, teasing and coaxing pleasure-filled moans from Julian's lips. Beckett's thick finger moved in him, making him quiver and squirm. He was more than ready.

"Please, now, I need you." Julian all but begged as Beckett continued driving him wild. "Condoms and lube are in the nightstand."

"Has anyone ever mentioned you're a little bit bossy?" Beckett murmured and placed a few soft kisses along the inside of his thigh then released his legs, reached over and grabbed a condom and lube from the bedside drawer. Julian scooted to the middle of the bed, making room for Beckett. Beckett joined him quickly, tearing the foil packet with his teeth as he settled on his knees between Julian's spread thighs.

He bit his lip in anticipation, watching as Beckett rolled the condom down his length then drizzled lube on his fingers and cock. Need coursed through his veins. The sight had him on the verge of crawling out of his skin, primed for Beckett to touch him again. If he wasn't careful, he could easily become addicted to this gorgeous man. He closed his eyes, hoping to get some kind of control over his feelings in this moment. There was so much to sort through in his head.

"Look at me, Julian." Beckett's words pulled him to the present, and he slowly opened his eyes. "Are you okay?" Concern filled Beckett's dark stare.

At first, the question confused Julian. It must have shown on his face.

"We don't have to…" Beckett started to pull back.

"I want this." Quick reassurance tumbled from Julian's lips. Beckett's fucking sexy thoughtfulness ignited his yearning, making it burn hotter. "Stop talking and make me come," Julian teased, trying to lighten the mood, to show how ready he was. Then he reached up, taking Beckett's face between his palms. "I'm more than okay." He pulled Beckett to him. Their lips met as Beckett settled between his thighs.

Julian licked into Beckett's mouth, taking time to savor every sweet flick of Beckett's tongue against his. The kiss grew hot and heavy, his mind spinning from the deep connection drawing them together. Beckett's mouth was so sure and demanding against his own. Julian slid his hands down Beckett's strong back.

"Fuck me."

"I love your filthy mouth." Beckett nipped at his lips, sliding those long fingers along the crevice of Julian's ass, driving him mad with need.

Julian lifted his hips, eager for Beckett to quench the fire raging in his balls. He moaned as Beckett dipped a finger inside him, teasing him mercilessly before another joined.

"Love how warm and tight you are. I want to feel all this heat wrapped around my dick." Beckett added a third finger, pumping the digits in and out of Julian's body a few times before pulling free and adjusting his position.

Julian drew his legs up toward his chest. His body vibrated with anticipation as the blunt head of Beckett's cock dragged up his crack then pressed at his entrance. He looked up to find Beckett's eyes on him. Watching. The tip of Beckett's cock breached him, sliding deeper and deeper, stretching and filling him as he lost himself in that intense dark gaze. He blew out a breath and reveled in the fullness.

"Ahh, yess…" Julian trembled with pent-up emotions. The pressure along his passage bordered on that sweet spot between pain and pleasure in such a decadent way. He'd always loved the sensation of being entered. His toes curled from the intense pleasure of it all. Beckett didn't move. He remained frozen, his eyes boring into him as if waiting for some signal.

"Are you okay?" Beckett asked, his voice raw with such concern Julian was caught off guard. It was rare to have someone so interested in his well-being, especially where sex was involved.

"More than." He bit his lip and grinned up at the beautiful man. The tension coiling in the muscles under his palms eased. He couldn't be certain the tremble running along Beckett's body was from straining to hold back or relief at his words. Julian reached up to stroke his cheek, hoping to reassure him.

Beckett kissed his palm and drew back. That uncertain stare remained locked on his as he glided in and out of his body. That thick cock dragged along every nerve ending in his ass, setting his body on fire.

"I don't ever want to hurt you, Julian." Beckett lowered his head and pressed a tender kiss against his lips.

"I'm so fucking good. You feel amazing, and I want more."

A sly smile slid across Beckett's lips as he slowly sank into him then pulled back and thrust forward again. Julian dropped his head back against the pillow, and Beckett followed him down, his kiss demanding and deep. He groaned into Beckett's mouth as his pleasure soared higher and higher. He wrapped his legs around Beckett and gripped his shoulders before drawing his nails down Beckett's back, taking everything the man offered.

Beckett nipped his lips and canted his hips, his thrusts growing faster. His cock hit that perfect spot every time his hips slid forward. Those fucking powerful hips rolled into him over and over with maddening precision.

"Yes, Beck… right there. Don't stop. I'm close." He untangled his legs from Beckett's waist, dropping his feet to the mattress, taking everything his lover gave him. Beckett buried his head in Julian's neck and changed the pace of his strokes, sending tingles scattering throughout Julian's body. Short, teasing strokes then long, slow ones left him gasping from the intensity. He clenched the muscles in his ass and pushed against the cock inside him.

"So good, Julian. I never want this to end." Beckett panted against his ear. That hot breath igniting sparks along his spine.

Julian rolled his hips in response, holding on to Beckett's shoulders as the sound of their bodies meeting filled the room. Completely at his Marlboro Man's mercy, then Beckett's hips sped up and stole the oxygen from his lungs. Beckett felt so good inside of him. If he died right now, it wouldn't matter. He'd already had a taste of heaven. Julian didn't attempt to slow the orgasm racing to the surface. He surrendered to the bliss.

Sliding his hands into the man's thick hair, he let his fingers tangle in the silky strands as he tugged Beckett's lips to his. Beckett's tongue invaded his mouth like the man invaded his soul, and he was helpless to stop it. The kiss deepened, and Beckett's thrusts grew more demanding. With every push, Beckett was claiming him, inserting himself firmly in Julian's heart.

"Please," Julian begged, "I need…"

"Shhh. I've got you." Beckett shifted his weight and wrapped a rough, warm palm around Julian's cock then stroked in time with his thrusts.

"*Yes*… Fuck me." Julian sank his fingers into the firm globes of Beckett's ass, trying to force him deeper. But Beckett never lost rhythm as he plunged in and out of Julian's body.

Their breaths mingled and their moans peppered the air as Beckett fucked him right to the edge. The waves of ecstasy built deep in his body as intense heat raced down his spine and licked at his balls, drawing them to his body.

"Harder, B, I'm…" were the only words he could manage. It didn't matter to Julian if it was the hand on his cock or the cock in his ass. He just needed it harder and faster.

"Come for me, baby." Beckett tightened his grip and snapped his hips against him, hitting that delicious bundle of nerves deep in his ass with every movement. He continued driving into him with a look of such devotion staring down at him. Beckett saw deep down into his soul. Julian let himself be swept away with that knowledge. This man saw the real him.

"Beckett," he cried out, squeezing his eyes shut as pleasure racked his body. His release slammed into him with such a force it bowed his body and left him spasming in sweet oblivion. His come coated Beckett's fist and his stomach as he succumbed to the rapture.

"That's it. Feels so good, Julian." Beckett panted, dropping his forehead to Julian's as he continued fucking him through his orgasm. His hips slowed, and his movements faltered. "So, fucking good, Julian." Beckett's dick twitched hard in his ass, drawing one last shudder from his overstimulated body. He held on tightly, clinging to him as his breathing slowed and the tension left his muscles.

Beckett pressed his mouth against Julian's lips in a soft, sweet kiss. A tender sampling of lips as their tongues slid together in a slow and deliberate dance. There were no words to describe the feeling bubbling up in Julian's soul. He'd never felt lighter, even with the weight of his Marlboro Man pushing him down.

Beckett pulled back from the kiss and stared down at him. "You're amazing. That was more than I'd ever dreamed it could be."

Julian smiled at the raw honesty hidden behind those words. He agreed it was more too. The connection and their chemistry were so off the charts it messed with his head even now. Could there be something more in the future? He pushed the wayward thoughts aside when Beckett lifted off him, that delightful weight leaving him.

He had to stop himself from protesting as Beckett slowly withdrew his softening dick and rolled to his side, gathering Julian in his arms and settling him against his thick chest. Instead of saying anything, he snuggled into Beckett, enjoying the tenderness of the moment. He lay in Beckett's arms with come drying on his stomach as Beckett's fingers caressed his skin.

"Are you sure you're okay?" Beckett's chest vibrated as he spoke, drawing Julian's attention.

Yeah. No. Maybe. Hell, he didn't know if he'd ever be okay again after tonight. He couldn't force himself to think about anything besides the comfort of Beckett's embrace.

"I'm not freaking out. No flashbacks, if that's what you mean. I'm more than okay. Well, other than the come drying on my stomach, I'm great."

"Yep, we forgot the towel. And I need to get rid of this condom. Hold on." The warmth against his back disappeared as the mattress dipped and Beckett stood from the bed.

Julian rolled over, watching that perfect ass flex as he walked to the bathroom. That man had an ass for days. His cock stirred at the thought of a second round. He would love to have Beckett as a client. When Beckett disappeared behind the door, Julian flopped to his back and sighed. What was he thinking? What was the deal with his emotions? Why was he so conflicted over wanting his old life back?

"I hope that look on your face doesn't have anything to do with my performance." Beckett's smile faded as he dropped down on the bed and wiped the warm wet towel across Julian's stomach.

"Your performance definitely received a standing ovation, and I'm hoping for an encore," he said quickly, slipping back behind the veneer of his old life. He would find his answers soon enough. Right now was a time for basking in the energetic end of such a long dry spell.

CHAPTER 32

The crown molding and crystal chandelier grandeur of the Georgian-style villa fit Julian to a tee. The early morning view of the bay from the third story balcony attached to the main bedroom did speak to Beckett's soul. He liked the scenery, envisioning breakfasts on the terrace with his love while watching the sun rise, but nothing else about the place attracted him. Beckett turned back to the gorgeous bedroom as he scanned the custom-made furnishings.

"It's not for you?" Brigit Dougherty, the realtor Beckett had hired and worked sleuth-like with, asked from the entry into the room. He could hear the disappointment in her voice as the planner in her hands slapped decidedly closed and her arms gathered at her chest.

"It fits one of us." Beckett shoved his hands in the front pockets of his slacks as he stepped fully back inside the room.

So many doubts plagued Beckett even as everything vibing

off Julian pointed toward the commitment Beckett was ready to make. He desperately wanted their happily ever after. A relationship so strong, nothing could break them apart. Only then would he truly be content.

Thinking along those lines reaffirmed his decision to find a place that would please them both. Images from the last twenty-four hours flipped like snapshots in his head. In action, Julian had given Beckett everything he wanted, but Julian hadn't said those three little words. It didn't truly matter; they both had recognized the magic they had shared when together. The sweet way Julian had clung to Beckett after sex… Fuck, Julian had a way of making Beckett feel special.

More than any other desire coursing through him, he wanted to care for Julian for the rest of his life.

Julian had to know that Beckett would bind them together if ever given the chance.

Maybe that was why Julian chose Beckett to be his first lover since the incident.

"Okay, I see you're really thinking about it," the realtor said. "I have one more listing for you to see. And I honestly believe it's the best suited for you." Brigit looked down at her watch then pivoted on her heels. "It's almost seven thirty. The next property should be available for a walk-through. The family wanted to wait until they left for work." She stepped toward the ornate stairwell. "After all the places we've seen this morning, I think 64 Spinnaker Way may be the one. It's a corner property with a gorgeous water view and has private access to a boat dock. It's a three-bedroom, two-bath, with a private patio that comes beautifully landscaped and a nice size swimming pool…"

Beckett stood at the railing, looking down over the spiral stairwell as she made her way to the front foyer. The elevator behind him was a nice touch to the house, but Beckett couldn't help thinking about himself. He'd feel caged in if he had to live there. Locked behind closed doors with Julian was one thing. A quite different story if he ended up living here alone.

If that happened, he'd have to sell the place.

Beckett turned around again, taking in everything about the fine home. It was so damn sophisticated. Most of the third floor was dedicated to the main bedroom. Julian's furniture would work well here.

His phone vibrated in his back pocket. He pulled it free; Julian's sleepy face filled the screen. Beckett swiped a thumb over the display, already lost in his handsome guy. "You're supposed to be asleep. Why are you awake?"

"My alarm went off…" Julian said, yawning as he fell back on the stack of pillows, bringing the phone with him. "To take you to the airport. Guess what? You snuck out and left me sleeping."

Beckett nodded with a small smile. "I left a note on my pillow. I thought we were using my phone alarm."

"Yeah. I didn't trust it. Are you at the airport? Is the flight delayed?" Julian asked, rubbing his eye. His flight home didn't depart until nine thirty this morning. That had been Beckett's deception. He didn't want to freak Julian out after the whole mountaintop confessions catastrophe.

"Yeah, something like that. I wanted you to sleep. You were up all night," Beckett said, his heart taking in Julian's bed head and thicker stubble. Every side of Julian was always so damn beautiful.

"Up with you. You have to be exhausted." Julian's eyes narrowed, and he brought the phone closer to his face. "Is that a dome?" Beckett hadn't really considered his surroundings when he'd answered. He looked up at the gorgeous stained-glass dome overhead. "Are you in a church?"

Beckett chuckled as he turned back to the phone, bringing it closer to his face to block anything else out. "No, definitely not a church." He wasn't sure he'd ever been inside a real church before.

"Beckett, are you coming?" Brigit called up to him, but Julian didn't seem to hear her. His hesitant smile grew as Julian's confusion furrowed his brow.

"What are you doing?" Julian asked.

"I'll tell you later. I gotta go. I'll text you when I land." Beckett nodded at Julian, trying hard to get Julian to just go along with it.

"*Okay...*" Julian hedged, and after another long skeptical pause, his face morphed from speculation to resolve. The image on his screen shifted as Julian turned the phone down the length of his nude body. "I planned for you to take care of this before you left. The big guy's gonna be frustrated if it has to stay like this until next weekend."

Beckett did the one thing he probably shouldn't have done; he quickly clicked the buttons on the phone to save a screenshot. He'd save the photo in his most private spot and tell Julian what he'd done later, when he had more time.

"Keep it just like that. I'll be back late next Saturday."

Julian chuckled and fisted his cock. "Talk to me, babe. I'll be fast."

Oh God... The high heels clicking on the steps heading his direction sent panic scampering through his stomach.

"Beckett?" Brigit asked a little louder.

Julian's phone jerked back to his face, giving a critical lift of one brow. "Is that a chick calling you?"

Beckett only had moments before the realtor could hear his phone conversation. He pointed a stern finger at the phone, attempting to dominate Julian. "You keep that for me. I'll take care of it when I call you back in about an hour."

"Yeah right," Julian hissed then cackled. "You have a lot to explain, mister."

They stared at one another for several seconds as the heels clicking on the steps grew louder. Just before she reached him, Beckett lifted a hand in a wave. "Bye."

"Bye, my Marlboro Man." Julian was the one to end the call with a wink and a press of the finger.

Clearly, Julian wasn't the jealous or prying kind. Beckett shoved the phone back in his pocket and started down the stairs, meeting the realtor as he went.

"I'm sorry. I had a business call. Let's go look at the last property. I need to get to the airport sooner than I planned." Another lie rolled off his lips as he took the steps down two at a time, leaving her to follow. Thanks to Julian, his cock was fucking hard as stone now too. If there was any way to squeak in a quick rub for both he and Julian, he needed to figure it out.

For the first time in a long time, Julian felt like he had his groove back. The club's Monday night attendance had always been weirdly high.

Many months ago, they had decided to turn Monday night into theme night for both the restaurant and the nightclub. It was the only time the restaurant ever let loose of its strict dress code. Mondays had taken on a cult-like following for the regulars, taking on a life of its own. Tonight was disco night. Donna Summer belted out a fun tune that had Julian shuffling his feet, dancing to the music before he ever reached the employee entrance door.

Julian's groove had come with the idea of doing a quick stop by his storage unit to find his iconic Travolta-esque polyester white dance suit. Of course, he had coupled the outfit with a black silk dress shirt.

Throughout the day, Thane had reminded him to have that conversation with Thomas. He wished he could remember Pat's Pub. He'd have that discussion then spend the rest of the night on the dance floor, living his life carefree and easygoing. He planned to drink freely and have the time of his life, all at Reservations' expense.

Honestly, there was no doubt about it, Julian was a changed man. So much so that he'd teasingly kept Beckett on a thin line all day. It hadn't taken him long to figure out that Beckett had been looking at new homes this morning. His sly guy had chosen the well-known landmark home that had been on the market for way too long. The one with the gorgeous dome that had given away his location immediately. The owners had put it up for sale with a crazy expensive price tag. But Julian hadn't let on that he'd figured it all out. Instead, he toyed with Beckett, making him squirm and forcing him to ride the lie. It was hilarious for Julian because Beckett was shit at lying.

Once inside the nightclub, Julian finally answered Beckett's last text message. His grin couldn't have grown any bigger. Beckett had sent him four additional messages since the last time Julian had responded over two hours ago. In that last text message, he'd questioned the real reason Beckett had left him sleeping. He'd implied that perhaps Beckett had snuck off to go see a woman. It tickled Julian so much he laughed as he read all of Beckett's responses.

"Julian. Of course, I didn't leave you sleeping to slip out and see a woman. We had a busy weekend. You barely slept a wink. I didn't want to put you out."

One hour later: *"Julian, don't be mad. Answer me."*

Thirty minutes after that: *"Our calendars are still linked. You aren't in a meeting. Answer me."*

Then twenty minutes later, which was also seconds ago: *"Okay. I met a realtor early this morning to look at a place more permanent for me. I didn't want to freak you out or make it seem like I was pushing you or us in a direction. I believe it would be more cost efficient to buy a place rather than stay at Escape. My company's contract has me there in training classes many times over the next year. It makes sense to buy. I'm sorry I lied."*

The three dots started drumming in the corner of the message, making Julian wait to see what more Beckett might have to confess. *"Of course, you can stay at the new place whenever you want. I had you in mind everywhere I went this morning. It wouldn't just be my place unless you didn't want to be there with me, then no harm, no foul."*

Those three dots continued blinking. *"I'm not suggesting we move in together unless you want to."*

What in the world? Beckett was working himself into a tizzy. Julian pushed the video option, calling Beckett in lieu of another text. His quick-draw guy answered on the first ring.

"Did you get my texts?" Beckett asked by way of a greeting. Julian lifted his phone's screen to a better angle to stare into Beckett's mesmerizing eyes. He swore he'd never met anyone who had shown such a depth of character in the reflection of their gaze.

"I did get them and stop stalker texting me." As much as Julian wanted to keep teasing Beckett while he rode the edge of sanity, he couldn't help his smile at so much concern and worry. "I figured out what you were doing about two seconds after we hung up this morning. I've been messing with you all day. I know you're not a liar, so I had to see how long you would hold out."

Beckett's eyes narrowed, which caused another burst of laughter from Julian. "So that's why you didn't answer when I got to the airport."

"That was a hard one—literally. I sacrificed getting off to give you hell. Don't make me do that again," Julian teased with a wink.

The tension instantly eased from Beckett's expression. "You should be ashamed of yourself." The happiness inside Julian couldn't be contained. He had to look like a damn Cheshire cat with how much he'd been smiling all day. "I spent the whole day either texting you or waiting on a text. I was thinking about coming back to Coronado. You got in my head."

"I'm sorry then. I knew you were keeping secrets. You're pretty transparent," Julian said and started down the long hall toward the club.

"And you aren't transparent at all." Beckett gave an exaggerated eye roll. The fatigue on Beckett's face replaced his worry, making Julian feel a minimal amount of guilt…very minimal. "What are you wearing?"

"It's disco night tonight. I'm at the club. You have to hear the music," Julian said louder as he drew closer to the club's main door.

"You look like a retro John Travolta. Where were you keeping that suit?" Beckett asked, letting go of a solid yawn.

"You'd be shocked at the costumes I have. I'll be here for a while. I'm back to myself, thanks to you. We had a great weekend," Julian said.

Beckett nodded, but of course, he never gave himself credit for anything. "You've come a long way, Julian. It's all you. You're doing great."

The hour must have turned, the music ramped up in volume, a tactic designed to lure the dinner guests into the club. He wouldn't be able to hear Beckett or be heard without yelling. "I've got to talk to the guy I told you about for Thane. I'll probably be late getting home. Do you want me to call you or wait until the morning?"

"Whatever you want," Beckett yelled. "Have Marc take you home if you drink too much. They can bring you back in the morning to get your car."

"You're always looking out for everyone," Julian said, not letting on that he'd already used the security team as his private transportation. They regularly drove Julian where he needed to be.

"Just looking out for you," Beckett corrected. "Thank you for putting me out of my misery. Go. I can barely hear you. Have fun!"

Julian lifted a hand to say goodbye. Beckett waved back before the video call ended. He wasn't sure how he had gotten so lucky to find such an extraordinary man.

CHAPTER 33

Two hours later, Julian feigned exhaustion on the dance floor when their DJ for the night paired Sister Sledge with "WAP" by Cardi B. You can bet there was a time when Julian would have done his best "WAP" dance, dropping to the floor to show his talents off, but those times were long gone. Besides, he'd appreciate the view far better from a distance.

"Ricco sent this over," Remington, Julian's waiter for the evening, said as he handed Julian a cocktail glass and a small stack of cocktail napkins. When he started to reject the napkins, Remington shook his head and pointed to Julian's forehead where beads of sweat had formed.

"I'm out of shape," Julian said, dabbing the napkins at his forehead.

"I think it's probably more that you aren't the young man you once were," Remington countered, taking the napkins and dropping them in the center of his tray. The quick quirk of

Remington's lips and sassy shift of his hips as he pranced away showed how easily Julian had been set up for the dig.

He promised himself he'd get the kid back before the night ended.

Julian took a long drink as his gaze turned back to the writhing bodies on the dance floor. They didn't disappoint. His cock stiffened, as he watched the younger crowd in their barely there clothes, popping their asses and gyrating on the floor to the suggestive sounds pounding from the speaker. He remembered a time he'd have put on a show for anyone interested in watching. Hell, these guys had nothing on Julian. When he'd danced, he'd made bank and filled his calendar with future dates.

"Boss, Thomas Peterson's here. He just took his seat." Julian nodded at Ricco before looking over his shoulder to table sixty-eight where Thomas sat. The man was older, graying in a distinguished way, and still, very well put together. Their gazes met, which wasn't anything new. Thomas always watched Julian. After a second's pause, Julian lifted his cocktail glass in greeting.

"Did you tell him I wanted to speak to him?" he asked Ricco, watching Thomas nod, giving his charming smile. It had never been a struggle to spend time with Thomas.

"No. Should I?" Ricco asked.

"No, I got it." Julian pivoted around, dismissing Ricco as he started Thomas's direction. "Bring us a round on Thane."

Thomas's gaze stayed fixed on Julian. Something suggestive crossed his brow, a look Julian hadn't seen for a long time now. Julian grinned a sexy smile, one he had mastered years ago, surprised at how awkward it felt on his face. Thomas swiped out a hand toward the empty barstool at his table, pulling it closer to him as Julian approached.

"You alone tonight?" Julian asked, lifting his thigh to take the seat.

"I am." Thomas cocked his head in such a way that his gaze slid up and down Julian's body as he leaned back in his seat, taking a complete look.

"Something's changed." Thomas's eyes narrowed as he took in Julian's face. "You aren't carrying the wariness any longer. What's happened?"

Julian drained his glass, letting an ice cube fall inside his mouth. Thomas's praise wasn't new. Everyone in his life had commented on the change they had seen in him. They also knew Beckett's involvement in bringing Julian back to his old self. Clearly, Thomas hadn't been in on the gossip. Julian struggled with how much to share.

"You don't have to tell me. The best part of our relationship was neither of us pried too deeply," Thomas said, lifting his nearly empty cocktail glass and taking the last swallow. "But if you've gotten back into the business, you need to know, your spot is still open."

Julian's heart stuttered at the words he had longed to hear for so long now. He gave himself the moment. Was he back in business? His head and his heart aligned then settled before both ran crazy rampant with unbridled excitement. His thoughts raced, going every which way as Remington placed a fresh drink in front of Julian then Thomas.

"Is that a blush?" Thomas asked, eyebrows raised. His fingertip caressed the line of Julian's cheek. All the old feels were there. Excitement and anticipation of an arousing night followed by a nice-sized monetary bonus left for him after a job well done brought conflicting but comforting ease that he hadn't had for a very long time.

Julian shifted his gaze up to a lingering Remington. He wasn't prepared for the look of concern on the waiter's face. As Julian read the confusion and judgment rolling off him, Remington seemed to remember himself, forcing a passive, disinterested look to drop in place as he said, "This round's on Thane. Can I get you two anything else?"

Remington refused to look at Julian, his gaze fixed on

Thomas.

"What's Thane have to do with any of this?" Thomas asked.

Remington's name drop had been done on purpose. Julian just wasn't sure why. "Julian knows." The waiter had been borderline rude when he punted off his explanation to Julian then turned away with nothing more than a judgmental cock of the brow and a disgusted harrumph.

What the hell was happening? No waiter had ever talked to him in that tone before.

Julian turned back to Thomas who had lost that mesmerized look. His gaze went from Remington to Julian and turned speculative as he sat back an inch or two and brought the cocktail glass to his lips, taking a small sip. If Julian interpreted it all correctly, Thomas was trying to figure out why Julian was at his table. Too bad. Julian could have used a few more minutes of Thomas's genuine flirting.

He gave a sigh and lifted his own glass. "Thane's looking for an introduction to Padraig Collins. He runs the bar at Pat's Pub. He believes you could make it happen."

"And how does he feel I could help him?" With the change of the song, the volume of the music increased. Thomas pushed back in his seat, inching away from Julian as understanding of a motive replaced the unabashed invitation being offered.

"Thane says you have a relationship with the guy," Julian answered.

The bark of laughter was unexpected as Thomas turned up the glass, draining its contents. "Why does everyone assume I have a relationship with Padraig? One picture, one time…" Thomas leaned in with his elbows on the table, lifting a hand to Remington, motioning for another round. "If I pretend to know him, can the drinks be on Thane all night?"

The humor and good times were back with a roar. "You can guarantee your night's on us. So, no connection or circle of influence with Padraig or maybe Pat?"

"Pat's the old man. His grandson goes by Padraig." Thomas lifted his hand in a scout's oath. "And if he and I were the only two men in a room together, I'm not sure I would know it was him. No relationship other than I've been to the pub and apparently took a picture that wound up on some influencer's page."

Julian nodded his acceptance of the answer.

"So back to more important things. You back in the business or stuck in the nine to five?"

Julian started shaking his head as he tipped the glass up for a drink. "I miss it more than you'll ever know, but my body's not the same. I have significant scarring."

Thomas nodded his understanding. What had happened to Julian wasn't a secret. Of course, he'd know, but his next words shocked the shit out of Julian. "I heard about the one on your thigh and also the chest, I believe. We all know. It's such a shame to mar such beauty, but there's also no one out there like you, Julian. You're a dying breed. Men today expect the cash and pleasure, then get clingy. You understand the arrangement. You give. The scars don't matter. You're gorgeous. You always have been. It's those eyes." Thomas leaned in further, close enough that Julian could smell the alluring scent of his expensive cologne, and whispered, "Let's get out of here. I have a suite at Escape. Spend the night with me. I'll make it worth your while."

Thomas clasped Julian's fingers in his, tentatively testing the hold. Julian's heart stuttered then turned frantic. This was all he had wanted in the world, and he never truly believed it to be possible for him again. Julian refused to let Beckett's warm smile and gentle, compassion-filled eyes compete with Thomas's handhold.

This moment was so damned empowering for Julian.

"We'll take it easy," Thomas reassured, misreading Julian's hesitation.

Beckett. The name reverberated through Julian's mind like an echo in a deep canyon.

Beckett had imprinted himself on Julian. He was in every thought Julian had, but his life goals hadn't changed. At a minimum, Julian needed to have a conversation with Beckett before he made such a move. It was only fair.

"Let me tell you what," Thomas said, in negotiation mode. "The Foundation Gala is next weekend in LA. Be my date like you used to be. It's a masquerade ball. Go with me. We'll see if the chemistry is still there between us."

Chemistry? What a silly notion. Thomas was a client. Julian had worked hard to build the connection they shared. Thomas liked to play the high roller, and Julian had pulled a mint of cash out of the guy. The inner struggle raged. Right versus wrong. Good versus bad. They all battled against his newfound awareness. He'd always done really well at the gala, discreetly gaining new clients from the hordes of wealthy men who attended the event.

He found himself nodding as he asked, "Black tie?"

"Yes. Tuxedo and mask." Thomas squeezed his hand, looking pleased with himself. "I can arrange those for you. My buyer will be in touch. Is your number the same?"

He shook his head. Julian had changed his phone number after the accident. Cell phones were so easily trackable these days. He didn't want to worry whether his attacker could use that information to find him. "No. I'll text you my number in the morning."

"Good. I'll send a jet to pick you up," Thomas said, then convincingly added, "I promise, no pressure, but the hotel is booked. You can stay in my suite."

"Twenty thousand dollars," Julian said the obscene total with more confidence than he had. With that much money, he was certain to be performing in many different ways.

Thomas laughed straight out loud. "Always so sure of yourself. Deal, but for that amount of money, I want in that ass. You and me, no one else."

Julian nodded his confirmation then took another much

smaller drink. He turned in his seat, pretending interest in the dance floor as the heat crept up his neck. He told himself, his uncertainty only had to do with Beckett. He had to always remember that he'd promised Beckett nothing. Nothing. He had even gone so far as to reiterate his hesitation in committing many times over.

Surely, at some point, hopefully soon, he would begin to feel good about this decision. How could he say no to getting back his old life when it was the exact thing he'd fought tooth and nail for? He couldn't.

Thomas's hand came to Julian's shoulder. He gently squeezed as he bent forward to whisper in Julian's ear. "You're always so damn elusive. You've made me happy tonight. Let's see how it goes, but in the meantime, come up with a number that will allow you to leave all this behind and be exclusive to me." The palm squeezed his shoulder again. This time a chill crept down his spine. "I'll be back. I'm going to call my assistant to get you set up."

Julian nodded automatically, wondering how this simple conversation had taken such a hard turn. Why wasn't he more excited? This was exactly what he'd wanted. He'd mourned the loss of his past life from the second he'd woken up in that hospital room.

Beckett...

Fuck.

The sweet, gentle wolf of a man who loved Julian in every possible way.

Of course, Beckett hadn't said the words but only because Julian hadn't wanted to hear them. Where Beckett may not have spoken the sentiment aloud, his actions showed the loving relationship just waiting in the wings for Julian to accept.

Julian's heart gave a twist at the pain he was about to cause Beckett.

This had been the reason he'd always been upfront, but the

situation still felt off in his soul.

"What are you doing, boss?" Ricco hissed. Julian hadn't even noticed his approach. He could hear the concern and recrimination in the manager's tone.

"Mind your business," Julian responded, never looking over at Ricco.

"I would've normally done exactly that before my boss…" Ricco hedged as he came to stand right in front of Julian, forcing his gaze up. "…found me and every other server in this room and taught us to look out for each other. That we're a family. Over the last month, I've never seen you so good and happy. So again, what are you doing, Julian?"

His back stiffened, ramrod straight, even as he understood the love and respect Ricco was using, only looking out for Julian's best interest. "Mind. Your. Fucking. Business. I do what's best for me."

"You're fucking up and self-sabotaging," Ricco shot back, putting his fists at his waist. "And I can see you're determined to go through with whatever you just planned. Tell Beckett. He's a good man and deserves the truth."

"Fuck off, Ricco," Julian said and rose from his seat, draining his drink before he started down to the dance floor. "Tell the gossip crew to keep this to themselves. I'll fire anyone who gives Beckett the heads up before I tell him. I'm not playing."

He lived by the rules he created, no one else's. By God, they could dump all the shame on him they wanted. He'd thrived under the world's condemnation before, and he could do it again. That had been the perfect exchange to seal Julian's fate. He was moving forward with the gala. Julian was back.

"Yes, sir," Ricco mocked in such a way Julian cut his gaze to the acting manager who cocked a frustrated brow as if Julian was nothing more than a nuisance, not a man who could fire him on the spot. He had always liked Ricco, so he let it go, dismissing him without a backward glance.

Holy shit, his whole body vibrated with anticipation. He remembered that sensation, and it felt almost as good as he thought it might, except for that niggling thought in the back of his mind that he wouldn't allow space to form. Fuck that. He was finally back in the game.

CHAPTER 34

A dark SUV drove slowly down the well-worn path leading to the camp's main house. Beckett worked with Randy, folding a tent, and split his attention between the task at hand and the vehicle carefully making its way down the rocky driveway that needed repair.

"Who is it?" Randy asked, standing to his full height.

"I don't know." Beckett also got to his feet, still holding the nylon, and squinted his eyes. The shiny black paint job clashed with the bright sun, making it hard to see. It wasn't until the back door opened and the long, dark hair flitted in the breeze that he knew exactly who it was.

"Mom," Beckett murmured, forgetting all about the tent and heading straight for the SUV.

He'd heard she might be coming to spend the rest of the summer with Dad, but he'd also heard those same rumors over and again throughout the last few years, and they had never come to be.

The melancholy of almost twenty-four hours without speaking with Julian instantly faded as Beckett started toward his mother, dusting off the layers of dirt from a hard day's work.

"Mom." How he loved his mother. Nothing about her had changed. Her long, shiny dark hair and bohemian style clothing fit her long, lithe frame, accenting her natural grace. Beckett pulled off his work gloves, tucking them into his back pocket as he quickened his steps. "I didn't know you were coming."

"My goodness, you keep growing, Beck, my boy." Her bright smile and larger-than-life hug enveloped him. She wasn't a small woman, but he still outsized her in every possible way, ultimately lifting her off her feet and into his arms.

"I didn't believe you were actually coming this time." Her sing-song laughter filled the air as his father's distinct footsteps clomped across the front porch of the main lodge.

"When my son has finally met his one, of course I must come see," she said, landing back on her feet, patting his chest with her palms. "You need sunscreen, son."

Beckett gave a full belly chuckle, thinking of Julian's attempt to repair his skin. "That's the second time I've heard that in the last week. I guess there's something to it."

His father's hand came to Beckett's back as he wound around him, taking his mother in his arms. As unorthodox a couple as they were, Beckett always felt the love they shared. He became chopped liver for the attention he received after his father took his mother into his arms, kissing her as if his life depended on their intimacy.

Randy came to Beckett's side, watching his father carry his mother toward the cabin, up the steps of the porch, and he suspected, to their bedroom. "He's glad to see her."

"Yeah. He missed her," Beckett said, watching them until the screen door slammed shut. Beckett looked down to see his mother's bags at his feet. Just by the sheer amount of luggage, he guessed she planned to stay awhile this time. He quickly pulled his wallet from his back pocket, handing over cash to the driver who was shutting the SUV's trunk.

"Thank you," Beckett said. The driver looked down at the twenty and gave Beckett an irritated shake of the head.

"Do you know how long a drive it is from the airport?" The driver's hand extended further toward Beckett for more money.

His boldness tickled Beckett, reminding him of Julian, and he pulled another twenty out for nothing more than to reward the brazen confidence. He placed the cash in the outstretched palm, but the driver didn't lower it. At the driver's expectant stare, Beckett glanced at Randy who looked at the driver as if he were crazy.

"Dude, get outta here," Randy barked as Beckett started thumbing through his cash again.

"Had to try." The driver's face changed into a silly grin as he tucked the bills in his pocket and turned away, going for the driver's side door. "It *was* a long drive."

"Let's get these inside without me having to hear or see anything that'll scar me for life," Beckett teased.

The momentary reprieve of missing Julian vanished with a vengeance as he again became hyper aware of his cell phone and how he hadn't spoken to Julian since last night at the club. Julian hadn't made one single response, either by text or call, to the half dozen Beckett had sent.

The damn cell phone grew heavy inside his pocket with all its burden. Beckett forced himself to push the lack of communication out of his mind. He just couldn't figure out why Julian hadn't responded.

Anxiety rippled over Beckett's every nerve ending as he hoisted the heavy suitcases and started for the house.

Julian lived near a large body of water for much of his adult life yet never realized how completely the constant churn of the ocean was reminiscent of the battle he fought between his head and his heart. He dropped down on the sand, dressed in his professional clothing, and watched the waves lapping against the shore, rolling forward then tugging backward again, never getting too far either way. It seemed the theme of Julian's life.

Goddamn Beckett. When had the man wormed his way through all of Julian's protective barriers to be so firmly embedded in his heart?

Julian had always wanted back into his old life. That desire had never wavered. He just hadn't thought it would be possible. He'd owe Beckett everything for helping him find his way back.

The gentle way Beckett had loved him had shown Julian that he had nothing to worry about. With his lip tucked between his teeth, he crossed his legs as the salt breeze filled his lungs and danced across his skin.

Maybe the next steps in his healing process were to tie himself to one man. Thomas could afford him. He hadn't blinked an eye at the twenty thousand dollars Julian had requested. Instead, he had licked his lips in anticipation. Julian grinned at the memory and dropped his chin to his chest, staring at the sand between his slacks-covered thighs.

He should be delighted right now. He wrapped his arms around his legs and dropped his forehead to his knees, blocking out the evening sun just beginning to dip into the ocean. Why did he have so much reluctance then? Where was it fucking coming from? Was it his own insecurities he still needed to overcome? Why did he feel so incomplete?

Thane had poured everything into making Julian's life

successful. Julian may have worked hard, but there were elements of escapism in all the hours he put in at Reservations. Thane had consistently reprimanded Julian, trying to whip his rebellious behavior out of him. The dear man had also promoted him when no other employee would have risen up in the ranks like Julian had, especially factoring in all his antagonism. How would Thane feel about this decision? But Thane wasn't the one who worried him the most.

No, it was that sweet, gentle giant who couldn't have been any better to Julian. Beckett. The name drummed through his head like an anthem. A deep exhale rushed from his lips as he dropped his legs back into the sand. A heavy weight made Julian's shoulders sag. His head dropped forward again. Why did he feel like crying? He didn't know, but no matter how he resisted, a tear finally built enough steam to slip from his eyes and fall to the sand.

His finger followed, mixing the drop in the sand, hiding his weakness.

Beckett.

Julian's brow wrinkled at the pain his actions would cause the sweet Marlboro Man. His heart hurt as he thought of the many texts he'd gotten today that, in his cowardice, he had chosen to ignore. Beckett had to be making himself sick with worry. Maybe that was Julian's desire speaking. This having his cake and eating it too attitude he'd adopted.

No, Beckett was worrying, and Julian needed to man up and call. Needed to tell Beckett not to come this weekend.

Did Julian have it in him to lie? He could go with Thomas, test the waters without telling Beckett the truth.

No. Julian wasn't a liar. And if he attended the gala and followed through with his weekend plans, his fate would be sealed. Beckett needed to be told. He owed him the truth.

"Julian." He lifted his head to see Marc standing over him.

He must have been sitting there longer than he'd realized.

The sun had dropped below the horizon without him noticing, darkness creeping in.

"You good?" he asked, his cell phone vibrating before he finished his question.

"Is that Beckett?"

Marc nodded. "He's texting me, worried about you. I told him I had you in my line of sight."

Julian nodded and pushed to his feet, dusting the sand off his legs. He hated sand and hadn't properly thought this through when he'd taken the seat. Julian swiped at his slacks before bending to gather his dress shoes, choosing to carry them and go barefoot. His toes in the sand had helped ground him.

"Can we not tell Beck I was out here like this?" Julian asked, lifting his head to the bodyguard. He looked down at the sand as they went. "I'll call him when I get home."

Marc's eyes narrowed as he tilted his head in Julian's direction. "I thought I'd gotten to know you pretty well, but you've been off. Did something happen?"

"You could say that," Julian confirmed as he fished his keys from his pocket.

"I didn't notice anything. What did I miss?"

"It's a personal thing." Julian veered off, heading to his car parked next to Marc's. Before he dropped in his seat, he took his phone from his back pocket. Once he was inside the confines of his car, he started the engine and pulled his messaging app up to read Beckett's latest text.

"When you see this, know I'm thinking about you and missing you. Whatever's going on, we can deal with it together this weekend. My mom showed up unexpectedly. It's great seeing her. We're having dinner together tonight. I'll be free early—by nine. Call me when you get settled. I leave in the morning for a training session. I'm really missing you. No pressure. Call me when you can."

Julian dropped his head back against his headrest. Beckett was a fucking saint, a consummate gentleman. Nothing was ever off about him. Not ever.

Knuckles rapped on his passenger side window, startling him. Julian pushed the button to lower the window for Marc. "I've known Beck a long time. He's a real good guy. He never asks where you go or who you're with, just that you're safe."

Julian blew out a breath and nodded then rolled the window up without saying another word. He needed no one's guilt. He dropped the car into gear and backed out of his space, berating himself with every turn of the wheel. He knew better than to get involved with the honest and integrity-filled people of the world. It was why he had ignored his attraction to Beckett for so long.

Fuck. Beckett deserved someone so much better than Julian. He would make the call tonight and end both their agony.

CHAPTER 35

"Congratulations!" Beckett said, taking the lead at his small family dinner party. He grabbed his longneck beer bottle and lifted enough from his seat to tap his father's then Randy's bottles in the center of the table. Beckett's mother clapped happily, smiling as broadly as the other four people at the table.

"A baby! I'm so happy for you," she said, clinking her glass of sweet tea along with everyone else's.

"We're nervous," Marly, Randy's longtime girlfriend, said with a hand resting on her belly.

"When did you find out?" Beckett asked.

"Two days ago," Randy announced proudly, lifting his brows toward his girlfriend for confirmation. She gave a patient grin and lifted three fingers. Randy continued, "We haven't told our families yet. She's barely two months along. We were thinking about eloping, so her parents don't have a fit."

Marly nodded. "They're very religious. They think I'm still

living at school. Like I would live on campus while working on my PhD.”

They all knew the details of Marly's life, and how she'd eventually followed Randy, tired of the long-distance relationship. Though her parents would never understand living in the wilderness while teaching at a small county school, Marly felt her life fit their small circle of family completely.

“Well, I couldn't be any more excited,” his mother said, grinning dreamily. His smitten father reached across the table, taking her hand in his. “I wish we had been able to have more children, daddy.”

Beckett's gaze slid to Randy's, lifting a brow, giving him a firm zip-it glare. Randy always made fun of his mother's endearments. He had a whole teasing joke, explaining to anyone around that Beckett's father was not really her father too. It was so overdone.

His phone rattled and vibrated next to his dinner plate. The few minutes of reprieve from the mounting anxiety slammed forward again as Beckett reached for the phone, not caring in the least at the panicky way he opened the screen to find a message from Julian.

Finally. A breath he hadn't known he was holding released. Beckett opened the message as he stood, his chair scraping across the linoleum.

“Can you talk?”

Why did such a simple text cause immediate alarm? Something wasn't right, and it didn't take a brain surgeon to figure it out. Since Beckett had first broken through Julian's barriers, they'd spent all their free time talking. Three words after days of silence wasn't good.

“I need to take this,” Beckett said, excusing himself from the table, walking toward the front door. He pushed the call button, forgoing a text message, and brought the phone to his ear. It took four rings for Julian to answer.

"Hey. That was fast."

Beckett stepped outside, held the door for Woofer to slip past, and shut the door firmly behind him. A million stars twinkled in the sky. His favorite time of the day. Beckett paid no real attention to anything other than the man on the other end of the phone. He took the porch steps down, sitting on the top one. Woofer stayed at his feet, his focus showing how well the dog sensed Beckett's unease.

"How are you?" Beckett said, worry taking its toll in his tone. "Is everything all right?"

"Yeah…" Which meant it wasn't.

Woofer's head came to Beckett's lap, most likely hearing Julian's tone.

"What's happened?" Beckett asked when Julian didn't say more. "If it can't wait until the weekend, I can come…"

"No," Julian said firmly. "I…"

Beckett could hear the struggle in Julian's voice as he cleared his throat and started again.

"I should have called you last night. I'm sorry I didn't. You need to see if you can cancel your flight this weekend."

Beckett's heart gave a solid dip.

"Okay. I thought we'd turned a corner after last weekend." Beckett stopped himself from saying more. It was Julian's seriousness more than the actual words that led him to believe Julian was actively putting distance between the two of them. He changed course, needing to know the problem before he could solve it. "What are you not saying?"

"Look. I've always been honest with you, even though I've let the lines between us blur. The truth is, I met an old client at the club, and he's offered me my old position back." The longer Julian spoke, delivering his devastating news, the harder his tone became. "It came out of nowhere. I didn't see the offer coming, and long story short, I accepted a date with him this weekend."

Beckett's entire body went numb.

What had he done wrong?

House shopping?

He had scared Julian.

His body's protective barriers broke like a dam, flooding his heart, mind, and soul with insurmountable pain. His stomach roiled at the thought of Julian moving on without him. His heart shattered into a million pieces as he tried to hold back the emotions overwhelming him. He'd known the score from day one. He was certain he could handle anything Julian threw his way, but he'd been so damn wrong.

"This hasn't been easy for me. I feel like I'm letting you down, but I can't deny this is something I've wanted since I woke up in the hospital bed…after the accident. I'm an escort at heart. It's what comes naturally to me, and I'm damn good at it. I owe it to myself to test the waters." Julian's voice was flat and final.

Beckett's mind raced, searching for something to say. He wanted to beg Julian to let him be his one. Beckett could buy Julian's time. They could pretend whatever Julian wanted.

"Say something. You're killing me." Even under all the heaviness of his own pain, he didn't like the worried concern pervading Julian's words.

"I can't say this wasn't out there between us." Beckett hoped to find common ground between them. "You know, I wish I was enough for you—"

"Beckett, please…" Julian interrupted.

"Let me finish, Julian." Beckett had to clear his mind and bring forward his determined side to get through the lie he was about to tell. "Go do what you have to do. I told you I would never ask you to change. A lot has happened to you over the last couple of years. You're an amazing, beautiful man. Go find yourself. I'll be here waiting for you."

"Goddamn it, Beckett," Julian barked, his frustration clear.

"What do you see in me that attracts you so much?"

Beckett stared down at the dog who tried to give him comfort. With as badly as his heart ached, he wished he could go back to the numbness. He reached out to run a hand over Woofer's head, smoothing the soft fur as he spoke his truth. "You're smart, fun, and caring. You have a drive to goodness that inspires me. You're always looking out for the people around you, even as you pretend not to care at all. You appreciate the smallest gestures as if they were grand and give back to the world in a way few can understand."

Julian let go of an anguished breath. "No one has ever accused me of such goodness before. It's my looks, Beckett. Men like my looks. I know that's who I am and what I have to offer. You've never seen me correctly."

"No." Beckett shook his head. "I see you better than you see yourself. You're beautiful inside and out, and you're also a good, gentle man. Your looks may have turned my head, but that faded pretty quickly after I watched you for so long then spent time with you. It's what lay underneath that hooked me."

The front door opened, light filtering over Beckett. He ignored it, concentrating on Julian's response. "You still want to be in my life?"

"Yeah," Beckett said and had to fight the giant lump threatening to take him under. "Always."

"Can I call you Sunday?"

Beckett was going to have to go five days without talking to his love. It seemed almost impossible.

"Yeah," he finally answered, not liking any of this. "I should probably fly there anyway. I don't want to get in your way, but I need my truck…" The lie fell flat on his lips and probably was a terrible idea. If Beckett happened to see Julian before his date, he didn't see himself above begging Julian to pick him. "I'll stay out of your way…"

"You can stay here," Julian offered. "You're never in my

way, Beckett. I'm flying to LA. There's a foundation gala he and I always attended together. I can hear the hurt in your voice. I'm sorry."

Beckett felt his father's palm come down on his shoulder, ending in a reassuring squeeze. He didn't look up and hadn't considered the windows of the cabin being open when he'd chosen this spot to have their conversation. Of course, they'd all heard.

"I'm okay," he said, trying for an upbeat tone for both Julian and his father. "I'm leaving in the morning. I'll be out until Saturday morning. My flight is scheduled to arrive about five thirty Saturday afternoon, I think. Take your safety precautions and remember what I taught you. You got this."

"Beckett…" Julian's voice radiated an agony that did nothing to ease the pain churning in Beckett's soul. "I shouldn't have started this with you. I fought our connection for so long. I appreciate everything you've done for me. I do, but I've always wanted my old life back. I didn't like it being taken from me against my will…"

Beckett's father took the seat beside him. That would just never do. He rolled his eyes and let out a huffed breath as he pushed off the porch. He doubted he would actually cry, but with his father's gentle approach, he wasn't going to risk it.

"I've gotta go. I'm still at the main house and Woofer, and I need to head to my cabin. Come on, boy," Beckett said as his mother, Randy, and Marly came out on the porch.

"All right. Call me when you get home tonight if you want to get off," Julian said quietly, in such a way that it felt like it was being offered out of pity.

"Be safe. Call me if you need me." Beckett was halfway to his golf cart when he ended the call. His heart had broken. The only sound that penetrated his haze was the grass and rock crunching under his boots. He motioned for Woofer to take his seat and started to drop down into his own when he looked up to see everyone staring at him. His mother started down the steps toward him.

"No, stay there. I'm fine." Beckett lifted a hand to stop her, but of course, she didn't. "Mom, really, I'm fine."

"I love you," she said, coming to the edge of the golf cart, taking him into her arms. Her warmth and sincerity helped. He loved his mother's hugs. "Love's hard, and you St. Clair men don't make it any easier on yourselves."

"I'm okay, Mom." He wrapped an arm around her waist and held her tightly for only a few seconds. He waved at the rest of them before he took off, lost in the uncertainty of what had happened.

CHAPTER 36

The pitter-patter of Julian's heart showed how much the finer things in life spoke directly to him on a soul-deep level. The splendor. The extravagance. One glance at the over-the-top amenities that came with a top floor suite at a posh hotel had Julian understanding exactly how much he had truly lost after his accident and how far he still had to go before he could own this life again.

If wealth had a scent, Julian was certain the smell continuously circulated inside this suite.

When Julian had arrived at the hotel, he'd been greeted with an apology note from Thomas, explaining his tardiness. Thomas's private plane had a minor mechanical issue, causing him to return to the private airport, pushing back his departure several hours until the repair could be made. Thomas was going to be late, giving Julian the privacy he needed to regroup from any worry or anxiety and overcome, which he had done in a big, big way with the help of all these lavish amenities.

A custom-tailored tuxedo hung in the closet, made from what Julian's fingers decided was the finest materials, and turned out to fit his frame like a glove—just like he had expected. The tuxedo accentuated all the right parts, as it should. He'd go ahead and call it. His ass looked great, as well as the outline of his cock. He'd been dressed to impress, and that he did.

Julian's hair was meticulously styled, and his beard trimmed with precision by a stylist who'd stopped by the room shortly after his arrival. He'd also had a manicure and pedicure timed perfectly after the stylist finished her job. There was a time Julian would have taken all this special treatment for granted. Not this evening, though. Now, he understood the pure joy of being so cared for and pampered.

The stylist had come armed with some essentials: eyeliner and mascara. Thomas had a thing for his blue-green eyes being accentuated with a dark eyeliner fringed in mascara. Based on the intricate mask hanging close to his tuxedo, the black eyeliner was a perfect choice to make his gaze pop.

This world of incomprehensible amounts of cash had a way of blocking out the realness of Julian's current life. Although Beckett hadn't left Julian's thoughts since he had made the decision to come tonight, he was also no longer carrying the guilt like he had. Maybe because he hadn't checked his cell phone since he'd boarded the flight to LA. Julian's buzzing anxiety was already at an all-time high before factoring in Beckett's pain. He pushed those thoughts away too.

A dilator kit had arrived exactly thirty-minutes ago, helping to remind him of his current job. Julian had to find then retain a single-minded focus to help get him through this night. Thomas liked his toys and enjoyed being the one to administer them. Of course, Julian had misgivings, but he'd deal with those when the time came.

A soft instrumental played throughout the bedroom, dressing area, and bathroom, coming to an abrupt halt with the tone of a beeping alarm. Eight o'clock. Time for the party. Julian had skipped the seated dinner. He had too many butterflies flittering away inside his belly to think that adding food would end well.

He reached for the mask, careful of his hair as he put it in place. He had to admit, the eyeliner did make his eyes pop and his full lips look plumper than normal.

His nerves were frayed, ready to get the night started, pushing Julian out of the suite to the bank of elevators leading to the grand ballroom downstairs. The sooner he got his night started, the faster he could find some ease.

Surely everything was destined to fall into place. After all, his dreams were coming true.

Julian rolled away the tension in his shoulders then swiveled his neck back and forth as the elevator doors opened to the first floor. He stepped out, moving with more confidence than he'd thought possible. Showtime.

Beckett pushed through the front door of Julian's condo, instantly sensing a coldness that he'd never experienced before. He flipped on the entry light and made his way further inside the condo to the kitchen, turning on all the overhead lights as he went.

Before coming to the apartment, Beckett had found himself stalling, killing time since his flight had arrived. He'd stopped to grab a bite to eat at a steakhouse in San Diego, thankful that he'd finally been able to put food inside his stomach. He wasn't sure he'd eaten a full meal since the night Julian had broken his news.

Beckett's melancholy attitude had him spending a couple of hours in the restaurant, not wanting to come to this empty apartment. It all felt so final.

The internal beratement that had started days ago hit Beckett again like a sledgehammer to his brain. His crazy thoughts careened from why in the world he'd thought he would ever be enough to keep a vibrantly beautiful man like Julian to what a sucker he'd been to think he could hang in the prestigious world of Reservations. Why was he always so damned naive?

He scanned the small space. It was tidy, with nothing out of place except for a folded piece of paper with his truck keys on top. He went there, dropping the house key on the small center island then reached for a note with his name scribbled on top in Julian's efficient penmanship.

B,

I'm truly sorry for hurting you. In time you'll see it's better this way. Stay as long as you like. There's no reason to drive all night.

Call me next week when you can talk.

X,

J

Dammit. Beckett was so damned fucked. As hard as it was to come to this apartment, it was equally as difficult to leave. With a heavy thump, his fist dropped to the countertop. The note floated out of his fingers.

Beckett turned and surveyed the condo. He had a sense of home being with Julian's furnishings. What if he did stay the night? Pathetic, yes, but no one needed to know. Why he'd let himself even consider being one of Julian's men. One of many paying Julian money to spend time with him. He couldn't, not after everything they shared.

He gave a hard, frustrated shake of his head to dispel the image of so many men chasing after Julian. He reminded himself for the millionth time this week that Julian had been up-front from the beginning. Why had he let himself hope he could be the one to change Julian's mind?

Beckett hadn't been wrong about wanting a long-lasting, committed monogamous relationship. He tightly fisted his truck keys, the metal digging into his palm, and started for the door.

This bullshit maniac whining he kept doing had to stop. He agreed he shouldn't drive all night, especially being sleep-deprived, but he also needed to grow a fucking spine and man the fuck up. So what that the man he loved didn't want him? That shit happened all the damn time. At least he'd fucking tried. Put himself out there.

Beckett flipped off the lights as he made his way to the front door. He turned the single lock before shutting the door tightly behind him. He took long, purposeful strides toward the parking lot. He had no regrets. He'd given Julian his all.

After two hours of mingling with the throngs of escorts who always attended these events, Julian found he was no longer the top cock on the walk. The more interesting revelation was that he didn't want to be. The silly conversations were nothing more than flaunting money they didn't truly have and bragging about possessions they'd never truly earned.

Julian experienced deep embarrassment, knowing he'd once been a lead member of this ridiculous and petty group. He had preened his imaginary success openly, just like all these men. And at the time, he'd believed every word. Exactly like these men did now.

Destructive thoughts took him down a dark rabbit hole. He knew, with all certainty, these same men had rejoiced in his pain after his abduction. No doubt glad to see Julian's clients open for the picking. He had no friends here. He'd sensed his disconnect from this lifestyle the moment he entered the ballroom then every minute after that chasm had grown.

As the night wore on, Julian learned exactly how much he had evolved. Apparently, he was no longer willing to engage in surface-level conversations. He wanted in on the business discussions. And to his credit, he held his own when speaking of the stock market and future trends.

What the fuck had happened to him?

Although he repeatedly asked himself that question, the answer didn't seem to truly matter. After fifteen minutes of pretending to be enraptured by the stories of sexcapades, Julian had edged his way to the crowd of uber-successful business leaders. He fit there far better. His inner Thane leaped to the forefront, shocking the shit out of him at exactly how much he had learned by living his life in Thane's shadow.

He quickly became the Reservations town crier, relentlessly chatting about the concept of the night club and restaurant, and their plans to expand nationwide then internationally. Julian was honored to have earned a lead role in the concept of creating a safe place for all types of men to meet one another. Probably most pleased to have helped in implementing the grueling application process designed to keep every member on the up and up.

Julian rolled his eyes and drained his near empty champagne flute before discarding it on a server's tray. Then he reached for his second glass of champagne for the evening. He took a sobering step back from the crowds.

He lifted the cold drink to his lips, only taking the slightest of sips as he scanned the large room. Marc stood along the far wall, close to the entrance, along with other private security members. His gaze connected with Marc's. He hadn't asked when or how Marc had decided to trail along after Julian, but Marc had accompanied him on the flight to LA. The guy seemed to work a gazillion hours and never tired of trailing after Julian. He hoped

Marc had eaten dinner. If not, Julian would take care of it once he got back to the room.

He jiggled his wrist, knocking his watch back in place to look down at the time. A quarter to eleven. Damn, it felt later than it was. Thomas wasn't scheduled to arrive until after midnight. Julian needed to be honest with Thomas. Apologize for the effort he had made to make this night special for the both of them. This was no longer Julian's life.

He lifted his gaze while doing the same with his glass. The backdrop of the room morphed into the dance club he used to regularly attend.

The room bristled with energy as he took a long drink from a cocktail glass in his hand after an extended dancing period while waiting for his new client to show. He could feel the recreational drugs pumping through his veins, causing the disco lights to pop a little brighter and the dance music to thump a little clearer. Molly had always been his drug of choice.

Moments later, his head swam, and the room transformed into his old favorite dance club. A forceful arm circled his waist, drawing Julian's body back against a hard chest. Cheap aftershave and the scent of unwashed male body assaulted his senses.

In this moment, caught between both the past and the present, Julian fought to catch his breath. His heart rate double-timed its frantic beat as a cold sweat broke out along his hairline. Everything slowed.

The cool fresh air around him became stagnant, the smell of mold and stale cigarettes thickened around him. A dirty flannel sleeve came into focus. Memories of a distorted, tattoo-covered face flashed in his brain. Julian recognized his abductor immediately.

Micah Abbott.

The son of his parents' pastor.

It had been years, but there wasn't any doubt in Julian's mind. Micah had sneered down at him with a menacing glare that sent chills racing down his spine seconds before a powerful fist had met Julian's jaw and he'd lost consciousness.

Holy hell.

His abductor was the kid he'd got caught fucking during a church service. Micah had done those things to him?

Julian's mind spun back to the present. His stomach churned. His head hurt so bad he worried he might pass out. He rocked back unsteadily on his feet as if that fist had traveled through time and connected with his jaw where he stood in the ballroom. The flute in his hand crashed to the floor, sending champagne and fragments of glass splattering every which way.

The reality and implications of his flashback slammed through Julian's entire body. Bile forced its way from his stomach and hung in his throat. He was going to be sick. He wanted out of this place and away from these people.

Beckett. He needed Beckett. Julian spun around, catching Marc's concerned gaze as he took long purposeful steps toward Julian. Every head in the room had turned at the crash of his glass. Now they tracked Marc on his way to Julian's side. Julian must have made a scene but couldn't care in the least as he ripped the mask off his face, tossed it away as he started toward the protection of his private security guard.

Julian opened his mouth to speak, but his breath caught in his throat, no words would come. The edges of his vision darkened. He refused to pass out, but he couldn't draw air into his lungs. *Fuck.* Julian reached for Marc's forearm to help steady himself, his fingers digging into the man's skin to keep him from dropping to the floor. His thoughts still whirled and his mind reeled from the shock of remembering…everything. His heart raced in his chest as he fought to remain standing.

"What happened?" Marc hissed. Julian gave a frantic shake of his head, starting to move them out of the room. At this rate, passing out was imminent, and he refused to do it in front of some many prying eyes. "Breathe, Julian. I got you."

He stared at Marc's dark eyes, not near as warm and inviting as Beckett's, but he still trusted Marc with his life.

"Beckett," Julian said through a constricted throat, taking long strides to the elevator banks. Shooting stars sprinted through his vision, increasing in size and speed. "I need to speak to Beckett."

Marc's protective arm came to Julian's back, keeping him upright as the bodyguard ushered Julian to the elevator. "Let's get you back to the room."

The elevator doors opened, and he hurried inside, thankful he'd managed to stay on his feet. He finally took a centering breath, anchoring him into his reality. "Find Beckett for me. Tell him I'm sorry and see if he can come."

Julian's hands shook as his world then turned desperate.

"Julian, are you all right?" Someone asked from outside the elevator as the doors closed.

No, he wasn't. Not at all.

Julian forced himself to pull it together, at least long enough to get to the suite. His mind spun as if it was on a continuous loop. Flashes of that tattooed face. The hate he'd felt when he'd looked into those eyes. It was Micah. Micah had abducted and assaulted him.

So many questions spun through his head. Why would Micah abduct him? Why would he want to hurt him? Why did he leave him for dead?

CHAPTER 37

Traffic was a bitch.

Beckett pushed back in his seat, trying to find some comfort as he draped his wrist over the steering wheel of his truck and came to a dead stop on the interstate. Again. The third traffic jam he'd encountered since leaving Coronado. He'd hit a congested spot in San Diego then again when he made it to the LA area. He thought he'd been home free. But Santa Clarita at close to midnight proved him wrong. A long yawn escaped as he reached for his cell phone, searching for the closest hotel with a vacancy.

He should have spent the night at Julian's place and gotten an early start home in the morning. *Should've, could've, would've.* The story of his life.

Beckett split his attention between his phone and the road, using one hand to google nearby accommodations. He blinked, confused, as Marc's name covered his search on the screen. His fucked-up head stared at the bubble as if it were a mirage until the ringtone followed. Beckett's brow wrinkled, and he stepped overly hard on the already pressed brakes as he pushed the green accept button, bringing the phone to his ear.

"What's up?"

"Something's happened. Julian's asked me to call you." Marc's tone sounded hard and clipped, but the words confused him.

Beckett's gaze riveted on the unmoving speedometer. Why hadn't Julian called himself? "Where is he?"

"He's on the phone with the front desk," Marc explained. He lowered his voice as if to keep his words private as he continued. "Beck, he's alone. I don't know where his date is, but he never showed. Julian seemed fine with that. He went downstairs on his own and spent much of the evening on the periphery of the guests. He never fully engaged with anyone…" Marc paused, but the puffs of breath let Beckett know Marc's mouth remained close to the phone.

Just above a whisper, Marc said, "You know, he has that way of looking at someone like he knows they're full of bullshit. He had that look all night. He and I made eye contact. He seemed fine then suddenly paled and wobbled on his feet. His champagne glass fell from his hand. I darted toward him, and he started toward me, asking for you. I don't know what happened, but his sole focus is for me to find you while he gets us a new room. He doesn't want me to leave his sight."

Beckett kept his foot rammed down on the brake pedal as his mind raced. "Can I talk to him?"

"Yeah, but whatever's happened is more than he can deal with. He's edgy. Frantic. Hanging on by a thread. Be careful," Marc whispered.

"Okay. Let me talk to him." Beckett's gaze shifted back and forth, from the dashboard to the center console, lost in the possibility of what could have upset Julian. He must have remembered something significant about his abduction. That was the only thing that made sense.

"Julian." Marc's voice still carried a soothing quality as he addressed Julian. "Beck's on the phone."

"They have a room for us. It's small, but they'll meet us on the third floor," Beckett heard Julian say. Julian's tone was all wrong. He spoke briskly and succinctly, not with his usual casual flippancy that he had mastered so well. "I need to pack. It won't take a minute."

Beckett's worry elevated. He took a deep, settling breath, trying to stay calm as he tucked his chin to his chest and waited for Julian to speak to him. It seemed like forever until he heard the sound of Julian's voice over the line.

"Beckett, it happened. I saw him."

Beckett's eyes lifted to the open highway in front of him. The honks coming from other vehicles finally penetrated his focus. He looked in the rearview mirror as cars navigated around his stopped truck. He flipped on his blinker and slowly edged his way over to the right lane and navigated to the closest exit.

"Who did you see and where did you see him?"

"Micah. In a memory. It's all back. At least the part I was conscious for." Julian sounded scattered and scared. Beckett could hear the background noise of Julian moving quickly, probably packing. "Can you come?"

"Yeah. I'm not too far away. I'll turn around now," Beckett said, finally getting into the exit lane. "Why are you getting a new room?"

"I can't do this. I just…can't."

What did that mean? He swallowed all his questions, no matter how the pounding of his heart demanded an answer. Julian seemed too close to the edge, but he was doing everything Beckett had taught him—stay close to Marc, find a safe place, then call him. Julian was clearly doing everything possible to hang on to his sanity. Beckett just needed to get to him, now. He'd figure the rest out later.

"That's fine," Beckett said, racing to take the curve back onto the interstate, heading toward LA. "You don't have to do anything you don't want to do. Just stay close to Marc until I can get there. Hear me?"

"Oh yeah. I'm not letting him out of my sight," Julian said, and a second later Marc was back on the phone.

"I don't know if you can tell, but he's moving fast to pack," Marc explained. "We'll be heading downstairs in the next few minutes."

"Stay with him." Beckett gunned the engine. "And text me the hotel's information. I'll be there as soon as I can."

He dropped the phone on the center console and gripped the steering wheel tight with both hands. Adrenaline had surged in his system, removing any lingering exhaustion that had plagued him during the traffic jams. His focus zeroed in on a single task: get to Julian. Then he'd deal with everything else. Right now, he had more questions than answers.

Julian stared out the large window of the new hotel room. The curtains were wide open, the rest of the small double room was dark, shadowed by the lamp between the two beds and the lights and sounds coming from outside. Marc had pushed the desk chair into the corner of the room where he now sat, watching him closely.

He'd freaked out the seasoned private security guard. Any other time, that might have amused Julian.

The man might be too much of a professional to admit it, but Marc's eyes had focused only on Julian for the last thirty minutes.

Hell, Julian had freaked himself out. His damn thoughts were scattered all over the place, jumping all around. He tapped his foot in the same frayed rhythm as his wayward thoughts.

He let go of the breath he held, crossing his arms over his chest.

Micah.

What a mind fuck.

At that dickhead's hand, a pastor's son, Julian had been badly abused, scarred for life. Yet Julian felt more pity for Micah than himself.

Whatever bullshit the leaders of that abusive church had put Micah through should be held responsible for his crimes. After hours of prayer and lectures from the pastor and deacons of the church, Micah had been sent to conversion therapy. Julian didn't stick around to find out what his parents had planned for him. Hell, they already treated him like a pariah. He'd been devastated when he'd realized their love was conditional. Their religion held more importance than his wellbeing.

Even with running away from home at sixteen, with little more than the clothes on his back, Julian had clearly gotten the better end of the stick, if Micah's actions were any indication.

All these little bombs of revelation exploding like unseen landmines inside his head had officially blown his mind.

More interestingly, Julian found his life was far better right now than at any other time before. He had depth. He had friends who loved him and accepted him for who he was as a person, not what he could give them or do for them. There were so many accomplishments that he had achieved on his own. His past felt very much in the past. All the men, trips, and money no longer held the same attraction it once did.

What crazy fuckery was happening?

A rap of knuckles tapped against the hotel room's door. Julian knew exactly who they belonged to. Marc stood, lifting a hand toward Julian to keep him in place as the guard moved his suit coat out of the way for better access to a revolver Julian had never known was there until that moment.

The sight of the gun brought the danger factor of his life roaring back into focus. Julian turned toward the door, crossing his arms tighter over his chest. Marc quietly checked the peephole before reaching down, unlocking the door, and opening it wide.

When Beckett strode through, Julian's entire world slowed. Relief washed over him. The turmoil running amok inside him settled. His Beckett had come to him. Julian's arms dropped, the tension in his shoulders easing. He saw his future so clearly playing out in his mind. Beckett was his one, always by his side, giving Julian strength, encouragement, and love through all the stages of their lives.

They'd be partners.

Friends. Lovers. Equals.

Julian would always be appreciated and unconditionally loved. He'd eagerly return that devotion tenfold for the rest of his life.

Julian's lips turned upward as he took long, confident strides across the room. Beckett's hurt and guarded gaze collided with his. The pain he had caused was reflected all over Beckett's face. Julian absolutely deserved that look but hated he'd been the reason for it. He didn't stop until he wrapped his arms around Beckett's waist and chest then stepped straight into the man.

As far as Julian was concerned, he still wasn't close enough to Beckett to ease his concern. "Tell me I'm not too late," Julian whispered into his chest.

Beckett. The name ran like an anthem through his head.

His sweet Marlboro Man.

The one person in the world who had literally done anything and everything he could to make Julian happy. He'd been given such a gift. What had he done in return? He'd hurt Beckett.

Beckett's tense frame didn't relax, keeping him at a distance, even as Julian tried to plaster himself against Beckett. Self-preservation was written all over his stance. There may not be any physical distance between them, but miles of emotional space separated them.

What if he had messed it up so badly that Beckett was done?

No…

Several heart-stopping seconds later, Beckett finally looped a single arm around Julian's waist. When Julian pulled back enough to see Beckett's face, confusion, sorrow, and pain marred that strong brow.

Beckett seemed lost to what was happening. Julian had been right about one thing; he didn't deserve someone this good.

Marc slipped out of the hotel room, whispering quietly as he went, "I'll be right outside the door."

"What's happened, Julian?" Beckett carefully lifted his tentative fingers to Julian's upturned face, moving several strands of hair off his forehead. "Tell me everything."

"I'm sorry. I'm so sorry. I should have never doubted what was happening between us. It was insane for me to come here. I'm nowhere near the man I used to be." Julian laughed, but there was no humor in it. "I fought to get back to who I used to be, but I've evolved from that person. I didn't understand that before tonight. I don't want what I thought I did. Tell me I didn't ruin everything for us." Julian wasn't above begging Beckett to let him turn back time to their happier days together.

"You had to give yourself a chance…" Beckett didn't finish his sentence. Julian could see the gears in Beckett's mind trying to catch up.

He knew Beckett had cared for him. Hopefully, Beckett hadn't lost the feeling in just a few days. Julian rose to his tiptoes, skimming his lips over Beckett's mouth. Julian searched Beckett's expressive gaze as he faced the beginning of his new life, head-on.

"I did have to try, and I hurt you in the process. I'm so sorry. I cherish you; I love you, Beckett. I'm the luckiest guy in the world to have found you, and I almost threw it all away. Tell me I'm not too late." Julian recognized the begging tone and the way he rambled, but he couldn't stop until he made Beckett see the truth. "If you give me a second chance, we'll do it your way. Commitment. A relationship. I don't want children, but then again, maybe I do if you do. I don't know. We'll figure it out—"

Beckett's lips were on his in an instant, his tongue plunging forward, dominating Julian in the hottest, most promising kiss of his life. Both of Beckett's muscular arms locked around his body, tugging him flush against Beckett's broad chest. The invisible distance between them instantly vanished.

Julian wrapped his arms around Beckett's neck, holding on tightly, as relief eased all the tension Julian had held on to. Beckett wouldn't kiss him as if his life depended on their intimacy if he didn't see their future as clearly as Julian.

Beckett devoured Julian's mouth. He had no real idea what the fuck was going on, but it didn't stop the most intimate, soul-searing kiss of his life. The chaos Beckett had expected to walk into had instantly shifted to a declaration from the heart and words Beckett had longed to hear. *I love you.*

He yearned for it to be the truth. He'd wished for that kind of commitment from Julian. But Beckett found himself holding back, if only a tiny bit. Julian had given him whiplash. What if this moment, this beautiful moment, declaring his intention for commitment, had been spurred on by the fear of whatever memories Julian had uncovered?

Julian climbed up his body. Beckett gripped Julian's thighs while those sexy legs locked around his waist. He held Julian as the crazy guy lifted above Beckett's face, making his head tilt backward to continue the ravishing kiss. Julian's palms pressed to Beckett's cheeks, angling his head as Julian dove into the farthest recesses of Beckett's mouth.

Holy hell. If kisses spoke, this one was driving every one of Julian's words into action, sealing their fate together.

Self-preservation made Beckett remember Julian was on the edge of an awful situation.

Beckett carefully pulled back from the kiss. Julian's mouth followed him, his hands like vises on Beckett's cheeks, tugging him back to the kiss.

"Julian...please."

"What, Beck?" Julian's tongue swept forward. Beckett forced the kiss to stay light until a frustrated Julian reared back, staying within inches of Beckett's face. "What's wrong?"

"Julian." Beckett's head told him to give this time, but his hands tighten their grip, keeping Julian's hard cock pressed into his lower belly. "How can we move forward until we get your deal resolved?"

Julian's face paled, his legs pushed against Beckett's hold. It was damn hard for Beckett to let Julian go.

"It's too late," Julian said with disappointed finality and started to move away. Beckett's sense of reason was lost to his desperation of making Julian happy at any cost.

He tightened his grip around Julian's upper arm. "Of course, it's not too late, but you've identified your attacker. We need to take this in steps. You've been through a lot tonight. Tell me what happened?"

Julian's nimble fingers raked through the silky strands of his hair. Beckett had never seen that from him before. When Julian stepped away, Beckett released him. Then watched as he headed for one of the two full-size beds.

As Julian took a seat on the edge of the mattress, he explained, starting from the beginning of the evening, leaving no detail unaccounted for. Beckett paced the small room, listening to each word until Julian finally got to the part of Micah's arm wrapping around his waist. As Julian continued, the memory seemed so real—the culprit to his current state of anxiety and fear. Beckett took a seat on the other bed, facing Julian. He reached out for Julian's hand as Julian explained he'd lost sight of the memory after the champagne flute shattered against the floor.

Silence held between them as they stared at each other.

Beckett had no idea what to say to make this moment better, so he squeezed Julian's hand and moved to sit beside him.

"I haven't properly thanked you for hiring Marc," Julian said quietly, nodding his head toward the door. "I don't know what I would have done without him here tonight. Having him with me eased the fear. He's very good at what he does."

Beckett brought Julian's knuckles to his lips, pressing a kiss there. "It was his idea to follow you tonight. I wasn't thinking clearly," Beckett answered, wanting to hold more of Julian than just his hand.

He couldn't imagine how Julian felt at having all the pieces come together like they had. How could a childhood friend cause Julian so much pain?

"Did the LAPD assign you an investigator? We should call them immediately."

"They did, but after that first few months after the accident, I never heard from them again." Julian had scooted into Beckett, moving closer until Beckett adjusted his position. Julian moved against his chest, resting his head against his shoulder. Beckett held on just as tightly. "I wouldn't know who to call."

"We'll work it out in the morning. Maybe Marc can find the answers tonight," Beckett offered, kissing the top of Julian's hair. Julian held on to him as if his life depended on it. "It's late. You should try to get some rest. I feel like tomorrow's going to be a long day for you."

"I need to talk to Thomas. I took off without saying anything to him." Julian reached past Beckett for his cell phone on the nightstand. A lot of things were going to happen but fuck Thomas. The guy could be left guessing from now until eternity for all Beckett cared.

"He'll figure it out," Beckett said, gently plucking the phone from Julian's hands, putting it back on the nightstand's charger. Julian smiled up at Beckett, his palm caressing Beckett's cheek.

"A jealous side?" Julian asked in a show of relaxation. He sat on his ass and kicked off his shoes before scooting back against the headboard.

"Not jealous necessarily. I'd rather say smart." Beckett got to his feet, giving Julian room to get comfortable.

"Come join me?" Julian said, patting the bed, giving his sexiest grin. Julian was always a vision, especially with the eyeliner so artfully applied.

He tucked that away and gave a playful eye roll before starting for the door.

"Let me get Marc. He's got a long drive home in the morning."

"You're firing him?" Julian asked as if that were the dumbest idea in the world. Beckett had to agree.

"No," Beckett said with his hand on the doorknob. "But I'm not letting you out of my sight until they make an arrest. Which means I have you covered."

"My Marlboro Man…" Julian murmured lovingly.

Beckett playfully rolled his eyes again, something he did a lot with Julian, and with the hand on the door handle, said, "I seriously don't get that nickname. I don't even smoke."

Julian's laughter was music to Beckett's ears.

CHAPTER 38

Julian sat at a tiny four-seater table inside a small conference room in the Los Angeles Police Department. The chill in the air did nothing to calm his nerves. At least it didn't appear to be a room set aside for interrogating criminals. Though that thought did little to help his current level of freak-out.

He'd been in the precinct for several hours, his right leg steadily bouncing, showing his anxiety. The room wasn't much bigger than the table, and it could sure use some color and a picture or two to spruce the place up.

He envisioned all sorts of violent interrogations happening behind various closed doors in the building.

He mentally beat back monstrous waves of anxiety as they threatened to topple him. He wondered if Beckett could feel it from his seat beside Julian.

The flashback had been so much easier to absorb than this early morning meeting with the LAPD.

"Maybe we came too early," Julian muttered, tightening the hold he had on Beckett's hand. Beckett didn't exhibit any of the nerves eating away at Julian. He seemed as at home in a police department as he did at the nightclub.

Did his Marlboro Man not get the difference between the two places?

Perhaps it was a gift of sorts to be so comfortable all the damn time.

Julian didn't have that ability, and his leg bouncing started double-timing again.

"You're good, Julian. Why are you so nervous? You've already done the hard part." Beckett's thumb continued to caress the top of Julian's hand.

Julian looked at Beckett as if he were insane, which honestly wasn't off the table as a possibility. "Last night, I was trying to get you back. Today, it's about a psychopath who tortured me. He's out on the streets, Beckett. Who else has he hurt?"

He didn't have one single qualm about leaving out his lifelong apprehension about police officers. He'd sucked off or been fucked by too many cops to get himself out of whatever offense they said he'd committed. There might be a decent officer out there somewhere, but he'd never met one.

Shit. Julian was losing his cool if he actively remembered his naughty antics back in his hometown.

Calm down. Julian narrowed his eyes, looking over at Beckett. Why did the voices inside his head sound like Beckett?

Beckett must have sensed his rising unease. He cupped his arm around Julian's shoulders, drawing his temple to Beckett's lips. Beckett kissed him sweetly. "I know, babe. This guy being out on the streets has been my fear since I found out what happened. Maybe try to think of something else. You look guilty of your own crimes."

Julian flipped his irritated gaze to Beckett. Arching a brow, he gave his love the death stare he deserved. "My anxiety is through the roof, and you're cracking jokes?"

"It wasn't a joke." Beckett's smile said something entirely different. "Drink your orange juice and relax." He nodded to the unopened bottle of juice from the vending machine down the hall, still sitting where Beckett had placed it along with the pack of little white donuts. Beckett ate like shit. "You've been through the hard part, giving your statement of what happened. After we talk to the investigators, we're done. I'm sure they're issuing an arrest warrant even as we sit here waiting. They'll get the guy off the streets and prosecuted. Don't worry."

"Shit." Julian's gaze shifted back and forth between the donuts and the OJ, not seeing either one.

A trial would bring his past to his present.

His stomach gave a hard twist, and his leg came to an abrupt stop. His world stilled, thinking about the possibility of seeing his parents and siblings again.

He never wanted to see those hateful backwoods people again. They had caused him too much pain. Luckily, before he traveled too far down that warped path of thoughts, the conference room's door opened. Two investigators dressed in street clothes came through the door. If their jobs were to blend in, they didn't nearly reach their goal.

"Mr. Cullen?" the female said.

Julian didn't remember her. He did recognize Detective Ryan as one of the first officers to speak with him when he'd regained consciousness in the hospital.

Beckett stood, causing Julian to stand on wobbly legs. He'd been too lost in downward spiraling memories, dwelling on the abuse and callousness of his family, to pay too much attention to her name. The hellfire and brimstone teachings of his religious family had caused their own damage and taken years to get past. Clearly, for Micah too. What that guy must have lived through as punishment for his perceived sins.

Julian sighed as Beckett let go of his hand to shake each

of the investigators' hands. He focused enough to hear Beckett explaining his presence, but mostly Julian's heartbeat ran rampant, thumping loudly in his ears.

"Take a seat, please." Detective Ryan nodded to the table. He held a couple of full file folders that he placed on the table in front of his seat, directly across from Julian. "You've been a hard man to reach."

Julian's gaze lifted to meet Detective Ryan's direct stare as he rubbed his trembling hands together under the table. All the confusion and insecurity of those first few weeks after the assault settled over him again. The battle Julian had fought to bring himself back kept his lips tightly shut. Beckett reached over, his comforting hand sliding between Julian's two palms to clasp their fingers together. Julian one-upped Beckett by wrapping both his hands around Beckett's, his life preserver in this dark stormy ocean he was drowning in.

"We're here this morning because Julian had a breakthrough last night. An officer took his statement," Beckett started when Julian hadn't spoken for a moment. "Have you seen it?"

Detective Ryan nodded and opened his folder. He didn't sugarcoat anything or lead in slowly. Julian drew in a sharp breath as his gaze riveted to an eight by ten photo of Micah Abbott. He recognized him instantly. Though, the years hadn't been kind. The youthful young man he'd once been had become something harder. His eyes were flat, filled with hate. He appeared mean and unyielding. He looked way older than his years. His face was ravaged, most likely by alcohol, drugs, and the skin art from a clearly amateur tattoo artist hadn't helped. Julian tightened his hands around Beckett's.

"Just so you know, your memory is spot on with what we've found. This is Micah Abbott. He was killed in an automobile accident in Coronado. At the time, we of course did not know his connection to Julian. He was killed while driving under the influence of alcohol and narcotics in the early morning hours. As the pieces have come together, we now know he was within a few blocks from your apartment when the accident took place."

As Detective Ryan spoke, he continued to turn photographs, letting Julian see the pictures of the accident. Julian lifted a single hand, stopping at one photo. He moved it closer for a better look. He stared at the smoke-colored Charger that had triggered his memory.

"I saw this car. It was my first flashback," Julian said, pushing the photograph toward Beckett. "He must have known where I lived."

Beckett nodded as a cold sweat beaded across Julian's forehead. Nausea bubbled. His emotions were all over the place.

"It wasn't until last week that we found the connection between you two," Detective Ryan continued.

"What do you mean?" Beckett asked, his hard tone commanding attention.

The female investigator reached over and flipped the next several photos. Their content caused Julian's heart to stutter violently in his chest. She scattered them around so Julian could get the full scope of what he'd been up against.

"Abbott rented a small apartment in San Diego a few months ago. When the rent wasn't paid, the owner walked in to find this and called us."

Julian inched his upper body away from the table as Beckett leaned in closer for a better look. The apartment had a wall filled with pictures of Julian. And not just recent photos. They spanned from the time he was a young boy to more recent as he walked from Escape to Reservations.

Beckett moved the police photos around, showing a collection of Micah's loose images of Julian walking into his apartment and others with Julian taking Woofer out for a walk. Beckett kept searching through the photographs that chronicled Julian's abduction. Several showed the faces of men involved in his rape.

A shiver raced down Julian's spine and bile rose up in his throat as he shifted his gaze away, not wanting to see anything more.

"He was tracking Julian."

Detective Ryan nodded his confirmation, even though Beckett had made a statement more than asked a question. The evidence painted the whole picture easily. Julian felt in his bones that Micah had planned to finish what he'd started. What a sobering reality.

"We believe he left the area after your abduction then came back about two months ago, per his lease and his cell phone records. His family has since verified our findings."

"He must have thought I died that day," Julian said, staring down at his and Beckett's joined hands. That touch had become a lifeline to reality, keeping him grounded. "And then found out I hadn't. He was coming back for more."

"Yes, we believe so," she explained. Julian looked at the table as she slid her business card across to Julian then one to Beckett. Marcia Bates. Julian reached for the card, placing it on the table right in front of him.

"So, it's over now?" Beckett asked, his words penetrating the horror circulating through all of Julian's thoughts.

"We're keeping the case open. There's information in these pictures that tells us where you were held and who else was involved. These men *will* be held accountable for their actions," Marcia said firmly. She was comforting and reassuring. Julian deeply appreciated the care she used in speaking to him, and the conviction that they would provide him justice.

He nodded, letting go of a deep sigh. "Thank you."

"We tried to call you," Detective Ryan said as he shuffled the photos into a pile. "But didn't have current contact information. We sent an officer by your home then over to Reservations last night, but you weren't there."

"No, I was here in LA," Julian confirmed and sat back in his seat. All the worry and fear he'd lived under all this time seeped out of him, leaving him exhausted.

"So, you believe the others were part of the abduction?" Beckett asked abruptly.

"We don't know, but most likely not. They committed other crimes, as evidenced in these pictures. But all indications are that they were opportunists rather than fixated on Julian specifically," Detective Bates answered. "Micah left a…manifesto of sorts. He had it out for Julian. Blamed him for his past problems as a young man that ultimately led him to a life of crime."

"Can Julian see the full report?" Beckett asked.

"I don't need to." Julian shook his head. "We grew up in the same Southern Baptist church. Last I heard before I left home and never looked back, was that Micah had been sent away to undergo extensive conversion therapy."

The silence at the table spoke to the understanding of the heavy consequences of such treatment.

"Okay. We now have your contact information," Detective Ryan said, shoving the documents back into his file and pushing back his chair as he stood. "If you change your phone number again, please make sure we have the information."

"Absolutely," Julian agreed, reaching out his hand for the business card Detective Ryan extended.

"I was new to this role when you were found. You were one of my first cases and by far one of the worst I've seen since then. I wasn't sure you would survive. I'm glad to see you doing so well and thankful this part is over for you."

Julian nodded and smiled as he got to his feet, letting go of Beckett to shake each detectives' hands. He appreciated someone noticing how much it had taken to get him back on his feet and moving forward with his life again.

"Can we have a few minutes alone before we head out?" Beckett asked.

"Take your time," Detective Ryan said, shutting the door as they left.

Julian rolled his shoulders then his neck as he turned toward Beckett. "It's done."

Beckett wrapped his arms around Julian, drawing him in. Julian clung to him, his body trembling. Of course, this moment would bring tears. Beckett tightened his hold, kissing Julian's silky hair, wanting to do nothing more than provide comfort.

What he didn't expect was the small rumble of laughter that followed.

"What's so funny?" Beckett edged away and looked down. Julian bent in to press his lips to the crook of Beckett's neck.

"Life," Julian answered as he unwound himself from Beckett's hold. "Something that had been hanging heavily over my head for a few years is just solved. If only I had known it was finished about the same time I started having my first flashbacks. All the training and money spent to protect me didn't have to happen. Micah could have grabbed me that morning."

"Woofer was on duty," Beckett said, trying to match Julian's jovial attitude, but he struggled. Had Micah gotten to Julian before Beckett, he'd have mourned the loss of a man he might not have ever truly known. Beckett cupped Julian's shoulders, caressing down to his elbows, continuing his path until he clasped Julian's hands. "I think you should take some time off. Come home with me for a few days and let me take care of you. You can regroup. Meet my family."

Julian's tension had truly melted away. He dropped in his seat and reached for his cell phone before he tilted his face up to look at Beckett. "You want me to meet your family? That's serious. I'm not sure I've ever met anyone's parents before."

"You'll do fine." As Beckett had held Julian last night, he'd researched the psychological effects of recovering from memory loss and finally being able to identify his attacker. Julian needed rest, relaxation, and a moment to just breathe. Beckett could provide those things in spades. He reached for his coffee cup and stir stick. "You should probably call Thane…"

"How much longer do I need to wait for an *I love you back*?" Julian asked.

Beckett's head snapped in Julian's direction. He sat there, casually crossing one leg over the other. The weight of the world no longer held Julian at a distance. He looked tired and beautiful and everything Beckett had ever wanted in the world.

"You're an awfully good guy. My Dudley Do-Right. I can see you not wanting to rock my boat until we got through this morning. It's okay if your feelings have changed. You certainly don't have to spend the next week with me."

Beckett placed the half-full cup into the bottom of the can before he stood to his full height. They were in the middle of an LAPD precinct. Minutes ago, Julian was quaking with uncertainty. His life was completely upended. Beckett narrowed his eyes and placed his hands on his hips. "You want to do this here?"

Julian looked around, his brows lifting. "If it goes in my favor, then we could probably wait. I was convinced this was an interrogation room, and they didn't believe my statement."

Beckett chuckled and went to Julian. "This is awfully nice to be an interrogation room."

Julian barked out a harsh laugh and got to his feet. "You certainly need to keep me around if you think this is nice." He straightened his clothes as he spoke. His hands then ran the length of his waistband down to the wrinkles at his upper thighs, pushing them away. Beckett was mesmerized. What an immediate, remarkable change. His guy was back, worried about his appearance.

Julian wouldn't like the deep circles forming under his tired eyes.

"I do need you, that's for sure," Beckett said and started for the door. "Come home with me. I'll call Marc and fill him in. You can call Thane while we're on the road. Plan?"

"I'm in if you'll feed me a decent breakfast," Julian quipped, reaching for the unopened treats Beckett had found.

"What? You don't like powdered donuts. They're the breakfast of champions!"

"*Pfft*," Julian tossed his hands in the air at such an insult to breakfast. He casually walked through the door that Beckett held open, no longer clutching him as if his life depended on their connection.

Beckett tucked his hands inside his jeans pockets and followed Julian out. At the front doors of the building, Julian found a child sitting with his parent. He nodded at the parent, asking for permission. When it was granted, he leaned down and offered the donuts and juice to the little guy.

Beckett couldn't contain his grin, seeing how caring Julian was with a child. Life was definitely going to be something special with this man by his side.

CHAPTER 39

The old trail leading to the main cabin had needed repair before Beckett and his father had ever started their business. It had always been on their need-to-do list, falling so low it never got done. Now he regretted that delay. No matter how slowly Beckett drove, the cab of the truck yawed from side to side from the deep dips and ruts. His sleeping beauty, who had conked out maybe ten minutes into the ride and had stayed asleep through every refueling and bathroom break Beckett had made, finally lifted his head, his tired eyes cracking open to look at Beckett.

They had made great time on their way back to his home. The sun was just beginning to set in the distance. The mountain range made a gorgeous backdrop with its rugged, majestic beauty. Beckett's soul filled with satisfaction and pride. He, his father, and Randy had really made something with their lives and the place had come alive under their care. Excitement bubbled within to finally have Julian not only see but be a part of his world.

"Where are we?" Julian mumbled. A jaw-stretching yawn tore

free. Julian stretched his body every which way he could inside the confines of the cab before Beckett had a chance to answer. Then Julian resettled into his reclined passenger seat, taking the soft blanket Beckett had packed for emergencies and pulling it up to his neck.

The next rut bounced the truck hard, causing Julian to jackknife forward in the seat.

"Sorry. I need to fix this road."

"We're already at your place?" Julian asked, confused, rubbing his fists against his closed eyelids. He gave a smaller yawn this time.

Beckett pointed a finger to the main lodge. Julian's face followed his arm and hand to where his family stood on the wraparound porch, waiting on his and Julian's arrival. He had texted them all before they ever left LA, begging his mom and dad to do a quick clean at his cabin. He then texted Randy, unceremoniously dumping every bit of his part of the business's workload in his friend's lap since Beckett planned to take the next few weeks off to be with Julian.

He did have some guilt, but figured Randy was ready to take the leap into a full partnership since he now had a baby on the way. With Randy being an equal partner, that also meant his old man would be looked after in Beckett's absence. At least, he hoped it worked out that way. They had a lot to talk about to help make the transition as smooth as possible. He didn't let his thoughts linger there. It would work itself out.

"Beck." Julian dropped the visor down to hurriedly check his appearance in the lighted mirror. "I look like hell."

"Right," Beckett scoffed as if the most gorgeous man alive could be anything but. "That's something that would never happen." His truck hit a significant dip, bouncing Julian until he bumped his head on the roof under the force. "I think one of our first goals should be to get some meat on your bones."

Julian cast a glaring side eye in his direction while rubbing the top of his head. "I think you'd be better off working on this road." He dismissed Beckett, back to pushing at the longer pieces of his hair. Of course, Julian's dark bed head fell easily in place. "Do they know I'm coming?"

"Yeah, I texted 'em," Beckett answered and lifted his ball cap, scratching his head as he took the last turn. At this moment, after the long night and equally long drive, he was Julian's exact opposite; Beckett didn't give a shit how he looked. He was tired as hell and ready to be out of this truck and back to his home. Julian gently pinched his own cheeks then slid his loafers on his feet. Beckett came to a stop maybe twenty-five feet from where his people stood waiting. "Don't worry. You look good."

Julian's freshly glowing face turned to Beckett as he finished with one shoe. "I can't believe I slept the whole way. I don't normally sleep like that."

"You needed it," Beckett answered, lifting the gearshift into park. "You'll probably do a lot of that over the next few days. It's supposed to be part of your recovery. Or something like that."

"You learn that on the University of Google?" Julian teased, chiding him with a cute quirk to the corner of his mouth. "You're too good to me."

"*Ha Ha*. I wanted to know how best to support you. Stop making fun of me." Smiling broadly, Beckett pushed open his truck door and stepped out, glad to be on stable ground again. Long drives always made him appreciate being outside any chance he got. Julian bent over in the seat, working the crease in his fitted slacks.

"I haven't met anyone's parents before. Do I look okay?" he asked, still bent over but cocking his head in Beckett's direction. The stalling tactic made Beckett smile. Julian was so damned endearing with his rare displays of insecurity.

The front porch door swung shut with a clap. Marly came out to stand beside Randy. His mother had started down the steps. Beckett placed a hand on the top of the truck and an arm over the edge of the door. He leaned in, talking quietly so no one else could hear. "You always look gorgeous. I don't think you could look anything other than amazing. Now, come on. They're coming toward us."

He shut the door, not giving Julian a chance to put this off any further, and started around the hood. If he could get to Julian's door first, then maybe he could offer some emotional support for his nervous guy.

His parents had other plans. They had hotfooted it to his truck. Beckett had been deemed chopped liver for how they cut him off without more than a glance, getting to Julian's door first. His father pulled it open wide, putting Julian in the spotlight and on full display.

Julian may have been the main attraction, but like normal, Woofer bounded around the house, drawing everyone's attention toward the rambunctious, speedy dog as he happily darted for Beckett's truck. At least someone wanted to see him.

Julian placed one foot on the ground then the other, sliding from the seat. As he stood, Beckett saw the exact moment Woofer realized Julian was there.

The dog came to an abrupt skidding halt then altered his course, speeding straight for Julian. Beckett pointed to the dog. Like the parting of the Red Sea, his parents and Randy and his girlfriend stepped apart, giving Woofer a straight line to Julian. Seconds before Woofer made contact, he launched himself off his back paws, his front paws aimed straight at Julian. Julian caught the large dog's weight with an *oomph* and stumbled back into the open truck door. Woofer wasn't put off in the least, whining excitedly and licking straight across Julian's lips.

It might have been the sweetest reunion ever. Woofer danced at Julian's feet. His tail tucked between his legs, mewling and whimpering in his excitement. His non-dog-loving guy instantly bent down, forgetting everyone else, giving Woofer all the love he'd missed.

"He's found his owner," his father said proudly as Julian gave the wiggling dog a good, thorough rub down.

"He's so happy to see you," his mother added, her beaming smile lighting her face. She stepped around his father to give Beckett a hug. "How was your drive? I'm glad you got here before dark."

"It was good," he said, wrapping an arm around his mom as he made the introduction he'd wanted to make for so long now. "I think Julian's gonna stay the week if I have anything to say about it. Mom, Dad, this is Julian. Julian, this is my mother and father. Call them Mom and Dad, everyone does."

Julian tried to wrangle an excited Woofer and pay proper attention to his parents, but he had to finally stand up and ignore the overly happy dog to shake his father's hand.

"It's nice to meet you," Julian said as Woofer refused to be ignored and leaped between them to keep the attention focused on him.

"Place, Woofer," Beckett said firmly, and for a few seconds, the dog did follow the command, dropping to his seat. His tail whipping back and forth. Beckett had no idea Woofer had missed Julian so badly.

"I've never seen him like this," Randy said, standing at a distance.

"Like I've always said, he's the worst emotional support animal ever," Julian teased as his mother came forward, bypassing Julian's outstretched hand to give him a tight motherly hug.

Just as quickly as she bent forward for the hug, she reared back, her palms going to Julian's cheeks. Beckett could only grin at Julian's confusion as his own nervous energy pumped through him. He loved his mom unconditionally, but she regularly startled people with her simple way of reading them.

Beckett lifted his ball cap and scratched his head again, watching his mother study Julian. Maybe as much as a minute passed as he turned the bill around and settled the cap backward on his head.

Should he intervene?

Perhaps it had been a bad call to stop by the main house first.

Whatever his mother saw must have made her happy. She pulled Julian to her again, hugging him as tightly as she'd hugged Beckett.

"It took you long enough. Our guy's been waiting on you. Welcome to the family. Call me Mom. You eventually will, so might as well start now." His mother said the words so quietly Beckett only heard because he was inches away from Julian.

Julian's gaze lifted to Beckett's, his brows arching in astonishment, making his father bark out a laugh. "She's good at what she does. I can never figure out how she does it, but I don't need to, I guess."

His mom pulled away, staying close to Julian's side as she wrapped an arm around his, happy as Beckett had ever seen her. Woofer moved to glue himself against Julian's side, his tail whipping Beckett's legs as his father shook Julian's hand.

"That's Randy and his future wife, Marly." Beckett directed Julian's attention to the couple hanging back to let his mom and dad greet Julian.

Julian lifted a hand, giving a bright, charming smile.

Beckett couldn't have been prouder, his heart soaring. He circled an arm around Julian, stepping in closer. Proud to have Julian there with him.

Man, Beckett was a lucky man.

"We have dinner in the oven at your place. We felt like you'd want to get home pretty quickly," his mother said before looking directly into Julian's eyes. "Happiness is coming. I promise."

"Thank you," Julian said with patience and kindness, probably because what else did you say to something like that?

Beckett let go of Julian to slap a hand on the back of his truck. Woofer immediately executed a jump maneuver, landing safely inside the bed of the truck as Beckett swung a handout to encourage Julian back into his seat.

"Randy, stop by tomorrow so we can talk about next week's Coronado training class. Not too early and call before you come," Beckett said as Julian hoisted himself into the truck only to have Woofer bound from the back. His paws landed on the gravel only long enough for him to launch forward into the front seat with Julian. They all laughed, including Julian, who had a hundred-pound German shepherd sitting awkwardly in his lap.

"Down, Woofer." Beckett's command fell short with all the humor flowing through him. Julian stopped Woofer from complying by circling his arm around the dog to keep him in place, sitting right beside Julian in his seat.

"I'm not sure I've ever had anyone miss me so much. Can he ride up here? I'll take the middle seat." Maybe Woofer wasn't alone in how much he missed Julian. Julian looked pretty taken with the dog. Beckett nodded, not sure his heart could hold any more love for Julian than it did right then. Once Julian and the dog got settled, Beckett shut the door, checking to ensure the latch held. He had precious cargo to protect.

Beckett mouthed a quick thank-you to his parents who nodded with big grins on their faces. Then he made eye contact with Randy as his mother reached up, stopping Beckett's retreat to give him one of her great hugs.

"Tell him soon. He's insecure," she whispered.

He had no idea how she did it, but she always did. He nodded to her and started for the driver's side of the truck.

Dusk edged out daylight quickly as Beckett pulled away from the main lodge, driving on a trail Julian swore wasn't there.

Julian stared out the front window, not seeing anything more than miles and miles of dark nothingness. No, that wasn't true. This was Beckett's world. The magic of the way Beckett had lovingly spoken of his home drew Julian into the mystique of this vast wilderness. He just wished he could see it a little better, but that would come soon enough.

Beckett reached an arm around his shoulders, drawing Julian closer to his side. Julian grinned, casting his gaze toward Beckett who kept his eyes focused out the windshield. Woofer readjusted his big body too, laying his head on Julian's thigh. A glance down showed the dog looking up at Beckett too.

His family. He riffled his fingers through Woofer fur and rested his other hand on Beckett's thigh.

The rightness of such a thought settled Julian, relaxed him into the drive. Julian was exactly where he wanted to be. Every fiber of his being rang ready to welcome the commitment he wanted to give. For the first time he could ever remember, he wanted to put down roots. Have someone to always be his plus one. And this dog waiting for them to come home. If a heart could smile, it did just then.

Julian sifted his fingers through Woofer's fur, petting him right behind his ear where Woofer loved it the most. "I can't believe I slept so long. I'm still tired."

"You should be. You've been through hell. I suspect you'll need quite a bit of downtime to recover. I don't know how you've done so well. Those pictures…"

Julian gently squeezed Beckett's thigh. Beckett had studied the investigators' photographs when they found him bloodied and abused, on the cusp of death in that dingy motel's bathroom. As he started to bring the subject up, Beckett turned the truck around a curve, the headlights illuminating a large structure in the distance.

"What's that?" Julian leaned in closer to get a better look.

Beckett chuckled, tilting his head toward Julian as if he should know this answer. "It's my cabin."

"Cabin?" Julian barked and changed his position, dislodging Woofer as he tried to glance this way and that until the truck aligned itself in the same direction as the two-story log cabin. "That's a sizable home. Cabin means one or two rooms max. That looks huge and has two stories. You built this?"

Beckett didn't hide his humor at Julian's surprise. "When you're in the closet, hiding from yourself and the world, you have lots of time on your hands. The upstairs is incomplete, but as I got started, it felt right to build up. I kept pretending I'd find a wife and have a pack of children someday," Beckett explained, pulling the truck to a stop in a gravel driveway. "There were holes in my plan. I had never dated a woman, and I lived in the middle of nowhere, so I don't know where this imaginary wife was going to come from."

He put the gearshift into park and unwound his arm to reach for his cell phone tucked into a cubby. "We have one of those Starlink satellites. You should be able to get coverage anywhere around here. My password is Julian. Don't judge me."

Beckett worked his phone's screen, and seconds later, the lights on the front porch and some of the trees came to life, guiding their way. The lamps in each window followed suit until the whole house welcomed their arrival.

"It's beautiful, Beck. I was expecting to have to battle varmints and bugs. I was afraid it wasn't going to end well for us." Julian stared at the gorgeous scenery. A picture-perfect place. If the inside was as tranquil as the outside, Julian saw nothing but relaxation in his near future.

"Varmints?" Beckett asked, turning his body as he stopped in mid step of getting out of the truck. "You been watching Gunsmoke or Yosemite Sam?"

"Rocky and Bullwinkle," Julian shot back, smiling at the happiness rolling off Beckett. He tenderly elbowed Beckett, pushing him out of the cab as Woofer bulldozed his way out of the truck in front of Julian. He ultimately scooted back, letting the dog go first, his paws and hair leaving Julian's clothing in disarray.

"Come on, slowpoke," Beckett teased. He took long strides toward the front door, laughing at their silly exchange as he pushed the front door open then moved to the side, waiting for Julian to join him. Woofer clearly knew the path. He trotted his way up the porch steps.

"Hey now," Beckett said to Woofer, who pushed past Beckett to get inside. Woofer turned in the frame of the doorway, sticking his head back outside, both his guys were watching, waiting for Julian to start their way. He did just that.

It had been a long twenty-four hours on top of a long couple of years. He took a shuddering deep breath as he stared at all the goodness in front of him. He digested the chaotic mess of his life. His life had been messed up for even longer than the accident. He couldn't remember a time that he'd ever been truly happy. Sure, it had taken a minute for him to recognize what he had, but with his heart pumping wildly in his chest and tears welling in his eyes, a certainty settled in his soul. This was what he'd been missing. The love embracing his soul: happiness. That honest, endearing man and that silly dog waiting for him made the tears spill over and trail down his cheeks.

"What's wrong, Julian?" Beckett asked, meeting him halfway across the porch. Julian rubbed his hand over his eyes as Beckett tenderly took him into his arms. His concern and confusion were Julian's only focus. He wanted to ease Beckett as much as he wanted to take his next breath. "What happened?"

"I'm a fucking mess." Tears flowed in earnest now. "I never cry. What the hell?"

Beckett let Julian go long enough to pull his cotton T-shirt over his head. Julian only rolled his eyes. It wasn't the hot, muscular chest that seared Beckett into his soul but the sweet man giving him the shirt off his back to wipe away the tears. A symbolic gesture that spoke of their future so clearly.

"Beckett." Julian took the shirt and wiped it over his face as Beckett hovered around Julian. His scent… That dick-pleasing cologne mixed with Beckett's naturally alluring aroma. It was intoxicating. Beckett's strong, gentle hand swept over Julian's hair, brushing it from his face. The back of Beckett's fingers slowly caressed down his cheek. Woofer nudged between their legs, wanting to offer his own comfort.

Julian melted against Beckett's broad chest, soaking up every bit of affection offered. He was a forever changed man. His road was always meant to lead him right here to Beckett. In the fucking wilderness. Julian glanced up, helpless, as he stared at the man before him.

"Months ago, when you first walked into Reservations, the first minute you came through the restaurant into the bar, I saw you. Something compelled me to look your way. I knew you were going to be trouble." Julian's tears cascaded down his cheeks again. "I want this to happen between us. I know I don't deserve…"

Beckett lifted his fingers to Julian's lips, stopping him from saying anything more. He took his damp T-shirt and haphazardly wiped it over Julian's face. With strong fingers, Beckett tilted Julian's chin, forcing him to meet his gaze.

"You have to know I've loved you since that very first moment. Every thought, every day since then, has revolved around you. I love you to my core." Beckett tried to smile, but it didn't come easy under the weight of his confession. "I've tried hard not to push you before you're ready, but when the time comes, I want us to be each other's one. To be bound together. You and me, facing the world. I liked everything you laid out last night in the hotel room. I'm so in."

Julian tossed his arms around Beckett's neck to tug him down to seal their fate with a kiss. Julian's legs gave out from underneath him as Beckett scooped him between his arms. Woofer barked as Julian gave a yelp and tightened his hold around Beckett's neck.

Beckett's face instantly flushed.

"You look lighter than you are…" Beckett said through a huffed breath then started, slow-footed, toward the door.

"Is that a fat joke?" Julian asked, cocking his brow inches from Beckett's face. "I'm actively trying to make myself heavier right now."

Beckett chuckled and edged them awkwardly through the doorway. "Not a fat joke at all. I'll take you at any weight. I'm afraid you're never getting rid of me."

Julian tightened his hold around Beckett's neck, aligning them face to face. "Good. That's just the way I want it."

CHAPTER 40

Three weeks later

Julian pulled into the parking lot in downtown Baltimore, coming to a rolling stop as he leaned into the windshield of his rental, looking over the combination restaurant and pub that Thane had had such a hard-on to buy. He tilted his head as he tried to make sense of what he was seeing. Thane owned some of the largest restaurant chains in the world. He negotiated with top business executives and world leaders to elevate his empire. The man would be a billionaire soon if he wasn't already.

Yet…this was Pat's Pub and Sunday's Side? He narrowed his eyes at the building before him. He'd heard the place was genuine. The patrons looked to be both old-timers and new customers. A dream clientele from an administrative perspective. It had been around for a long time, but the construction looked new to be so generationally beloved.

They must have had a radical facelift. No shame in that. Julian had already marked on his calendar app the day, twenty-nine years from now, when he planned to gift himself a facelift.

He sat back in the seat and repeated the question he'd been asking himself for a while now. What alternate universe had he landed in? From his own personal changes to Thane wanting this restaurant and bar, all reasonable signs were pointing to the world entering a new dimension. Life as Julian knew it had come to a screeching halt. Life was changing and all he could seem to do was hang on for the ride.

The honk from behind reminded Julian he was blocking the entrance, urging him into a nearby parking space. He sat there, fishing out his cell phone from his pocket, jonesing for any kind of communication with his boyfriend. Warmth seeped over Julian at the *Daddy Bear* title he had given Beckett's contact information. It had been six hours since he'd left Beckett at the airport in San Diego. Their departing was a melodramatic display with Beckett clinging to Julian, not wanting him to leave for his three-day on-site intensive training at the Dishology headquarters in Ellicott City. And by Beckett clinging to Julian, he really meant Julian clinging to Beckett.

He'd learned over the last three weeks that once love's arrow struck, the serum spread rapidly, leaving him a major codependent baby who wanted Beckett within reach at any given moment. Meaning Beckett's job seemed to be at Julian's beck and call. His Daddy Bear spent hours a day inside Reservations, and Beckett was one hell of a handyman. Julian recognized his ridiculousness, but it didn't seem to matter. He couldn't get enough of his man.

He checked his phone to see if Beckett had responded to his arrival text. Beckett had stayed in Coronado to close on their new house. The coveted corner lot Beckett had seen without him had turned out to belong to two members of Reservations who had recently expanded their family. Julian had been to the home many times and had negotiated thousands of dollars off the asking price. Beckett was lucky to have him. The crazy man would have shelled out so much extra cash, which was unacceptable since that money could be spent on Julian himself.

He cut the engine, reached into the backseat for the gifts he'd gotten Luke and Logan, and left the car. He tucked his phone in his pocket as he went inside to meet Thane, Levi, Logan, and Luke. He had planned to stay in a hotel while in town, but Thane and Levi were butt-hurt because he didn't want to stay with them in their new home. Even though that seemed weird, he'd caved and agreed to spend his nights there.

This Walker-Silva family genuinely believed Julian was one of theirs and had only come to town to visit them. Now, the baggage of family obligation weighed on his shoulders.

Julian cast his gaze down, avoiding the bright sun as he made his way inside.

"Julian!" He heard his name shouted before the door even closed behind him. Luke, apparently his new best friend or so you'd think with the daily update emails he'd been getting since Luke had moved out east, lifted his hand, then jumped from his seat, the chair teetering until it clattered to the floor. Luke glanced behind him at the chair. "My bad."

Everyone in both sides of the place looked at Luke then at Julian. He couldn't hide his grin as Luke hurriedly righted his chair. The rest of the Walker-Silva family stood. Except Logan who was shoveling the last bit of food on his plate into his mouth.

"Am I late?" Julian asked, sticking out a hand to shake Thane's, looking at the empty plates on the table.

"We had a change of plans," Luke said, breaking Julian's handshake with Levi from across the table. Luke wrapped his arms around Julian, giving his side a full-body hug. "The university can see us early. It's cool right?" He was a tall, lanky kid, who looked to have grown since Julian had seen him. "I'll graduate from college about the same time I graduate from high school."

"I knew you were smart no matter what they said about you," Julian teased, handing over the gift he'd brought. "I felt like a university guy needs something special."

Logan finally looked up at Julian, chewing a mouth full of food. The look was very clear. Logan was starting at the university this semester along with his little brother. Where was his gift?

"I got you too," Julian assured. "Don't worry."

"Logan, look. It's the new Samsung Galaxy." Luke lifted both boxes from the sack before wrapping himself around Julian again in appreciation.

"Thank you. Thane, look. Julian got us phones. It's cool to have rich friends," Luke said unabashedly, tightening his arms around Julian.

"We have to go," Levi said, chuckling behind Julian. "Let Julian go, Luke."

Luke did, his smiling face looming over Julian. "Thane said you're staying with us. I'll see you tonight."

He wasn't sure why Luke liked him so much, but it had been like that since the first time he'd met the kid, and Luke *was* a kid, almost sixteen years old.

"Thanks, Julian. This is clutch," Logan said from behind him.

"Anytime," Julian said and patted Luke on the arm before moving around him. "Get going. I'll see you later."

The twinkle of humor lit Thane's eyes. Julian's boss was having a great time at his expense. He pushed from his seat and stood. "Why don't we go into the bar. You can have lunch there, and we can talk."

"Like explaining why you'd want to buy this place. It seems off brand," Julian said as Thane swept out an arm in front of him, urging Julian to go first.

"Have you seen their Yelp rating?" Thane asked from behind him. "I've never had a place where customers are so devoted. I need that in my lineup."

"It looks new," Julian said, not remembering a time Thane had ever talked reviews as a reason to buy anything. He scanned the busy establishment, trying to see what Thane saw.

"Is this someone new to try to talk us into selling?" The bartender asked with a sarcastic quirk of the mouth as Julian took a seat at the bar.

Thane chuckled as he took his seat. "Padraig, meet Julian. And no, I'm done trying to convince you to sell to me. I've been turned down enough."

"Yeah, since we hired Logan as a busboy a couple of days a week. Who buys a bar because a teenager likes it here?" Padraig shook his head as if that was the dumbest thing he'd ever heard as he ran a rag over the bar top.

Julian's gaze slid to Thane's in astonishment. "Are you serious? You put me through hell because you wanted to impress one of the Silva boys?"

Color rushed to Thane's cheeks. He jerked his head toward the bartender. "You got me drunk, and I told you that in confidence. I'm never gonna live it down, am I?" He hooked a thumb over to Julian. "The food is great, and he needs a menu. I'll have my usual."

"What about you?" Padraig asked Julian.

"How about a Diet Coke? I need to be sober to retain all the facts so I can spread them far and wide," Julian teased, his entire focus still on Thane. "What happened to you, man?"

A cackle came from the center seat of the bar. An old man reading a romance novel, based on the picture of the half-naked girl and guy on the cover, slapped the bar. "Walker's an arrogant one. He needs someone in his life to knock him down a peg or two."

"Pat, meet Julian. He's one of my general managers. Pat's family owns the pub. Padraig's his grandson," Thane said, waving a hand in the air to stop the conversation as he hooked an arm on the bar and turned fully toward Julian. Thane wore a smug grin. "What happened to me is the same thing that's about to happen to you with Beckett." Thane shook his head ruefully. "Reformed players become sickeningly devoted creatures. I can't even stand myself. You'll see."

Julian picked up the menu without saying a word. He wasn't about to disagree because Thane was usually right. Julian could already see the writing on the wall. A smile tugged at the corners of his mouth, and his heart filled with happiness at the thought of a lifetime devoted to Beckett. *Bring it on.*

The End

Julian isn't done. Follow him in Luke's story.
Hopefully, out 2022.

(Honestly, it's probably going to be more like early 2023 but we can hope.)

NOTE FROM THE AUTHOR

Send a quick email to kindle@kindlealexander.com and let us know what you think of Breakaway. For more information on future works, sign-up for our new release newsletter or come friend us on all the major social networking sites.

✦ Facebook ➜ https://www.facebook.com/AuthorKindleAlexander/
✦ Twitter ➜ https://twitter.com/KindleAlexander
✦ Instagram ➜ https://www.instagram.com/kindlealexander2.0/?hl=en
✦ Book+Main Bites ➜ https://bookandmainbites.com/KindleAlexander
✦ Goodreads ➜ https://www.goodreads.com/author/show/6421828.Kindle_Alexander
✦ Amazon ➜ https://amzn.to/2JXnKRF
✦ BookBub ➜ https://www.bookbub.com/profile/kindle-alexander
✦ Newsletter ➜ https://www.kindlealexander.com/contact-us/

BOOKS BY KINDLE ALEXANDER

If you enjoyed *It's Complicated* then you won't want to miss Kindle Alexander's bestselling novels:

Breakaway
Reservations
Painted On My Heart
The Current Between Us (with Bonus Material)
Closet Confession
Secret
Texas Pride

Always & Forever Duet
Always
Forever

Nice Guys Novels
Double Full
Full Disclosure
Full Domain

Tattoos and Ties
Havoc
Order

Better If Read Together
The Current Between Us
Secret
Painted On My Heart

ALWAYS

Winner, Book Excellence Award, 2020

Book of the Year 2014 Member Choice Awards ~Goodreads MM Romance

Book of the Year 2014 ~Sinfully Sexy Book

LGBT Book of the Year 2015 eLit Awards

Born to a prestigious political family, Avery Adams plays as hard as he works. The gorgeous, charismatic attorney is used to getting what he wants, even the frequent one-night stands that earn him his well-deserved playboy reputation. When some of the most prominent men in politics suggest he run for senate, Avery decides the time has come to follow in his grandfather's footsteps. With a strategy in place and the campaign wheels rolling, Avery is ready to jump on the legislative fast track, full steam ahead. But no amount of planning prepares him for the handsome, uptight restaurateur who might derail his political future.

Easy isn't even in the top thousand words to describe Kane Dalton's life after his father, a devout Southern Baptist minister, kicks him out of the family home for questioning his sexual orientation. Despite all the rotten tomatoes life throws his way, Kane makes something of himself. Between owning a thriving upscale Italian restaurant in the heart of downtown Minneapolis and managing his long-term boyfriend, his plate is full. He struggles to get past the teachings of his childhood to fully accept his sexuality and rid himself of the doubts brought on by his religious upbringing. The last thing he needs is the yummy, sophisticated, blond-haired distraction sitting at table thirty-four.

HAVOC & ORDER

(Tattoos And Ties, Book 1)

Keyes Dixon's life is challenging enough as a full patch member of the Disciples of Havoc Motorcycle Club but being a gay biker leaves him traveling down one tough road. With an abusive past and his vow to the club cementing his future, he doesn't believe in love and steers clear of commitment. But a midnight ride leads to a chance meeting with a sexy distraction that has him going down quicker than a Harley on ice.

Cocky Assistant District Attorney Alec Pierce lives in the shadow of his politically connected family. A life of privilege doesn't equal a life of love, a fact made obvious at every family gathering. Driven yet lonely, Alec yields to his family's demands for his career path, hoping for the acceptance he craves. Until he meets a gorgeous biker who tips the scales in the favor of truth and he can no longer live a lie.

Can two men from completely different worlds…and sides of the law… find common ground, or will all their desires only wreak Havoc?

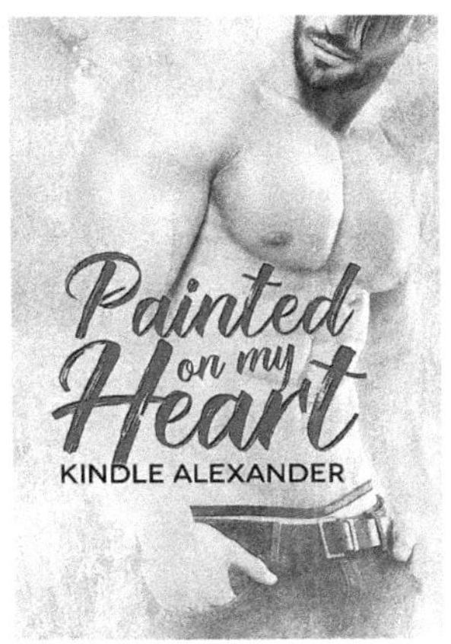

PAINTED ON MY HEART

Winner of the 2017 eLit Award Romance category
Winner of the 2017 eLit Award LGBT Fiction category

Artist Kellus Hardin let love and loyalty cloud his past decisions, a mistake he definitely won't make again. Now, lost and alone, he's left to pick up the shattered pieces of his broken heart while facing the truth of his reality.

Arik Layne exudes power, confidence, and determination. But when an encounter with the guarded artist shakes him to the core and alters all his future goals, he finds more than just his heart on the line.

For Kellus, opening himself to love isn't an option.

All Arik wants is to make the artist his.

Can love create a masterpiece when it's painted on your heart?